Reckless Behavior
Meghan French

MEGHAN FRENCH PUBLISHING

Copyright © 2026 by Meghan French.

All rights reserved.

No part of this book may be reproduced in any form or by any electronic or mechanical means, including information storage and retrieval systems, without written permission from the author, except for the use of brief quotations in a book review.

Without in any way limiting the author's exclusive rights under copyright law, any use of this publication to "train" generative artificial intelligence (AI) technologies to generate text is expressly prohibited. The author reserves all rights to license uses of this work for generative AI training and development of machine learning language models.

This book is a work of fiction, created without the use of AI technology. Names, characters, organizations, places, events, and incidents are either products of the author's imagination or used fictitiously.

This one's for the quirky girls, who wear their personalities like a badge of honor.
Thanks for making the world a brighter, more eccentric place.

Contents

About Reckless Behavior	1
1. June	3
2. Asher	11
3. June	18
4. June	30
5. June	34
6. Asher	42
7. June	46
8. June	59
9. Asher	64
10. June	65
11. Asher	68
12. June	80
13. June	84
14. Asher	91

15.	June	99
16.	Asher	104
17.	June	114
18.	Asher	131
19.	Asher	134
20.	June	141
21.	Asher	163
22.	June	178
23.	Asher	189
24.	June	199
25.	Asher	209
26.	June	214
27.	Asher	220
28.	June	226
29.	Asher	229
30.	Asher	231
31.	June	236
32.	Asher	249
33.	June	252
34.	Asher	262

35.	June	269
36.	Asher	273
37.	Asher	278
38.	Asher	286
39.	June	296
40.	June	301
41.	Asher	312
42.	June	318
43.	Asher	320
44.	June	323
45.	Asher	326
46.	Asher	327
47.	June	335
48.	Asher	340
49.	June	346
50.	June	349
51.	Asher	355
52.	Asher	366
53.	June	370
54.	Asher	374

55. June	379
56. Asher	388
57. June	393
58. Asher	405
59. June	416
60. Asher	419
61. June	421
62. Asher	425
63. Epilogue: June	436
Want More?	445
Acknowledgements	446
About the author	448
Also by Meghan French	449

About Reckless Behavior

Reckless Behavior is the fourth and final book in the Chicago Foxes series of interconnected standalones. They can be read in any order but are best enjoyed in order of publication (Casual Now – I'll Look After You – The Way You Say Good Morning – Reckless Behavior).

JUNE:

I work hard and love hard, so sue me. Few things in my life have gone according to my plan lately. It's bad enough that I had to leave what I thought was my dream job when the company suddenly folded, necessitating a move back in with my parents. When my professional baseball player brother hooks me up with a job in Chicago working for the team there, there's finally a ray of hope in the shambles that have become my life. My brother even arranges my housing for me. There's just one small problem: I have to live with my brother's best friend, who may or may not be my childhood crush and the boy who gave me my first kiss, only to immediately break my heart after.

All I have to do is make it through the season. With one season under my belt, I'll have enough experience and money saved up to venture out on my own, until my new roommate suddenly has ideas of his own.

ASHER:

It's my first full season as the starting pitcher for the Chicago Foxes and I'm finally settling into a groove. I've got friends, my team is doing well, and I'm pitching the best I ever have in my life. So when I finally decide I can relax enough to focus on my love life (or lack thereof), I dip my toes in the dating pool only to discover complete humiliation. Apparently, my nerves surrounding the *extracurricular activities* after I take my date home translate into a fumbling, awkward mess, leaving all parties dissatisfied. In a desperate attempt to regain control of the narrative spreading throughout the city that I'm bad in bed, I agree to allow my roommate to give me lessons, as long as her brother never finds out.

Because what her overprotective brother and my best friend can't know–ever–is that I've been in love with June Demoranville since I was a teenager. I've kept her at a distance since then, and that's where she will remain. Forever.

CHAPTER ONE
June

"**O**pen up and take this cock."

My reaction is so visceral, so immediate, that I barely make it to the bathroom before vomiting. Because no one should *ever* hear those words coming from their parents' bedroom.

After heaving the contents of my breakfast into the toilet, I brush my teeth and close my eyes, vowing to move out as soon as possible. It's a welcome thought, after what I just heard, but the logistics will be a nightmare. I moved back into my parents' home only three weeks ago. Moving out without a new job isn't exactly an option, but with no one biting on the applications I've already sent out, I'm getting desperate. I was already desperate *before* I learned just how active my parents' sex life is. I suppress a shudder and fight another roll of my stomach. Then I rush back into my bedroom, lock the door, and pull up my laptop to resume my desperate hunt for employment. Anything to get me out of here.

"Your last name is rather unique, Ms. Demoranville," Deb says over the video call. "I just have to ask, any relation to the baseball player?"

I cringe internally, and only just manage to maintain my poker face. It was only a matter of time before this question came up. I was hoping maybe Deb simply worked for a baseball team but didn't really know anything about the sport. I'm not ashamed of Devin; quite the opposite. I'm still my brother's number one fan and he deserves every ounce of the insane success he's earned. I had just hoped that I wouldn't have to question my own skills as it relates to this job interview. I want to earn my new job, not have it handed to me because Devin is good at his.

I plaster a smile on my face. "Actually, he's my brother." I shrug, hoping it comes off as playful and nonchalant, without inviting further questions about my brother's personal life. Deb smiles indulgently, as if she knows what I'm thinking.

"I only asked that because I think you'll be great for the job. I'd like to recommend you to my bosses, but if you prefer I keep your family relationship out of that conversation, I'd be happy to. However, knowing that you have a firsthand understanding of baseball life and its stressors, I might suggest that you allow me to divulge that. I think it will only help your case."

I want to believe Deb. She's right; seeing Devin's progress through college baseball, to signing a minor league contract with San Francisco, to getting traded to New York, to coming up through New York's farm system, it's all been a learning experience not only for Devin, but for the rest of my family. I'm a huge baseball fan; in my family, it's practically a requirement. But prior to Devin going pro, I had no idea there were so many levels to the minor leagues, from rookie ball to low A to high A to all the As. Of course, Devin skipped a few levels, as do many players, but still. And yes, I'm sure my experience of being a family member to a player could be insightful, but it's a happy coincidence. I have the degree, the skills, and the experience to do this job, regardless of whether my brother is a professional athlete or not.

I smile, and watch myself on my screen, careful to mask any strain on my face. "Whatever you think would be best," I reply cheerfully. Deb nods and promises she'll be in touch by the end of the week.

Closing my browser, I drop my forehead to the desk. I'm in my childhood bedroom and the size of this desk is not exactly conducive to adult use. It's better than nothing, though. I'm glad my parents didn't hesitate to invite me back home when things ended at my last job. Having to pay rent on an apartment while not having a steady paycheck is not exactly what I want to do.

I love my freedom. I loved my apartment. I had it decorated exactly as I wanted it; its bright colors showcased my personality, and the space gave me the independence I was looking for. The shame of moving back in with my parents only a year after moving out is something I relive every night when I close my eyes. Which is why I've been applying for jobs like crazy. When Devin suggested I look for something with his team, offering for me to live with him in Manhattan, I initially balked, then let my imagination run wild.

Living with Devin again would have been a dream. Sure, we'd probably have had to set some ground rules, because from the articles Whitney and Christine occasionally send me, Devin is a gigantic man-whore, and I do not need to see the steady stream of women he no doubt brings home each week. But getting to be with my big brother day in and day out? Even thinking about it now makes me smile.

Admittedly, we grew apart when he went off to college, and even more so when I did the same. We still texted each other regularly, but even those texts spaced out from multiple times a day to only once or twice a week. Both of us were so busy, and now that Devin is a big-shot ball player, he's even shorter on time. But he made time for me when I told him about the debacle with my last job and their "downsizing." In that phone conversation, he came up with the idea of me joining him in New York.

Unfortunately, the New York Mustangs had no openings. There's a baseball employment portal across all Major League

Baseball, which lists every professional teams' openings, and that's where Devin stumbled upon a posting by the Chicago Foxes, in their family support program. Program management has always been my dream. It's what I did when I worked for the psychology clinic most recently, running their community and charitable programs division. I snort to myself. I was the only employee in my department, but they insisted on calling it a division.

Deb, the Foxes Family Program lead, seems nice. The entire interview went well, but I'm getting desperate. A move to Chicago might be what I need. This morning, I woke to the sounds of my parents having sex *again* and I was *thisclose* to shoving a drill in my ear and mashing the contents of my brain. The problem is, in order to move to Chicago, my new paycheck needs to be big enough to cover moving costs *and* finding a place to live in the city. Seeing as I'm only two years out of college, I haven't accrued the experience necessary to demand a high enough rate of pay to cover everything I need it to. Devin insisted that was a problem for Future June to worry about.

As if he can sense me thinking about him, my phone buzzes with an incoming video call from the man himself. I swipe to answer it.

"How'd it go?" Devin demands, skipping all niceties and greetings.

"Hello to you, too," I grumble. He rolls his eyes but still doesn't give me a greeting. He just waits. "Jerk. It went well, I think. The program lead said she was going to recommend me to her bosses, so that sounds hopeful, right?"

"Fuck yeah, Junie! I knew you'd kill it." I can't help but grin at my brother's unwavering enthusiasm for me.

"Don't get too excited. I don't have an offer or anything." I'm telling myself this as much as I'm telling Devin, because with no other interviews scheduled, most of my eggs are in the Foxes basket. "How's the Valley of the Sun?" I ask, changing the subject before I can get too anxious about jobs.

"Sunny," he answers with a shrug. "I'm trying to enjoy it while I can." He's a few weeks into Spring Training in Arizona, but we both know New York springs are notoriously fickle. Philadelphia springs too, I think, as I look out my bedroom window into the gloomy haze. "I'm meeting up tonight with a few of the guys from college who stayed around here. Oh! And Asher!"

I snort. "Why are you excited about going out with Asher? You see him all the time. I wouldn't be surprised if you read bedtime stories to each other every night."

Devin's glare is scorching, but I've been on the receiving end of it for twenty-three years; it's nothing I'm not already used to.

"We do not."

I can't help the laugh that escapes my lips. I obviously knew they didn't, but I guess it's nice to have official confirmation that my brother's high school best friend does not require a bedtime story.

"*Anyway*," Devin continues. "Seeing Asher is important because he's with the Foxes!"

Shit. I forgot.

It'll be fine. Even if I do get this job, I work with players' families, not the players themselves, so what are the odds Asher and I really will see each other? Besides, I haven't seen Asher in a long time. In fact, I haven't seen him in years, and even before that when I did, he's been super awkward and seems to go out of his way to avoid me.

"Not only is he with the Foxes," Devin plows on. "He's been kicking ass. He was up and down last year, but he helped them to win that World Series this past year." The Foxes faced off against Devin and the Mustangs, and the series was neck-and-neck for most of it. It killed me not to see Dev's team win, so much so that I forgot Asher was even on the opposing team at the time. "He's for sure making the Opening Day roster this season."

Devin is the kind of friend (and brother) everyone wants in their corner. His unwavering loyalty and support are someof his greatest features, and I'm happy to hear his excitement for the success of one of his oldest friends. I'm happy for Asher, too. Despite his weirdness around me, he's worked incredibly hard to get where he's at. He's been sent up and down frequently in the last couple of years, hovering in this weird limbo between Triple-A and the major leagues. Devin's natural talent, unbreakable work ethic, and a consistent string of good luck allowed him to fast-track to the highest level of professional baseball; I know very few athletes are that lucky. Asher's trajectory is still more impressive than the average athlete's, even if his upward movement was slower than my brother's.

"Good for him," I tell Devin, meaning it.

"The point is, Junie, you can probably live with him!" My jaw literally drops open. Whether Devin sees or not, he doesn't acknowledge it. "Think about it! I'm sure he's got a decent place, given that he's been on the forty-man roster forever. Living with him wouldn't be that different from living with me!" I try to wipe the disbelief off my face. Living with Asher, however improbable, would be *nothing* like living with Devin, and for good reason.

Devin is still rambling, but I haven't heard the last several sentences. I'm still recovering from the shock of having my brother play apartment matchmaker with unsuspecting landlords.

"Sorry, what?"

Devin tsks and rolls his eyes. "I *said,* I'll ask him tonight. We're scheduled to hit the driving range after the game."

CHAPTER TWO
Asher

The heat must be getting to me. Arizona in the spring is usually nice, hovering around eighty-five degrees at its hottest, but we've been experiencing an unusual heat wave for this time of year. The extra ten degrees makes a huge difference, and my golf swing is evidence of that. I forgo the frosty beers sitting in the bucket on the table behind us and ask the server if they have any electrolyte drinks. I recognize it's an odd request, as this place is half-bar, half-entertainment complex, but it's still a driving range, so I'm hoping they have some sort of sports drink.

The waitress directs me to a vending machine near the stairwell. Loading my arms up with chilled bottles, I return to the group Devin organized on the top floor. I've known most of the guys here for a couple of years, because Devin insists on hosting this reunion every spring. They're not bad guys, but it's only a matter of time before the conversation changes to my two least favorite topics. The inevitable questions about who I'm seeing (no one) and when I'm going to be a permanent fixture in the big leagues (trust me, I'm trying) are wearing after hearing them year after year. While most of these men played baseball with Devin in college, he's the only one to successfully go professional, and he did it in record time. I'm still making strides toward my own big-league career, but whether I make it or not is limitedly within my control. There are so many factors—including management style, roster spots, salary caps, and egos—in addition to my on-field performance.

By the time I make it back to our lounge area behind our bay, Devin is finishing a god-awful swing. You'd think he and I would be playing better, given that we (he, more so than I) swing bats around for a living, but apparently, I'm not the only one affected by the heat. I wordlessly hand him a red Gatorade, knowing it's his favorite. I unscrew the cap off my own blue flavor and down half of it in one go.

"Thanks." Devin sits heavily on the couch and I follow suit. I'm starting tomorrow's game, so I avoid the greasy, fried onion rings on the table in front of us, but I can't resist a particularly cheesy bite of nacho. I tell myself it's healthier than an onion ring because it's got chicken on it and Allie, one of our nutritionists, is on me about upping my protein intake. I snap a picture of the loaded tortilla and send it off to her with a quick message.

Me

> See? Already increasing my protein.

Allie

> <facepalm emoji> Not what I meant.

Allie was the dietician at Triple-A with me last year, and we struck up a professional friendship. I think she was almost as bummed as me each time I got called up to the majors, only to be sent back to our minor league affiliate a few weeks later. It's the nature of the beast, especially when we have a strong major league club, but it still stings. This spring, I've been working my ass off to make the Opening Day roster. I did last year, but only because another player's injury opened a temporary spot for me. I was promptly sent back to the minors after a couple of weeks. This year, I'm determined to make the team and stay there. I have no plans to be back in the minor leagues. Ever.

Working my ass off this offseason and Spring Training means I rarely make time for social outings such as these. I'm sure Devin is a little worried about me, but he knows this is the way things go. He's the obvious choice for New York's Opening Day catcher, so even though there are still two weeks of Spring Training left, barring injury, he's got nothing to worry about for himself.

"You've got nothing to worry about, Ash," Devin tells me, reading my thoughts. "Your ERA is low. You're looking confident on the mound. The fifth spot is yours." Last year, I served a middle reliever role, coming into the games after the starting pitcher was done. I'd pitch for an inning or two before the closer came in to seal the deal. This year, the manager had the idea to stretch me out for a starting position. I was thrilled when Samuel "Benny" Benjamin, the Foxes' manager, called me and proposed the suggestion. I grew up playing starting pitcher; the idea of throwing ninety pitches a game doesn't scare me. I'll do whatever it takes to make it to The Show.

It's taken a lot of work this offseason, working remotely with my strength and conditioning coaches to build my stamina, working with local pitching clinics in Philadelphia and making the drive into Manhattan twice a week to work with a pitching specialist Benny recommended. The work has paid off, though; I feel better than ever, and Devin's not wrong: my confidence on the mound has never been higher.

"So, Asher, are you seeing anyone these days?" Tom, one of Devin's old teammates, asks. I'm immediately reminded that my confidence on the mound does not translate to confidence with the opposite sex. I shrug.

"Nah, I've been focusing on work." Tom nods, as if he really understands the single-minded focus it's taken me to get here.

"You can do both," Tom tells me. He playfully shoves Devin. "This guy does both all the time. I'm telling you, man, when I visited him in New York last year, women practically threw themselves at him. It was like shooting fish in a barrel."

Devin frowns. He might get around, but he's never been disrespectful toward the women he's with. Tom, however, is a bit of an ass.

"But I guess that's why Asher's got the World Series ring, not you, huh, Dev?" Like I said, an ass. He's mostly harmless, so Devin and I ignore his remarks, and he shifts to the high-top table next to us and engages in conversation with them, repeating the same story and looking for a laugh.

"I wanted to ask you a favor, Ash." Devin's tone is suddenly serious. "June's last job was kind of a shitshow. I don't know all the details, but it crashed and burned hard and fast, so she moved back to Philly and is desperately looking for a new job."

"Okay..." I say. I'd probably have a more sympathetic response to June's plight if Devin wasn't giving me his best puppy dog eyes. It sucks that she needs a new job, but I'm not sure what that has to do with me.

"I tried to get her to move to Manhattan with me, but she wasn't thrilled about the job prospects. But she found an open position with the Foxes. She interviewed today and I think she's gonna get it."

"Oh, wow. Good for her." I've kept the loosest of tabs on June since she went off to college in New Jersey. I don't remember what her major was, or what field her career is in. I've done my best to tune out as much information on her as I can. Writing maybe? Shit, I hope she's not a reporter. I've gone through media training, but the idea of talking to June after every start is already giving me heart palpitations. Devin's still talking and I missed the last part of what he said.

"...obviously will need to move to Chicago." I nod, pretending I didn't just space out for a moment there. "You still have that two-bedroom, right? Can you do me a solid and let her move in with you?"

He's looking at me expectantly, and what can I say? *No?* Devin's been my best friend since we were fifteen and it sounds like June is in a real bind. When I don't say anything, he starts up again.

"I'll cover her rent, utilities, all of that, so this doesn't put you out more than it already is." I scowl. This is not about the money. I may not have officially made the Opening Day roster, but I am on the forty-man, meaning my union benefits dictate I make the league minimum, which means a good paycheck. Certainly enough to afford rent on a two-bedroom apartment in Lakeview. Certainly enough where I don't need my roommate's brother covering the minimal additional expenses living with June will require.

Shit, what am I thinking? I haven't even agreed to this. And it's not because of the money. The idea of living with June is making me sweat more than the Arizona heat is already doing.

"Please, Ash. She needs a win."

"I don't even know if I'll be there. I haven't made the team yet." I tell him lamely, grappling for an excuse. He smiles, knowing as well as I do that if that's the best I've got, I've pretty much agreed to his favor.

"You will. I've lived with June most of my life; she's an easy roomie. She won't cramp your style."

I swallow. I nod, because what else can I do? It's not like I can tell Devin his sister can't live with me. I already have the apartment leased through the season, whether I make the team or not.

I guess we're doing this. Assuming she gets the job. Knowing June's tenacity, I'm sure she will.

Fuck.

CHAPTER THREE
June
Age 15

"Shh, she's coming!" Christine's voice carries more than I'm sure she wants it to, seeing as it's me she's talking about. I don't mind too much, though, because I know she's not talking shit. Sighing, I realize I might prefer it if she was, because the only other topic she and Whitney ever discuss is far less preferable. Climbing the metal bleachers to get to them, each of my steps echoes in an unflattering clunk, culminating in an even larger thunk when I drop my backpack onto the empty row in front of my two best friends. Whitney's flushed cheeks confirm what I already know: they were discussing my brother.

In an objective way, I get it. Tall, strong, and on the varsity baseball team, I guess he's what some girls would consider conventionally attractive, with his sparkling green eyes and wavy chocolate hair. If he weren't my brother, I might be inclined to agree. But he is, so it's gross and annoying that both of my closest friends have developed raging crushes on him. I'm pretty sure he's aware of it, too, but he hasn't said anything.

Like we do every day, we gather on the bleachers outside of our high school baseball diamond. We're supposed to be working on homework, but we mostly end up chatting, gossiping, and watching boys in tight baseball pants practice whatever skills their coaches deem critical that day. The boys still have another forty-five minutes before they're released for the day, having already completed an hour doing who-knows-what in the weight room.

I take a bite of what's left of my churro, having come straight from Spanish club. I offer a bite to both of my friends, but only Whit partakes. Christine is still distracted by the over-the-top stretching Greg's doing in front of the dugout. At least Greg acknowledges us, even if he's a little obnoxious.

Slapping the excess cinnamon sugar from my hands, I lean back, bracing my elbows and upper back on the row behind me, soaking in the early April sunshine. It's unseasonably warm today and while the sun feels good, I hope it doesn't make me sweat too much. The last thing I need is a sheen of sweat to accompany my already embarrassing mouth full of metal and the newly emerging pimple on my chin. Just once, I'd like to show up to my brother's practice feeling as confident as my friends do. They're not the least bit self-conscious as we all gawk at the teenagers in front of us.

Devin is crouched in a squat behind home plate, decked out in his red and white catcher's gear. It's no surprise that, at two years older than me, he's playing on the varsity team. He's played on it since freshman year. I'm not just supporting my brother when I say he's really good; he's already been scouted by colleges, and his junior-year season has barely started. He thinks he's going to go pro one day, and he's probably right. Literally every goal Devin has set for himself, he achieves. I'd feel jealous if he were cocky about it, but he's really down-to-earth.

I love my brother. He's looked out for me since we were little, and he's (mostly) tolerated the way I've tagged along after him in pretty much everything we've done growing up. Even now, when our age difference and interests have us diverging more often than not, he still always slings an arm around my shoulder as we walk to the car together after his practices. I could take the bus home if I didn't want to wait for him, but Dev got his license last year and the excitement of having him drive me around still hasn't worn off. Plus, having my friends here to hang out with while I wait for him to finish up makes it fun.

I tug my pink polka-dotted backpack open and rummage around until I find my cat-eye sunglasses. Plopping them on my face, I'm hoping they make me look cool and casual and sophisticated and mature. Because as much as I love my brother, I am *not* here for him.

My covered gaze slides to the pitcher's mound where the most beautiful boy on the team stands, his own gaze locked on my brother. Devin lobs him the ball and he catches it easily, gracefully. Gripping the ball in his right hand, he adjusts the brim of his hat with the same fingers. If I tried to hold something in my hand and adjust any part of my clothing, I'd be a fumbling mess. Instead, Asher Incaudo looks relaxed, comfortable... gorgeous. While I can't see his hazel eyes from my vantage point in the stands, I know they're narrowed on my brother's glove as he starts his windup. He releases the ball and it sails directly into Devin's mitt, before Dev pops it out and tosses it immediately back to the mound.

My brother has been playing baseball with Asher for as long as I can remember. They weren't always close, but once they started playing on the high school team together, they have been an unstoppable force both on and off the field. They have similar class schedules, so one is usually with the other when I catch sight of them in the hallways. Devin always greets me with a lift of his chin, but sometimes, I swear Asher doesn't even know I exist.

I know he exists, though. My spidey senses are highly attuned to Asher's presence. Now that they both can drive, they rarely hang out at our house on the weekends like they used to, instead preferring to go out. The invitation is never extended to me. Which is fine by me, mostly. Christine, Whitney, a few of our other friends, and I usually keep fairly busy ourselves, but once, *just once*, I'd love to be a fly on the wall to see what Asher and Devin get up to in their free time.

Asher is the perfect balance to Devin's more intense personality. Whitney describes my brother as "brooding," whatever that means. Asher is more carefree, in a quiet, sidekick kind of way.

My thoughts of Asher are broken by Whitney's whispered "damn" when the boys run back toward the dugout. I know not to ask what she's referring to. Yesterday, she said something similar and when I asked what she was talking about, she went into far too much detail about the tightness of my brother's uniform and how it shifted over his body as he popped to standing. Part of my tuna salad sandwich from lunch had threatened to make a reappearance. I pointedly ignore today's remarks.

By the time the guys finish, Whitney's mom has already picked her and Christine up. They, too, could ride the bus home, but they've convinced their parents they're in clubs as well. In all honesty, the level of enthusiasm they bring to their very own varsity baseball fan experience might count as a legitimate club experience. Membership is at an all-time high of just the two of them. I don't consider myself a part of their little club because my fangirling is limited only to the pitcher, but they don't know that. I keep my crush on Asher under wraps, not just from Devin, who I'm sure would first laugh himself silly if he found out, followed by needless threats to leave his friends alone, but my secret is kept from my closest friends as well. I'm not sure why, but I just want a piece of Asher for myself.

It's technically summer, and our freshman year ended with the varsity Redwings making it all the way to the Pennsylvania state championships. Not only did they make it, but they practically swept the whole thing. The team played well, obviously, and Devin took home the coveted MVP designation, after he hit two home runs in one day, including the walk-off homer to win the championship.

The road to the win was fun, mostly because I got to tag along. The state championship was in Pittsburgh, which is a straight shot across I-76, but because it was nearly five hours away from where we live, my parents made the trip too, booking a room in the same hotel as the team. Of course, Devin and Asher roomed together, and Dev didn't bat an eye when I asked if I could join them in watching a movie in their room the night before the big game.

Devin had laughed at how jumpy I was while we watched Taken, a movie I'd seen before. But the truth is, I only jumped because Asher's arm brushed mine when he crouched next to my spot on the tiny loveseat to get another soda from the cooler. He and Asher were watching from their respective beds, and every once in a while, I would watch Asher from my periphery, the plot of the movie entirely forgotten. Like the creep that I am, I watched his broad chest rise and fall with his breaths. I watched the way his throat worked as he swallowed down a gulp of Sprite. Then, I watched him play absently on his phone and pay me absolutely zero attention.

But apparently a night of sugary soda and thriller movies makes for championship material, because the boys won. Now that the state champ trophy is firmly secured in the locked halls of our high school, the team is looking to continue that celebration.

Greg's parents are notoriously absent, which means he's hosting tonight's celebration. I'm not a drinker, and neither is Devin–he's too concerned he might do something stupid while drunk and mess up his chances at the big leagues. Me? I'm just too scared to get in trouble. Armed with Whitney and Christine, though, I'm feeling a little more confident. My braces came off yesterday morning, and I can't stop running my tongue over my teeth. They feel so hard and smooth and slippery, and when I catch glimpses of my new smile in my reflection, the two years of torture were worth it.

I'm wearing a new pair of skinny jeans and a scoop neck tank top that's loose enough to hide my stomach chub but tight enough to show off the girls, but my confidence is coming mostly from my new smile and equally new pair of espadrille wedges. I'm average height, but the wedges give me the inches I didn't know I was missing. Plus, they make my not-so-average-sized butt look great.

Never one to miss an opportunity to showcase at least one quirky feature, my tank is proudly emblazoned with a sparkly green cactus and the words *Don't be a prick*. My hazelnut locks are curled in loose, brushed out waves and I've perfected my winged liner to the point where I know I'll never be able to replicate it ever again. I'm glad I was able to pull out all the stops on a night where I know Asher will be around.

The three of us waltz into Greg's house behind Devin. We all know we wouldn't be allowed in if we didn't come with him, seeing as we're barely no longer freshman, but we all pretend that we were personally invited. Whit and Christine are planning on sleeping over at my house after, and I know both of them are planning on drinking for the first time.

Devin peels away from us as soon as we cross the threshold of Greg's enormous house. He's immediately beckoned by a gaggle of girls to join them. My brother may not drink or smoke, but he can't resist the allure of the opposite sex. I don't even want to know the number of times he's had sex, despite both Whitney and Christine musing that the number must be high enough that he knows what he's doing. *Barf.*

The girls and I do a lap around the main floor, taking in the various groups of people grinding in the living room, mixing drinks at the kitchen counter, partaking in the enormous amount of snacks set out in the dining room, and the group of stoners smoking out Greg's dad's study. Outside in the backyard, music is playing, and Greg and a group of seniors I don't recognize are lounging in their underwear in the hot tub. Christine lets her eyes linger, but I hurry Whitney along to get back inside. There's no way I will be taking off any of my clothing in front of anyone else tonight, thank you very much. I'm all for women owning their bodies, but my self-confidence is not that evolved right now.

"I need a drink," Whitney mutters, and it's hard to disagree.

"I'll get one with you," Christine agrees, ripping her eyes away from Greg's torso. He smirks, knowing the effect he has not just on Christine, but on the other girls in the water with him, too.

Drinks in hand (Sprite for me), the three of us smoosh together on the loveseat in Greg's basement. Devin and some of his teammates are playing pool while a raucous group plays some sort of team/first-person shooter game on the couches next to us. It's my first real party, but somehow, it doesn't feel much different from my usual hangouts with Whitney and Christine with the backdrop of a party surrounding us. Christine sucks loudly through her straw, and it makes a rattling noise, alerting us all to its empty status.

"I can go get us some more," I announce. I need to get off this couch; it's hard not to feel a little disappointed that this party hasn't lived up to the hype. Maybe it's because we hardly know anyone here, or that none of us are extroverted. I don't know what I was expecting when Devin allowed us to tag along, but I guess I was expecting a bit more…excitement?

Entering the kitchen, I swear the music fades into the background as I lay eyes on Asher. He's leaning against the kitchen sink, one ankle crossed over the other. His Redwings baseball cap is pulled low over his eyes, but I can just make out the gold flecks in their hazel backdrop. His Pearl Jam tee is stretched across his chest in a way that is tight without being too small. He looks relaxed, bicep bunching when he palms the back of his neck, deep in conversation with Michael, the first baseman, and his girlfriend, Luna. I watch, entranced, as Asher brings a beer bottle to his lips. When he pulls it away, I stare as his tongue, in slow motion, darts out to catch the drop of liquid on his top lip. I finally break my stare when someone bumps into me and I fumble Christine's empty cup, crunching it loudly in my attempt to maintain my grasp. At the sound, Asher's eyes flick to me.

Dammit, why couldn't he catch me doing something cool, like laughing while surrounded by my adoring fans?

I lamely hold up Christine's cup, giving it a little shake. "Just, uh, getting some more," I explain, as if an explanation was necessary. Grabbing the closest liquor bottle–vodka–I tip it into the cup. I have no idea what I'm doing or if this is enough. Too much? I don't even know if Christine was drinking vodka earlier, and I vaguely remember hearing something about how you shouldn't mix liquors.

"Whoa, easy there, killer." Asher's deep voice sounds over my shoulder. He takes the bottle from my hand and sets it on the kitchen island. "You trying to get wasted or just die tonight?"

"Oh um," I stutter, peering into the cup now half-filled with liquor. "It's for Christine." I sigh, deciding to be honest instead of trying to cool-girl it with Asher. I'm pretty sure I already failed on that front. "I have no idea what I'm doing."

"Let's just…" He trails off, pouring more than half of the cup's contents into an empty cup from the stack nearby. "That should be plenty."

"Thanks," I say, tucking my hair behind my ear. I crack open a can of Sprite and fill the rest of the cup. I want to say more, but I have nothing left to say.

"Smile at me," Asher instructs abruptly. Even if he didn't tell me to do so, I would have. Smiling seems to be my face's automatic reaction upon seeing him. The boy in question smiles back at me, cataloguing my shiny new teeth. My cheeks flame at the undiluted attention, and I realize this is the Best. Party. Ever. "Looks good, June. How does it feel to get your braces off?"

"Good. Really good, actually. Thank you for notic–" I start, but my words are cut off by a shout.

"Hey, Ash! Callie and Lexi think they can take us in darts! Come down here!" My brother's voice booms up from the basement stairs. Asher turns, winking at me before he goes.

"Try not to die tonight, June, yeah?"

The rest of the night passes in a short succession of watching Lexi flirt with Asher while keeping an eye on Christine getting progressively more drunk. I never considered myself a jealous person, but I hate that Lexi bitch.

I sigh.

Lexi is probably a nice, normal girl. I just hate that she has Asher's attention.

This has gone on long enough, I tell myself. It's true. I've had this huge, going-nowhere crush on my brother's teammate for the whole school year. He's polite enough to greet me, acknowledge me, when I'm around Devin, but other than that, I'm pretty sure he's not even aware of my existence. It's time I let him go.

Chapter Four

June

Age 16

I try to blink back my tears, but it's no use. Just as the first tear pushes past the boundary of my waterline, I paste on a fake-ass smile so big it crinkles the corners of my eyes. I hope it's passable. I hope these tears will be interpreted by everybody, especially my brother, as tears of happiness. Because it's what he deserves. I quickly wipe my eyes with the sleeve of my cable-knit sweater.

Devin has officially signed his letter of intent to attend college in Tempe, Arizona. It's a great school, an incredible baseball program, and almost as far from Philadelphia as physically possible. I am genuinely happy for him, but I am so sad for myself. I've never not had my brother around, and while I always knew he'd go off to college without me, I've been in denial about just how soon that will be happening.

The local newspaper covered all the student athlete signing-day news today, so it was cool to see Dev have his moment in front of the cameras. I'm glad I got to be here to see my brother's official signing, since it happened to occur during my lunch period in the lobby outside the main gym, next to the cafeteria.

Shadows cross my periphery as a tall, lanky body comes into view. I glance up, taking in Asher's large form next to me.

"That stupidly handsome face was made for the media, huh?"

I grin. "I was thinking the exact same thing. It's disgusting how comfortable he looks up there with everyone fawning over him."

"Better get used to it, June. That kid's going places."

"I hear he's not the only one." I give him a pointed look and he smiles in response.

"Yeah. Devin's already planning when he can come visit me in Baton Rouge next year. He's already researched the shuttle that will take us to New Orleans."

I chuckle. "I'm not surprised. He's probably stocking up on Mardi Gras beads. Pig."

"I'm pretty sure he's already bought them in bulk." Asher and I fade into a comfortable silence. I can feel his eyes on me, but I make no move to face him. "You okay, June?"

"Yep!" My tone is overly cheery. Asher's not buying it, but that's probably because I fail to hide the tiny sniff after it.

"He's gonna miss you, too, you know." His voice is quiet, somber. "He's already lectured the younger guys on the team to keep an eye out for you. Of course, then he followed that immediately by saying he'd find out and murder them if they laid a hand on you." I snort, believing every word.

"No wonder I'm still single," I mumble, trying for funny, but it just comes out a little sad.

"Ah, come on." Asher bumps his shoulder with mine. "He's just protective. It's how he shows his love." I hum noncommittally.

"Are you ready for tonight?" I ask, intentionally changing the subject. Part of me wants to blame my lack of romantic prospects on Dev's overprotectiveness, but the truth is, I think he'd step aside if I asked him to. The thing is, I've never had an opportunity to ask him to, because no one has shown an interest in me. I try not to think about it too much, which is a nearly impossible feat.

"As ready as I'll ever be," Asher says, and I'm grateful he doesn't say anything about my abrupt change in subject. Tonight is the school talent show and Asher's last year to perform. He plays guitar every year, sometimes singing and sometimes performing as part of the many bands he's been involved with at various points. I didn't go to his shows prior to attending high school with him, but if last year's performance is any indication, Asher will blow it out of the water again this year.

Asher did more than just blow it out of the water. He brought the house down. He played lead guitar and sang a cover of "Sometime Around Midnight" by The Airborne Toxic Event. Lexi played violin in the small band Asher assembled just for the show, but my eyes were drawn to him and only him the entire time. He infused the perfect amount of emotion into his voice to convey the anguish behind the lyrics. Then, at the end of the show, he led all of the talent show performers in an ensemble rendition of "Good Riddance" by Green Day. It's only February, but the members of the senior class in the audience were misty-eyed.

Suddenly, all the work I did to forget about the feelings I held for Asher went out the window, and I'm right back at square one, desperately hoping for something, *anything*, to distract me from my feelings for Asher Incaudo.

Chapter Five
June
Present Day

"I'm looking forward to it, too. Thank you again," I tell Deb sincerely. After hanging up, I set my phone down carefully on my too-small childhood desk, push my chair back, and silently do a happy dance in my seat.

I got the job. I got the job!

After the shitstorm that went down at my job in Tampa, my confidence was on shaky ground. It's nice to get a win. It's nice to be reminded that others value my skill set, that I *am* good at my job. In my interview, Deb had explained that this job was pretty much an amalgamation of all of my skills: organizing events, establishing charitable connections, supporting players' partners and families, coordinating support services, and beefing up player perks like family babysitting. My Spanish skills will be utilized frequently too, which was something I was concerned about losing when I moved away from Tampa. After the interview, I tried not to get too excited, but now that the job is mine, I can firmly say it is everything I've ever wanted in a job. A sharp reminder not to get too excited sticks to my ribs; I thought the job in Florida was all I could want, too.

Still, I need to share the news with someone. My parents are both at work, so I dial Christine. She's in her second year of law school and her free time is extremely limited, but she made me promise to call her as soon as I heard back from the Foxes. She picks up on the first ring.

"Tell me it's good news," she demands.

"It's good news," I say, unable to keep the grin out of my words. "They want me to start next week. They asked if I could start before then, but getting to Chicago is going to take a bit and I'm pretty sure my parents would murder me in my sleep if I tried to leave tomorrow."

Opening Day for the Mustangs is next week, which I'm assuming means the Foxes start the same day. Deb told me the Foxes start the season on the road, so if I start next Tuesday, it should give me a couple days to get my feet wet before the team rolls in.

"Do you have a place? Are you going to take Devin up on his offer to reach out to Asher?"

"Ugh, I don't know. I feel like that's my best option, right? This job doesn't pay that well, but it's what I want to do. I don't know how else I'm going to live in an expensive city. I could find a roommate on the internet, but you know, murder." Christine makes a sound of assent.

"I know you don't want to take advantage of your brother's friend, but I thought you and Asher got along well? Why are you so hung up on this? It could be fun."

"Yeah, we did get along decently well, I guess. I suppose living with Asher would be better than living with a stranger. And he'd be on the road half the time anyway, so I'd probably mostly have the place to myself when I'm not working." I'm thinking aloud, but Christine is making small, agreeable noises to let me know she's still listening. I hear her shuffling papers in the background, though, so I know I'll have to cut this short. "Look, I'm just worried things will be awkward," I finally blurt out.

"Why? Because of your ginormous crush on him in high school?" Christine is clearly distracted, but her tone is still amused.

"You knew about that?" I roll my chair back further as I take in the revelation that my biggest secret was, apparently, not so much of a secret.

"Girl, everyone knew about that."

"Do you think *Asher* knew about it?" I shriek.

"Relax. Probably not. Men are oblivious. Remember how Devin didn't even know Whit and I were obsessed with him until you told him, like, two years ago when we got drunk at your parents' Christmas party?" I let out a slow breath. That is true. Men really are oblivious. Because my crush on Asher was *definitely* more subtle than hers on my brother.

"Okay, first of all," Christine starts, and I can envision her ticking off her fingers as she talks. "It was, like, *seven* years ago. He's probably forgotten about it. And you should, too, considering you've dated, like, a ton of people since then." I scoff, but don't correct her. What can I say? I love love, and I'll give it every opportunity to cross my path. "Second of all, so what? It's just a crush. I mean, I fucked your brother at that Christmas party and we can still be in the same room as each other."

"Ex*cuse* me?" I'm shouting now. "You did *what* with my brother?"

"Guess you're not the only one keeping secrets, huh babe?" She dissolves into a fit of laughter. I should have known; Devin fucks anything with a vagina and Christine's been practically advertising hers to him since we were freshmen.

"I hope you wore protection," I mutter.

"So do you want to hear how good he was?" Christine's laughter is reaching hysteria; I'm pretty sure she's struggling to breathe.

"No, gross. Fuck off. I'm done with this call." I hang up on her, and a moment later my phone buzzes with her text.

Christine

> Love you. <angel emoji> <kissing face emoji>

> Seriously, don't worry about this Asher thing. It's only weird if you make it weird.

I put off calling my brother with the news of my job for the rest of the day, but I should have known my parents would get to him first. I decline his video call, but call him back on audio. I have a decent poker face, but Devin has always been able to read me like a book. Still, I've kept the secret about my crush on Asher. I don't need him to find out about it now, seven years after the fact. As far as Devin knows, I'm a blushing virgin who's still waiting for her first kiss. I snort, just as he answers the phone.

"I see how it is. You reject my video call but can't resist reaching out anyway."

"I just got out of the shower," I lie, but he doesn't question it.

"So, when were you going to tell me about the new job?" He sounds like a disappointed dad, and I'm almost sad he can't see my face to watch how hard I roll my eyes at him.

"I just got it today, Dev. Relax." I can feel him warring with himself, wanting to guilt me about making him wait but also wanting to show me just how excited he is. The excitement wins out.

"I'm so proud of you, June Bug! I knew you'd get it!" In the back of my mind, I still have a lingering doubt that my last name had something to do with the job offer, but the rest of the interview, before Deb asked if I was related to Devin, seemed to go well too.

"When do you start?"

"Next week." I can feel my own grin spread across my face. It's nice to be excited about a new job again.

"That's great, sis. I'm happy for you. And hey, I talked to Asher already and he said he'd be thrilled to have you as his new roommate." I snort. I doubt those words came out of Asher's mouth; I suspect he took some convincing, but I appreciate the gesture nonetheless.

"Thanks for asking him, Dev. I promise, I'll be out of his hair as soon as I get a couple paychecks under my belt and can afford something on my own. Will you tell him that?"

"You can tell him yourself. I'll send you his number. But June, you know this isn't just about the money. If it were, I would have just covered an apartment for you myself." He pauses, hesitating. "I'm worried about you, Junie. It's hard to move to a new city where you don't know anyone. You've seemed a little…sad…lately. Maybe living with someone–who isn't Mom and Dad–might do you good."

My eyes fill with tears and I'm once again grateful I declined the video option of this call. I know Devin means well, but I don't need him treating me like some fragile little doll. So what? My last job went down in flames, which just so happened to coincide with a rough breakup, causing me to flee the state in shame. It happens to a lot of people, right?

"Promise me you'll stay at Asher's at least through the season. Then you can figure out the rest, but starting a new job, in a new city, trying to make friends and get your feet under you? It's a lot, all at once."

"'Kay," I say, my throat tight.

After I hang up with Devin, he sends me Asher's contact info. Swallowing, I figure I might as well get this over with sooner rather than later. I tap out a text quickly, hit send, and promptly throw my phone on my bed to avoid overthinking.

> Me
> Hey Asher! This is June Demoranville! Dev sent me your new number. He told me about your "offer" to let me stay with you in Chicago, and I hope he didn't torture you too much to get you to agree! Anyway, I really really appreciate it!

Ugh. *Lay off the exclamation points, June.* I sound like a psychopath.

My phone chimes with a response almost immediately.

> Asher
> You're welcome.

That's it. You're welcome. Followed by the dreaded period.

Three hours later, I still don't have any information about Asher, his place, or anything else. I hope that Devin will fill in the blanks for me. I'm not sure how living with someone who seems intent on still avoiding me, all these years later, is going to go, but I don't really have another choice.

CHAPTER SIX
Asher

> Me
> Let me know when you're close and I'll meet you downstairs to help with your things.

An hour ago, June had given my message a thumb's up. I scroll to the top of our text exchange. It's sparse at best. June's use of exclamation points reminds me just how bubbly she can be. I grind my teeth in response. I need to get control of myself; I can't be an asshole to my best friend's sister. She's going to be living with me, for Christ's sake.

June sent me another text a couple days ago, letting me know she got the envelope I overnighted to her, containing keys to the apartment and the garage door opener. It's a small building, set on top of an underground parking garage, and I like the security. I didn't know when June would be getting here, because I didn't bother to ask, so I sent the essentials, including the address, in the envelope. It was probably a douchey thing to do, but I don't really know how to navigate this. She told me she'd be arriving today, which is an off day before our home opener tomorrow, and like a fool, I've been opening and closing my texts all day, just in case I missed a message from her announcing her arrival.

Three little dots pop up, telling me she's typing.

June

> Getting off Lake Shore Drive now!! ETA is 10 minutes!!

I unfold myself from my couch, scanning the living room to make sure there's nothing out of place that I missed in my earlier scans. I could say I'm a nervous cleaner, but the truth is, I just like things organized. And while I'm a little nervous for Opening Day tomorrow, I'm not pitching, so there's little for me to be nervous about.

Two weeks ago, Benny pulled me aside and told me the fifth spot in the pitching rotation was mine, and I wanted to hug the man. I remained professional, shaking his hand instead, but I wanted to laugh and cry and let out a whoop of joy.

Last year, I made the Opening Day roster, but as a reliever, with the understanding that as soon as the injured player I was replacing healed, I was to head back down to the minors. This year, there is no such condition hanging over my head. I'll be the man on the mound every five days, and I'm determined to let Benny and Foxes ownership know they chose the right man for the job.

I may not be pitching tomorrow, but I'll be starting the day after, and while I'm nervous, I also can't wait. I feel like a kid before the first day of school. Sure, technically baseball season already started when we played three games on the road in Kansas City, but a home opener in Chicago? I'm pretty sure that's what heaven is made of.

The slow-moving Prius rolling down my street tells me that's likely June looking for the correct address. When I see her flick on her turn signal into the parking garage from my third-story window, I take the stairs down to the garage to meet her. My long legs eat up the distance from the stairwell to where she's pulling in, and I direct her to one of the two reserved spots assigned to my unit.

She clambers out of the car and leans back into a full-body stretch. She's been driving since early this morning, making the twelve-hour trek in one go. I'm reminded of my days in the lower-level minor leagues, where we bussed from one location to another. Brutal.

After stretching, June grins and greets me with a crushing hug. Her scent, apple and something else I can't quite place, envelops me. I can't help but smile back as I breathe her in. It's been years since I've seen her, yet she's still somehow the same June I've known for the last ten years. She looks like a freckled version of Aidy Bryant, with her long, wavy hair and pretty, blue eyes. The shirt stretched across her torso says "Dogs > People." Her warm embrace erases the tension that's been bracketing my mouth and shoulders since Devin convinced me to let her move in. Maybe this won't be as bad as I envisioned.

Releasing her, I step to the trunk and open it. "Let me help you with your things." She goes to pull out a suitcase, but I stop her with a gentle hand on her shoulder. "You can get the doors."

Loading two duffels across each of my shoulders, I drag her roller bag behind me and up the stairs, thankful for the extra workouts I put in this past offseason. Trailing behind her so she can open the doors for me, I don't realize what a terrible idea this is until June's a few stairs above me on the steps, putting my eyes directly in line with the wide expanse of the back of her thighs and her perfect, round ass.

Fuck. Me.

Rooming together is going to be exactly as hard as I thought it would be.

Chapter Seven
June

I was pleasantly surprised when I got out of the car a few minutes ago and it seemed like the years dividing Asher and me melted away. The years have been good to him. His dirty blond hair is long, almost to his shoulders, and with his blue ballcap, he looks every inch a baseball pitcher. And he has a lot of inches. Google told me he was six and a half feet tall, and I believe it. He's still lanky, all long arms and legs, but his form has filled out a little more, and the extra bulk looks good on him.

He allowed me to hug him when I arrived and his smile upon seeing me seemed genuine. I'm almost convinced that I made up the idea that he's been trying to avoid me for the last seven years. Maybe I was reading into things too much. Regardless, I decide to let it go. We're adults now, and we're starting fresh. I really am relieved to have a friend by my side as I start my next chapter.

Asher insists I stay in the apartment while he brings the rest of my things up from the car. I didn't bring all that much; admittedly, most of my bags contain clothes. Devin assured me Asher's place was fully furnished, which is just as well, considering I left all my furniture in storage down in Florida.

Before he left to grab another load, he gave me a brief tour of the apartment. It's not huge, but it's appropriately sized for just one or two people. Two bedrooms fan out from the open living room and kitchen. In-unit laundry and a bathroom are on the opposite side of the living room, along with a door to a small back deck where Asher keeps a charcoal grill. His place is tidy and organized, and I hope he didn't feel the need to clean for me.

I haul my biggest bag onto the queen-sized bed in the guest room. Unzipping the sides, I begin to unpack, placing my clothes in the simple black dresser and hanging my dresses in the small closet off to the side of the room. Asher has kept the entire apartment simple but nice, the only decor consisting of a few well-loved acoustic and electric guitars held up on mounts against the living room wall. I wonder if he'll find it condescending if I tell him that I'm proud of him for earning the last spot in the rotation. It's the truth; I've seen him work hard for the last ten years, and I can't imagine getting here was easy. No doubt he's had to sacrifice a lot.

I hear the front door open and close before Asher steps into my room, depositing the last of my bags. My stomach chooses that exact moment to let out the loudest grumble. Pressing my hands to my abdomen in an attempt to quiet it, I grin sheepishly at him.

"Guess the fast food I had for lunch wasn't enough," I joke, but feel my cheeks heat nonetheless.

"I'm glad you're hungry. I made dinner," he says, beckoning me into the kitchen. The actual kitchen space is somewhat compact, but it opens into the living room, giving the feel of it being larger than it is. Three brown leather bar stools stand sentry in front of the large counter that houses the sink. Asher turns to the cabinets and begins pulling down plates and glassware. It's then that I catch the bubbling, cheesy goodness on top of the stove.

"You made me lasagna?" I try to keep my emotions out of my words but fail miserably. Asher just shrugs.

"I had the day off and you've been driving all day." He says it like it isn't the most thoughtful thing someone has ever done for me. Asher grew up in an Italian household; it wasn't uncommon for Devin to come back from hanging out with him, his arms weighed down with leftovers, all of which were gourmet. Devin told me long ago that Asher's mom finds cooking and feeding others therapeutic, and she's apparently passed her talents along to her son. I, myself, like to cook, so I know exactly how long it takes to make a lasagna, and Asher shrugging it off like it's not a big deal doesn't fool me for a second.

"Thank you," I tell him genuinely as he hands me a fork. When he dishes out the lasagna, he gives me a big enough slice to feed me for several meals. I start to get in my head about it. I'm a bigger girl, and while I recognize giving me a large slice is Asher's way of taking care of me, he clearly thinks I eat too much. I'm learning to love the body I'm in–I've always been this way–but some days are easier than others. However, when I see Asher has dished himself an equally large slice, my nerves settle. Apparently he simply has no concept of normal portion sizes. As we sit side-by-side at the counter, engaging in small talk, Asher's giant lasagna quickly dwindles from his plate. I guess it's not that he doesn't know about portion sizes–it's that he assumes everyone has an appetite as large as his. Something about that causes me to breathe a huge sigh of relief.

I tell him about the new job, and how I'm expected to go in early tomorrow morning. It's Opening Day tomorrow, and I really didn't do myself any favors by not coming to Chicago earlier, so that my first day didn't have to be the craziest day of the year, but I wanted to spend the extra time packing and saying goodbye to my parents. Deb was more than understanding about the adjusted timeline. If I'm being honest, I wanted as little downtime in Chicago as possible, out of fear that living with Asher would be exactly as awkward as I imagined it. So far, I've been pleasantly surprised.

After dinner, Asher just nods when I ask if he'd be okay if I headed to my room to get ready for bed and call it an early night. I really am exhausted from a full day of driving, and the heavy dinner makes me want to faceplant into my pillows instead of finishing unpacking.

"It is *so* nice to meet you!" Deb throws her arms around me in a genuine, although not-entirely-professional hug. "I cannot tell you how glad we all are to have you here, me especially. I've been asking to expand the program for years. You're about to find out that the expansion is long overdue." Deb begins walking and I scurry to follow her. Asher lives about a ten-minute walk from the ballpark, so I walked to work today. My sensible flats are already rubbing my pinky toes raw, and I try to hide my hobble as I hurry after her.

Deb, I'm learning, is like a caffeinated squirrel. She's small and incredibly sweet, but excitable doesn't begin to describe her personality. She clearly loves her job and is the social butterfly of the office. She takes me from office to office and cubicle to cubicle, introducing me to my new coworkers and divulging happy little anecdotes about their role and background, all while my head spins and I just try to keep up. If Deb is having trouble managing her workload to the point that she needs an assistant, which is only sort of what I am, I can't imagine what I'm walking into.

Most of the employees in this office, located on the third floor of the building next to the ballpark, are middle-aged, but everyone is dressed nicely. Deb assures me that everyone is simply pulling out all the stops due to Opening Day, and that the dress code is normally casual. I run a hand down my plain black slacks and thin olive sweater; I wasn't thrilled with my outfit choice when I got dressed, noting it didn't have much personality, but I look professional, so I guess that's something. When we reach the back corner of the office, Deb introduces me to Priya, Liam, and Faye, who thankfully look to be around my age. I can get along with anyone, but it's nice to see there are likely people here I can relate to.

Priya is the social media manager; Liam and Faye are legal interns, working on everything from contracts to HR support to legal-related operations at the field. I silently repeat their names in my head over and over, hoping to at least remember these ones. Sensing my overwhelm, Priya gives me a warm smile.

"You'll get used to it. Deb's been around here forever. She built the family program into what it is today. Don't feel like you have to remember everything today. Besides, today is a good day to start. They bring in the good catering on Opening Day!" She gestures to the room across the hall, where, through the doorway, I can see tables laden with platters upon platters of food. Craning my neck, I watch as two chefs set up warming lights for the carving station. This is an over-the-top situation. I feel a little weird. It makes me excited to start, but I haven't earned any of the success that everyone here is celebrating, so I feel like an awkward bystander.

"Welcome to the team," Liam says, giving me a small wave as the three of them make their way toward the food.

"I can't believe I didn't show you your office yet!" Deb looks at the jacket and bag I've been awkwardly shuffling between my hands as I greet my new coworkers. With an excited clap of her hands, she is on the move again, power walking through the sea of cubicles we just came through. At this rate, I'll lose ten pounds from the cardio of trailing after Deb's short but quick strides. I wish I had worn my hair up, I think, as a trickle of sweat trails down the back of my neck.

"Here we are!" Deb announces cheerily. My "office" can hardly be described as that. It's more of a glorified broom closet, but it has a window overlooking the crowds already forming outside the ballpark. The game doesn't start for another three hours, but with the Foxes having won the World Series last year, there are sure to be other festivities and ceremonies prior to game start. Setting my bag and coat on my desk chair, I turn to Deb and tell her I'm ready to get started.

"Great! Let's go to my office and go over the game plan for today. I've already drawn up most of what we'll need, but a lot of today will be socializing, networking, and flying by the seat of our pants. Are you up for it?"

I grin. "Definitely."

Deb wasn't kidding. After we reviewed the morning plans, she filled me in on her vision for my role. While sometimes I'll be assisting her in her various projects, I'll be heading up my own projects, including securing charity partnerships the WAGs–wives and girlfriends–can get involved with, soliciting donations from local businesses for both charity functions and gifts for the families, planning outings and events for the families, and rebuilding some of the less functional aspects of the family program.

"Basically, we need to beef up our family program because it is so instrumental to the recruitment of players," Deb explains. "It's hard on these athletes to uproot their lives, and if we can ease that transition in any way, they're more likely to sign with us over another team. Of course, every other team has their own family support programs, but ours is the best." Deb winks. "We offer free babysitting and meals for the kids during the games, so the children don't grow restless and bored after their fiftieth baseball game. During the games, we check on the family members and build relationships with them. They all have my phone number, and we can get you your own work cell if you don't want to share your personal number with the families. Of course, your number is already in our Foxes address book in the cloud, so the players and staff members all have access to your number automatically."

I filled out all my onboarding paperwork through HR last week. The hefty NDA I needed to sign was unreal, but I suppose that's what needs to happen when you work with multimillion-dollar athletes.

Deb hasn't stopped talking, which means my head hasn't stopped spinning. "Let's get bundled up and head over to the family room. It's across the street in one of the brownstones behind center field. It's where babysitting and kids' crafts go on during the games." I hustle back to my office for my coat, stopping only to wedge some tissue between my baby toe and the wall of my flats; I doubt it will do much good, but something is better than nothing. Returning to Deb's office, coat in hand, I notice that she is wearing sneakers, which is a far smarter idea than these stupid, albeit adorable, yellow flats.

She ushers me into a beautiful but nondescript brownstone. Aside from a ballpark security guard standing near the fenceline, there's no indication that this building is anything other than a neighborhood home. Entering, that's exactly what this is: four stories of beautiful home, but used for temporary purposes. Deb takes me on a brief tour; each room is relatively small to account for the limited real estate in this area. Altogether, though, the square footage is that of a typical family home, just stacked on top of each other.

The basement is entirely devoted to crafting and craft supplies, neatly organized into clear plastic containers on shelving. Long tables are spread across the room, already set up for the day's craft, which looks to be various paper crowns and other cut-out accessories. Deb explains that if crafting is my thing, the staff here are always looking for new ideas.

Taking the stairs back to the first floor, Deb introduces me to two workers who are stocking the refrigerator in the small kitchen with sodas, waters, and wine. The kitchen table, pushed against the back of the couch in the small living room, is laden with chocolate-covered strawberries, dried fruits, nuts, and the widest assortment of cheeses I've ever seen. The counters hold various vegetables, crackers, breads, and more dips than I can count. Deb explains that the family members will be showing up here shortly to partake in the season kickoff, so we should head upstairs for the rest of the tour.

On the second level, there are two bedrooms that have been converted into a nursery with three small cribs ("In case the littles need to nap," Deb explains) and a "zen den" ("where the older children can go to rest"). The zen den competes with the craft basement for my favorite room in the house: fluffy cloud material covers hanging bulbs; the whole room is made to look like an outdoor oasis. Two small fabric tents sit in the corner of the room. Another wall is covered by a bookshelf overflowing with children's books.

Deb ushers me to the third-floor landing, where another door leads to roof access ("locked when kids are here") and a large bedroom converted into a movie theater. Despite its lack of adult bedrooms, I want to move in. I can only imagine how much the children love it here, and I'm sure I'll stop by during many games to see it in action.

And action there is. By the time we descend the stairs to the main level, family members have started to filter in. A little boy who looks to be about four years old, with the chubbiest cheeks I've ever seen, rushes toward Deb, who crouches down to swallow him in an enthusiastic hug. When she stands, Deb greets the few women who have come in the door, hugging one of them. She introduces me to them all, and I really try, but I forget all of their names as soon as they say them. It doesn't help that they introduce themselves and immediately tell me their partner's name and position; the flood of information makes their names whoosh right out of my brain.

"It's June's first day, but she's a quick study," Deb tells them with a wink. I'm not sure she has any evidence of that, but I accept the compliment anyway. I help her pass out welcome back gift bags to each of the families, inviting them to partake in drinks and snacks before the game starts.

Every few minutes, I'm introduced to another face, another name, and I'm having trouble keeping up, so when the influx of people entering the brownstone slows, I find myself relieved.

"It's a lot, and you picked the most intense day to start, but you'll get the hang of it." Deb reassures me. "Most of the partners are heading back to the field to see their husbands get announced before the game."

I know from Devin's first year that Opening Day is a big deal, but seeing it from this side makes me realize just how much preparation goes into making it perfect for the players, their families, and the fans. Deb flashes a badge at security as we walk over to the field, bypassing the lines.

We spend the next several hours chatting with the families, touring the ballpark, and checking in on the family room. Considering the chaos of the first several hours, the second half of the day is a breeze. Deb finally settled; either her caffeine finally wore off, or her hyperspeed mode was due to nerves. I have a long note started on my phone with all the information I want to remember and the questions I'll eventually want to ask.

By the time the game is solidly in the seventh inning and Deb invites me to go back to the office with her, I'm ready to collapse. My brain has been firing on all cylinders since I woke up at five this morning. We finally take a break, grabbing plates and loading ourselves up with the leftover catering, which is still plentiful. Taking a seat together in the mostly empty conference-room-turned-catering-lounge, I finally get to enjoy the silence, only to have it punctuated by the television broadcast of the game.

Deb smiles at me. "You'll get used to it, and I promise it's not normally this chaotic. The families are great. Every once in a while, you'll get a family member who is a little…needier…than others." Deb chooses her words carefully, and I suspect this is one of those years where she must cater to a "needier" wife. I'm not concerned about it. After working for Karen and her sister, Louise, the original mean girl duo in Tampa, I can handle anything.

Deb and I catch the tail end of the game from the conference room. The Foxes manage to win by a run. The celebratory shouts from outside the conference room indicate we're not the only ones watching the game. I feel like I'm back in high school, watching Devin play, getting caught up in the celebration.

Growing up, I was always a fan of Devin's team, rather than following a particular professional team. I like baseball, but mostly because it was ingrained in me from Dev. It feels nice to belong to a team of my own now.

CHAPTER EIGHT

June

AGE 16

I hum along to Lake Shore Losers' latest release thumping through my earphones. Adalina Esau can sing like nobody's business, and I'm identifying particularly hard with the angsty lyrics today. It's just one of those days that only music can cure. I'm not particularly musically talented. I can clap along to a beat, but I can't carry a tune. Lyrics, however, are the key to my heart. As soon as I hear a new song, my brain starts transcribing the words, memorizing as I go. If I can't decipher all the words on the first go around, I look them up, filling in the blanks. It doesn't take much for me to remember each word because it's not just my brain that remembers the lyrics, but my soul. I guess there is something to the saying of learning it by heart.

I'm so lost in the lyrics as I pull open the refrigerator and take out a bottle of water that I don't notice Asher on the other side of the door until I shut it. I let out a little squeak, scrambling to press pause on the music streaming in my ears from my phone.

"Asher, jeez!" I press a hand to my chest. He raises an eyebrow at me, watching me struggle to open the bottle. It's a humid day, the kind of humid that even when you're inside with the air conditioning blasting, your water bottle sweats as soon as you remove it from the fridge. My fingers slip and slide in their grip on the bottle. He curls his fingers in a "give it here" gesture. Wordlessly, I hand him the bottle, and he opens it with ease. He hands it back to me, placing the cap on the counter next to him.

Asher always looks good, but there's something about him today that looks particularly delicious. I'm guessing it's his backwards purple baseball hat that brings out the gold in his eyes, but it could be the veins crisscrossing his forearms, on display in another band T-shirt. My mouth suddenly dry, I gulp down half the water bottle before pulling it away from my lips. Asher tracks the movement, probably because I look insane.

"Devin's at work," I tell him. In the last few years, Asher has taken to walking into our house unannounced. Devin says he does the same thing at the Incaudo residence, and I have no doubt he does. He can be so rude sometimes.

"Oh, okay. I thought he was off today?" Asher frowns, but even that looks handsome on him.

"He was, but he was asked to pick up a shift last-minute this morning."

"Ah." Asher glances at my phone. "What are you listening to?"

Instead of answering, I hand him one of my earphones. It's not wireless, so he has to duck his head closer to mine to listen. I tap the play button on my screen, and Adalina and the rest of the Lake Shore Losers filter through our ears. Asher grins when he recognizes the song. Eventually, he softly sings along to the lyrics while I close my eyes, absorbing the moment. Asher has a beautiful voice. I could listen to him sing forever.

The song fades, its final notes ringing in our ears as we huddle together. I slowly open my eyes to find him looking down at me, a soft expression on his face. I gaze back at him, unblinking. He's just so attractive. I lick my lips and his eyes follow the movement. I pull in a soft breath. The air around us is charged. The kitchen is empty, save for us, but there's an electric feeling. If I looked down at my arms, I'm sure I'd see them covered in goosebumps, but I'm afraid if I break eye contact with Asher, I'll ruin the moment, and I'm not willing to let this go.

I feel like this is the first time Asher has really looked at me. Sure, he's given me glances. We've had plenty of conversations over the years. But he's never looked at me like this, and I'm not sure what it means. If anyone else looked at me like this, I'd think they wanted to kiss me. But Asher? I'm afraid to hope.

He removes the earbud and straightens but doesn't move his body away from me. I continue to watch him, craning my neck. Slowly, so slowly, he reaches his hand toward my face. He uses his thumb to pull gently at my bottom lip, which I didn't realize was held firmly between my teeth. He releases it from its confines and dips his head. I'm afraid to move, afraid to breathe and break whatever spell has him bringing his lips impossibly closer to mine. And then it's happening.

His soft lips are on mine, and it's the gentlest, softest, sweetest thing I've ever experienced. I actively suppress a moan. His hand still gently cupping my cheek, he angles his head and deepens the kiss, licking the seam of my lips the tiniest bit. On instinct, because I have no idea what I'm doing, I open for him.

And it's everything.

Fireworks ignite in my belly. My heartbeat flutters in my chest. I'm not sure if I'm breathing, or if I even remember how to. But it's okay, because if I die at this moment, I will die happy. Because Asher is finally noticing me. And Asher is finally, *finally* kissing me.

"Hey, June! I need you to move–" Devin's voice shatters the little bubble Asher and I found ourselves in. We both jump away from each other just as my brother rounds the corner into the kitchen. I snatch at my phone and in my haste, knock over the half-full water bottle, spilling its contents all over the island and the floor.

"Shit! Fuck!" I cry out, slapping at a nearby dish towel and frantically mopping up the mess.

"Hey man!" Asher says, a little too loudly. "I thought you were working?" Devin watches me in amusement as I do a terrible job of cleaning. Oh well, the water will dry. The amusement on Devin's face is good, though. It means he didn't see Asher giving me my first kiss.

CHAPTER NINE
Asher
Age 18

F uck.
 I should *not* have done that.

CHAPTER TEN

June

AGE 16

"You better call me before every game," I threaten, but we both know I have no way of enforcing my threat.

"Seeing as we don't have games until February, that gets me off the hook for a long time." He smirks as he says the words, knowing they will rile me up. I punch him playfully in the arm. "Hey! That's my throwing arm!"

"Good thing you're not a pitcher then," I tease back. My mind instantly and automatically goes to the best pitcher I know, as much as I hate it.

Two months ago, after Asher kissed me, I saw the look of terror in his eyes when Devin walked into the kitchen. It was then that I knew, no matter how perfect that kiss was, we would never, ever be repeating it.

At first, I wanted to get in my head about it. Am I bad at kissing? Is that why Asher and I never spoke of it again? But I know, I *know*, Asher enjoyed it as much as I did. I've replayed in my head a thousand and one times, and I know he initiated it. He deepened it. He wanted it and enjoyed it and then immediately pretended it never happened.

What I don't know is *why*. I know Devin is probably responsible for most of Asher's retreat, but I deserve to know if that's the whole reason, or if there's more. But I never see Asher without Devin's presence, so I've never had an opportunity to ask. I have a sneaking suspicion that Asher is ensuring he and I are never alone together since then either. Even if the three of us are hanging out and Devin gets up to go to the bathroom, or to grab some snacks, Asher insists he has to make a phone call or offers to help Dev in the kitchen. It's like he's afraid to be around me.

I'm sure he regrets the kiss, because he's acting like he regrets the kiss. I get it, he got caught up in the moment, and it wouldn't have happened in literally any other situation. But don't I deserve to know that? I've spent so much of the last two years pining after a guy I knew I'd never have. Then the second I get him to kiss me, he snatches himself away as if I've suddenly burst into flames and he can't afford to get burned.

I'm done questioning the kiss and everything about Asher now. Because Devin leaves for school in an hour, and Asher leaves tomorrow. Asher will go off to Louisiana, meet some beautiful southern belle, and forget (again) about my existence. What did I expect? That after one kiss, Asher would profess his love to me and ask me to be his girlfriend? That he, *a college student*, would be interested in dating someone who just got their driver's license, who's only a year out from braces, who is still *in high school*?

Once again, I find myself in the familiar and disgraceful position of having to shove Asher out of my heart and out of my life.

CHAPTER ELEVEN
Asher

PRESENT DAY

I'm not a terribly superstitious man. Compared to some of my teammates, I'm positively practical. Still, I haven't pitched a game since high school without falling asleep the night before to whale songs, eating a bowl of Frosted Flakes for breakfast, and tucking my mother's note of encouragement into the brim of my hat. I gently finger the folded paper, soft and almost fuzzy in its age, before getting ready to step onto the field for warm up tosses.

My mother has offered to rewrite the note for me at least a dozen times, but I've turned her down each time. She wrote me a new one at the beginning of every season in high school, so when she was unable to get coverage for her shift, she wanted her words to bring me some sort of solace. Many years ago, she left me a note on the kitchen table before running out the door for an early shift at the diner. When I tucked it into my hat later that afternoon, I had to rip it down to size, carefully tearing around the most important words before tucking them inside the back of my hat. *I love you always.*

As an adult, I can recognize it's a little cheesy, but my mother's words have carried me through college, the minor leagues, and now, my very first major league start. It's not my first time pitching at Foxes Field, but it is my first time starting a game here, and I'm trying not to let my nerves get the best of me.

My mother is the hardest-working person I know. She worked two jobs while I was growing up, first serving at my grandparents' diner each day to help during the breakfast rush and again at night for the evening crowd, then working between shifts as a dental hygienist. It was a rare occasion when she missed one of my games, but even when she did, she made up for it tenfold. As a single mother raising an only child, I don't know how she did it. Sure, she had help from her parents, but she did most of the heavy lifting herself. Keeping the note tucked into my hat is less of a sentimental reminder of my mother's unwavering faith in me, and more of a reminder to myself of all the sacrifices she made to get me where I am.

My grandparents are in the middle of trying to sell the diner, to officially retire and sail off into the sunset, and an interested buyer is coming today, of all days, to look at the place. Otherwise, I know my mother would be here in the stands to cheer me on. I like to think her life has gotten better since I started playing professionally. I don't make the highest salary, but my signing bonus, paired with earning the major league minimum, allowed me to pay off the mortgage on her and my grandparents' houses. Flying my mother out to catch a game is an easy enough task, if not for the sale of the restaurant. I feel like a shitty son to admit that a part of me is secretly the tiniest bit relieved my mother is watching from Philadelphia instead of inside the stadium. Not because I don't love her, but because I still haven't quite bested the nerves that plague me each time I set foot on the mound at Foxes Field.

I don't lack confidence in my game. I know I'm skilled; I know I deserve to be here. But there's a certain pressure that comes with pitching that is notably absent for my position-player teammates. When you pitch, whether you're a starter or a reliever, the direction of the game largely depends on you. Sure, you don't win a game without scoring runs, and luckily, I don't have to bat, but if Hayden Oliver has a bad game, it's not quite the same as if I have a bad game. A position player's bad game doesn't always equate to a loss.

Pitching every five games is both a blessing and a curse. If Oliver, or Perez, or Edwards have a bad game, their stats (and thus, their longevity with the major league club) are relatively unaffected, as they have far more opportunities to course correct than I do. But if I fuck up even a couple times, my job is in jeopardy. I suppose that's how it goes for people in the real world and their jobs; there's just a lot more of those types of jobs around. There are only thirty Major League Baseball teams, with a handful of pitchers on each team. So yeah, the pressure sometimes gets to me.

A heavy arm drapes across my shoulders. Its owner slaps me on the chest with the arm not slung around me. "You've got this, Incaudo. You've earned the rotation spot. Clear your head and get out there."

I nod, letting Kyle Crawford's words sink into my mind. He's been a mentor and friend to me for the past two years, and he seems to know I need the smallest of pushes to get me out there. I appreciate him taking me under his wing a bit; he's a veteran of the game and I've learned so much from him already. He releases me with one last squeeze of my shoulder. I heave out a heavy breath and climb the dugout stairs and jog to the outfield. Edwards, my catcher, isn't out here yet. I like to get out here early to catch my breath and center myself. I take the extra solitary time to do a few dynamic moving warm ups. I've already warmed up earlier with my strength coach, but the extra hip mobility exercises settle my nerves and make me feel prepared. I have one of the league's highest leg kicks during my pitch delivery, and I like my hips to feel loose. Eventually, Edwards joins me, and we lob the ball back and forth to each other in the outfield, warming our arms up. It's not long before the national anthem is playing and we're taking our positions on the field.

The first three innings go well for me and, by extension, the Foxes. I give up a walk and a hit, but the game remains scoreless on both sides. The fourth inning doesn't quite go as I plan, and I admittedly let my nerves get the best of me. I allow the bases to load before Edwards runs out to the mound and talks me off the ledge. He doesn't have to say much; he's able to read the situation enough to know I need the extra time to gather myself. When he steps back behind the dish, I deliver back-to-back strikeouts and a popup to JJ Jeffers for the third out. Now in the sixth inning, I've settled into my rhythm. I know Benny, the manager, and Will Dyer, my pitching coach, are keeping a close eye on my pitch count. My goal was to make it through the fifth inning, so as long as the Foxes can maintain or add to their two-run lead by the time I'm pulled from the game, I'll be happy.

I'm a simple guy. It doesn't take much to make me happy, but June promised she'd make me brownies if I pitched well. I don't need the extra motivation, or pressure, but in all the years that I've known June Demoranville, I have yet to turn down one of her brownies. They're gooey and soft, and sometimes she swirls peanut butter in them. She sometimes gets fancy with them, but she never puts nuts or anything healthy in them; her brownies are perfect and unblemished by obstacles. She once sent Devin to a high school game with a plastic container filled with them; I'm pretty sure I ate half of them. When she found out how much I loved them, she insisted on making them for me for every start I made in high school. I would have built that into my game-day superstitions, but once I graduated from high school, June stopped making them for me. I'm all too happy to pick that tradition back up.

Living with June, at least for the last day and a half, has been easier than I thought it would be. We've slipped into an easy camaraderie, the years and distance between us melting away like vanilla ice cream over one of her warm brownies. We've always gotten along well, and she hasn't mentioned our awkward teenage kiss, so I'm sure she's long forgotten it. Far be it from me to bring it up and make things weird between us. I'm probably misremembering how good she tasted anyway.

The ball smacks into Edwards's glove with an audible slap. Instead of throwing the ball back to me, Tyler jogs halfway to the mound and flips it gently to me. Message received. He called for a slider and I threw a fastball. That's what I get for thinking about June instead of keeping my head in the game. Shaking my head to rid myself of any non-baseball related thoughts, I spin the ball in my fingers, setting up for my next pitch. Edwards calls for a slider again, and I adjust my grip so my index and middle fingers are pressed together. It sails across the plate and the batter whiffs just before the ball smacks into my catcher's glove.

I make it out of the inning alive, but my pitch count is at ninety, and I'm certain Benny and Dyer won't let me see the seventh inning. I'd pitch until my arm falls off if they'd let me; it's not just the pressure to prove I belong here, but my love of this game and everything it's given me. Still, I recognize that pitching more today will jeopardize my ability to be ready for my next start, so I don't argue when Benny slaps an encouraging palm on my back and tells me to rest.

I remain in the dugout for the next inning but watch the rest of the game from the weight room. Jameson Bates, our closer from last season, looks even better this year. He's a good guy, but a little on the quieter and moody side, so I mostly give him his space and let him do his own thing. I get along with everyone, but it should surprise no one that I'm closest with Crawford and Edwards. I finish my shoulder and forearm exercises, working to cool the joints, ligaments, muscles, and tendons in my overworked arm.

We managed to maintain the lead, giving me the win for today. When Benny walks into the weight room after the game, he tells me I'm requested to speak at the press conference, but assures me he'll be sitting next to me the whole time. Other than minor interviews following our World Series win last year, I've done very few media interviews in Chicago. Mariah, my publicist, insisted on putting me through rigorous media training two years ago, but seeing as I have had few opportunities to practice those skills, my nerves resurface. There are few monsters quite like the beast that is Chicago media. Devin has also tried to prepare me for the kinds of questions I might get asked, but seeing as I haven't slept with half of Brooklyn, I'm guessing the questions I'm asked won't be all that similar to the interest shown in Dev. Still, I'm grateful for a manager like Benny, who will help me ease into press conferences instead of throwing me to the wolves. I've seen Benny jump into pressers to rescue his players from embarrassing or awkward questions; he's such a naturally charismatic guy that the reporters hardly realize what he's doing until they go home and remember that the player never ended up answering their question.

Luckily, both the Chicago media and Benny have mercy on me. I get asked softball questions, like how I like starting compared to relief pitching (very much more; I appreciate the opportunity the Foxes have given me), how I feel after my first start (great; I'm ready to do it again in five games), and how I like Chicago and its fan base (it's the best city in the world). I didn't even have to stretch the truth with any of my answers.

After meeting with the media, I return to the training room to continue my recovery work. Our massage therapist starts working on my arm, but it's never the relaxing massage I hope for. He kneads and scrapes my arm and shoulders, digging into a particularly stubborn knot under my right armpit. It makes me want to rethink the friendly relationship I have with him. By the time I'm finished with cryotherapy, I'm ready to go home and sleep for days.

As promised, I come home to the smell of melted chocolate. My mouth waters before I finish unlocking the door. I ate the postgame meal, but I always have room for dessert.

"Congratulations! You looked amazing!" June squeals when I walk through the door. Her cheeks bunch, crinkling her eyes at the corners. She's standing behind the kitchen counter wearing a Vote for Pedro T-shirt and jeans, a pan of brownies cooling on the stove in the background. I'm suddenly struck by how nice it is to come home to a friend. I haven't had a roommate since my earliest years playing in the low minor league system, right out of college. Last year, even when I pitched a great game, it was a little lonely coming home to an empty apartment, which is probably why I spent so much time going out after games with Crawford and the rest of the bullpen. Unlike my mentor, however, I always came home alone.

"Thanks," I say, suddenly feeling awkward. June's genuine happiness in response to my performance isn't unexpected, but I'm still not used to someone gushing over me. "You didn't have to make me brownies though, you know."

"What! Of course I did. We've got to keep some traditions alive. Or do you no longer eat brownies?" Her eyes twinkle, no doubt remembering how much I loved her brownies growing up.

"Actually, I'm allergic to chocolate." June's face falls immediately. I try and fail to stifle a grin before she realizes I'm joking. She throws the nearby oven mitt at me, hitting me squarely in the chest. "Do you not remember the multiple times I nearly put myself into a diabetic coma from eating practically the whole pan of your brownies?" I raise an eyebrow at her.

"Well, I don't know! People develop all sorts of weird allergies at random times in their lives!" Tiny patches of pink pigment her cheeks; it's fucking adorable. "I guess you *don't* want my brownies anymore!"

"No, please. I'm sorry, Junie. Don't take them away from me." I show her my most contrite face, pouting out my lower lip. It's ridiculous, but it must work, because she slides the pan toward me. I groan when I see artful swirls of light brown interspersed among the chocolate. "Ungh, you put peanut butter in it. Marry me, June."

She laughs, attempting to cut a piece for me, but I grab the pan possessively. She huffs a sigh of resignation before opening my silverware drawer and producing a fork. I'm about to dig in when I remember to snap a picture. I tap out a quick text and hit send.

Me

> See? Peanut butter brownies! I'm getting good at this protein thing.

Allie's text arrives just as I'm putting the first gooey bite in my mouth. I groan as sweet chocolate and salty peanut butter explode on my tongue. The brownie is warm and melty and everything that's right with the world. June's eyes dance with amusement and pride as she watches me dive in for another bite, and another. When I finally surface for air and respond to Allie's text, a quarter of the pan is gone, and I have no plans to slow down.

Allie

> You're lucky you burned 1,000 calories today because there's no way the protein in that outweighs the sugar. Or fat.

> Me
> You're just jealous I won't share with you.

"Did you want some of this?" I say to June around a particularly thick bite.

"Uh, no. I have no intention of losing a hand, which is the inevitable outcome if I get between you and your beloved brownies."

"Your loss," I say, picking up the pan and sauntering toward the couch. "Tell me about your day." I want June to love her new job. Dev didn't tell me much about her old one, and she hasn't divulged much either, but from what I understand, it didn't end well for her. June is one of the nicest people I've ever met; she deserves a win. I know her first day yesterday was chaotic, so I'm hoping she starts to feel settled soon.

"It was good. I'm still reeling with the number of people I've met and there's so much to do. I want to jump in and do everything right away, but I know I need to pace myself. I got to spend some time at the family room during the game, but don't worry; they have the game on all the televisions there, so I didn't miss a pitch!" June's excitement over her job is contagious. In our own ways, we both are starting new jobs at the same time.

"You know you don't have to watch just for me," I say, rubbing the back of my neck. I'm finally starting to slow my dessert consumption. She gently pries the pan out of my fingers and places it on the coffee table. I scoff but realize she's probably right. My stomach will thank her later, as much as my taste buds are currently protesting.

"I like supporting you guys. If I can't watch Dev, I might as well watch you," she tells me playfully. I nod, wiping my mouth with my thumb. I lean back against the couch cushions. June looks like she's about to say something but stops herself. After a pause, she whispers, "Thanks for letting me stay with you, Ash. Coming home to an empty house, in an unfamiliar city would be a little depressing."

The smile I give her is genuine. "Anytime."

CHAPTER TWELVE
June

Some days, I've decided, I hate my job. Those are the days that I'm woken up early on my days off to attend a Feel the Burn Bootcamp. For work. Luckily, I've forced Priya to attend with me, convincing her that this is *for sure* an excellent opportunity to record additional social media content. However, we're only halfway through the class, and I feel like dying. I should get hazard pay for this.

It's the second road trip for the Foxes this season, and the wives and girlfriends are attending their first official Foxes Family Program event. Apparently, a survey went out during Spring Training, asking family members about the types of events they'd like to see this season, and this one topped the list. I'm on my third set of crunches and I cannot for the life of me figure out why this is deemed a desirable activity. At least the trainer is hot. But he's ruthless, pushing us to our physical limits all while happily circulating the room, giving praise and redirection as needed. I'm praying he keeps his perfectly toned ass on the other side of the room, far away from me.

The class is titled "Sweatin' with Ryan," and it is not the kind of sweating I'd like to do in front of a male audience, ever. The WAGs are all in incredible shape, and I can't help but feel self-conscious in my biker shorts and oversized Foxes moisture-wicking polo. I tried to blend sporty and professional in my attire, but given the amount of sweat pouring off my body, I'm fairly certain I've failed spectacularly. Most of the wives seem nice. They are a kind, grateful bunch, and in another life, I might have been friends with them. You know, if supermodel-caliber good-looking people were friends with regular people.

I've paired up with Priya for partner work, but she periodically abandons me to do her job, snapping photos of the WAGs for social media. I'm starting to suspect she chooses these moments of content creation when she's supposed to be doing the most challenging exercises. Fine; if Priya is off the hook for this set, then so am I.

"Come on, June!" Ryan's overly cheerful attitude makes me want to slap his excessively beautiful face. Why can't he let me collapse onto the floor to drown in my own sweat and die quietly? "I'll be your partner!"

Ugh, the last thing I want is an exquisitely muscled beefcake making the exercises that will surely put me into an early grave look easy. Sensing my hesitation, Ryan grabs a nearby medicine ball and stands opposite me, refusing to take no for an answer. In his defense, I don't have enough air in my lungs to say no, but I'm sure my face conveys the message clearly enough.

The medicine ball comes sailing my way, and I catch it with a soft "oomph." I squat once, before tossing it back to my self-appointed partner. He squats with it five times before tossing it back to me. I'd scowl at him for being a show-off, but his extra work allows me a few precious seconds to catch my breath before I'm forced back into this labor camp masquerading as a fun group activity.

I can feel myself being watched. This is truly my nightmare. Looking up, I see Melody Malone, one of the wives, watching me, her face the epitome of judgment. I don't know any of the WAGs very well yet, so I haven't figured out if Melody has an unfortunate case of resting bitch face, or if she really hates me, because her face perpetually looks like that when she gazes upon me. Her lip curls into a sneer, like my panting and sweating *in a fitness class* offends her. I want to roll my eyes at her, but I can't, because she's technically my client. Besides, I don't *know* that she dislikes me. Maybe that's just the way her face looks.

Lost in my thoughts, the weighted ball Ryan lobs my way catches me off-guard and knocks me on my ass, literally. The wireless microphone curved around his face catches his gasp of surprise and his follow-up apology, causing all heads to turn my way. I can feel my cheeks and chest heat under the newfound attention as I scramble to my feet, only to accidentally kick the medicine ball away from me. I run across the room after it, feeling like a helpless toddler running after a stray rubber ball, the heavy lifting we did earlier slowing my steps to an awkward, lumbering gait. I squat, reaching my fingers further to grab this stupid fucking ball. As I do so, I tip a little too far forward on my toes. I'm off-kilter, but seeing as falling flat on my face—at work, in front of the most gorgeous, coordinated women in the world! —would be the most embarrassing thing to ever happen to me, I attempt to avoid it at all costs. I do, but only for a moment. Instead of falling face-first, I tip to the side and fall in a weird sort-of-slow-motion, half landing on my hip, half on my ass. The ball dribbles once again away from me, and the only acceptable solution is for a sinkhole to suddenly appear and swallow me whole.

Fuck. This.

I'm never working out again.

Chapter Thirteen
June

The perks of my new job include an interesting schedule. Especially when the team is on the road, I have the flexibility to work from home if I want. However, my wonky schedule means that I have inconsistent days off, which vary from week to week, depending on the game schedule. My days off are never when the team is playing at home, but I don't mind that so much, seeing as my only sort-of friends in Chicago also work for the Foxes.

The bad thing about a wonky schedule is that if I die, no one will know. I might be on death's doorstep right now. It hurts to move. It hurts to breathe. I knew I should have asked for hazard pay after yesterday's event from hell; I wonder what the Foxes will pay out if I keel over and die?

I need to pee, but if I try to sit up, I know I'll hurt even more than my overstretched bladder feels right now. I brace myself for the movement, but even that is painful. I know I wasn't supposed to work my toes yesterday, but somehow, even those are sore. If I could move, I'd march myself down to Feel the Burn and give Ryan a piece of my mind. The only thing more painful than my physical body is the memory of my humiliation near the end of class, made worse only by Ryan's gentle suggestion that maybe I should sit the rest of class out. It didn't take a genius to realize what a safety risk I was.

Pitiful groans and moans spill out of my mouth on the way to and from the bathroom. I'm just glad Asher isn't here to see my rapid deterioration toward my imminent demise. It was bad enough to see twenty or so pairs of eyes witnessing my disgrace yesterday. I suppress a shudder at the memory and divert my path back to bed to the couch instead. All I want to do is curl up (or maybe stretch out? Will that hurt less?) with a book and allow visions of my newest favorite storyline to drown out the embarrassment of yesterday's memories.

Glancing at my phone, I'm surprised it's almost noon. Say what you will about Ryan being the devil incarnate, I haven't slept that long or deeply since high school. It must have been my body's way of trying to slowly piece itself back together after the horrors of labor–I mean boot–camp. I'm in the middle of placing a delivery order to the noodle shop around the corner when a text comes across the screen.

Priya

> Hey girl, you alive after yesterday?

Me

> Nope. This is June's disembodied ghost. Still not sure if it was the physical terrors or the emotional trauma that finally did her in.

> Damn. It was nice knowing her for these last few weeks.

> If you're not too busy haunting Ryan's ass, do you want to come to a show with me Friday night?

> A show? What kind of show?

> My sister's boyfriend is in a band and they're in town this weekend. Free tickets?

I'm not musically talented myself, but I am an admirer of just about every genre. Over the past few weeks, Priya and I have developed a little bit of a friendship. Liam and Faye are great too, but they have very limited time to socialize with us outside of work.

> I'm in, assuming I don't lose the fight against these grievous bodily injuries.

> Please don't die. I need someone else to take the heat of Melody Malone's glares off me.

I'm glad I'm not the only one she's glaring at, but it sucks that we're both subjected to Melody's judgmental glowering.

My phone alerts me that the Foxes game starts in twenty minutes. A couple years ago, Deb worked with the guys in the tech department to develop a Foxes Family Program app. It's still in a bit of beta mode, mostly containing a calendar and helpful links, but it conveniently alerts me to game information too. I pull up the app and see that Asher is starting again today.

Shit, I probably should have texted him sooner. I know Devin has his phone with him in the clubhouse until he hits the field about fifteen minutes before game time. I'm not sure if Asher is the same, or if he's got some sort of unique pregame ritual or responsibility. Fuck it, if I'm too late to text him, at least he'll see it after the game.

> Me
> Good luck today! I know you'll kill it. I already bought more brownie supplies in preparation!

Three little dots appear and disappear before reappearing, then disappearing again. I restarted the brownie-making trend as a way to jokingly entice him to perform better, but now it's sort of become our own thing. He hasn't won every start he's made this season, but I give him the dessert anyway, transforming the victory brownies into the occasional brownies of commiseration. He comes home after tomorrow night's game; I'm already planning on making my salted caramel swirled version. I know Asher enjoys peanut butter swirl, but I'm trying to expand his horizons.

> Asher
>
> Thanks. How was your first event?

Asher talked me off the ledge before he left on the road trip. Deb handed me the reins for the bootcamp class, and I took it and ran with it. I had cute little sweat towels printed for us, scheduled the class with Evil Coach Ryan, and organized the smoothie delivery afterwards. I even put together little gift bags with the towels, bottled water, electrolyte tablets, and scrunchies in Foxes orange and blue. The WAGs were really enthusiastic about it. All in all, the event seemed to be a success. If only I could move today.

> Well, it hurts to move everything but my face, but I think I'll live to see another day. I think the wives liked it all.

Again, the dots appear and disappear over and over. I wonder if now isn't a good time to text him.

> When you go in to work next, run down to the training room in the clubhouse. I have a massage gun in there you can bring home to use. It's got my name on it. Just ask one of the clubhouse attendants to borrow it.

> There's no way I can go into the training room to steal your stuff!

> Why not?

>> I don't know, it's weird! I don't even know if I'm allowed to live with you, or hang out with you, or whatever.

> Why wouldn't you be allowed to live with me?

>> In my onboarding paperwork, I had to sign something saying I wouldn't fraternize with the players.

> Fraternize?

>> Yeah. I don't know. We need a divide between us at work.

> Separation of church and state?

>> Exactly.

>> Don't you have a game to play or something?

> On it. See ya later, Junie.

I turn on the Foxes game, which at the moment consists of the announcers speculating what will happen once play begins. I mute the television and settle deeper into the couch, opening my book.

I'm in my most comfortable off-day joggers and *Book Boyfriends Do It Better* T-shirt. I stay immersed in my book, every once in a while peeking at the game to see how Asher is doing, for the next several hours. I don't have a romance subgenre preference. I read it all and as long as the male main character experiences a heavy dose of longing, I'm there. And this book delivers longing in spades.

Chapter Fourteen
Asher

J J Jeffers is dancing far too close to me in this clubhouse. We're in Miami, and normally I'd be excited to explore a new city, but I didn't pitch well this afternoon and the humidity from the current weather has seeped into the locker room, giving everything a gross, sticky feel. Outside, the storm clouds match my mood.

The Foxes managed to win the game, giving me a no-decision to add to my stats. It's better than a loss, but it's not great. I slept terribly last night, too. But I'm still in my rookie season, and I can't exactly be grumpy toward our unofficial team captain, especially given how well he played tonight. His two homers in back-to-back plate appearances are one hundred percent the reason why I didn't get the loss today, but I'm still irritable.

I turn my back on a gyrating Jeffers, but it does nothing to block out the sounds of a whooping Caleb Andrews, cheering on his best friend. I sigh quietly, but not quietly enough, because beside me, Crawford picks up on my misery.

"Shake it off, Rook. It wasn't that bad," he says under his breath, careful not to draw attention to my lack of enthusiasm. He's downplaying my disastrous outing, but I appreciate the lie nonetheless. If I didn't have excellent defenders on the field behind me, things would have been much worse. Even through the haze of my foul mood, I am grateful for my teammates. "Come on out with us. We're going to Little Havana tonight. You, me, Edwards, anyone else who wants to go."

I shrug. I'm not in a partying mood, but the alternative is sitting alone in my room or drinking alone at the beach bar at the hotel. "Yeah, all right," I agree reluctantly. Crawford claps loudly, drawing the team's attention.

"Little Havana tonight for those that want to join. I'll see if Alan can get us a dinner reservation. Who's in?" Hands go up and Crawford counts quietly under his breath before leaving to find our traveling secretary about getting a last-minute reservation for twelve of us. My phone dings and I brace myself for the consolation texts.

> June
>
> <photo>
>
> I hope you can find something similar to drown your sorrows tonight.

I can't help but grin at the goofy look on June's face as she holds an unopened bag of chocolate chips up to her face, pretending to pour them into her open mouth. Her purple glasses with rhinestones in the corners catch the flash from her ridiculous selfie.

Something in my chest loosens. Instead of sending contrived platitudes about my performance, June tells it like it is, but in a way that's genuine and somehow, still uplifting. It's what I need. I don't need someone to tell me they're sorry about my shitty performance. I don't need someone to tell me lies, that it wasn't as bad as I'm remembering (it was; I lived it), or that I'll get 'em next time (I know I will, but it doesn't stop me from being annoyed right now). Apparently, what I need is an acknowledgment of my performance, a little joke, and permission to move on. I don't know why I expected anything less from June; she's been living that life with her brother for as long as he's been in baseball. While it's true you can't win them all, it doesn't make the shitty games less shitty, and somehow, strangely, June's recognition of my lackluster performance helps lift some of the clouds on my mood.

Dinner tonight helps too, but that might be due to the massive number of mojitos our poor server keeps bringing to the table. It would have been more efficient for the wait staff to set up an assembly line from the bar to our table with the way we have been putting them back, but with twelve professional athletes, what did you expect? The blended mojitos, a house specialty, are particularly helpful in chasing the post-game blues away. The blender whirs serve as a steady backdrop to the laughter and conversation that flows around the table just as easily as the booze.

"Are you going to finally put yourself out there this season?" Tyler Edwards eyes me.

"What do you mean?" I ask, swirling my straw in my drink. I haven't been drinking fast enough. The heat and humidity on the covered patio melt the blended concoction, but the massive fans set up around the perimeter of the dining area keep us at a comfortable temperature. Edwards cocks an eyebrow.

"What do I mean? Jesus, man. Start dating!" I'm going to need another drink for this conversation. I suck down the one in my hand, grimacing when I get a mouthful of all rum in the rapidly separating cocktail.

"Yeah, I don't know. It's easy for you to say when you've had a girlfriend for the last four years."

"Fiancée," he corrects me. Tyler and his girlfriend got engaged during Spring Training.

"Fiancée," I agree. "But you guys have been together forever. It's hard to date once women find out you're an athlete." He nods sagely. I'm not a highly suspicious person, but I've learned the hard way that a healthy dose of skepticism and distrust can be helpful in my line of work. I've experienced it myself and I've seen various teammates go through it as well. There are plenty of cleat chasers in baseball, looking for a free ride to wealth and notoriety by bagging a ball player. I don't mean to minimize all women to gold-diggers, but in general, the available dating pool has had me wading through gold-diggers or women unwilling to put up with the grind of the baseball schedule. It's not something I really want to put myself through, not when I should be focused on building a lengthy career.

"Who says you need to start dating?" Crawford interjects. "Start with hookups. As long as you're clear upfront that you're not looking for a relationship, it's great." Crawford would know; the only bigger man-whore than Devin is Kyle. I'm not judging them, but I already know that's not the lifestyle I want for myself. Still, I can admit that some nights, my hand just isn't cutting it anymore. It might be nice to dip my toe into the dating pool, if I can do it without feeling completely used.

"I don't know, man. You're not worried about getting a girl pregnant or something?" Kyle straightens, tension lining his entire body.

"Do not put that out into the universe," he hisses. He grabs the table salt and pours a generous amount into his hand before tossing it over his shoulder and performing some sort of complicated, Kyle-esque sign of the cross. Edwards and I laugh at him. Given the amount that he sleeps around, it's likely only a matter of time before he ends up with a kid.

"I wrap my shit up tight," he tells us.

"James, back me up." Across the table, Warner James, our right fielder, has been watching us quietly, taking in the conversation. He raises an eyebrow at Crawford's insinuation. "Shit, no disrespect to your wife. I just meant that before you and Alicia got together, you got around, too."

Warner doesn't deny it. Instead, he shrugs. There's no question in my mind about his complete devotion to his new wife, but I know he dated quite a bit before he met her.

"Were you, uh, worried about sleeping with someone else? How did you know they weren't trying to entrap you or something?"

Edwards shakes his head. "Jesus, *Dateline*, we're not talking about jailbait."

"I meant with a baby!" I protest. Shit. This is not coming out right and I'm looking like a sleazebag. "One of my college teammates got a chick pregnant. Apparently, she lied about being on birth control and was hoping to get pregnant. She had the baby, but the relationship didn't last. He loves his son, but after everything went down, she told him she was only in it to bag a ballplayer."

"Yeesh." The guys look chagrined but not surprised. Growing up with a single mother, I already know there's no way I'd do that to a woman. If I sleep with her, I have to be ready to face the consequences for the long haul. It's the biggest reason why I've avoided sleeping around. My teammate's relationship woes instilled in me a strong distrust of women who suddenly become interested in me when they find out my profession and earning potential. My life is complicated enough with the threat of moving up and down within the organization; no need to drag someone else (or worse, an innocent child) into the mix.

"Condoms are your friend," Warner says simply. Easy for him to say. "Not every woman wants a child anyway. Few are manipulative enough to purposely get pregnant just to tie you down."

"I know that. I'm not really that cynical. I just don't know how to sift out the good ones."

"How about a dating profile?" Andrews leans in, forcing his way into the conversation.

"That's the worst idea I've ever heard," Edwards says, voicing my thoughts exactly.

"Nah, we'll make your profile, set your preferences to a super high standard, and only put you on the sites where you can date other higher-profile individuals. Benny was on one of those sites for a while, before he met Delaney."

Before I can say no, Caleb plucks my phone from where it's been sitting face-down on the table next to me.

"Smile!" he says, taking what I'm sure is an unflattering photo of me. Looking at it, he deletes it immediately. "Eh, we'll get your profile pic later." Great. This is off to a fantastic start already.

In what must be record time, Caleb has shouted down the table for Benny to give him a referral code, downloaded an "exclusive" dating app, and written a relatively bare-bones profile for me. He shoves my phone back into my hands, telling me to upload my own photos and hit "publish." I scroll half-heartedly through my photo album, settling on a few that make no allusions to my job: one of me playing guitar, next to a snowman my mom and I made last winter, and a close-up of me smiling next to Dev. I crop my best friend out of the last photo. Wincing as if my phone were suddenly going to turn into a rabid dog and bite my hand, I press "publish." Caleb whoops loudly.

I really hope I don't regret sticking this.

CHAPTER FIFTEEN
June

Baseball season is in full swing, which means my job is, too. There are times when it's chaotic and stressful, but in general, the work is relatively easy and a lot of fun. There are a lot more perks in working for a professional baseball team than there were working for my shady clinic in Florida. Deb is an awesome boss, even if she is a little hyper sometimes. She's kind and respectful and a lot of fun. I have no idea how she maintains her high-energy lifestyle, as she's got to be pushing sixty years old. Priya and I joke that it might be cocaine.

Walking into the family room, I breathe in deeply. There's something about being in this brownstone that feels like home. I've gotten to know a lot of the kids, and they are all lovely. Kaito Soji's son teaches me how to write a new Japanese word every time I see him. Samuel Benjamin's kids are here for this homestand, too. The oldest two don't visit the family room unless they're picking up or dropping off their young sibling, but six-year-old Scarlett has already got me wrapped around her little finger. Yesterday, she made me promise to play Princess Babies with her. I'm not sure what that is, but I already agreed, so I'm sure I'm about to find out.

"Hi, Harper!" I greet Melody Malone's three-year-old daughter enthusiastically. "Hi, Melody." Melody gives me a tight-lipped smile and a brief nod before crouching before her daughter. Harper is all round cheeks and fierce independence; I love it. Three- and four-year-old children are my favorite age, because that's when you really get to see their little personalities develop. I've been babysitting since junior high, and toddlers have always been the most fun, but I love children of all ages. Harper nods at her mother's words, promising to be good. When Melody stands, I crouch to get on Harper's level.

"Today, the kids are making superhero masks in the basement." I found the foam masks on sale at Michaels the other day, and scooped up enough to bring over here. One of my favorite parts of my job is designing craft ideas for the kids. Deb said I could leave it up to the babysitters if I wanted, but they always seem grateful when I drop off materials and suggestions. "Upstairs, the kids are going to watch 'Finding Nemo' if you want to do that." I catch a flash of red hair walking through the back door. "Or, if you want to join us, Scarlett and I are going to play Princess Babies!"

I brace myself as Scarlett practically tackles me in a hug. I just met her yesterday, but we hit it off immediately and now are, apparently, the best of friends.

"Scarlett, you're going to break someone's neck one of these days, baby girl," her stepmother, Delaney, admonishes jokingly. "Hey there, June." Delaney offers me her hand and helps pull me to standing. "Hi, Melody," she greets the other woman. Melody blinks, drops a kiss on her daughter's head, and walks out the back door.

"Hi Delaney, it's great to see you," Delaney mocks. "Bitch," she adds in an undertone. Her response is so genuine but so unexpected that I'm not prepared to stifle my giggle. The wave of relief I feel upon discovering that one, Melody is a jerk to everyone, and two, I'm not the only one who doesn't like her, is palpable.

"I wonder if she knows just how slappable her face is when she gives me that look," Delaney continues. I don't know Benny's wife well, but I like her immediately. She grabs a banana from the counter and peels it, handing it to Scarlett. "Are you staying here the whole game?" she asks me.

"I'm not sure yet. I'll definitely be here for the next hour or so."

"Scar's been talking about playing Princess Babies with you all morning. You're a big hit in our house." Delaney breaks off a piece of Scarlett's banana and pops it in her mouth.

"Ah, well, I'm a big fan of Scarlett too." I whisper behind my hand to Delaney, "but what's Princess Babies? I agreed to do it, but I don't know what it means."

Delaney shrugs. "No one does. I'm pretty sure she made it up, but I guess you'll find out!" She bends, kissing Scarlett on the cheek and telling her she loves her to the moon and back. You wouldn't know that Delaney isn't Scarlett's biological mother; sure, they don't look alike, but the love between them is strong. Deb told me that Scarlett's biological mother, Benny's first wife, is also incredible.

I end up staying in the family room for most of the game, only heading into the ballpark in the eighth inning. I sit in the family section with the players' families, catching up with a few of them. Other than Melody, they all treat me with respect. The game ends in a loss, a complete blowout. It's never fun to be on the receiving end of a shutout like this, but the wives seem to take it in stride, seeming more relieved that the game is over and they are put out of their collective misery.

I walk with them to the gate that lets them on the field. Priya joins us, snapping photos here and there. After a loss, especially one as massive as today's, no one really feels like doing Priya's fun little quizzes or social media games, so she takes videos of the kids running the bases. It's something that's offered after every weekend game, and children of all ages partake. There's even a small group of high schoolers elbowing each other as they race around the bases, carefully dodging the smaller kids.

Tomorrow is an off-day for the team, which means the families and players are milling about lazily along the foul lines, chatting and swapping off-day plans with each other. I'm already planning on working late tonight so I can take a half-day tomorrow. I'm trying to set up a wine tasting event for the WAGs next month, and while I have lots of ideas to make it cute and fun, in order to work within my budget, I need to get a little creative, which requires more research on my end. I've got plans to come into the office tomorrow; I haven't asked him, but I'm sure Asher would prefer to have the apartment to himself tomorrow instead of having to work around me. I promised Priya, Liam, and Faye I'd bring in iced coffees from the adorable empanada cafe a few blocks from Asher's and my apartment.

They don't know that I live with a player, and I'd prefer to keep it that way. I'm still not exactly sure if living with Asher counts as fraternization. I thought fraternization just meant I couldn't sleep with Asher (ha!), but when I looked up the definition, I realized it also meant hanging out with him. Seeing as I can't really afford to live on my own, I'll be taking my living arrangement secrets to the grave. While I'm sure Priya, Faye, and even Liam would be cool with it, I've been burned by coworkers before, so I'll be playing this one closer to the vest. Super separation of church and state.

Chapter Sixteen
Asher

June worked late last night and is working a half-day today. As much as the empty apartment feels weird without her, I'm grateful for the time alone. Her scent permeates the apartment, and it's one I've closely associated with comfort. No one else smells like June does, but I have yet to identify all the notes. She smells like fresh apples and something else, but I can't figure it out. I've even Googled "what scents go with apple?" but none of the suggestions seem right. I feel like a pervert, sneaking into her room to find her perfume, but I've got to know. The mystery is driving me crazy.

I hesitate at the threshold of her room. She keeps her door open unless she's sleeping, so I can see inside from where I'm standing, debating how creepy I want to be. We're friends now, long since having bypassed the awkwardness of our teenage attraction, but I wonder if this is crossing a line. It's not like I'm sifting through her underwear drawer, I tell myself, but that thought heats my blood. At least I know that's one line I won't be crossing. I can only imagine Devin's reaction. I'd have to observe it from the afterlife though, because there's no way he'd let me live if I did that.

June left for work an hour ago, so there's no way she's coming home soon enough to catch me. I suppose I could *ask* her, but what would I say? *Hey roomie, I love the way your skin smells. Tell me what your perfume is made of?* Even in my head, I say it with a creepy, raspy voice. I've worked hard to put her firmly in the box of "only friends;" asking her what she smells like for sure opens the box again.

I waffle at the doorway before finally striding briskly across the room. If I walk fast enough, I won't talk myself out of it by the time I reach her dresser. The room isn't large, but she's kept it well organized and neat. On top of her dresser sits a line of quirky little barrettes in different hues. I can't resist touching one with a tiny frog face on it. I've never seen her wear that one.

June's personality cracks me up. Between her unconventional T-shirts, multicolored hair accessories, and sparkly glasses, she's always wearing something memorable. While the comforter and bedsheets on June's bed are mine, she's left pieces of her own style on top. A knitted yellow blanket with white daisies is folded at the foot of the bed. A beat up, one-eyed stuffed yellow dog sits front and center against a smattering of velvet throw pillows in various shades of green. I can't help my smile; June has always been unapologetically herself. It's one of the things I've always loved about her.

Turning back to the dresser, I find the bottle I'm looking for. It's nondescript. Literally. There is no label on it. It's just a rectangular, cobalt bottle. The bottle itself is pretty, with geometric diamond patterns etched into the glass. I pick it up, hoping to find a brand name or something written on the bottom, but come up empty. I pull the cap off, unable to resist taking in a lungful of my favorite, unidentified scent. It's definitely apple, with something else. It's clean and sweet at the same time, just like June. I find myself infuriated with the lack of answers. I wonder if Google can tell me a non-creepy way to ask June about it.

Relegating it to one of the great mysteries of the world, I plop onto the living room couch. I've been putting off a different kind of online research for as long as I could, but it's time to face the music. I lift the lid of my laptop and type in the offending words; it takes me a couple tries to get the spelling right, but I find what I'm looking for. The website that appears is not what I expected.

Black banners surround hot pink writing. The font is slightly blurred around the edges, giving the letters the look of neon signage. FOXY FANATIXXX, the top banner proudly proclaims. Underneath it: "Your primary source for ALL the dirt on Chicago's finest men!" I'd roll my eyes if I didn't feel like throwing up.

When I left my date's apartment last night, I heard her muttering, "Foxy Fanatics was right about that one." Not knowing what she was talking about, but hearing the derision in her tone, I left, feeling more defeated than after last week's date.

Despite my teammates' encouragement, dating is *not* going as expected. Or maybe the problem is that it's going exactly as *I* expected it to go. Several mojitos deep, I allowed Crawford to drag me to the bars in Little Havana where I practiced flirting but went home alone. I can flirt with the best of them; I've been doing that since I was fifteen. Maybe even before then. Picking up women is not the problem; it's everything that comes after that makes me so nervous I can't get out of my own way.

Last weekend, I met up with Celeste, a drop-dead gorgeous meteorologist in Cincinnati. I matched with her on the dating app Caleb set up for me, and the conversation we had via the app messenger was easy and uncomplicated. The conversation in person after the game was similar. By the time we made it back to Celeste's apartment, I was so in my head about sleeping with her that I couldn't seal the deal. If I'm being completely honest with myself, I didn't want the night to end in sex anyway. I'm certain sex will still bring about too many complications that I'm just not ready to deal with. But I still haven't figured out a way to communicate "I'm interested in hooking up with you, but draw the line at sex, but it's not you, it's me." In high school, it was so much easier because sex wasn't the expectation. I've hooked up with my fair share of women, but since college, my dating life has been sparse, to say the least.

Celeste, it appears, interpreted my hesitation as some sort of performance anxiety on my part, and to be fair, she's not wrong. It just has nothing to do with my sex drive or my dick not working properly and everything to do with my own head not letting me relax enough. I overthought everything. We kissed at the bar and it was good. When we kissed at her apartment, it was amazing. Celeste's body, which she quickly bared to me once we made our way into her bedroom, made my brain short-circuit a bit. But even when I touched her, my movements were slow and clunky, rather than the practiced and smooth she was expecting. I was already trying to figure out how to extract myself from the situation without sleeping with her, and it showed.

My experience last night with Hattie, a local social media influencer, wasn't any different.

Both women, it seems, had something to say about it. And it seems they chose Foxy Fanatixxx, a crowdsourced blog featuring Chicago athletes, most of them Foxes players, to do so. Unfortunately for me, the posts are sorted in chronological order, which means my face stares up at me from the top of the page, fresh from Hattie's "review."

Each word I read pushes me closer to the edge of humiliation, until I've tipped over into a pool of absolute mortification. How do I shut down the entire internet? Is it easier to change my name, become a hermit and live in a cave somewhere, never to show my face again?

Celeste and Hattie didn't hold back. Words like *utter letdown* and *boring* and *lackluster* and *couldn't find my clit if I handed him a map and GPS* float around in my head. I know where the clit is, thank you very much. I just find it hard to focus on it when I'm consumed with letting the girl down easy.

I am so fucked.

And not in the good way. I extend my punishment, forcing myself to read every word each woman wrote. Neither woman considered that I was distracted or nervous. While Hattie was a little more tactful in her delivery than Celeste, they both basically said the same thing. They both commented on my lack of verbal feedback, and they might be on to something there. I'm not exactly silent in the bedroom, but what am I supposed to say or do? *Would it kill him to produce a little dirty talk?* Celeste had written.

I go down another rabbit hole, Googling dirty talk. Whichever FBI agent gets stuck reviewing my search history has my condolences. There's apparently a whole subsection of TikTok devoted to the subject, which blends seamlessly into an area called BookTok, which sent me down an entirely new rabbit hole before I realized I'd strayed from my mission.

I open my notes app on my phone, starting a new checklist to catalogue my research. Dirty talk tops the list. I add in positions, how to relax in the bedroom, and oral tips, just to be on the safe side. I've never had any complaints about my oral skills, but I also never considered that I should be voicing the litany of dirty thoughts in my head while hooking up with a woman either, so what do I know? I'm horrified, reflecting on the girls I've been with over the years (admittedly, aside from Hattie and Celeste, there haven't been any since college) and wondering if I'm terrible in bed and just don't know it.

Website after website sends me on a wild, kinky adventure through the internet, but I'm not turned on. I'm confused. Overwhelmed. Surprised. Okay, a little turned on, too. I'm so engrossed in my research that I don't hear the door to the apartment open and close. I, apparently, also don't hear June calling my name several times.

She dives onto the couch next to me, startling me. "Fuck!" I exclaim, slamming the lid of my laptop shut. I'm not on porn sites, but I'm not on anything remotely PG either. June laughs, the sound filling the room.

"I called your name, like, three times. What were you looking at?" She wiggles her eyebrows as if she already knows.

"Nothing!" My quick denial is drowned out by more laughter. I'd bask in the sound if I weren't so embarrassed. She tries to wiggle the computer free from my grasp, but I'm gripping it so hard I'll probably crack the screen.

"You know it's okay to watch porn, right?"

Nope, I don't need those words coming out of June's mouth. The "only friends" box I've shoved her in over the last few weeks shifts dangerously in my mind. The top flap lifts, just the corner. In my head, I slam it shut and cover it with packing tape, sealing all the edges.

"Maybe next time, do it in your room?" She's still talking. About porn. My eyes bulge when I find myself wondering if *she* watches porn in *her* room. The one that shares a wall with *my* room. I mentally take the box and throw it into a closet, covering it with a blanket.

"It's not porn!" Why is my voice so loud? My face feels hot and I don't need a mirror to know I'm blushing.

"Okay, it's 'not porn,'" June says, putting ridiculous air quotes around the words.

I thought the Foxy Fanatixxx website was bad enough. This is a new level of shame I'll never recover from. Maybe I'll just move; there's got to be plenty of available apartments in Chicago. It was fun being friends with Devin for the last ten years, but that's got to go, too. It was nice while it lasted.

"Asher, are you okay?" June rests her hand on my forearm, her neon green fingernails lightly scratching my skin, sending a shiver skittering down my spine. Her face is concerned, probably because I've stopped breathing.

"It wasn't porn," I repeat adamantly.

"Okay, it wasn't porn," she agrees quickly. Too quickly. I wouldn't believe me either.

"It was...research." Her eyes widen at my admission and I realize she still thinks I was looking at porn. I sigh deeply. There's no way to salvage this conversation without telling her everything. If I do tell her the whole story, she'll never look at me the same way again. Maybe I *should* let her think it was just porn.

Wordlessly, I lift the lid of my laptop again. When I log in, the incriminating websites spring to life, including an absurd GIF of a man with a cartoonishly giddy expression on his face. His index finger repeatedly slides in and out of the circle he's made with his other index finger and thumb. June quirks an eyebrow but waits for an explanation. Cringing, I navigate to the first tab, where Celeste and Hattie spill their secrets on my less-than-stellar performance to Foxy Fanatixxx. I hand my computer to June and wait for her to laugh at me.

Her eyes flit back and forth, scanning each line, reading every humiliating word the girls have to say about me. I shift uncomfortably next to her while I wait for her judgment. When she finishes reading, she looks up at me. I brace myself for laughter that doesn't come.

"Oh, Asher, are you okay? What a cruel thing to have happen to you." She touches my forearm again, and this time, her touch burns. She's not supposed to be nice about this. Then, to my horror, I realize she *pities* me.

"Don't pity me, June. Please." The last word is whispered, reeking of desperation. Her eyes soften.

"I'm not pitying you, Ash. But I am sympathizing–*empathizing*–with you based on how these women treated you. I'm sorry you had personal information broadcast on the internet without your consent. I'm sorry that these women weren't kind in the ways they chose to describe you. I'm sorry you were thrust into this situation."

She doesn't say it, but I imagine her words anyway. *I'm sorry that you suck in bed.* Instead of wallowing in self-pity (because whether she calls it pity or sympathy, that's what it is, and I've gotten enough pity from June to last me a lifetime), I move forward in trying to solve my own problem.

"Anyway, I really was researching. And not porn."

"Right. Never porn," she says with a stiff nod. "Porn is the devil. Got it." I can't help but crack a smile. We lapse into silence. It's not strained, but it's not comfortable either. June's eyes cloud with worry when she looks at me, and I can't stand it. I throw my thumb over my shoulder.

"I'm just gonna….yeah…" I stand, grab my keys, and walk out the door.

Chapter Seventeen
June

H uh.

I never would have guessed that Asher was bad in bed. His broad shoulders and large hands led me to believe he'd be a monster in the sack. Not that I've thought of him in bed often. Oh, who am I kidding? I've thought of it often. As much as I try to deny my schoolgirl crush on Asher, the more it digs its stubborn heels into my heart. I've given up denying it and have accepted it as part of my fate. I must have done something mildly bad in a previous life that I need to atone for. I probably drove a loud muscle car or never recycled. Now, I'm paying for it by living with my crush and, it turns out, said crush is bad in bed.

Asher told me not to pity him, and I really don't. Not for his lack of bedroom prowess anyway. I feel terrible for the way he had to find out about it, though. Hell, maybe *I'm* bad in bed, too. I've never been told that, but my skills have also never been publicly reviewed online (I hope). At least Asher is a sweet person.

My mother's voice rings in my ears. *You can be taught a lot of things, but you can't teach nice.* It's true. I've met my fair share of extremely competent assholes. You can teach just about any skill, but you can't teach someone to have a great personality. All Asher needs is a little help, and you know what, good for him for listening to feedback (even if it was delivered in the most horrible way) and working to better himself. As someone who has slept with some, ahem, *less-than-talented* partners, I have to give Asher a lot of credit for not getting defensive. When my partners aren't cutting it in bed, I try to gently encourage them to give me what I need; it's the ones that don't listen that don't get a repeat date. All this to say, I recognize that Asher isn't taking the easy way out and is willing to do what will benefit him (and many women) in the long run. Good for him.

I decide to tell him just that when he gets back from his walk or wherever he went. Except he doesn't come home. Hours pass and the sky slowly darkens. I'm not sure if he left on foot or took his car, but when fat raindrops hit the living room windows, I hope it's the latter. I debate whether I should reach out to him, just to check if he's okay, but decide to give him space.

I pour my leftover pasta into a glass container and put it on top of the one I've already filled for Asher. I sliced Italian sausage and peppers in the sauce like I know he likes, but he never makes it home for dinner. It's not until I'm lying in bed, hours later, that I hear him creep in, locking the door quietly behind him. I know he's avoiding me, but I'm not sure how to make it better. Maybe by the time we both wake up tomorrow morning, this will have blown over, and we can both forget what we learned yesterday.

Spoiler alert: we both did not forget.

I'm in the middle of a bowl of Frosted Flakes with frozen blueberries, my favorite weekday breakfast, when Asher lumbers out of his room. He reaches for the box and pours himself an extra large serving. I hand him the milk and hold up the bag of frozen fruit, silently asking if he wants any.

"In my cereal?" He says around a mouthful.

"Yeah, it's my favorite. It keeps the milk extra cold and the berries juicy." He doesn't say anything else but accepts the bag from my outstretched arm. He mixes in the frozen berries, taking another oversized bite. His eyes widen in surprise as he immediately digs in for another spoonful. It's stupid, the amount of pride I feel right now.

"So, um, are we going to talk about yesterday?"

"There's nothing to talk about. And I'd really rather not think about it. I'm starting today and need a clear head." I nod, forgetting that it's Asher's day to pitch. It's probably for the best that we don't discuss anything heavy right now. I want him to do well, but I also can't wait to tell him about the idea I came up with in the middle of the night. It'll have to wait until later tonight. He's already tilting his bowl of purplish milk to his lips, having inhaled the cereal in record time. I'm not sure if he's hungry or just trying to get away from me. He places his empty bowl into the dishwasher, steps around me, and begins gathering his things to head into the ballpark.

He usually rides his electric scooter to work, but tonight's weather report promises more rain. When he snatches his keys from the hook by the door, he finally meets my eyes.

"Do you want a ride?"

"No thanks. I'm not going in as early today. Priya and I are rollerblading together before we go in if the rain holds off. She's convinced I'll like it." His eyes dance as the corner of his mouth twitches.

"Wear a helmet." Without another word, he ducks out of the apartment.

Rollerblading with Priya was not as terrible as I thought it would be. While I technically swore off exercise after the Sweatin' with Ryan debacle, the weather is slowly becoming warmer and it's a nice day out. My neighborhood is the perfect location for rollerblading on the sidewalk; the pathways are wide and smooth, making it a far safer option than the street. Priya is patient with me as I learn to establish my balance. I'm slow and wobbly, but once I learn to relax into my stride, things go much smoother.

Last week, I mentioned to Devin that Priya wanted to introduce me to rollerblading. The next day, a pair of teal and purple rollerblades and matching helmet showed up on the front door. Thanks, overnight delivery! The matching helmet might make me look like a giant dork, but Devin and I both agree that it's important not to sustain a traumatic brain injury.

My ankles are sore by the time we finish an hour later. Knowing my experience with boot camp, I mentally prepare myself for tomorrow's soreness, too. Priya comes up to our unit with me, changing in the bathroom before she drives us to work. Luckily, she doesn't ask any questions about my roommate or my current living situation.

We make it to work about an hour before the game starts. Foot traffic is heavy around the stadium, and the air is filled with the scents of grilled meats and popcorn. As much as I want to get started in the family room, I know I have to buckle down and secure some donations for our wine tasting event if I want it to turn out the way I have it planned in my head. I've been answering emails, balancing budget spreadsheets, and fielding phone calls for so long that I didn't realize that the game had already started. Looking up at the muted televisions in the main area of the office, I'm startled to see the Foxes are already in the fifth inning.

The game is flying by at an unusually quick pace. That usually means one or both pitchers are doing well. As if the broadcast crew can hear my thoughts, they post a recap of Asher's performance so far. He's been lights-out. He's given up one hit, one walk, and thrown seven strikeouts. He's having an incredible game, and I've missed most of it. Guilt gnaws at me, and I decide to take a break, pulling up the game on my laptop in my office. As part of their hiring package, the Foxes gave me a subscription to their online broadcast of games. I haven't used it yet, so it takes me a moment to set up my account before the game filters through my screen.

The announcers are singing Asher's praises. He's somehow managed to keep his pitch count low enough that I wouldn't be surprised if he plays late into the game. Another replay from earlier in the game reveals Hayden Oliver and Carter Perez both hit solo homers. They're responsible for the only runs scored in the game, and while some insurance runs here would be helpful, the small run margin doesn't seem to be bothering Asher. He looks almost *relaxed* on the mound, as the camera zooms in on his face. He's dialed in; I don't think I've ever seen him so focused. My phone buzzes with a text, but I'm afraid to rip my eyes away from the broadcast, worried I'll miss a crucial element of the game.

Devin
> Ash is looking good today. Hope you didn't die while rollerblading.

Me
> I didn't! Alive and well, thank you very much. My ankles want to murder me, but Priya and I already have another session planned for next week!

> Glad you had fun.

> Good luck at your game tonight. Love you.

> Love you too.

Devin doesn't play for another three hours. I have my baseball app on my phone set to alert me anytime he makes a play during his game. With the amount of rollerblading Priya and I did earlier, I'm not anticipating staying awake to watch all of his game, but I'll hopefully catch the first few innings.

My attention returns to the game on my computer in time to see Asher pump his fist, striking out the third batter this inning. I'm relieved to see him pumped up; after how deflated and defeated he looked last night, Asher could use a win, in all senses of the word. I make a mental note to swing by the grocery store on the way home to pick up more brownie ingredients.

Somehow, I make it home before Asher does; with the pace of today's game, I'm home well before the threat of storm clouds becomes anything to worry about. I'm cleaning up the last of my baking mess when Asher's key turns in the lock. I'm planning on frosting tonight's brownies with a peanut butter buttercream because the store had a blue-and-orange sprinkle mix on sale, so I called an audible. Tonight's recipe will still have peanut butter, but in a different format from Asher's favorite. We'll see how it stacks up against peanut butter swirls.

He groans when he steps into the apartment, smelling the rich aroma of chocolate.

"Tell me there's peanut butter in this batch," he says as he kicks off his shoes.

"Not yet, but there will be. I made a peanut butter buttercream frosting, but it might still be a little warm to finish just yet."

"Mmmm," Asher lets out another moan and closes his eyes, savoring the idea of frosted brownies. Hearing his excitement and feedback about my baking is one of the main reasons I keep making them for him. It's always more fun to bake for people you know will appreciate it.

"I figured you deserved a more special batch after today's game. You looked great out there, Ash. How do you feel?" I spread the frosting over the top of the brownies. It only melts a little, so I toss the sprinkles indiscriminately over the top.

"I feel good," he tells me honestly. I can't help my wide smile in response.

When we sit down to eat our brownies on the couch, the television already tuned in to Dev's game in the background, he makes a point of snapping another photo of his brownie before he digs in. A whooshing sound informs me he's sent the photo in a text or email to someone.

"Who are you sending my brownies to?" I suddenly feel self-conscious, because if Asher is sending photos of my food to his mother, I need to step up my game. No one can cook like Ms. Incaudo.

"My nutritionist, Allie. We have this running joke that I need to take in more protein, so I send her photos of ridiculous protein sources. You know, cheesy nachos with a single, tiny piece of chicken, or brownies with peanut butter."

I roll my eyes and laugh. That is a very Asher thing to do. "Are you supposed to be getting a lot more protein? I can see if I can swap in some protein powder into the next batch or something."

Asher looks affronted. "Don't you dare. You'll ruin the desserty integrity of my brownies."

"Desserty integrity?"

"Yes. It's a real thing. These brownies are perfect. The frosting melts perfectly. You're an amazing baker, Junie. Don't change a thing."

I can feel my cheeks turn pink at his words. It's high praise coming from Lorelai Incaudo's son. As if he can't take the wait any longer, Asher picks up his brownie and shoves half of it in his mouth, groaning in pleasure at the taste. I try to keep my preening to a minimum, but it's hard not to take pride in his reaction. I take a bite of my own and set it gingerly back down on my plate.

On the screen, Devin saunters up to the plate, bat in hand. It looks chilly in New York, the late spring warmth likely dissipating with the setting sun. Devin looks strong and focused, and I'm reminded of Asher's laser-like focus earlier today. We both watch silently, rooting for my brother. With a crack of the bat, he hits a dribbler to the third baseman. Despite his hustling, he's thrown out by a mile. Asher laughs.

"That wasn't even close. Big boy is gonna need to work on his leg speed." He snorts before tossing the rest of the brownie into his mouth. I turn back to Asher, now that the only reason I have for paying attention to the game in New York is back in the dugout.

"I'm only going to ask this once, and if you don't want to talk about it, you can forget I brought it up. But do you want to talk about yesterday?" I wince. I feel like things were awkward at breakfast with us, so I want to talk about it, but at the same time, Asher just pitched one of the best games of his career, so do I really want to bring him down with this conversational topic?

"We can talk about it. There's not much to say, I guess. It's not really a secret I haven't dated much since college. I've been so focused on making it to the big leagues, and I didn't want any distractions. Not that women are a distraction, but you know. I needed a singular focus to get here." I nod. "Now that I'm here," he pauses, choosing his words carefully. "In Miami, some of the guys convinced me to set up a dating profile. And I obviously went on a few dates, and they obviously did not go well."

"When you say you haven't dated much since college, what does that mean?"

"Like, not at all. No dating, no random hookups. I may not have made it to the big leagues as fast as your brother, but I was still on a fast track to get here, and when you're pegged for success, it's hard to know who really wants you for you, and who wants you just to get a piece of you."

I can understand that. It's got to be stressful, constantly questioning the people in your life and if they really want to be there or if they have ulterior motives.

"I somewhat intentionally kept my social circle small. After a pregnancy scare for one of my teammates, I was even more intentional with who I allowed in my company. But seeing my current teammates have successful relationships, it makes me wonder what I'm missing out on. It'd be nice to come home to someone who loves me for who I am."

My heart breaks a little bit for Asher. We've all got our own issues, but I didn't realize he was lonely.

"What about Allie? You seem to have a good relationship with her. Would you consider dating her?" Asher levels me with a look.

"Hard pass. Not because Allie isn't a great person–she is. But dating someone I work with is messy. That, and she's engaged to someone else."

"Oh." I think for a moment. "Do you think the whole website thing was just because you're out of practice? Maybe it's something that will come back to you with time. Like riding a bike."

"No, June, I don't think that's what it is." There's something in his tone that makes me pause. It's almost...sadness?

"What is it, do you think?"

"When I was with Celeste, or with Hattie–the girls from the dating app–I was so in my head. I was overthinking everything. Not because I was worried about my own performance, although I guess I should have been, but because I was consumed with coming up with an exit strategy. I was so distracted, worrying about how I could extract myself from the date without sleeping with them."

My eyes widen at the realization sleeping with them wasn't part of Asher's original plan. Sensing my confusion, he continues.

"There was a really messed up situation with my college teammate that kind of scared me straight when it came to the whole accidental pregnancy thing. I don't know that I can trust someone enough to believe they aren't trying to manipulate me into staying, now that I'm tied to money and a modicum of success."

"I never thought of it that way," I respond thoughtfully. "I mean, obviously most women will probably not be trying to do that, but how do you figure out which ones are genuine and which ones just want a piece of you?"

"Exactly!" Asher's immediate and enthusiastic response surprises me, but I'm pleased to hear that I understand him well enough. "That's only part of it, though." He takes a deep breath, as if he's steeling himself to tell me the next piece. "I've never…I mean, I'm…a virgin." He says the last bit quietly, but not shamefully. I school my face, trying to temper my shock.

"But you had so many girlfriends in high school. College, too, I assume?" Asher picks at a loose thread on the couch cushion, refusing to meet my eyes.

"Yeah, but I didn't sleep with them. The good ones accepted my excuses about needing to focus on baseball. The bad ones pressured me constantly until I eventually broke it off. I mean, sure, I did other things with the girls I was seeing. I'm not completely inexperienced. But there's always been a level of attention on me, ever since I started getting scouted in high school. It made me question who I could trust. And when I wasn't sure if my girlfriend was in it for me or for the eventual payout, or the notoriety, or the status, or whatever, it was just easier to avoid sleeping with them altogether. I resisted them until there was so much anxiety around the act itself that it just wasn't worth it." His voice is quiet as he reveals his final truth. "The last thing I wanted was a girl getting pregnant because of me. Not because I don't like kids. I do. But to be saddled with me because of them? Because if I don't make it, if I don't live up to the hype surrounding me? I won't be able to look at the mother of my child if I thought I would see her regret."

I sit with Asher's truth for a long time. His gaze remains on the television, but I can tell he's not really focused on it. I replay his words in my mind, letting them sink into my consciousness. I always knew he was committed to the game, but I never quite realized the weight he was carrying around with him. A small part of me wonders if that's why Devin engages in meaningless hookup after meaningless hookup: if you never slow down enough for someone to really get to know you, they can't reject you, and they can't regret you.

My heart wants to break even more for Asher, for the things he's held himself back from experiencing in the name of self-preservation. At the same time, I'm proud of him for trusting himself enough to know what he's willing to risk and what he's not. When I tell him just that, he seems surprised, like he's never viewed his actions as something to be proud of.

"Well, I'm proud of you, Asher. Whatever your reasons, no one should ever pressure you, and I'm sorry that happened to you. But your reasons are good, and they make sense. And they've probably helped you get where you are."

Finally meeting my eyes, his hazel ones reflect gratitude for the shift in perspective. I'm happy to be Asher's sounding board—and brownie maker—for as long as he lets me.

"Can I ask you something?"

"Anything," I tell him honestly. I don't have any major secrets, but I want him to feel comfortable around me.

"What do you smell like?"

"What?" I snort. Whatever I thought he was going to ask me, it wasn't that.

"Ugh, I don't know how to ask this. Your perfume smells really good, and I know it's apple, but I can't figure out what else it is and it's driving me a little bit crazy."

I howl with laughter, mostly because the turn of subject from serious to unpredictably unimportant throws me off so much. Asher joins me with a chuckle, and it's nice to bring some levity to the conversation. As our laughter dies and I wipe a tear from the corner of my eye, he pleads with me.

"I am serious though, June. It's driving me nuts. Just tell me what I'm smelling and why I can't identify it."

"It's a custom scent. Whitney, Christine and I went to France the summer after high school. We went to a perfumery and had custom fragrances created for us. It cost a fortune, but it was clearly worth it. They've saved the scent profile and every year since then, I reorder a bottle for myself for my birthday. It's my little treat to myself." Asher waits expectantly, circling his wrist in the air, urging me to go on. I momentarily debate fucking with him, or at the very least, prolonging the suspense, but decide he's been through enough lately. "It's apple blossom, pear, and green grass."

"Grass. Fucking grass! I can't believe I didn't identify it. I'm only around freshly mowed grass every day of my life." Asher facepalms, shaking his head at himself. I smile, and we both return to watching the game.

After a few minutes, I finally decide to just go for it. Shifting my body to sit sideways on the couch so I'm facing him, I take a deep breath and blurt it out.

"Look, if you're really feeling…rusty, or whatever. I can help you. You know, build your confidence back up so even if you don't end up having sex with your dates, you can at least get out of your head a little bit?"

Asher is silent for so long that I'm convinced he's trying to find the words to let me down easy, to tell me that's the worst idea he's ever heard and to never talk to him again. I wish I could rewind time or snatch the words out of the air and shove them back into my mouth. Asher's mouth is open in a small "o," but he still says nothing.

"Sorry, forget I said anything. I just plowed right through that boundary, huh?" I unfold my legs, preparing to retreat to my bedroom, bury my head under the pillows and resurface when Asher's lease is up and I have to move.

"No, it's okay. It's not a bad idea, I'm just…uh. Wow. I wasn't expecting that. Can I, um, think about it and get back to you?"

"Yeah, no worries," I tell him when, in fact, I am all worries. I'm so filled to the brim with worries that I'm surprised they aren't spilling out of the top of me, soaking into the couch and dripping onto the floor. "Just, uh, let me know." I wave my hand around, as if that clarifies anything I'm trying to communicate. "I'm gonna head to bed. Goodnight, Asher."

I scurry off to my bedroom without a second glance behind me.

Chapter Eighteen
Asher
16 years old

"Huge tits, am I right?" Greg's voice rings out over the music pumping in from the weight room. In the background, shower water splashes against the tiles, yet somehow Greg's voice comes through loud and clear, even though he's halfway across the locker room. He's holding his arms in front of his chest, his hands cupped as if to demonstrate just how large Sarah Wilder's chest is. He's not wrong, but I'd like to think I wouldn't be so crass about it.

"I don't know man, I'm more of an ass man myself," Evan Jones replies. His eyes take on a faraway look. "Now give me a Lillian Hoffman any day."

I share a look with Devin. We don't really have room to talk; he and I have both hooked up with our fair share of classmates, but we don't gossip about it in the locker room. Our high school isn't that big; there's bound to be overlap between the girls we've dated when that dating pool remains the same for four years. Devin's face is hardened and I know what he's thinking. He's already expressed concern that his sister will be joining us here at school next year and he doesn't want her talked about the way Greg and Evan are currently talking about Lillian and Sarah.

I can't blame him. I don't have sisters, or any siblings at all, but I've seen June. She's what my mother calls "early developing," and I already feel terrible that my asshole teammates and probably many other guys are going to look at her and see a pair of tits long before they discover she is a human being with an actual personality.

Devin clears his throat. He has to do it twice more to get everyone's attention, but eventually, the background chatter dies down as everyone focuses on our starting catcher.

"Alright everyone. Listen up. I'm not gonna tell you what to say or do in regard to other girls, but my sister is starting here next year." Devin stares down each of our teammates, his eyes flicking from one to another with intensity. "Let me be clear: my sister, June, is off-limits. There will be no discussing her in here or anywhere else. There will be no looking at her the way you look at all the other girls in this school. And there certainly will not be anyone on this team fucking asking her out. Understood?"

He again makes eye contact as each of our teammates nods or gives some sort of verbal indication that they get it. The last person Dev locks eyes with is me. I obviously nod as well. I guess Devin's sister is pretty, but I'm not dumb enough to be interested in my best friend's kid sister.

Especially when that kid is sister to Devin, the world's most protective older brother. It's what makes him such a good friend and an outstanding catcher. It's not a surprise that his naturally protective instincts drew him to a position in which protecting the plate is of the utmost importance.

I know Devin's protectiveness would never go so far as to tell June who she could or couldn't date, but telling our teammates to steer clear? I'm fine with that. I agree with him. Some of the comments they make about girls are downright disrespectful. And hell, half the time, June acts like my little sister, too.

Chapter Nineteen

Asher

Present Day

*I*f you're really feeling...rusty, or whatever. I can help you. You know, build your confidence back up.

What the hell does that even *mean*? Did June just offer herself up on a silver platter to me, her brother's best friend? And if so, tell me why I'm considering it like it isn't the worst idea in the history of roommates?

Tell me why I want to dig out that "only friends" box from my closet and fling it open? Because I'm dangerously close to feeling that way and once I open it fully, there's no going back. And despite my confusion on what, exactly, June offered me last night, I *know* she wasn't offering anything more than a friendship.

I run my fingers through my hair, gripping the strands tightly, as if it will help ground me to reality and find a way to respond to June's proposition.

"Don't do it, man," Crawford's voice has me snapping my head up, worried that I somehow accidentally voiced my thoughts aloud. At my confusion, he says, "Don't rip your hair out. You've got that California surfer look going. It'd be a shame to ruin it."

I shake my head, dropping it between my shoulders where I'm sitting, leaned over in front of my locker. The game ended an hour ago and the clubhouse is slowly emptying out. Crawford and I are the only ones left in the locker room; even the noises from the nearby weight room are fading. I'm already showered and have no reason to stay at work any longer, other than the fact that I'm avoiding my roommate.

"Can I ask you something?" Crawford and I have known each other for a few years. If anyone knows the answer to my conundrum, it'd be him.

"Sure, what's up?"

"What can you tell me..." I hesitate, wondering if I'm going to regret this. "About dirty talk?"

Crawford is silent for a moment, processing, before he tips his head back and lets out a loud, deep laugh. I'd feel discouraged if I wasn't confident his laugh is one of shock rather than mockery.

"Of all the things I expected you to say, Rook, that wasn't even in the top five hundred." I grin. At least I have the ability to surprise him. "Whew. Okay. What do you want to know? Why are you asking?"

I end up telling him about the Foxy Fanatixxx disaster. I give him the highlight reel, a brief synopsis, rather than the play-by-play.

There is no way I will be telling Kyle Crawford, god's gift to women, that I'm still a virgin.

"Ah, shit, that sucks. Stick with me, young grasshopper. I'll teach you what you need to know." He pauses for a moment, then adds thoughtfully, "You're smart to start with dirty talk."

"I am? Why?"

"Think of dirty talk as your foundation, the building blocks to being good in bed. Men and women are built a little differently. We can get ready to go at the drop of a hat. At the mere mention of sex, we're a few pumps away from getting off already. But women? They're a different animal, and it takes them a little more to get going. Enter dirty talk: your secret weapon to getting a woman wet and ready to go without even touching her."

I hate that we're discussing this in a locker room, of all places. But we're alone and I'm desperate for any help I can get, and Kyle is being helpful for once.

"I get that, but what do I say? And when? And how do I know she'll be into it?"

He thinks for a moment before taking the seat next to me. "Okay, there's no guarantee that every woman will like it, but in my experience, almost every woman is into it. If you're doing it right." I sigh, feeling like I should be taking notes, given how out of my element I feel. "Okay, think of it this way. When you're hooking up with a woman, or you see someone you want to hook up with, what thoughts are running through your mind?"

"I don't know?"

"Yes, you do. Think about it. Your dream girl walks in here right now. You're all alone; she's half-naked and giving you very clear signals that she's down for it. What are you thinking?"

Unbidden, an image of June pops into my head. Her long chocolate waves spill over her breasts, her plump lips pink and glossy. She walks toward me. With each step, her tits jiggle just the smallest amount–I slam my eyes shut, and along with it, the mental image of June gets thrown back into its cardboard box. I throw a heavy bag on top of it, since taping it up clearly didn't work, and shove it to the back of my mental closet.

"Yes, exactly," Crawford is nodding when I open my eyes again, as if he knows what I'm thinking. "What, specifically, explicitly, are your thoughts? What do you want to do to her?"

"I want...to undress her. And have my way with her."

Crawford tsks. "No, you don't."

"I don't?"

"In that exact same scenario, my half-naked dream girl walking in here, all alone? I'm not undressing her. I'm ripping her clothes off, watching her nipples tighten into hard little buds before I suck them into my mouth." I whip my head around, ensuring that we actually are alone. Kyle continues. "I'm going to wrap a hand around her throat while my fingers slide down her panties so I can find out exactly how wet she is for me. I'm not 'having my way with her,'" he says with disdain. "I'm bending her over and shoving my cock so deep in her that she feels it in her throat. I'm reaching around to strum her little clit so she explodes around me, her pussy milking me for all I've got. Or maybe I'm falling to my knees to eat the best fucking pussy I've ever tasted, licking her until she's a shaking, screaming mess on top of me, dripping down my face. *That's* what I'm doing to her. Don't give me any of this polite, tentative bullshit."

Fuck. Crawford's description has me half hard. He's leaving very little to the imagination. I swallow.

"Women don't want your hesitation. Obviously get your fucking consent, but once you have it, be confident. Tell them exactly what you want to do and then pay attention to their response. Does she moan when you talk about eating her out? Then you know she wants that. Does she stop breathing or increase her heart rate when you tell her you want to choke her while sucking on her tits? Then do that. It's not hard. I know you've already got the thoughts running through your head, just voice them."

"But what if she doesn't like dirty talk?"

"Like I said, man, I haven't met a woman yet who doesn't. But if she's not into it, then stop. You're making things more complicated than they need to be. If she likes it, do it. If she doesn't, don't. You can check in with her and ask, but do it in a way that conveys your confidence."

"What do you mean?"

"Would you rather have sex with a woman who constantly asks, 'Is this okay? Is this good?' or who says, 'Tell me what you like.'"

"The second one."

"Fuck yeah, the second one. The second one empowers her to get exactly what she needs, while promising that you're the man to deliver it. The first one is meek and unsure and it makes her feel like she has to keep reassuring you. If you're in your head about it, it makes *her* in her head about it, and no one has a good time."

I take it all in, suddenly wishing I'd had the foresight to record this conversation, so I can reflect back on it, while simultaneously feeling grateful that there is no permanent record that we ever talked about this.

Crawford stands, squeezing my shoulder. "It's less about skills, I suspect, and more about confidence with you. I have no doubt you know what you're doing. And if you don't? Well, I'm gonna start charging you for lessons and start calling myself the love doctor."

"Get the fuck out of here," I say, rising to stand and shoving him away from me.

As I ride my scooter home, the breeze lifts my hair off my neck and clears some of my thoughts. Crawford might be the world's biggest fuckboy, but he knows what he's doing. I scanned enough of the Foxy Fanatixxx articles to know he's a fan favorite for more than just his baseball skills. I wouldn't be surprised if my head was more of the issue than my physical prowess when it comes to pleasing women, but I have no way of knowing that for sure unless I hook up with women and get their specific feedback.

Which brings me back to my original conundrum: is that what June is offering, and if so, can I say yes?

My dick responds with a resounding yes, but he's wanted June since I was eighteen. My head, on the other hand, is a bit more cautious. I won't know for sure what I can handle until I know exactly what June is offering. Maybe she'll just talk to me about strategy or something, like Crawford just did. I can handle that. But if I'm supposed to touch her or, god forbid, do anything more, I'm not sure I'll survive, and not just because her brother will murder me.

CHAPTER TWENTY
June

My knitting needles click together over and over, creating a pleasant little ASMR soundtrack that I can hear between songs. I'm listening to Priya's sister's boyfriend's band, Thistle Whiskey. Their show was great, and their lyrics are some of the best I've heard in a long time. I'm happily in my zone, despite my novice knitting skills. One summer in high school, my grandmother taught me to knit. I made one shabby scarf, which took me most of the summer, but once school started up again, I promptly abandoned all attempts and forgot about my skills. In Tampa, I decided to revisit my craftier side. I'm still working on the wobbly hat I started last year, but I'm making progress. More and more, it's starting to resemble an actual article of clothing, instead of a wooly blob. Maybe I'll finish by the time it starts to snow again.

The break between songs is punctuated by Asher's key in the lock. Lately, I've been beating him home after games. I prefer to go in earlier to work and leave once the game is over. I tend to work better in the mornings, and dragging myself back to the office once the game is over leaves me feeling unfocused and inefficient. Deb is flexible enough that as long as my work gets done and I'm at the games to support the families, she doesn't care about my hours. It's a refreshing change from being micromanaged.

"Hey," I say when Asher steps inside and tosses his backpack on the kitchen chair.

"Hey," he says. "I didn't know you could knit. What are you making?"

"Knitting is a relative term, I'm finding. I'm attempting to make a hat. I'll report back on my success in three to six months once I finally finish this." I hold up the purple yarn that is sort of maintaining its cup-shaped form. "If you squint really hard and use your imagination, you can kind of see where I'm going with it."

Asher's eyes remain wide as he lies through his teeth. "I can see it. It looks great." He sits on the opposite end of the couch as me and takes out his phone. Tension lines his body as he taps and scrolls away on the device, but I can feel his eyes periodically dart to me and away. I wonder if he's as apprehensive as I am about our conversation yesterday. I don't want to take back what I said, because I really will help him if he wants it, but I also don't know if my offer made things irreparably awkward between us. He clears his throat. I glance up at him and he sets his phone down on his lap, turning his torso toward me. I set down my needles, anticipating I'll get my answer now.

"June, what did…" He starts, then pauses. He picks at his fingernail and tries again. "What did you mean when you said you'd help me yesterday?"

Shit, is he going to make me spell it out for him? I thought it was obvious that he needed help in the bedroom. I'm not sure how I could have misread that.

"Did you not, um, feel like you wanted help? I'm so sorry to have assumed you wanted to change that."

"No, I do. I just…before we get into anything, it's probably important for me to understand what exactly you're offering. How you're planning to help." Asher swallows audibly. I give him what I hope is a reassuring smile.

"I guess it can be whatever we make it. However you want the help. If you have specific questions about things, or want pointers or something. I'm sure I could find some helpful resources if you're looking for something specific. I just thought you'd want a female point of view, if that's who you're hooking up with."

Asher smiles. "Yes, June. I'm straight, if that's what you're asking. A female perspective would be great. I don't want you to feel obligated though."

I wave my hand in the air in front of me. "Ash, I wouldn't have offered if I wasn't willing to provide the help."

His shoulders sag with relief. "Honestly, Junie, I'll take whatever help I can get. I'm feeling a little desperate here."

I pat his arm gently. "We'll have your reputation restored in no time." When he lifts his head to look at me, his hazel eyes are filled with an undefinable emotion.

"It's not really about my reputation. I mean, yeah, that part sucks, too. More than that, though, I want to be good for my partner. I don't want any woman to regret coming home with me." I want to squeeze Asher and his tender heart. Those Foxy Fanatixxx women don't know what they're missing out on. If I hadn't already offered my help to him, that one statement alone would have made me want to. Asher is a kind, dedicated, hard-working soul; he deserves to have the world view him favorably. He also deserves to have fun having hooking up, instead of this anxiety-fueled stress-fest that it seems to be for him right now.

"How do you want to do this? Do you have questions about things?" He quirks an eyebrow at me and laughs.

"So many questions. I'm not a total novice, but now I'm second guessing everything I do know. Crawford is helping me with some things, but maybe you can give me the female perspective, like you said." I nod. Say what you want about Kyle Crawford's extracurricular reputation, he's probably one of the best men for the job to teach Asher a thing or two. "But we should probably talk about boundaries or whatever, too. Because the last thing I want is for you to look at me differently at the end of this."

"I hope you won't look at me differently either. I'm not exactly a blushing virgin. No offense," I add on hastily. Asher's eyes crinkle in the corners as he lets out a small laugh.

"No, that's just me. Okay, no matter what, we stay friends, yeah?"

"Of course," I promise. "And let's keep this our little secret, too. Devin doesn't need to know the dirty details of my sex life."

"Devin doesn't need to know that *I'll* know the details of your sex life," he points out. He pauses a beat. "June, don't hate me for what I'm about to ask. I just really, really need a clear picture of what we're going into here. And if I'm misinterpreting, there's no pressure whatsoever. Just tell me. But, um, is this like something where we're just going to talk about things, or are you like...going to show me, too?" He visibly cringes as his words come out.

Oh.

I didn't think about it that way. I guess I just assumed we'd talk about things. My brain is already telling me this is a dangerous idea, but my heart and my lady parts are chomping at the bit to tell Asher yes and ask what his schedule is like and when he can start. He must sense my inner conflict, because he shakes his head.

"Sorry. Clearly, that's now how you meant things. Forget I said anything."

"No, wait. It's okay. It just threw me for a second. I think I'd be okay with that, actually."

I mean, fuck it. I can keep things separate in my mind; Asher wouldn't be my first situationship. I haven't done the friends with benefits thing in several years, but I wouldn't be opposed to it. After my last boyfriend, I've been somewhat apprehensive about getting back into the dating game, but this might be just what I need to get a little kickstart.

"Are you sure? I don't want to complicate things or mess up anything."

"I think as long as we keep some boundaries in place, we'll be good. Obviously, it's not just Devin we have to keep this from. I'm fairly certain this would definitely fall under that nonfraternization clause in my contract." Asher huffs his agreement.

"What else? What other rules do you need?"

"I don't know that we need that much more, as long as we promise to be honest with each other every step of the way. If one of us wants to call it quits, for whatever reason, then it's a clean break. If something is jeopardizing our friendship, we break it off and go back to being friends only. If either of us is uncomfortable for any reason, we have to voice it." Asher nods along.

"Definitely. Agreed. To everything." He takes off his hat and runs his fingers through his hair before replacing it once more. "Thanks for doing this for me, June. I'm forever indebted to you."

"Psh, it's fine." I wave my hand in the air again. "I'd do it for any of my friends." *Lie.* While Christine, Whitney, and I don't shy away from talking about our sex lives, I'm not exactly teaching seminars to anyone. Asher is in a league of his own when it comes to the things I'm willing to do for him. He always has been.

Asher left for his road trip right after the game today. I won't see him for another week, which will hopefully be enough time for him to read through the book I shoved at him yesterday. While I doubt I'll ever regret my offer to him, I did have a moment of trepidation when I realized that my near-lifelong crush on Asher might rear its ugly head if we go down this road. Then, I told myself I could handle it as I started sprinting down said road as fast as my legs could take me.

At the same time, I recognized that last night was not the night to start anything between us. I needed a clear head and some time to figure out how we were going to go about this. Asher told me he's working with Crawford on dirty talk. The idea alone almost made me start fanning myself right there on the couch when he divulged that little nugget of information. Two insanely hot, tall, athletic men sharing dirty talk tips? To be a fly on *that* wall.

Still, I thought it was pretty smart of me to give Asher an impromptu homework assignment for his road trip. The book I threw at him was chosen simply because it was the first one I came across when I got ready for bed last night. I don't know how much time Asher will have for reading, or if he's even going to be into the type of romances I read one-handed, but it's as good a place as any to start. The author is one of my favorites, and it's an easy read. It's heavy on dirty talk and worshipful longing and contains no miscommunication: my all-time favorite combination.

I close my book. I've been reading the same paragraph over and over, with nothing penetrating my brain. I'm distracted thinking about Asher's and my arrangement. Priya and I have plans to rollerblade again in the morning, so I might as well call it quits for the night anyway. Asher pitches tomorrow, too. I wonder briefly if he's staying in his hotel room tonight, reading my book instead of going out with the guys. I shake my head. Who am I kidding? Even I would rather hang out with baseball players than read, and there are very few things that can tear me away from my beloved cliterature.

I never should have fooled myself into thinking I am graceful. I don't know how that thought ever popped into my mind, or why it persisted for more than a laughable, crazy moment. And yet, here I am, strapped into my teal and purple boots on wheels, which will inevitably whisk me away toward certain death. At least, those are the thoughts running through my mind as I cross Lincoln Avenue, a few wobbly paces behind Priya.

I probably should relax; Chicago drivers won't really run me over if I'm still in the crosswalk when the light changes, right? Then again, I'm pretty sure that's a risky bet to take in any major city. In Philly, they'd for sure mow me down. They'd probably make a game out of it: ten points for every fallen wannabe athlete, five if you hit her when she's already down. There's only so many fingers I can cross that the mild Midwestern mannerisms I've experienced in Chicago so far translate into driving styles (doubtful, seeing as I've driven around here, too).

"Oh god, oh god, oh god," I chant as the crosswalk light starts its countdown. I've still got half of the intersection to cross. Priya, with her stupidly athletic legs and good balance, reaches the safety of the other side of the street as I make classic mistake after classic mistake. First, I look down, which throws off my balance. I know it will, but I can't help it. The thickly painted lines of the crosswalk make for uneven terrain under my wheeled feet. My second mistake is to stiffen my body. That, too, I can't help. Straightening my legs might sound counterintuitive, lifting my center of gravity, but I know the strength (or lack thereof) in my legs, and there's only so long I can hold a bent-knee position. My third and most fatal mistake, however, is rushing. Again, this one was not my fault either. With the countdown of death signaling my impending doom, I apply a heavy dose of internal pressure to get my ass to the finish line.

Instead of reaching the finish line, however, my ass just reaches the pavement. As in, *she's going down. Timber!* Everything happens so fast, so I'm not sure how exactly it happens, but I throw my left arm out on instinct, causing shooting pain to rocket through my arm all the way from my hand to my elbow. Rather than dwell on the physical pain, though, I scramble to my feet in what I'm sure is the world's most uncoordinated and least graceful endeavor, because right now, the emotional pain and humiliation is worse.

Look, I'm not lacking confidence on most days. But most days I'm not engaged in feats of strength and balance in front of an audience. Even though I know I'll realistically never see any of these drivers again, I can't help but cringe.

Priya comes gliding back to me in a panic.

"Oh my god! June! Are you okay?"

"Yep," I grit out through clenched teeth, because I'm now realizing I need to take back my thought that the emotional pain and embarrassment is worse than the physical pain. Priya takes my hand and guides me to the curb, where we sit together.

"Where does it hurt?" I hold up my throbbing wrist. I don't miss the irony in Asher and Devin both having concerns about me hitting my head while wearing these death traps, but my head was the one thing that didn't touch the pavement. If it had, maybe it would have knocked me out so I wouldn't have to remember this entire experience. Priya helps me out of my rollerblades and we head home so I can ice my arm. I don't care that I look ridiculous walking down the city street in socks, while carrying a single rollerblade (Priya took the other one); anything is better than hobbling along with wheels of misfortune strapped to my feet. Every block or so, I can feel Priya's eyes on me as she scans my body for additional injuries.

Maybe I got off relatively unscathed, all things considered. I didn't get run over by a car (thanks, mild Midwestern mannerisms!). My wrist is the only thing really bothering me. Both my palms and the side of my leg got a little scraped up in the tumble, but nothing compares to the pain in my wrist. I've made it twenty-three years without a broken bone; are rollerblades really going to be the thing that takes me down? In my head, my sad little consciousness changes the sign that says "__ days without an accident" to zero. To be fair, the previous number wasn't that high anyway, considering the spill I took while sweatin' with Ryan, but that was more of an injury to my pride than anything else.

After an hour of icing my wrist under Priya's nervous gaze, we both agree that things are not improving, and we might need to go to urgent care. Priya assures me the urgent care around the corner can probably take X-rays, and we set off on foot. In shoes. Because there is no way I'm getting in those rollerblades ever again. Come to think of it, bikes might be off the table for the foreseeable future, too.

"Good news! It's not broken!" The doctor at the urgent care is cheerful and bubbly, and if I were dealing with anything life-threatening, I might find it more annoying. But her infectious smile is contagious, and I find my own making an appearance. "The bad news is it looks like a pretty bad sprain. There may be some bone bruising, but only an MRI will show that." I nod, as if I had any idea that was the case. Priya, too, nods along. Look at us, a couple of adorable little bobbleheads.

"So, what now?" Priya asks. It's sweet that she's taking the reins here, but I suspect it's because she feels guilty for suggesting rollerblading today, but my coordination challenges aren't her fault.

"We're going to put it in a splint for you. You'll need to keep it splinted until you can see a doctor. You can go to your PCP, but we really recommend an orthopedic doctor. Here's a list of some doctors in the area." She hands me a paper with a long list of names and contact information.

By the time I'm bundled up in a splint and shuffled out the door, I'm really wishing I had the forethought to shower before coming here. The sweat I built up during rollerblading has long since dried on my skin, leaving me feeling crusty and gross. I hope I don't smell. All I want to do is go home and take a shower, but with my arm looking like I shoved it in the middle of an oversized marshmallow and wrapped it in bandages, I don't think that will be happening tonight. A bath it is, followed by spending the rest of the evening calling orthopedic doctors to see who can get me in the fastest so I can get this thing off me and take a proper shower.

Priya insists on setting up the couch in the living room for me like I'm some type of invalid. She props pillows up, fills my water bottle, brings out a stack of books (at least she avoided bringing out my knitting needles), and puts the television remote on the nearest table. When she offers to go out to get me soup, I draw the line.

"It's just a sprained wrist, Pri. I'm not dying."

"Yeah, but you said your roommate is on a business trip! I just want to make sure you're able to get by without him." She still doesn't know Asher is my roommate. I feel bad for withholding that information from her, but I feel less guilty when I think about how my job could be at risk if anyone finds out about my "fraternizing" with my roommate.

"I'll be fine. Honestly, I just want to take a shower and get an appointment with a doctor so I can swap out this monstrosity," I hold up my puffy splint, "for something that doesn't make my arm look like the Stay Puft Marshmallow Man." Priya snorts.

"Are you sure there's nothing else I can get for you?"

"Honestly, no. I'm good. Thank you though. And thank you for coming to urgent care with me."

When she finally leaves, after making me promise her several more times that I'll call, email, text, or notify her via carrier pigeon if I need anything, I lock the door and plop myself on the couch. I turn on the television, just to have some background noise. The pregame for the Foxes is on, reminding me that Devin's game is probably finished. I snap a quick picture of my arm and text it to him.

> Me
> Guess we should have splurged on wrist guards instead of a helmet.

The text hasn't been sent for ten seconds before Devin is video calling me. I spend twenty minutes on the phone with him, assuring him I'm fine, that I didn't hit my head, that I don't need him to do anything (not that he could from his hotel in Minneapolis anyway), and that yes, I still am fine. Sometimes, it's nice to be cared for so fiercely by my brother. At other times, I have to remind him that I already have two parents, as he should know, since I share them with him.

I muddle my way through a bath. I can't wash my hair, which is perhaps the biggest tragedy of the day. I don't wash my hair every day, but after rollerblading and sweating in the sun, my scalp could use a good scrub. By the time I settle in bed for the night, I'm exhausted. I have an appointment in six days with a Dr. Levinson. His office was the only one with availability within the next week, so I took it. I'll have to trek halfway across Chicago to get there, but that's a problem for Future June. Present June just wants to find a comfortable position in which to doze off.

The universe, however, seems to have other plans.

First, Whitney calls, having finally seen my text earlier. I sent her the same photo I sent Devin, warning her of the dangers of physical fitness. As soon as I answer the phone, I'm greeted with a hard truth.

"Should have stayed lazy, my friend." Whitney's dry tone makes me laugh.

"Ain't that the truth. Remind me of this exact moment the next time I try to convince you to try Pilates or pickleball or anything more strenuous than a walk."

It's good to hear Whit's laugh. She's been working her ass off trying to get her event planning business off the ground. She's doing well for a newcomer to the field, but her crazy hours mean I don't get to catch up with her as often as I'd like. We both take the opportunity to fill each other in on our lives. I finally blurt out my new arrangement with Asher to her, too. It feels good to talk to someone about it. The silence that greets me once I tell her everything, though, has me nervous. We're not on a video call, but

I can somehow feel her penetrating gaze as if she were in the room with me.

"How do you feel about this?" Her words are measured, careful. They betray nothing of her true opinion on the matter.

"I think it'll be fun. Exciting, even." I didn't tell Whitney about Asher's virgin status. It's not my news to tell, and even if it were, she would never believe it anyway. We saw the never-ending stream of girls lined up for a chance to just talk to him. Hell, I *was* one of those girls at various points in my high school career. "What aren't you saying, Whitney?"

"I agree. It could be really fun. I just don't want you to get hurt. Christine and I saw you fall in love with him a million times over when we were younger." Her words hang thick in the air around me. I sigh.

"Does everyone know about my crush on Asher?" I grumble. "I'm not going to fall for him this time. I'm not some teenager with her head in the clouds. This isn't my first time with a friends with benefits situation, or whatever this ends up being."

"I know. But Asher isn't just some guy. He's simultaneously your first love and the one that got away." I scoff. I was just a kid back then. Sure, Asher is even more beautiful now than he was at seventeen, but I can keep my emotions in check. When I don't say more on the subject, she changes her approach. "So, what are you going to do when he gets back in town? Quiz him on the book you gave him?"

"Honestly, I don't know. This isn't your normal case of friends with benefits. I'm supposed to teach him things. I know I've got skills in the bedroom, but how do I convey that to him in a totally normal, won't-ruin-our-friendship-or-our-living-situation kind of way?"

"I'm always partial to the whole dressing-like-a-naughty-schoolgirl thing," she suggests. I snort out a laugh. Don't I know it? In college, the amount of times Whitney told us about her roleplaying adventures could serve as its own road map for the kink. I've been known to dabble myself, but it's not my thing the way it's Whitney's. I'm surprised the girl didn't become an actress. "Okay, if you're not going to fulfill his hot-for-teacher fantasies, what is your plan then?"

"I don't know. I guess we could just start talking about the book? Or the dirty talk he's learning from Crawford?"

"Kyle Crawford is teaching Asher dirty talk?" I give her a moment to sit with the idea. She hums happily into the phone. "I'd let that man do all sorts of nasty things to me. Nothing is off-limits." She's quiet again and I'm worried she's lost in her thoughts of filthy vampire role plays, or whatever she's into these days, with Kyle Crawford. "What if he watches you?" she asks thoughtfully.

"Crawford?" Whitney's giggles fill my eardrums, reminding me how much I've missed her.

"No, not Crawford. Asher!" When I don't respond right away, she plows forward, increasingly convinced of her brilliant idea.

"He wants to get better in bed, right? To do that, he needs to know what women like."

"Obviously," I say. I already covered this with her earlier.

"What better way to teach him than to *show* him? Have him watch you touch yourself. Bring yourself to the brink of an orgasm right in front of him. First of all, it'll drive him wild because it's hot as hell. But then you'll be able to dip your toe in. If you can't handle the awkwardness of *that*, then you definitely won't be able to handle sleeping with him."

She has a point. If I can get over my initial doubt about him scrutinizing me, it really is the best way to try it out. It's not like I haven't done the same thing at the request of my past boyfriends (well, not the teaching thing, but they've definitely watched me). But there's something about *Asher* watching me that makes me ten times more nervous while also making the situation a thousand times hotter. I adjust the neckline of my sleep shirt, emblazoned with the phrase "My Flabbers Have Been Gasted" in bright pink lettering. It's suddenly much warmer in my bedroom.

As if he can feel me thinking of him, my phone beeps with an incoming call. I pull the phone from my ear to see Asher is calling me. Asher never calls me. We text mostly, with the exception of one video call when I couldn't find a cheese grater that he insisted he had while he was on a road trip. With his video call guiding me, I found the grater in no time, leaving our non-texting phone communication limited to approximately a minute and a half.

"Hey, Whit, I gotta go. Asher is calling." I hang up with her before clicking over.

"Hey, Ash. I was thinking of a mocha brownie this week to celebrate tonight's win. What do you think?" My ears warm, as if he could somehow know what Whitney and I were discussing before he called.

"June! Are you okay?" His voice is panicked. Loud music and shouting voices rumble behind him; I imagine he's in the visiting locker room, celebrating the win with the rest of the Foxes.

"Uh, yeah, why?"

"Dev told me about your arm!" Oh. Duh. Thinking about showing off for Asher pushed all thoughts of my injury from my head. That and the good drugs they gave me before I left urgent care.

"Oh, yeah. I'll be okay. I'll know more once I visit the orthopedic doctor next week. You wouldn't believe how hard it was to get an appointment. I have to go all the way to Bridgeview, and even then, I have to wait six days! I'm stuck in this annoying splint till Thursday."

"Tell me exactly what they said." The urgency in his voice makes him sound commanding, and I might just be the teensiest bit turned on from it. So I do what he says. I tell him about Priya taking me to urgent care and setting up the apartment for me. I tell him about the sprain and the potential for bone bruising. I even tell him I was bummed that I couldn't wash my hair tonight.

"Okay. I'll talk to the team doctor here and get you in to see him. He'll be better than whoever you booked with."

"Oh, you don't have to do that. I'm sure Dr. Levinson is good."

"June, this guy is *good*. The best of the best. I'll have the trainers get me his contact info and get you in to see him before I even get home. Then you'll have answers and a treatment plan sooner," he says, imbuing even more sternness into his voice.

I don't know what to say, so I agree. Asher's never been particularly bossy or strong-willed. He's always been easy-going and relatively laid back. Sure, I've seen him laser-focused on the mound when he's pitching, but other than that, he's generally pretty mellow. A small part of me likes being taken care of. I didn't really have that when I moved to Tampa, and if I'm being honest with myself, I was worried I wouldn't have it when I moved to Chicago either.

"What else do you need? I can place a grocery order. Did you have dinner? I can have something delivered to you right now."

"Ash, I'm fine." What is with Priya and Asher treating me like I'm dying? "Thank you though. It's very thoughtful."

"I don't want you to make me brownies, either. You've got enough to deal with without trying to stir or crack an egg or something." I hum noncommittally. He's too chill to be taking this bossiness thing this far, but I'm not about to argue with him over the phone.

"Agree to disagree." I pause, debating whether to dive into the deep end or not. "What have you been up to on this road trip?

Read any good books lately?" His deep chuckle sends electricity across the airwaves and straight into my heart.

"I might've read a few chapters of something good this morning," he says, somewhat evasively.

"Oh really?" I'm not normally one to flirt with Asher, because hello, it's Asher. But there's something about tonight–maybe it's our new arrangement–that makes it so easy to slip into it.

"Yeah. JJ lent me his copy of *Lord of the Flies*." He pauses, waiting for my reaction, as I work to try to figure out if he's fucking with me or not. His stifled laugh is answer enough for me. "I'm kidding, Junie. I'm reading your book."

"And...?" I ask expectantly. I pick at a loose thread on the comforter, as if it will dispel my nervous energy.

"It's good, Junie. Really good. I'm getting all sorts of ideas." Asher's voice is quieter, darker somehow. It scrapes against my eardrums in the most delicious, alluring way. I clear my throat. It's better to rip the bandage off when he can't see me cringe if he says no.

"I was thinking when you get back, I could show you what I like. If you'd, uh, like to watch me." I wait with bated breath. Seconds, maybe hours, pass before he responds, in a notably more strangled voice than earlier.

"Yeah, June. That would be, uh, yeah, that would be great. I'd like that. If you're cool with it, too." Somehow Asher's stammered response makes him that much more endearing.

"I'm cool with it."

Chapter Twenty-One
Asher

"Well, well, well. What do we have here?" Crawford plucks the corner of June's book out of my grasp, pinching it between his thumb and index finger, as if he's afraid to hold it fully in his hands. The cover is a cutesy cartoon depiction of what, in my mind, is a loose interpretation of the main characters.

"Some light reading, eh, Incaudo?" As if the thought dawns on him for the first time, his eyes widen. "You're doing research, aren't you?" he hisses.

I whip my head around like I'm afraid to get caught with a book, of all things. We're on the plane home. I am hoping to settle into the next few chapters while the rest of my teammates are occupied with the poker game in the back. Not everyone participates, but my seat is near the middle of the plane; pretty much everyone behind me is focused on gambling. I didn't get nearly as far in the book as I had hoped. It was such a slow start that I found myself impatient to get to the sex scenes, but now that I'm in the thick of it, I find myself drawn to the storyline between the characters, not just the kinky sex. Fisher is magnetized to Paige, has quietly worshipped her from afar, and now that he's gotten a taste of her after their first night together, he vows never to be apart from her. I'm itching to read more, not just to learn about dirty talk (of which this book has plenty) and what makes women go crazy, but to find out how they overcome the potential challenge of the rodeo cheating scandal, of which Fisher is thrust front and center.

"Whatever, man. It's good." I purposely keep my voice low, but with Crawford thumbing through my book while standing in the middle of the aisle, he's drawing more attention to it, and thus, me.

"Whatcha reading?" JJ Jeffers, our shortstop, peers over the back of his seat. He never gambles on the plane, preferring to sit with Caleb Andrews and play video games. I don't know why tonight, of all nights, he couldn't be engrossed in Mario Kart instead of my reading habits. "Oh, I've read that one."

The speed in which both Crawford and I whip our heads toward JJ is so forceful I'm surprised one of us doesn't pull a muscle. "*You've* read *this?*" I don't mean for my tone to come out judgmental, but it definitely does.

"Yeah. Amy had me read one or two while we were dating. Sometimes I'll pick up one of her books just to read on my own. Especially if she gets very quiet and very still while reading it." He smirks, but Crawford and I clearly aren't in on the joke. "It means she's turned on by it. She's fully engrossed in it; she barely moves. That's my cue to read it when she's done. I've learned a lot."

I swear, my mouth is hanging open. Like JJ Jeffers had anything left to learn about sex or women before he met his wife. The man is a walking, talking sex symbol; what could he possibly get out of these books that he doesn't already know? As if he can read my mind, he shrugs.

I reach across Kyle to tug my book out of his hands, but he tightens his grip. He's got the book flipped open to a random page, but I can already tell what part of the story he's at based on the amount of underlined text I can see. I don't know how June will feel about me marking up her book, but if she has a problem with it, I'll buy her a new one. Right now, I'm treating this novel as my textbook. And I've always liked to take notes when I study.

Crawford brings his hand to his mouth, rubbing his stubble. The action does nothing to detract from the shock in his eyes. I'm going to have to research this author later. To have both JJ Jeffers and Kyle Crawford pausing to rethink their own strategies with the opposite sex is quite the feat. June may have thrown me into the deep end with this one, but it's clearly been vetted by the best of the best.

"Are you guys reading the girls' book club rec?" Caleb Andrews turns, half-kneeling on his seat in the row in front of me, to face us. Jesus Christ. I didn't mean for this to become a thing. Five minutes ago, everyone was so preoccupied with themselves, I was certain no one would notice that I was reading, let alone *what* I was reading. Now, I'm gathering quite a crowd. I move to snatch the book away from Crawford again, but he anticipates the move and ducks out of the way. He spins and plants himself in an empty seat in the row across from mine. Tyler Edwards was sitting there for takeoff, but the seat has long been vacant since the poker game started. As much as I want to lunge over there and rip the book from his hands, that would call even more attention to this situation, and already JJ, Caleb, and Crawford knowing about my reading list is three people too many.

Crawford remains there for the rest of the flight, rapidly flipping through the pages. I've never seen someone read anything so quickly, but I see the way his eyes scan the words and know he's not faking. So much for preparing to see June tonight.

It's late anyway. She'll probably already be asleep by the time I get back home. We never agreed on when, exactly, we would start our new arrangement, but I'm guessing it will be soon. Now that she has invited me to watch her, I want to get started immediately.

When I walk into the apartment, though, it's mostly dark, save for June curled under a reading lamp in the corner of the couch.

"Hey, all-star," she greets, unfolding herself and standing. Her wavy brown hair is down and styled nicely, and I'm immediately reminded of how Fisher wrapped Paige's hair around his fist as he shoved his cock down her throat. Then I'm immediately ashamed to be thinking about sex when my eyes catch on the brace on June's wrist.

I drop my bag at the entrance and rush toward her, gently taking her hand in mine. "Hey, how are you feeling?"

"I'm fine." She waves me off with her good hand. Her left hand is encased in thick, inflexible black plastic and fabric. It looks impersonal, almost industrial. June herself is wearing a green T-shirt with a cartoon skateboarding cucumber on it. Little wobbly lines are drawn near the cucumber's stick knees and "Cool as a Cucumber" is written beneath the miniscule skateboard. He's wearing sunglasses and a beanie. It's ridiculous and adorable at the same time, much like June. She's not wearing any makeup, which makes the freckles across the bridge of her nose stand out and her blue eyes more striking.

I sit beside her on the couch, careful not to jostle her. "What did the doctor say?"

"Dr. Katchel said it was a mild bone bruise. I have to wear the brace for two weeks to stabilize it, but I'm mostly just resting it. It's more annoying than anything else. Thank you for referring me to him, by the way."

I smile; it was literally the least I could do. When I called, I spoke with Dr. Katchel himself, rather than his office staff. I was happy to use my connections to get her in to see him in two days. I'm also confident in his skills. I'm sure the other doctor June found would have been good too, but why settle for good when you can have the best?

"Right. Well. Ready to get started?" June scoots herself to the edge of the couch. The movement is more of a wiggle as she tries not to use her injured arm to help her off my deep couch.

Her words sink in. I guess we're just jumping right into things. It's late and I'm sure she wants to get to bed. It's a night game tomorrow, but I have no idea how early she's planning on going into work.

"We can do this another time, June. It's late. If you want to go to sleep..." I let my words trail off, unsure how to finish my statement. I may be learning about dirty talk from Crawford and June's book, but I'm still a little self-conscious about just blurting out sex talk in the middle of a conversation.

"Nah, let's just rip the bandage off." She's already standing and walking to her bedroom. Like an eager little puppy, I follow, and not just because I know she's going to get naked. I'd follow June wherever she wants me to go. When we get in her room, I don't know what to do. I know I'm only going to watch her, but this is her show. I don't know how close I should stand, or if I should sit down somewhere. I don't want to awkwardly hover over her, but I also don't want to give her the impression I'm aloof or uninterested. I'm way the fuck interested, thank you very much.

"Where do you want me?" I'm a nervous, sweaty mess. A part of me is glad we didn't agree to me touching June, because my palms are slick. My throat is suddenly dry, and it makes my words come out raspier than I intend, but if June picks up on how turned on I am, she doesn't show it. I don't even care that I'm coming off as a total virgin right now; June deserves to know the effect she has on me.

"Probably the foot of the bed will give you the best view." Her voice betrays nothing. I have no idea what she's feeling. Is she as nervous as I am? Probably not. There are few women as confident as June. She wears her quirky style as a badge of honor; she is unapologetically herself. Where I'm lacking in confidence in the bedroom, she makes up for in spades. She slides her cotton sleep shorts down her thick thighs. My swallow is audible. Her panties go next, and I'm greeted by the sight of neatly trimmed, light brown curls. Forget my dry throat; my mouth literally waters at the sight. It's been a long time since I've been able to look at a woman's cunt and feel no worry about how I'm going to pleasure her while somehow magically avoiding the outcome of sex. I have no such concerns tonight, and the saliva pooling on my tongue confirms as much. June whips off her shirt to reveal the most perfect breasts I've ever seen. Large and heavy, her nipples already hardening in the air-conditioned room. I tell myself that it's because she's turned on for me, when I know it's really that she's turned on for herself. For what she's about to do.

She clambers onto the bed. It takes everything in me not to help her, given her wrist injury, but I'm afraid if I touch her now, even in a nonsexual way, I won't be able to stop. Just the sight of her naked body has my cock straining painfully against my zipper. I jerked off in the hotel shower this morning, after reading about Fisher bending Paige over in the tack room, but that was so long ago, and my dick is begging for another round. Tonight, however, is all about June. I fist and unfist my hands at my sides. I release my jaw, which had clenched so tightly I'm sure I'll be sore tomorrow, but it's all I could do to stop a groan from releasing when she straightened up and stepped out of her bottoms.

June props herself up against the headboard. Her hair spills over her shoulders and down her full tits. The sight is mesmerizing. It takes all I have in me not to palm my cock. He's screaming at me for even the tiniest bit of relief. June shifts, tossing her hair behind her shoulders and I'm pleased to discover the smattering of freckles across her nose that I love so much is twin to the ones scattered across her chest and collarbones. I rake my gaze across her, taking in her puckered nipples, her soft belly, the mostly hidden curls between her legs as she stretches out in front of me.

"How do you want me to do this?" she asks. Her voice is quiet, like she's under the same spell as I am. It comes out soft, but I don't mistake it for self-consciousness. June is in her element. This morning, right after I got out of the shower, she sent me a photo of her nightstand drawer, filled with vibrators and dildos of varying thicknesses and colors. I assume different ones do different things and thinking about that made me so hard that I turned and immediately hopped back into the shower, where I came again in record time.

"How would you do it if I wasn't here?" My voice is still raspy, coated in lust. I clear my throat, but I'm not sure it will help. "Just do whatever you would normally do."

"If I'm looking for quick relief, I just use my hand." I tip my head back and breathe deeply. I'm hoping that the lungful of air will also carry with it some sort of restraint, because I feel my own slipping. I'm a rubber band stretched taut; one more tiny tug, and I'm sure to snap. I've never felt this way. I've always had some level of control over myself, but June's naked body is testing my long-held belief that I'm not an animal. "But sometimes, if I want to draw it out, I choose one of my battery-operated boyfriends."

"What do you feel like tonight?" I don't care what she chooses. At this point, I'll take whatever I can get. But the greedy side of me wants her to draw it out. I want to commit every second of tonight to my memory. Never have I wished for a photographic memory so badly.

She turns, balancing on her elbow, as she opens her bedside drawer and rummages around. The movement allows me a side view of her luscious ass. When Fisher first saw Paige naked, he described feeling like he swallowed his tongue. I can absolutely relate. My chest rises and falls rapidly as I try in vain to regain some control over my breathing, my heartrate. I don't even realize I've moved closer to the bed until my hands are tightly grasping the footboard. June resurfaces, pulling a light blue vibrator with her. Is it weird that the first thing I notice is that it's the same shade of blue as her eyes?

The vibrator has two small prongs off the front, likely to stimulate her clit. While the shaft is somewhat long and thick, I'm pleased to see I'm packing more than my silicone competition. Not that June will ever know or see mine, but I'm filled with a sense of male pride nonetheless. She spins a knob on the bottom and it buzzes to life. I watch, entranced, as she slides it not between her legs, but toward her chest. The vibrations are soft, quiet, and matched only by June's hum of pleasure when she drags the vibrator down her chest, circling one nipple, then the next. I breathe deeply through my nose. I'm practically panting at the foot of her bed. Beneath my fingers, the wood groans under the tightness of my grip. I don't let go. I'm not sure what I'll do if I did.

Over and over, June circles her tits with the toy before her knees fall open, exposing her wetness to me. If I thought my mouth was watering before, it's practically a faucet now. I swallow, the sound deafening in my ears. June drags the toy down her chest, her belly, and between her thighs. Her pussy is as drenched as my mouth feels, and I can't help imagining the exquisite sounds we'd make if she would let me join the two. When she circles her clit once, twice, three times, I swear I stop breathing. A nuclear bomb could go off right beside me, and I wouldn't know it.

June presses the toy to her entrance and slides in, just an inch. I feel myself leaning over the footboard to get a closer view. She pulls it out, then slides it in another inch. The shaft is coated in her arousal and I want to lick it from the silicone. Anything to get even the briefest of tastes of her. In and out, in and out, slowly, torturously she works the toy into her wet cunt, until it's finally seated to the hilt. Then, she spins the dial on the bottom, ramping up the vibrations. The toy slides out of her a bit as she does so, she's so wet and working with only one hand.

Then the show really begins.

June bucks her hips at the increased vibration. The little prongs are aligned perfectly with her clit and I can only imagine how intense it feels for her there. I didn't limit my research to June's novel and Crawford's words. I've spent almost every free moment of the last road trip doing some sort of study on the female body, sex, and ways to improve myself in the bedroom. I learned that the clitoris has over ten thousand nerve endings, compared to the roughly four thousand in the head of a penis. It's been a long time since I've received a good, thorough blow job, but I know just how much I enjoy it when a girl sucks hard on the head. Knowing June has more than twice as much sensation going on somehow makes me even harder. The realization hits me as suddenly as a lightning strike: I want June to always feel good. I should have realized it sooner, based on my reaction to Devin telling me she hurt her wrist. I feel like I went a little crazy when I heard that news. I was initially upset that she didn't tell me first, but I realized, why would she? I'm just a roommate. The thought leaves a sour taste in my mouth, and I close my eyes.

"Eyes on me." June's voice is thick with the lust I feel coursing through my veins. My eyes fly open immediately. There was something so commanding in the way she told me to watch her that I couldn't not comply. I watch her drag the silicone cock in and out of her. The room is quiet, save for my heavy breathing and the wet squelching sounds that have my dick ready to explode. June's hips buck as she chases her release. Her thrusts become more erratic, and she brings her protected arm across her chest. Her soft whimpers turn to huffs of frustration before I finally figure out what's going on.

She needs more, but with her injured arm, she can't get it. Before I can think about what I'm doing, I'm walking to the side of her bed.

"Scoot forward," I instruct, in the same commanding voice June used on me earlier. She doesn't hesitate, which is how I know she's desperate. Neither of us want to think right now; we both just want June to feel. I climb onto the bed behind her, settling my legs around her and pulling her back to my chest. I didn't plan on touching her at all, but her little growls of frustration are killing me. In this position, I can touch her and make it feel like she's doing it herself.

I can't see as well from this position, but luckily, I'm tall enough to see the vibrator disappear between her thighs.

"Tell me how you like it," I whisper in her ear. I don't miss the responding shiver that works its way across her body. "Where do you need me?"

"I need...my tits." June's words are stuttered. I may not be able to see all of her pussy from this angle, but the up-close view of her tits is unparalleled. They're heaving. I can imagine their heavy weight in my hands. There's no hiding my erection at this point. June's ass and low back are pressed against it, and her rocking hips against it make my eyes roll back in my head.

The whole time ignoring the debate in my head about whether this is a bad idea or not, I reach down to cover June's working hand with my own. Gently, I pull her hand, still clutching the vibrator, away from her center. I groan at the sight of the toy, shiny with her arousal. It's all I can do not to press my fingers inside her, but that's not what we're here for.

"Show me." My breath ruffles the hair by her ears. She releases her hold on the vibrator as it continues to buzz against the mattress. I bring her hand to her breast, pressing it firmly before releasing it. I watch as she kneads and massages herself, as I mimic her movements on her other breast. The feeling is sensational. Soft and pillowy, yet somehow still firm. I mirror her movements as she pinches her nipple and she releases a needy moan.

"Just like that," she whispers. Her praise has me batting away her uninjured hand with my free one, ready to take over. With both hands on June's huge tits, I feel like I've simultaneously gone to heaven and hell. Heaven because it obviously feels good to me and incredible to her. Hell because I know I'll never get to feel this again. A stab of guilt slices through me at the knowledge that I've crossed a line with my best friend's sister, but I shove it away. I won't let anything ruin this moment. In my mind, teenage Asher is high-fiving twenty-five-year-old Asher, ready to do a keg stand.

With June's good hand free to restart its previous attention on her pussy, it does. She resumes working herself over with the vibrator with renewed gusto, now that her perfect tits are getting the attention they deserve. I maintain a steady rhythm of pressing, pulling, and pinching as June writhes in front of me. I take in the show, noticing the way she thrusts the toy harder and faster as she reaches her peak. Her hips buck faster as she buries the toy deep, circling it over and over. Her breathing becomes shallow, rapid. I can't help it; I pinch both nipples hard because it seems like the right thing to do.

Her mouth drops open in a silent scream, her hips still bucking relentlessly. The parts of her face I can see from my elevated position behind her are screwed up in such undeniable pleasure that I'm in awe. I've seen women come before, both from my fingers and tongue a long time ago and in the porn I admittedly do watch, but nothing compares to the view of June falling apart in front of me. Her pleasure is so apparent I can practically feel it coursing through me at the same time.

Except it's not June's pleasure coursing through me, it's my own. *Oh, fuck.* The realization hits me seconds before it happens, but I'm powerless to stop it. June's ass writhing against my cock, her obvious pleasure, the feel of her glorious tits in my hands. It's all too much.

RECKLESS BEHAVIOR

Fuuuuuuuuck. I stifle my groan as I spill into my pants.

Chapter Twenty-Two
June

I'm not an idiot; I know what I look like naked. Some men are into it, being with a woman my size. Some men are unbothered by it. But each time I undress for someone new, I can't help feeling a little on edge–not because of the sex, but because I really, really need them to like what they see.

I love my body. I really do. I spent years in junior high and high school doing whatever I could to try to change it before giving up and embracing what genetics gave me. I'm a lot happier now that I'm not killing myself in the gym or starving myself in the kitchen, but that doesn't mean I'm not apprehensive about showing off the goods to someone else. I know what society says about women my size. It's taken a lot of work to tune out those voices and listen to body positivity, and I still fall into body-shaming pitfalls, but I am working on it. It's why I undressed so quickly, before I lost my nerve.

I shouldn't have been worried tonight, though. Asher's face when I stripped down was the definition of hunger. His eyes held such obvious need as they drank in my naked form. Huh. Maybe Asher is one of those guys who likes bigger girls.

More so than Asher's face when I got naked, though, was his face when I started playing with myself in front of him. He looked almost angry as I slid the vibrator in and out of myself. His intensity turned me on more than I've ever felt before. He looked like he was trying not to blink, afraid to miss even a fraction of a second of the show I was putting on for him. I've never felt so desired.

And when he took over touching my boobs? I've always enjoyed nipple play, but until I couldn't do it myself tonight, I didn't realize how much I needed it to be able to come. Asher was a quick study, too. I couldn't see his face, but even now, two days later, I imagine the intense concentration on it as he first watched me, then perfectly copied my motions. The fact that he could get both breasts at once while I worked the vibrator intensified everything.

That night, I came harder than I ever have by myself. Although I guess I really wasn't by myself, with Asher's huge, strong hands splayed across my chest. I swore I saw stars as I pulsed around my favorite vibe. I basked in the afterglow of that orgasm for an hour. Shortly after I came, Asher hopped out from behind me and practically ran from the room.

I tried not to take it personally. The orgasmic afterglow seemed to help. Now that I'm a few days removed from the incident, though, my thoughts catch up to me. Maybe my O face looks weird, or my moaning and groaning sounded weird. If that's what made Asher run, then fuck him. If men are weird about a woman taking her pleasure into her own hands (literally), then that's on them and not me. Even as those thoughts filter through my mind, I know that's not the case.

I know Asher was into what we did. I know he wouldn't have positioned himself behind me and pinched the hell out of my nipples if he didn't want me to feel good, so I doubt that's the reason he ran.

More than likely, Asher is struggling with the post-sex clarity of realizing he touched his best friend's sister. Devin would absolutely lose his mind if he knew, which is precisely why he'll never find out. That fucking hypocrite fucked my best friend, so Asher groping me while I masturbated in front of him is hardly anything for him to be upset about. Still, I can't help but feel a little weird at the swiftness in which Asher left my room.

We haven't talked about it. I don't want to or need to talk about it, and apparently Asher feels the same way, because neither of us has brought up that night since then. I don't know if that means he got the information he needed and he no longer feels the need to repeat the other night or what. I keep telling myself that he left so quickly because he was so turned on and wanted to return to the privacy of his room to jack off, but even I'm having a hard time believing that.

Who knows. I keep telling myself to shove those thoughts away and not to worry about it, but in moments of downtime, the thoughts still come creeping in. It usually starts with a simple memory of the night. The way Asher looked at me, pupils blown wide. The white-knuckled grip he used to hold on to the edge of my bed, as if he was actively trying to keep his hands to himself. The rapid rise and fall of his chest as I inched my way closer and closer to an orgasm. His giant, talented hands on my tits, his growl in my ear, the feel of his thick erection against my back.

Fuck. In revisiting the thoughts just now, I realize what I repeatedly fantasize about are the elements of *Asher* in my bedroom that night. Not about the intensity of my orgasm or the liquid, floaty feeling afterward. Not even the intense pounding of the toy in my pussy. No, ever since that night, my memories are of Asher.

Luckily, he seems to be none the wiser. He came out of his room the next morning as I was packing my work bag, his hair messy and voice deep and rough with sleep. He offered to drive me to the ballpark even though he wasn't going in for a few more hours. I declined but accepted his command to wait for him to make coffee. I thought he'd want to talk about the night before, but when he emerged from the bathroom, he just smiled and began making coffee like nothing had happened.

I was honestly so relieved. After we crossed that line from roommates and friends to…something different…I didn't know how we'd handle it. I don't like the term "friends with benefits." I've never had a problem with it until now, but seeing as I was the only one who got off that night, it hardly seems like the correct term for whatever it is Asher and I are doing. But "instructor and student" just seems wrong.

Asher had made us coffee while he chatted conversationally. I pointed out the pan of brownies that I had made the day before. I had meant to give them to him the night before, but they remained on the counter, long forgotten when we became otherwise occupied. Then, travel mug in hand, I left for work.

When Asher came home last night after the game, I was already in bed. Perhaps it was the coward's way out, to avoid a potential conversation about it, but I told myself I was exhausted. Which was true. But then I couldn't sleep, thoughts of my last orgasm filling my brain and consuming my cognitive resources. I told myself I shouldn't feel bad about reaching into my drawer last night and pulling out my thickest, girthiest vibrator; I refuse to be a woman ashamed about her physical needs. I may or may not have intentionally chosen my loudest vibrator while I sat alone in my bed, knowing Asher was in his on the other side of my wall.

I was playing with fire, wanting to see if he would say or do something about my obvious antics, but I never even heard his bedroom door open. If he wanted to join me, I wouldn't have stopped him, but either he wasn't interested or was already asleep, because by the time my orgasm crested, the only Asher in my room was the one I conjured in my mind.

Today's afternoon game is going to be hot and my schedule is packed. Caleb and Jenny Andrews are hosting their annual dog adoption event prior to the game. It's a great strategy, bringing dogs to the field before the game starts, allowing open entry to the ballpark in order for residents to interact with the pups.

Priya and I have been out here the whole morning. Many of the other WAGs are here, too, helping Jenny and Caleb as they promote the local rescue. I've been a dog lover my whole life. Muffin, my childhood golden retriever, holds a special place in my heart. As kids, Devin and I didn't fight much, but the recurring argument about who got to have Muffin in their bed each night got so bad that my parents had to develop a calendar system to denote nighttime custody of the world's best dog.

While, technically, this isn't a Foxes Family Program event, I feel my presence is required. Besides, these dogs aren't going to pet themselves. Some of the players filter through the ballpark as they arrive for the day, stopping to say hi to Caleb or their significant others and to pet some pooches. Most only stay a few minutes before heading into the clubhouse to get ready for the game. Asher, however, has been here for more than an hour. Not that I'm keeping tabs on his presence. It's just hard not to notice a six-foot, six-inch behemoth lying on the field and letting a litter of pitbull puppies attack his face with kisses. Anyone would find it adorable.

"Hi, June!" Amy Jeffers's cheery voice breaks through my thoughts. "How are you?"

Amy is one of the sweetest wives. Most of the WAGs (aside from Melody Malone) are easy to get along with, but Amy has a way of seeking others out to make them feel welcome. She seems to make it a priority to ensure everyone is having a good time.

"Jackson adopted Bruno, our rottweiler, from this event a few years ago," she tells me. "He was just a baby then. His mom had been rescued off the streets as a pregnant stray, so Jackson has known Bruno for most of his life. But now I'm Bruno's favorite." Amy cackles and I can't help but join in.

"No loyalty, that dog," JJ says, coming up behind his wife and hugging her. Her face lights up when she realizes he's arrived.

"He's loyal!" she protests, then with a wink at me, she adds, "He's loyal to the ones he loves best."

The dog event continues for the next hour before they pack it up. I'm sure the grounds crew isn't thrilled about dogs and fans running amok on the field before a game, but they obviously don't have enough sway to prevent it from happening.

With promises to meet back in the office with Priya for a late lunch later, I head to the family room to help set up. Everything takes me nearly twice as long with this stupid brace on my arm. While I can wiggle my fingers, carrying anything in that hand, unless I smash it between my forearm and my body, is impossible. I'm not used to forcing myself to slow down, especially when my job started at the beginning of the season at breakneck speed. Now that spring is bleeding into summer, I've settled in, but it doesn't mean I've slowed down. I hate having to account for additional time to do something as simple as setting up this afternoon's craft project (homemade kaleidoscopes) or typing out an email.

Deb has been supportive and patient; *I* have not. At home, I can take off the brace to shower, which is great. What is not great is the pain I feel when trying to use my hand in the shower when said brace is off. There's only so often I can go to the dry bar and get a blowout. As it stands right now, my two blowouts have already eaten way more into my budget than I'd planned. And forget putting my hair up in a ponytail; that requires maneuvering with two usable hands, and we've already established my coordination is not where it should be for me to even attempt some sort of one-handed hair wizardry. Two weeks can't come soon enough for me to heal better. In the meantime, I clunk around with my arm in a brace.

I briefly debate cancelling my date tonight. Okay, I more than briefly debate it. As I set out rhinestones, beads, sand, and confetti for the kaleidoscopes, I wonder how Asher might feel about me going on a date tonight after what we did the other day. Then I realize how ridiculous that is. We didn't even hook up. We never had any expectation of hooking up, or exclusivity, or anything of the sort. My task was to teach Asher, to show him what women like, and I completed said task. Asher has no right to claim my time or mental energy outside of a normal, roommate situation.

I've been chatting with Paul through the dating app off and on for the last couple weeks. Am I entranced by the conversation? No.

Am I excited about tonight's date? Also no. But I do like meeting new people, and even if there isn't a romantic connection, maybe Paul and I can be friends.

Woof. The fact that I'm already planning on a friendship outcome doesn't bode well for this date. But sometimes you just need to meet with someone, and maybe the spark that was missing during text conversations will be present in person. One can only hope.

After the game ends, Priya pulls my hair back for me into a high ponytail. It's cute. It's not the way I'd ideally wear it for a first date, but my hair has been under a baseball hat all day, and I'm leaving straight from work to meet Paul at an Irish pub a few blocks away. I won't have time to stop home and change, which is why I brought a change of clothes in my work bag. Instead of my normal Foxes polo and jeans, I'm in a cute yellow sundress and denim jacket. My earrings, shaped to look like cherries on a stem, hang from my ears, giving me a little pop of color that matches the bright red of my new lipstick. I feel ready for summer, even if I'm not totally ready for this date.

"Hey, how's it going?" Asher asks as soon as I get inside. He has a blue electric guitar on his lap. He's changing out the strings, a slight frown on his lips as he slides the wire through the string post. When I plop onto the couch next to him, he looks at me with concern. I had texted him earlier today, letting him know I was going out after the game, so he wouldn't worry if I didn't come home. He's done the same for me before.

"It's going," I admit. He raises an eyebrow at me, silently asking me to explain.

The date was less than stellar, and I have no desire to be friends with Paul, either. It started out okay. Paul looked like his profile pictures, so that was good. Unfortunately, that's about where the positives stopped. Individually, I could have overlooked (sort of) his near-constant boasting about himself, the rude references to his ex being "crazy," or the lack of questions about me, but some things you just cannot sweep under the rug. The second time he used the R-word to refer to something he just didn't like, I knew it was my cue to leave. I wasn't sure I heard him correctly the first time, but there's no excuse for using an ableist slur, so not only was the date bad, but Paul was bad, too.

Of course, Paul didn't get the hint that I was uncomfortable literally any of the times I expressed that I'm sure his ex wasn't crazy, but had probably dealt with a lot of frustrations regarding whatever she was upset about, or when I plowed forward with my personal details following awkward pauses in conversation in which Paul did not ask the normal follow-up questions. The second use of the R-word had me interrupting him, letting him know I'd had a long day and really just needed to get home. He looked at me weirdly at my abrupt exit but didn't try to change my mind. He did, however, open his arms for a hug. I hate that I hugged him.

The number of men I've hugged when I didn't want to, just to keep the peace and ensure my sanity (or safety) is alarming, but not unusual. I just hate that I didn't have the courage to call him out on his bigotry, but I still had to walk home and didn't want to risk him getting upset and potentially following me.

Rather than say all that to Asher, though, I just shrug. "Bad date. Might swear off men later, who knows."

Asher's hazel eyes flash. "What do you mean, bad date?"

"Calm down, *Dad*," I say, holding up a placating hand. "Nothing terrible. Just general douchebaggery. Nothing I can't handle." Asher's shoulders visibly relax.

"Did you eat dinner? I picked up a few burritos on the way home but didn't eat the last two." I'm grateful that he doesn't push me to discuss the date. I'm tired, my hair is starting to get greasy, and my bed is calling my name.

Chapter Twenty-Three

Asher

To say that I'm annoyed that June went on a date tonight is putting it lightly. I know I have no right to feel annoyed, but I do. While she was out being wined and dined by some chucklefuck, I was thinking of her, the way her tits perfectly filled my hands, and the way she looked when she came.

I also know I have no right to think those things about my roommate either. I had no right to listen to her through the wall while she got herself off last night, but here we are. I felt like a total perv for putting my book down and listening through the wall when I heard the familiar whirring and buzzing of her "battery-operated boyfriend." I felt like even more of a creep when I stroked my dick to the small sounds she made as I imagined her face, screwed up in pleasure once again.

The "just friends" box I had put June in when she moved in isn't even a box anymore. It's a shredded pile of cardboard that I keep scooting around in my mind, pretending I didn't completely destroy it the other night.

I want to tell June not to go on any more dates. I can pretend it's coming from a place of concern for her safety, which is true, but it's not the only reason why I want to tell her to delete her dating apps. I want to tell her to swear off men, but come to me when she wants her physical needs met.

Actually, that's not a bad idea.

"Are you really considering swearing off men?" She shrugs, taking a bite of the chicken burrito I bought especially for her. Chicken, cheese, extra pico de gallo, and the hottest salsa possible. It's been June's go-to Mexican order since high school. She swallows her bite, but instead of elaborating, she dives in for a second.

Feeding June is slowly turning into one of my favorite things. Growing up, my mom showed her love through food, and I've definitely inherited that trait. There's just something about providing nourishment to those you care about that fills your soul in a way nothing else can. It's better if I can cook for her myself, but providing restaurant food for June is a close second.

"Well," I sniff, trying to buy myself time to say what I want to say tactfully. "If you do decide to do that, and you need some help getting your needs met, you know where to find me." I stretch the A string across the frets, pulling it taut. I study the action intensely. At this point, I could probably restring a guitar in record time with my eyes closed, but I suddenly feel the need to inspect the pegs and bridge with eagle-eyed precision. Anything to avoid watching her reaction.

"Are you proposing an addendum to our agreement, Mr. Incaudo?" I let out a small breath. She didn't stand up and slap me in the face for my audacity, so there's that.

"If you're interested." After a brief pause, in which I study one of the machine heads that needs no studying, I add, "It would probably help me apply the skills I'm learning from your books."

She chews, thinking it over, while I want to crawl out of my skin at the suspense. When she swallows again, I hold my breath. It's not so much that I want June to say yes, it's that I don't want her to hate me for asking.

"Okay," she says with another shrug.

"Okay," I tell her with a grin.

"But Devin never finds out." I wrinkle my nose and give her a look as if to tell her that statement was obvious and unnecessary. I string the rest of the guitar at lightning speed.

When June finishes eating, she balls up the foil wrapper and throws it away before walking toward her bedroom. With one last look behind her, she tosses a "You coming?" my way. I scramble off the couch to follow her. Normally, I'm meticulous about my guitars; they get hung up on the wood mounts on the wall when not in use. It's not about their monetary value; I have strong emotional attachments to my guitars, going so far as to name each of them. But right now, Lucille can hang out where she's precariously balanced on the couch cushions. I've got places to be.

When I enter June's room, her scent envelops me. Apple and fucking green grass. It's the scent that fills all my fantasies now. June looks up at me through her rhinestoned glasses as she perches on the end of her bed. I want to tell her that her little yellow sundress makes me want to both devour her and pick her up and put her in my pocket. I don't understand how something can be so adorable and so sexy at the same time, but I chalk it up to just one more of the many mysteries surrounding June.

I reach for her and stop myself, unsure how to proceed. I want to grab her, touch her, kiss her...I want to do everything all at once. She's temptation tied up in a little yellow sundress, and I just want to unwrap her. My hesitation is not because I'm nervous and trying to gently and smoothly extricate myself from this situation like usual. No, my hesitation is simply because I don't know what I want to do first. I take a faltering step forward.

"Can I touch you?" She nods. "Kiss you?" She draws in a quick breath and I hope she's remembering the last time I kissed her. I know I am. She nods again. I have to bend low to bring my face to hers, now that she's sitting, but I'd happily fold myself in half for this woman. I cup her cheek in my hand, stroking it with my thumb, savoring this moment. I've replayed our kiss in my head countless times over the last seven years, but I never dreamed I'd get a repeat. This is a prime opportunity to get in my head about it, needing to make sure it's good for June, to ensure that it lives up to the standard I set when we were teenagers, but for some reason,

I'm not. I'm relaxed, sure in my conviction that because it's with June, it's going to be good. It's a given.

When I press my lips to hers, I know I'm right. Her plump lips mold perfectly to mine, and my suspicion that we would move perfectly in sync with one another is confirmed when we both open at the same time, deepening the kiss.

It's everything.

It's more than everything. I wondered if, over the years, I had built our kiss up in my head to be more than it was, but I know now that I remembered everything exactly correct. June's tongue slides against mine as I match her stroke for stroke. She lets out a small moan and pride surges through my chest, knowing I made her make those sounds. No one else did that.

Still kissing her, I press her back onto the bed and step between her widened legs. Her feet are propped on the sideboard of the frame, creating the perfect shelf of support for her and the perfect feeling of being surrounded by her for me. Her hands start to roam while I groan my agreement. She slides her hands under my T-shirt, caressing the skin on my back as I shift my lips to her jaw, her neck, her collarbone. I suck gently below her ear and her hips rock against mine. I make note of that spot, intending to revisit it later. Later tonight, tomorrow, next week, for as long as she lets me.

"Off," June murmurs, tugging my shirt up. I can't rip the fabric off my body fast enough. She happily peruses my body, and I let her look. June seems pleased with what she sees. She sits up, pressing soft kisses against my abdomen as I stand in front of her, running my fingers through her hair. I pull the hair tie out and drag my fingers across her scalp. She hums in appreciation. Ever since I grew my hair out, I know the feeling.

When she starts unbuckling my belt, I grab her wrists. "Not until I get a taste first," I tell her. The surprise on her face is evident, but she lies back on the bed, allowing me to pull up the skirt of her dress to reveal white cotton panties. They're not objectively sexy. They're simple, plain. But the sight of them makes me want to bite my fist. For half a breath, I wonder if it's just because it's June wearing them that makes my dick that much harder.

Sliding my hands up the outside of her dimpled thighs, I tug the material down as she lifts her hips. As much as I want to bask in the glory of this moment, I don't want to deny myself or her for a second longer. I drop to my knees, using my shoulders to widen her legs. She takes it upon herself to put them on my shoulders and I can't help but grin. I love that she's doing what she needs to make it good for herself.

I don't hesitate. I don't build the anticipation. I don't kiss my way up her thighs or drag out the moment. Because all those things are for a man who can wait. I don't have that much restraint. There will be time, so long as June doesn't change her mind, for slow and restrained and patient. Now is not that time.

I dive in.

Holy fuck.

God, I missed this. I haven't eaten good pussy in years.

I wasn't kidding when I said I needed a taste first. I needed it like I needed my next breath. Now that I've had a taste, I'm not coming up for air anytime soon.

I drag my tongue through her folds, lapping at her arousal as her breath stutters above me. Her fingers spear into my hair as my own spear into her entrance. She's so wet that my middle and ring finger slide in with ease, and even though it's a somewhat snug fit, it turns me on even more. I focus my tongue on her clit, pressing and sliding along it like the rabbit ear prongs of her vibrator did the other night.

This isn't my first time eating pussy, and god willing, it won't be my last. This is a no-holds-barred feast, a smorgasbord of filthy, epic proportions. I'm not hearing any complaints from June, but I resurface briefly to verify her pleasure.

"Tell me what you need, baby." I jackknife my fingers in and out of her, the movements closely mimicking the intensity with which she fucked herself with her toy the other day.

"So good...so fucking good. Just like that, Asher, please."

Good enough for me.

I suck her clit into my mouth, rolling the bud between my lips and over my tongue, never letting up the speed in which my fingers fuck June's perfect pussy. She's writhing against me, her grip on my hair almost painful as she rides my face toward her release. I crook my fingers inside her. I'm pretty sure she is speaking in tongues at this point. Occasionally, I catch a nonsensical word here or there.

"Fuck...so good...god...damn...tongue..."

With my free hand, I tug the neckline of her dress down, exposing the swell of her breast. Her bra is white and lacy and so girl-next-door I feel my cock twitch in response. I don't bother tugging the bra down; I can tell she is close by the erratic rhythm her hips are rocking against me. Through the thin fabric of her bra, I pinch her nipple hard, just like I did the other night. The scream that leaves June's lips almost causes me to come in my pants again. Her pussy flutters around my fingers, drenching my hand. I maintain my ministrations, only slowing when she shoves my face away from her oversensitized cunt.

I swipe my forearm across my mouth as I stand, grinning down at her. She's the very definition of freshly fucked. Her hair is a mess, her clothing disheveled and half twisted, a dreamy expression across her pretty face. She looks so satisfied, I want to burn the image into my brain forever.

I did that.

"Holy fucking *shit*, Asher. You've been holding out on me." I love the breathy giggle to her voice as she works to regain control of herself. It drives home the meaning behind her words.

I can't help the laugh that escapes me. Seeing June this relaxed makes up for the way she came through the front door an hour ago, discouraged and withdrawn. Nothing like some food and oral sex to cheer a woman up. At this point, I don't even need June to reciprocate, but when she sits up and starts clawing at my jeans, I'm not gentleman enough to stop her.

"Are you sure?" I croak out as my pants fall to my ankles.

"So sure," she tells me confidently. "Are you?" I just nod, worried my brain and my mouth lost their connection. June is perched daintily on the edge of the bed. I prefer her this way to her on her knees, and with our height difference, the bed is the perfect level for her mouth to wrap around my cock. The thought alone has me clenching my teeth.

She palms me gently through my boxer briefs, cupping my balls. When she hooks her thumbs in my waistband and tugs them down my legs, it's all I can do to hold on. She's close enough that I can feel her warm breath on the head of my cock. All four thousand nerve endings in my head stand on edge as she stares at me, taking me in.

Her tongue darts out and licks the precum beading on the tip, and that view alone has my soul leaving my body. When she sucks my head into her mouth, I'm sure I've died and gone to heaven. There's no other explanation for the arousal coursing through my body. It feels like my first ever blow job–the sensations are overwhelming.

June pulls all of me into her mouth. I watch as her lips stretch to their limit, pulling me deep into her throat. I feel her gag before I see it. When she takes me deep again, I give up watching, no longer able to stop my eyes from rolling into the back of my skull. June fondles my balls while taking me deep, over and over. I clench my ass to keep myself from coming immediately. She bobs over me, up and down. My orgasm barrels toward me as I run my hands lovingly through her hair, praising her efforts.

"So good, June. God, you're so good at sucking cock." I rub my thumb along her cheek, feeling my cock on the other side. New kink unlocked: feeling my own erection under June's skin. She pulls back, sucking hard on the head and I see god before erupting, spilling into her perfect mouth on a groan. She licks up every drop of my cum. Watching her do that is enough to turn me on all over again.

"I'm so sorry I didn't warn you. It happened so quickly. You're so fucking good." I tell her between breaths as I help her to her feet from the edge of the bed. She pushes her glasses up on her nose and smiles. Then that vixen licks her lips.

Chapter Twenty-Four
June

I don't know who these Foxy Fanatixxx bitches are, but they're either liars or missing nerve endings in their erogenous zones (although my money is on the former), because Asher Incaudo does, in fact, know what he's doing. Sure, he fumbled a little bit in the beginning before he kissed me, but that was clearly due to nerves more than anything else. Did they not give him a second to collect himself? Or did he build up his arsenal since he last hooked up? Maybe Asher really is a quick study. Whatever the explanation, the man is good. With his fingers, with his tongue...I can only imagine how he uses the anaconda between his legs. My inner harlot starts rubbing her hands together greedily. I can't wait to find out.

After Asher finishes in my mouth, he helps me out of my dress and into bed. He tucks me in, takes off my glasses, and presses a kiss to my forehead. It is everything I could have ever wanted. A moment later, he returns with a glass of water. With a final squeeze of my arm, he turns and leaves. I'm sure I misread the look in his eyes. I swear I saw adoration, longing even, but it was probably just a post-sex glow. I know my own body is humming with a soft, contented energy as I drift off, certain I'm going to have the best night's sleep in a very long time.

The next morning, I am out the door before Asher even emerges from his room. My wrist injury has put me in a little bit of a funk lately, and riding my orgasm-induced relaxation from last night, I want to take advantage of my elevated mood. I call Devin on my walk to the craft store. It's been over a week since I talked to him outside of a text (other than the panicked video call when I injured myself), which, during the middle of baseball season isn't that unusual, but my head has been filled with nostalgia for the old days ever since Asher and I crossed that line. I chalk it up to wondering what it would have been like if we had pursued something after our first kiss.

The craft store, and talking with my brother, leaves me feeling refreshed and ready to take on the day. The normally crisp spring air has started to turn warm; I fumble to put on my sunglasses, lifting my eyeglasses to rest on the crown of my head. The sunshine on my face fuels my soul. That, or the killer orgasm from last night. I don't know what it is about last night's release that puts an extra pep in my step. I'm no stranger to orgasms, as my bedside drawer proves. But there was something about last night that was different. Maybe it was the fact that I haven't had good oral in years, or that our amended agreement has the potential to provide orgasms on tap for the next little bit. Either way, I'm not complaining.

At the craft store, I stock up on supplies for a new knitting project. It's probably ambitious, seeing as even holding a knitting needle in my left hand causes me to grimace in pain right now, but I have big plans for when I'm healed enough. I was making progress on my wobbly hat before I got injured, so I will hopefully be able to finish that quickly. I found a Pinterest pattern to make my own knitted cactus, stuffed with cotton fluff. I know I'm overprojecting my skills with this craft, but I'm up for the challenge, especially now that rollerblading is off the table for me. Forever.

Exiting the craft store, I window shop at a nearby romance-exclusive bookstore. I wandered past it a few weeks ago, but I always seem to walk by when it's closed. As I'm admiring the themed display of purple-covered books, an employee clicks the lock on the front door and flips the sign to open.

I enter, trying not to seem so eager as to pounce the second the store opens, but I can't help my excitement, which is only matched by the awe I feel upon entering. The store is small, but the black shelves lining the perimeter are filled with romance novels of all kinds. The shelves are organized by subgenres: mafia, small-town, closed-door, hockey, billionaire, LGBTQ+, workplace. Myriad hot, mostly shirtless men grace cover after cover. Near the back of the store, a small table sits with candles and book-themed knickknacks. The best part, however, is the built-in reading nook near the back wall. It contains comfortable-looking chairs and a completely Instagrammable wall background.

A giant, three-dimensional papier mache tree protrudes from the wall, the ceiling covered with an awning of leaves. The back wall is covered in faux ivy, the greenery making the neon pink sign proclaiming *This Must Be The Place* pop. Beanbags and floor pillows surround the base of the trunk. Would it be weird for me to say I want to live here?

I started reading romance novels with Whitney and Christine in college. I can't remember who discovered them first, but we were all instantly hooked. It's those books that I credit with my true sexual awakening.

Prior to reading romance, I was constantly self-conscious, worried about my size in the bedroom even more than I dwelled on it in the real world. After reading romance, I learned to harness the power of my body–no matter its size–and channel it into the incredible entity that it is. I learned how to not only be good in bed, but how to communicate what I wanted, what I liked, and most importantly, what I didn't. More than that, though, romance books gave me hope. Hope that a plus-sized woman could find her happily ever after, and that decent men do exist. Being surrounded by books featuring men written by women, I found a little healing from the unexpected breakup of my last boyfriend.

Dating Trevor wasn't terrible. Even looking back now, I can see that. But I also know that my rose-colored glasses were firmly in place up until (and a little after) the breakup. Trevor was handsome and funny and so unlike the guys I usually dated. He was one of the administrative assistants at the clinic in Tampa, and after a few weeks of heavy flirting, we finally hooked up. One thing led to another, and I was falling for him hard. I like to think he fell for me too. At the time, I was sure of it. With the way things ended, though, I'm not so sure anymore.

"Are you looking for anything in particular?" the sales associate asks me. I realize I've been zoning out, staring at a wall of baseball romances for the last few minutes, lost in my memories.

"Oh, no. Just browsing. There's a lot to choose from."

"I know, it's a little overwhelming at first. Is this your first time here?"

"It is! I've walked by a few times, but always at really weird times, so I've never been inside. I'm so glad the timing worked out today."

She flicks through a stack of flyers in a holder on the wall. "We're having a few events later this month," she tells me. "I'm not sure if these work for your schedule, but we have a neighborhood book club and a couple new author release parties, if you're interested."

"Oh, wow. That would be great. Thank you so much." I take the flyer and, after reading it thoroughly, fold it and place it carefully in my purse. "Any books you would recommend? I'll read anything but baseball romance."

The saleswoman raises a brow at my random avoidance of such a small subgenre, but she doesn't ask any questions. There's something about baseball romance that makes me cringe. Maybe it's because, after seeing Devin's life, I am bothered by the inaccuracies portrayed on the pages. Like, there's no way Devin or the rest of his team are setting foot inside an airport terminal to travel to their games; it's chartered flights all the way. And there's no real mention of just how hard the players have to work to maintain healthy bodies for all one-hundred-sixty-two games in a season. There's definitely no references to strength and conditioning coaches, or massage therapists, or the million other staff members that really make up a team. And there certainly are not curfews for the players to be in their hotel rooms on road trips. Seeing behind the curtain can ruin some of the magic, I guess.

By the time I pay for my three new books, none of which are baseball-related, I realize I've spent almost an hour in this tiny shop. It's my day off, so I don't mind, but I am surprised at just how much time got away from me while lost in my own bookish world.

I swing by the grocery store to get more flour for the inevitable brownies I'll have to make for Asher this week. I also pick up mini marshmallows and graham crackers, planning to make him a s'mores brownie for Asher's start tomorrow.

I'm feeling energized. It's been a great morning. The only thing that brings me down is my greasy scalp. I eye the blowout salon on my walk back from my errands. I can't stop now, seeing as I have eggs in my bag that need to get in the refrigerator, but I plan to call once I get home to see if they have any last-minute appointments available.

When I walk in the door, fumbling with the lock due to my one-handed status, Asher launches himself off the couch to help me. I'm pretty sure he'd help even if I didn't have my arm in a brace, and the gesture is appreciated. He lifts the grocery bag with ease and sets it on the kitchen counter.

He's dressed in athletic shorts and the softest looking Foxes tee. A darkening ring around the collar is evidence of the sweat he worked up when he had to go into the ballpark this morning. Asher always does some sort of sprinting drills and plays catch the day before he starts. I don't know if it's the line we further crossed last night or my uplifted mood, but I want to rub my face against his soft gray shirt.

Whoa.

Down girl.

But it's not even a sexual thing. For some reason, I'm craving Asher's nonsexual touch, too. Which is weird. I'm probably just touch-starved. I remind myself that I need to put more effort into making friends in Chicago, aside from Priya and Asher. Both of my friends here are lovely, but I need to expand my social roster, so I'm not always relying on the same people. Maybe getting some hugs from others will settle my non-sexual urges when it comes to Asher. I make a mental note to look into the book club.

Asher helps me unpack the bags, eyeing the covers of my new books with interest. The cover of the thick romantasy tome betrays nothing of the extremely spicy contents within, but the mafia and historical romances both have hot-guy covers. There's no hiding what kind of books those are.

"Do you have any plans for today?" Asher asks me as he lifts the egg carton out of the bag and into the fridge. I gesture to the books spread across the counter.

"You're looking at them. That and a blowout, since I got paid on Friday."

"A what?" Asher chokes from behind the refrigerator door. I look at him in confusion, unsure what the problem is.

"A blowout?" I start to giggle, understanding his misinterpretation. "It's not sexual. I want to go to a salon where they'll wash and dry my hair for me." I hold up my wrist. "I can't exactly do it myself. It's expensive, but a necessary cost these days."

Asher's expression morphs from alarm to a softer kind of concern. "You can't wash your hair?"

"Not really. I tried it myself and it hurt my wrist too much, so I switched to one-handed. To say it was a disaster is putting it lightly." There's only so much of my thick hair I can scrunch in one hand while trying to lather up enough shampoo in between my thumb and fingers to be effective. The end result was a half-clean, fully tangled mess. Tears sprang to my eyes when I tried to comb it after–half tears of pain due to the rat's nest my hair had become, and half tears of frustration and self-pity. It wasn't my proudest moment, hence my frequent trips to the salon ever since.

"I can help you wash your hair," Asher offers gently. It's sweet and alarming at the same time.

"Thanks, Ash, but just because we hooked up once doesn't mean I'm ready for you to take a completely platonic shower with me." I don't miss the way heat momentarily flares in his hazel eyes at the reference to last night. He quickly covers it when he processes my rejection.

"It doesn't have to be a shower. You can stay fully clothed. I can wash it at the sink here." He shrugs, nodding toward the kitchen sink. It's not the worst idea. I feel bad asking him to do it for me, but at nearly one hundred dollars a pop once I factor in tax and tip, going to get regular blowouts isn't exactly financially sustainable. I've only just paid off my credit card bill, which incurred a bunch of fees for breaking my lease early in Tampa, so funds are a little low right now.

When I don't say anything, he removes his hat and shakes out his blond hair, as if to advertise his skills in this area.

"Come on, June. You know you're thinking about it. You, too, could have luscious locks like this." Asher does have pretty hair. It'd be even prettier if he styled it, but I know that's asking too much. "I can figure out a blow dryer, right?"

I snort. My confidence in his skills doesn't extend that far, but at this point, I'm looking for cleanliness more than anything else.

"Okay," I finally agree.

"Great." Asher claps his hands. "I'm gonna hop in the shower real quick. When I get out, you get what you need and we'll get started."

Chapter Twenty-Five
Asher

After dressing from my shower, I leave my bedroom to find June has brought her shower products into the kitchen and lined them up neatly by the sink. She has two kinds of shampoo and a hair mask, which I'm assuming works like a conditioner. I may have read the back of it while I was in the shower a few minutes ago. It's good to be prepared.

I help her onto the counter. It's hard for her to press herself up to sit on the edge, and while it would be easier and far more satisfying for me to just pick her up and place her there, I don't know if that would make her uncomfortable. Things haven't been awkward since we hooked up last night, but I'm toeing a dangerous line. If this were a regular friends-with-benefits situation, I could just text June when I'm feeling horny. But it's not, because we live together. And since I'm pretty much always horny these days, I'm not sure how to navigate living together and friendship in addition to when I want to hook up next.

And the way June walked through the front door in her plaid dress, looking every inch like my naughty librarian fantasies come true? I want to hook up again as soon as possible.

But first, we need to take care of June's hair.

I help her ease into a lying position on the counter, her head hovering over the sink. I grab one of the kitchen towels and fold it into a tight roll, placing it under her neck to allow for some cushioning. The counter isn't huge, limiting the space we have to work with against the wall. Her legs are bent, her bare feet flat on the counter. The hem of her dress rides up her thighs, revealing black biker shorts underneath. Those, too, seem to have ridden up a bit, and I admire the way her pale skin bulges slightly around the tight seam of the shorts. Ripping my gaze away, I focus on finding the perfect water temperature before she catches me staring.

I can't help but stare at her. She looks incredible like this, splayed out on the counter, hair spilling into the sink. She looks like a reclining goddess. She's taken off her glasses and closed her eyes to protect from the light spray from the faucet. Her brow is furrowed and the skin beside her eyes crinkled, though, so I know there's a part of her that's not nearly as relaxed as she could be.

I pull the hose attachment out from the bottom of the faucet and drag it over to June. The water is one click warmer than room temperature as I drag it slowly over her scalp.

"Is the water okay?" I ask, cringing at the rasp in my voice. I quietly clear my throat.

"Yeah, it's good, thanks." I use the hand not directing the water to smooth her hair, careful not to get any spray near her eyes. My thumb swipes away some water that has escaped the confines of her hair and dribbled onto her forehead. I hear June release a deep breath at the same time her facial muscles relax.

I pump the first shampoo into my hands, creating a soft lather with the blue solution before gliding my fingers through her hair. She releases another breathy sigh. Now is *not* the time for my cock to jump to attention, but he somehow didn't get that memo. This is an innocent hygiene routine between friends and roommates. Nothing more.

When June's hair is fully coated in suds, I turn on the faucet again, rinsing thoroughly. With her eyes closed, it's the perfect time for my eyes to drink their fill of her pretty face. The constellation of freckles across the bridge of her nose, her plump lips, her dark lashes. I don't think June realizes just how incredibly beautiful she is. But those are inside thoughts, so I keep them to myself.

I repeat the shampooing ritual with the second bottle, setting both aside. The clean, expensive smell of June's shampoos fills the kitchen. It's a scent I didn't even realize I had associated with her, with comfort. When I think of her scent, I think apples and green grass, but the unmistakable fragrance of her shower products is a close second on my list of favorite smells in the world.

"That feels so good," she says as I'm raking the hair mask through her long strands. I will definitely be playing with her hair more. Not that I need another excuse to touch her.

"Good," I murmur, swiping some excess product from her temple. I probably used entirely too much shampoo and conditioner.

June's hair is so much longer than mine that I knew I had to glob a lot more onto my hands but given the massive amount of suds that accrued on her scalp earlier, I probably used too much. I'll remember for next time, I silently vow. "It says to let it sit for three to five minutes. Do you want to keep lying here or should I help you sit up?"

Her blue eyes open, connecting with mine immediately. The air feels charged, electric. "I should probably stay here so I don't drip water everywhere." She bites down on her lower lip, and before I can stop myself, I use my thumb to gently coax it free. Nostalgia washes over me, remembering the last time I did this, seven years ago. June's sharp intake of breath tells me she remembers it, too.

My hand glides down her neck before I pull it away. It's not like I can start anything right now, anyway. We still have at least two minutes to let the mask work its magic. I roll my shoulders back and clear my throat.

"I'll just clean up a bit while we're waiting." There's very little to do, but I still take my time bringing June's products back to the bathroom and wiping up the excess water that splashed onto the counter. I comb through her hair, something my mom suggested to me when I started growing out my hair.

The additional sitting time on the mask goes both quickly (when I'm admiring June with her eyes closed once again) and incredibly slowly (when June's eyes are open and we're sharing another charged moment), but I cherish it nonetheless. Like I said,

I don't know how to navigate hooking up with June again–or if she'll ever allow it again–so every moment I get to bask in her presence is precious to me.

When the conditioner is finally rinsed and I lovingly wrap June's hair in a towel, I help her to sit up. She replaces her glasses, the tiny gemstones in the corners glinting off the overhead lighting. Reaching for her, I lift her slowly to her feet. I have no doubt she could easily hop off the counter by herself, but we both pretend she needs the assistance.

She loosens the towel, her hair tumbling in wet waves past her shoulders. When she looks at me again, the air recharges once more. Is this how it's always going to be between us now? Sharing glances, the air heating around us, while we learn to be in each other's spaces after my head was buried between her thighs and my cock slid down her throat? I'm not complaining; I just need to know how to handle this.

Now that she's back on the floor, she looks up at me through her lashes. I'm a very tall guy. I'm used to being taller than most people, especially women. But there's something especially sexy about the way June looks up at me. Her blue eyes blaze.

"Ash," she whispers. In that instant, I know she's feeling the electricity the way I am. In the half-step it takes me to reach her, I release a breath of relief that I'm not the only one feeling this way. Before she can say another word, my lips are on hers and her fists cling to my shirt, as if she's afraid of what will happen if she lets go.

Chapter Twenty-Six
June

I don't know how a hair wash can be erotic, but here we are. Or, more specifically, here I am, drenched in more ways than one as I stand in the kitchen, my hair dripping wet. Asher's mouth is on mine and my body buzzes with a carnal energy that started as soon as he ran his fingers through my hair.

His long fingers worked their way through my scalp in a way that was both highly arousing and insanely comforting. I didn't know whether to jump on him right away or sink into the relaxation he was inducing with his magic hands. I kept my eyes closed most of the time to really remain in the moment, soaking in every sensation. But when I opened my eyes?

Holy fuck.

I've seen Asher's intensity on the mound, both from the stands and in close ups when I watch his games on television. But to be on the receiving end of such intensity? I wanted to fan my face and cross my legs, but both would have been weird in the middle of our kitchen, so I swallowed down my pornographic thoughts and pressed my eyes closed again.

But after we were done, when Asher lifted me off the counter like I weighed nothing, setting me gently on my feet? I could no longer ignore the unbridled lust coursing through my veins. Luckily, Asher seemed to be feeling the same way, because his name was only halfway out of my mouth before his full lips were on mine, swallowing my whimpers and moans.

I'm not sure how long we stand there kissing (what's with us kissing in kitchens?). It could be minutes. It might be days. I cling to him because it is the only thing I can do to prevent myself from climbing the man like a tree.

When we finally resurface for air, Asher's shorts are tented in front of him and I try not to preen with pride that I did that. He doesn't miss my pointed gaze, but he just smirks in response. Asher has never been cocky, but he's also never had an issue with confidence in almost all aspects of his life. It's nice to see his confidence bleeding over to other areas, too. He runs a hand down his face, as if trying to compose himself. I kind of like seeing him hanging on to his last shreds of control. I wonder what it'll take to push him over the edge.

What can I say? I've always enjoyed playing with fire.

"Fuck, baby. Are you going to let me touch you again?"

I both love and hate the way Asher calls me baby–he's only done it once before, but it makes the boundary we're already crossing that much harder to uphold. With the way he is looking at me now, though? I'd let him call me whatever he wants.

My voice choked with lust, I let out a shaky "Yes."

"June, baby. I need more than that. I want to do this only if you do. I don't want to be a pity fuck."

I don't miss that Asher said "fuck" instead of "hookup."

"Do...do you want to have sex?"

Asher approaches me where I stand, propped against the counter. His hand flexes and clenches, as if he's fighting a battle not to touch me.

"June. I want to run my hands up these gorgeous thighs till I reach your wet heat in the center. I want to run my tongue through your drenched pussy and taste how sweet I know you taste. And if you'll let me, I want to plunge my cock inside you. I trust you."

The silence hangs heavy in the air. If his dirty words weren't enough, his last sentence stills the breath in my lungs.

There's nothing more meaningful he could have said to me right now, and I don't miss how monumental this is for him. I'm honored to be his first.

"Will you let me?" The sincerity in his voice almost breaks me.

"Asher. I would love that."

He wastes no time hauling me to his chest and once again, lifting me with ease. My legs wrap around his waist automatically as he walks us to my bedroom. Setting me gently on the bed–far gentler than I expected, given the heat in his eyes–he wastes no time leaning over me, pressing his mouth to mine.

Our earlier kiss was soft, gentle, sweet. This is anything but: it's passionate and lustful and frantic. It's a claiming. Asher's tongue thrusts into my mouth as his hands find my breasts. Palming them both, he groans and thumbs my nipples.

Holy shit, I *ache* for this man.

I claw at his shirt, and he breaks our kiss only long enough to pull it over his head and toss it in the corner of my room.

"Your turn," he tells me. "I'm dying to see all of you again. To touch all of you again." Sitting up, I pull my dress off; the material is stretchy enough to easily tug overhead. My sheer lace bra is more for show than function. It makes me feel sexy, but nothing compares to the sexy I feel when Asher is looking at me like this.

Before I can lean forward to unhook it, he latches his lips over my nipple and sucks hard. My back arches involuntarily and a fresh gush of arousal coats my panties. I can't help the moan that escapes my lips.

"Yes, baby. Show me how you like it. I want you to be loud. Show me what you like."

"Asher…" I'm panting.

He switches to my other breast. His arms on both sides of my torso cage me in as I lower my back to the bed. In this position, his hips are too far away for me to do anything but lie here in pleasure.

"Can you take your little shorts off for me?"

I nod, unable to form coherent words. As if he can read my mind, Asher strips out of his shorts and boxers, too. Every rational thought flies out of my brain as I sit here watching him stroke his thick length. I scoot to the edge of the bed, reaching for him.

"Can I..?" I ask, licking my lips.

"Junie, you can do whatever you want. But I need to taste you before you taste me. Please." He did this last night, too. Asher has never asked me for anything in our entire lives, and this is what he asks—no, begs—for? Who am I to deny him? I stroke him once, twice, watching ecstasy wash over his features before pulling back to finish undressing. He squeezes the base of his cock as he watches me shimmy my shorts and thong down my legs. I sit back on the bed and lean back on my palms, widening my legs so he can stand between them.

Prior to last night, it had been a long time since I received oral sex, and an even longer time since I've received good oral sex. I had resigned myself to being chronically disappointed in that area of my life, but that was last night, before Asher's tongue worked me over and obliterated that plan.

With one long, sweeping lick just now, I can already tell he's going to have me coming faster than a bullet train. He's kneeling in front of me and eating me out with such enthusiasm, I'm worried about my cardiac health. Remembering his words from earlier, I supply him with the praise he craves.

"Asher, oh god. That's so good. Just like that, just like that, just like that!" My words go high-pitched and jumbled as he sucks my clit into his mouth and I explode.

Holy fucking shit.

I need to hook up with more virgins. They're so eager to please.

Asher keeps up the pressure, licking and sucking as I ride out my orgasm. When he finally pulls away, he presses soft kisses against the insides of my thighs.

"Thank you," I whisper, surprise lacing my tone. He chuckles.

"I may be a virgin, but I've gone down on plenty of girls." My wrinkled nose has him correcting, "Not too many girls. Just the perfectly normal, correct amount. And I definitely won't talk about other women while in bed with you."

"Asher."

"Yeah, baby?"

"Shut up and let me suck your cock."

Chapter Twenty-Seven
Asher

I wasn't lying when I told June I've had plenty of hookups without sex. But when June wraps her kiss-swollen lips around my cock, every memory of every other blow job I've ever received flies out of my brain to die a quick death. I scramble to hold on to the memory of what she did to me last night, but even that is clouded by an overwhelming amount of pleasure.

This. This is the type of blow job that could kill a man.

I watch as June swallows me down, hollowing out her cheeks as I fight not to come immediately at the thought of painting her throat with my release. June needs to teach a master class on sucking cock.

I slide my fingers through her hair as she bobs forward and back on my dick. She moves my hand to the back of her head, silently urging me to take control.

"Are you sure?" My voice comes out strangled. June's voice is muffled as she nods against me. "Tap my leg if it's too much."

Grasping the sides of June's perfect face with each hand, I hold her still and thrust into her mouth, over and over. Occasionally she gags, and I give her a moment to catch her breath. And just like she was vocal with me, I feel the need to praise her, too.

"That's my girl, Junie. You're so fucking good. That mouth feels so good."

She cups and caresses my balls and I see stars. A few more thrusts having me hanging on the edge, debating if I should just say "fuck it" and come down her throat. But a glance down at June's thick folded thighs and the way she's clenching and squirming beneath me tells me she needs more, too, so with superhuman willpower, I pull out of her mouth with an audible pop.

Breathing deeply, I pull her up from under her arms and kiss her roughly. I don't care that I can taste my salty precum on her tongue. I want to give this girl everything—she deserved everything—the way she went to town on my shaft, my head, my balls.

"Baby, that was…so good." Giving me a self-satisfied smirk, she climbs back onto the bed.

"There are condoms in the nightstand…if you still want to do this," she adds. As if I'd change my mind now.

"Fuck yeah. Still with me?" I confirm.

"As long as you're good, I'm good." She grins.

I yank open her nightstand and am met with the Shangri-la of sex toys. Vibrators and things I don't even recognize line the inside of her drawer.

"They should be just on the side," June tells me, a gorgeous pink blush coating her cheeks.

"We'll be coming back for these later," I promise her. I find the box of condoms and the caveman inside me is pleased to see it's unopened, the plastic coating still intact. I rip it open and pull out a condom, taking care to rip off just one from the strip.

June takes it from my hands and rolls it on me, saving me from the embarrassment from fumbling with it. It's been a long time since my sophomore year health class where we put condoms on bananas.

Coming to rest between her thighs, I press a soft kiss against her lips. It's slow and sensual and I hope that it conveys my gratitude for doing this with me. Everyone says that their first time is awful, but I can't imagine anything with June being less than perfect.

I just hope it's good enough for her.

She cups my cheek gently with her palm and I can't help but close my eyes at the contact.

"Asher," she whispers. I slowly peel my eyes open, not wanting to break the moment. "I have to tell you something."

I take a deep breath, preparing for her to tell me she doesn't want to do this anymore, that this was a mistake. Instead, she surprises me with her next words.

"You were my first kiss. I'm honored I get to be one of your firsts, too."

My brain feels fuzzy with the revelation. I don't allow myself to focus on her words and what they mean, so I kiss her once more before slowly, so slowly, pressing into her. For a moment, I'm afraid I'm hurting her. But then her face morphs into pleasure and she wraps her legs around my waist.

"Keep going, Ash. It's so good. You're doing so good."

I wonder for a moment if I had had June cheering me on, encouraging me, I would have made it to the Majors a lot quicker. I'd do anything to hear her praise me again. I thrust in another inch and she groans at the stretch. I'm girthier than most, so I watch her face carefully for any sign of discomfort.

"Please, Asher. I need more. You feel so good."

I thrust in the rest of the way, getting lost in the heat of her. This is heaven. I'm almost a little mad at myself for denying myself this intense pleasure for so long. But if I had indulged sooner, I probably wouldn't be doing so now with June, and doing it with June makes everything worth it.

Dropping to my elbows, I pick up my pace, pressing my mouth to her neck. I can feel her pulse going haywire under my lips.

"Baby, you feel so good. Tell me what you need." I need this to be good for her. It's bad enough that I'm fucking my best friend's little sister. I'll die if this isn't good for her.

"Asher, honey. You're doing so good. Just keep going. Please don't stop."

So I don't.

I keep going, gritting my teeth to stave off my own release. My cock drags in and out of her tight channel, her walls gliding over my shaft as she rocks her hips in time with my own. June's moans get louder, more frequent. I snap my hips faster, not caring that I'm breathing heavily in her ear. Her nails rake up and down my back and I've never felt anything so good in my entire life.

"Asher, I'm so close. Go hard. Please, go hard."

So I do.

I slam into June over and over again, and just when I think I can't hold off any longer, she tenses around me with the most exquisite tightness in the world. She screams loudly with her release, my name falling repeatedly from her lips. Her fingernails dig into my shoulder blades and I spill into the condom with my own sighs of pleasure.

"Juniper..."

I collapse on top of her and about ten seconds later, my brain catches up with my body, and I realize she probably can't breathe like this. I move to roll off her, but her hands tighten on my ribcage.

"Stay. Just. Stay here," she whispers softly, her voice thick with emotion.

So I do.

I kiss her softly against her neck, her shoulder, her jaw. I lift my head to reach her lips and when I do, I catch a tear squeezing out from the corner of her eye.

"June! Did I hurt you?" I scramble off her, pulling out and barely remembering at the last second to grasp the condom against me as I do. "I'm so sorry, Junie. I'm so sorry, baby."

My apology is frantic. I had no idea I was hurting her. I want to die knowing I did anything to harm her.

"No, it's okay." She gives me a watery smile. I'm not sure I believe her. "I promise. It was just really, really good."

Chapter Twenty-Eight

June

*J*uniper.

I know I shouldn't be reading into anything with Asher, especially considering it was his first time having sex with anyone, but it's hard not to feel a little...confused. I don't know what I expected from our first time sleeping together, but Asher calling me by the wrong name wasn't it.

My name is June. Four letters. It's never been anything more than that, unless Asher or my brother lengthen it to Junie, and even then, it's the obvious choice for a nickname. But Juniper? I can't even pretend that Asher thinks that might be the full version of my name. He knows my birthday is in June, and that I was named after my grandmother.

It's hard not to feel the smallest bit sad or disappointed that, in what was supposed to be a monumental moment, Asher called out the wrong name. But listen to me. I've long entrenched myself in the camp that virginity is a social construct, a way to make people (mostly women) guard something that doesn't need to be guarded. By inventing the concept of virginity and entwining it so thoroughly with the concept of purity, men have been controlling women and sex for centuries. That, paired with the fact that most people's first time is not that great, makes the whole concept of losing one's virginity a way bigger deal than it should be. It's just something that happens to most people at some point. And while I like to think I did everything I could to make Asher's first time good, and memorable, and pleasant, I can't help but feel a bit...off...about the way it ended.

Don't get me wrong, the actual sex itself was incredible. Really incredible, when you consider Asher has had no practice and somehow managed to pull off some of the best sex of my life without having anything to go off of.

I need to get over this Juniper thing.

I knew what I was getting into, even before Asher dropped the bomb of wanting to have sex with me tonight. He and I agreed to a particular relationship. We didn't say the words "no strings attached," but it was heavily implied. I'm here to serve the role of mentor, teacher, helper, and if I get some Os in the process? Amazing. And while I don't exactly feel disrespected by Asher's misnaming, because I can convince myself it's some sort-of iteration of my own name, it kind of cheapens the whole interaction.

Which is ridiculous, because the whole thing was pretty transactional. I shouldn't be feeling off about this, because regardless of what Asher called me, it's a friends-with-benefits situation, and

I'd do well to remember that my past crush on Asher needs to stay exactly there: in the past.

CHAPTER TWENTY-NINE
Asher

Sex with June was incredible.

Of course, I long suspected it would be, but I already know that sex with June will be different from sex with any other woman. I don't have any hard evidence to go on, given my extremely limited experience, but the feeling deep in my gut tells me I'm right.

I never, not for one second, had that feeling of awkwardness or confusion or, let's face it, *blind panic* that I've gotten before when hooking up with a woman. The level of trust I have in June is unsurpassed. It's not lost on me that my trust in her–and hers in me–led to what can only be described as mind-blowing sex (and I'm not just saying that because any sex is better than no sex). Seeing June let go like that, in a way I've never seen her before, was the sexiest, most fun thing I've ever seen. I want to see it again, and not just because it will mean I get to have sex with her again, but because she was in her element. She was every inch the dream girl I've been fantasizing about since I was seventeen.

For the last eight years, I've been dreaming of the moment I could touch June the way I've always wanted to. I never thought I'd be allowed; June is so far out of my league, we're not even playing the same sport. For the last eight years, when I've wrapped my fist around my hardened cock, it's with her name on my lips and her face in my mind.

Seven long years have passed since that kiss. I've kissed other women since then, and I'd kissed girls before June, but none hold a candle to that kiss in the middle of the Demoranville kitchen. It's not just nostalgia or misremembering or building it up in my mind to be something it wasn't. Because when I kissed June again tonight, this time in my own kitchen, every feeling from that earlier kitchen came tumbling back into my head, into my body.

The kiss tonight was even better than that summer kiss. It sparked a kinetic energy into every molecule of my body, down to the tips of my fingers and toes. It was as if the universe was whispering right into my ear, "This. This is *right*."

Who am I to fight universal involvement?

CHAPTER THIRTY
Asher

Now that June and I have had sex, it's like I have awoken a long-slumbering piece of my libido. I can't get enough. I don't think it's just sex. It's sex with *June,* and it's incredible.

When I'm not inside her, I'm thinking about the next time I can be. All I want to do is bury myself between her thighs, make her scream my name, and do it all over again.

I shove another bite of s'mores brownie in my mouth, not caring that the crumbs dribble onto my naked chest and into my bed. June just left, insisting that sleeping in the same bed, despite sleeping together, is a line we shouldn't cross. It's hard to disagree with her. The lines are blurry enough as it is.

Last night after the game, we skipped our usual ritual of eating brownies after my start. We won, I pitched okay–but not great–but when I got home and saw June standing in the kitchen, wearing only a pair of tiny sleep shorts and an "Iced Coffee Please" shirt stretched across my favorite tits in the world, it was all I could do not to bend her over the counter and fuck her right there. Instead, we made a responsible decision and went into her bedroom so I could bend her over the bed and fuck her there.

The tray of brownies lay forgotten on the counter.

Even tonight, after we both got home, we prioritized sex over brownies, so I haven't had my first taste of her newest recipe until now. It's ironic. In high school, June used to call these "better than sex" brownies. Nevermind the fact that neither of us had had sex to compare them to at that time. Now that we are having sex, I can confirm the name is a lie, despite June's incredible talent in the kitchen. There's just nothing in the world better than June's incredible talent in the bedroom.

Normally, I'd be bothered by crumbs in my bed. I hate feeling like I'm sleeping in sand. But tonight, I can't bring myself to care. I absentmindedly brush the crumbs to the side. I'll change my sheets tomorrow. As it is, there's a wet spot on the bed that I'm pointedly avoiding. As soon as I finish this oversized slice of heaven, I'm passing out. The day after I pitch is always reserved for rest, recovery, and treatment, so my physical activity today was limited to bucking up into June as she rode me like a rodeo queen.

I love my job. I know I'm one of the small percentage of lucky (yet hardworking) people that have made it to the major leagues. Every day, I feel grateful that I get paid to play my favorite sport in the world. Even coming up through the minor leagues, where pay was pitiable and I had to work odd jobs in the offseason just to survive (and that's while I was living rent-free in my mom's house), I felt so damn lucky.

Tonight, however, I'm finding it a little harder to be grateful when I have to be on the road and away from June. I'm well aware that this line of thinking is extremely dangerous. I shouldn't feel anything about leaving my roommate for a few days for work.

But June has never been "just" a roommate. To be honest, June hasn't been "just" anything for me since I was seventeen. At seventeen, I stopped thinking of June as "just" Devin's sister, "just" one of our friends, "just" someone we hung out with occasionally. Even still, if I leave emotions out of it, June isn't just a roommate, now that we've started hooking up. It hasn't complicated things yet, but I know that it could. I think we're both conveniently ignoring the possibility that things could get messy.

So when Devin texted me, not knowing I was out of town, asking if I was home tonight, to wait up for June to make sure she made it home from her date okay, I shouldn't have felt frustrated that June didn't swear off dating like she said she might earlier. And I definitely shouldn't have felt jealousy.

June may have started off seeming like my little sister. Until she wasn't.

After I started seeing June as more than a friend, I didn't say anything to Devin about his overprotectiveness of her because it benefited me. I've never been a jealous guy except when it comes to June. So, while I haven't said or done anything to prevent June from going on her dates, I can't pretend it doesn't gut me. There's a big, very real part of me that understands Devin's reluctance to see his sister date someone. But she's her own person, and she deserves to meet new people and find what makes her happy, even if I wish it were me.

I'm not an idiot. I know what this situation is. I know what June *should* be to me, versus what she is (and more importantly, is not). Still, my knee-jerk reaction to ask June not to go on a date isn't helpful. I've longed for June for so long that I've become an expert at swallowing down my emotions when it comes to her. I just need to keep doing that. My head has long since gotten the memo that we will never really be together, but my heart somehow missed that one. Sometimes, I wish I could rid myself of my feelings for her, and other times, I want to hold tight.

It's like trying to hold sand in your fist. The tighter you grip, the more the sand spills out. Right now, I don't want to let go of June, but I have no right to ask her to stay home, either. She owes me nothing. I'm sure she'd be mortified if she knew my real feelings for her anyway.

So, for the next week, while the team is in Dallas and Houston, I ignore my repetitive thoughts about June, knowing my feelings aren't reciprocated. By the end of the trip, I've almost convinced myself that I'm misremembering my feelings for her. I'm mostly convinced that I'm just feeling nostalgic. I just needed time away to get my head on straight and when I go back home, things will be back to normal. It's probably just a combination of nostalgia and post-sex glow that's addling my brain and confusing my heart.

I shove away my brain's sneaky reminder that I've had a thing for June for eight years.

CHAPTER THIRTY-ONE
June

I really did mean to swear off dating. I truly had no intention of going on another date so soon. I even deleted my dating apps, but when Priya begged me to go on a double date with her, I couldn't say no. Mostly due to the underhanded way she tricked me into agreeing. I have to hand it to her: it was a great strategy. She waited until we had some downtime at work, then asked me if I was free for dinner the following week. Only after I had agreed did she mention that she would be bringing this new guy she was talking to and his roommate, and would I pretty please do her a solid and join her on this double date.

I had rolled my eyes and reluctantly agreed. It was a nice time. Priya and Henry seemed to get along well, and I didn't *not* get along with Henry's roommate. He was a nice guy. Honestly, he seemed great. He was cute, polite, and a good conversationalist. I just wasn't feeling a spark. I was horrified to discover, halfway through the date, that I found myself subconsciously comparing him to my roommate. I shut those thoughts down immediately.

When Priya sidled up to me after the date, when the guys walked a few feet in front of us, she wiggled her eyebrows and asked me what I thought. I felt terrible for shrugging and saying, "He seems nice." Priya had wrinkled her nose, knowing that "nice" was codeword for "no future." At least she got the hint. The truth is, there was no issue with him. I feel bad that I wasn't feeling it, but not bad enough to agree to another date.

Priya also seemed to get the hint that I'm not interested in any more double dates. It's been more than a week, and she hasn't asked again, despite seeing Henry multiple times since then. At least now when she asks me to join her for a meal, she's upfront about it not being a surprise double date.

Today is a day off for both of us, and the team has an off day, too. They flew in from Texas last night, but I was already asleep by the time Asher got home. I was also out the door for breakfast and a hot-girl walk with Priya and Faye before he woke up.

When I walk in the apartment after our morning activities, Asher is sitting on the couch, acoustic guitar slung across his chest, singing a song I've never heard before. It's been a long time since I've heard Asher sing. I've been home when he's taken one of his guitars down from the wall and played around with it. I've heard him strumming quite a few songs, humming along, but this is the first time I've heard him sing in a long time.

The song is beautiful, haunting almost, in the way he infuses a sense of longing and grittiness into his voice. I've never been able to sing. I love music. My memory for song lyrics is the extent of my musical prowess, though. It makes Asher's singing beyond impressive. The fact that he can play guitar is notable, but singing and playing at the same time requires a level of coordination I can never hope to achieve. I listen quietly at the door. He knows I'm home; he gave me a small head nod when I walked in, but he knew I didn't want to interrupt him. The song is sad but beautiful. His voice rings clear as his fingers pick away at the strings. Goosebumps rise on my arms when he gets to the bridge and his voice takes on a raw quality.

When he finishes it, I'm tempted to demand he play it again for me, from the start. Instead, I ask, "What song is that?"

"It's just a song I heard a few years ago that I've been wanting to learn for a while."

"Who sings it?" He seems hesitant to tell me. Probably because he knows I'll obsess over the lyrics for the next two weeks. It's just what I do.

"Have you ever heard of The Gaslight Anthem?" I shake my head. "You'd like them. The song is called 'Break Your Heart.'"

Later, when I look up the song on YouTube, the haunting tone of Asher's voice is amplified with a greater understanding of the words. The lyrics speak of heartbreak, longing, whispered secrets, and unreturned love. I wonder what it would be like to feel so deeply, so longingly, for someone I may never have, before abruptly realizing that perhaps the reason that song is so haunting to me is because I felt it as a fifteen year old, toward the exact roommate whose voice breathes life into the words.

A soft knock at my open door reveals Asher leaning against the frame. The ceilings are high in this apartment, but even still, his slouched posture is the only thing that prevents his head from grazing the top of the extended doorframe.

"Are you going to be around for dinner? I was thinking I was going to make my mom's chicken ravioli. I got fresh sheets of pasta at this Italian marketplace I went to this morning." I groan.

"You're too good to me, Asher. That sounds amazing." I feel terrible. He had a start in Houston, and I still haven't made him brownies to celebrate. Granted, he didn't pitch a great game and the Foxes ended up losing, but brownies are our tradition, and I've grown accustomed to developing a new recipe every week. I had planned on making a cherry cheesecake swirled brownie, but time got away from me. Now that my brace is off and my arm is mostly healed, I've been trying to make up for lost time. It's never felt so luxurious to wash and dry my own hair, or to knit my ambitious projects, or simply open food packages without resorting to frustration-fueled violence. Asher insisted he didn't mind that I forgot to make his brownies, but I still feel bad.

"If you make me ravioli, I'll make you brownies. Deal?" I stand from the bed, closing my laptop.

"Deal." Asher's eyes twinkle. It's fun to see him in this light, now that we are living together. I've always known he's been a rock-solid friend, a bit of a mama's boy, and musically talented. But living with Asher has allowed me to discover his love of cooking and his gentle way of caring for others, whether it's the way he insists on making me coffee in the mornings in my favorite *Maybe Today, Satan* mug, or the way he sweetly washed my hair when I was injured. I know there's still so much to learn about him, but I can't help feeling surprised with each new discovery.

Like how he blocks my path on my exit from the bedroom, heat blazing in his eyes as he slides a finger under the thin strap of my top.

"Not so fast," he says darkly, and immediately my mind conjures all sorts of dirty thoughts. I've seen sweet Asher, eager Asher, I swear I've even seen glimpses of a longing Asher. But a dominant Asher? That I've yet to see, but I am. Here. For. It. "Look at you," Asher tsks. I swallow, unsure of his meaning. "Walking into this apartment in this sexy little number. Do you have any idea how much you drive me crazy?"

I can't help the smirk on my lips. I bought this athleisurewear onesie at the shopping event I organized for the WAGs last week. It was a little out of my price range, but the sales associate pressured me to try it on. Delaney and Amy were particularly vocal in their support of the bright pink one-piece with tennis skirt overlay. It was such a self-esteem boost that I convinced myself it was well worth the price tag. And the way Asher is looking at me now? Confirmed.

His eyes peruse my body while his fingers continue to slide up and down the shoulder strap. He towers over me; he always has, given our height difference, but today, I'm acutely aware of just how he's using that height to convey a sense of dominance and need.

"Junie. Tell me you'll let me fuck you again. Please."

Holy shit. How this man can go from dominant to begging and make it work for him is beyond me. I'm ready to start begging myself, but I'm also digging the power I feel, knowing Asher is this way for me and only me. Someday, he's going to make another woman very happy, but right now, that woman gets to be me. I may or may not arch my back, ever so slightly, pushing my breasts further toward Asher's hand.

"Hmm. I'm not sure," I lie. "Tell me what you want to do about it." I know I'm playing with fire. I can see the way Asher is hanging by a thread. But I also know the few times he's used dirty talk in the bedroom, it's made my heart race and my panties wet. What can I say? I love me some good dirty talk.

"I don't know what I want to do about it, baby. I can't decide if I want to shove my cock so far down your throat I'll feel it from the outside with my hand around your neck. Or if I want to throw you onto the bed and pound into your dripping pussy from behind, making you come hard and fast, or if I want to fall to my feet and worship you the way you deserve."

Yep. That'll do it.

Asher has worshipped me before and he's fucking amazing at it. But seeing as I have yet to experience a bossy, rougher Asher, I opt for the first two. When I tell him that, his pupils blow wide and dark before he commands me onto my knees.

Holy shit.

Just a few weeks ago, Asher was a little unsure and now he's ordering me to my knees so he can take what he wants, just from seeing me in a sexy new outfit. I'd like to think I had something to do with this transformation. Watching Asher harness his confidence in the bedroom is a level of sexy I didn't think I'd experience, but he is right. I'm not just wet as a result. I'm fucking dripping.

Without backing up into the room, I lower myself to my knees right there in the entryway. Asher reverently strokes my cheek.

"Fuck, you look so good down there on your knees for me." His thumb pulls at my lower lip. "Before you take me out and suck me off, I need you to tell me you know I respect you." I look up at him, confusion etched into my features. "Tell me you know I respect the hell out of you, Junie. Please. Because I'm about to fuck your throat like I don't, and I'm barely hanging on here, baby."

I smile, loving the effect I have on him. I make a mental note to send Kyle Crawford a fruit basket or something, because Asher brought his dirty talk A-game today.

"I know, Asher," I tell him honestly. Then, because I'm sometimes a little bit evil and I like to toy with him, I lick my lips slowly, never tearing my eyes from his. His whispered *fuck* is all I need to know I've got him right where I want him: teetering on the edge.

The blow job isn't pretty. It's loud and rough and sloppy. Quite frankly, it's everything a blow job should be. He wasn't kidding when he said he wanted to feel himself in my throat. The way his large hand circles my throat as he pounds into me feels like a brand in the best way possible. I've never minded rough sex, but now I have a feeling I'm going to crave it.

The few minutes I spend sucking Asher's cock is as much foreplay for him as it is for me. By the time he spills into my mouth, I'm a whimpering mess, turned on beyond all belief. He isn't gentle when he lifts me to my feet and tosses me onto the bed, and I don't want him to be.

"Strip." He may have come down my throat a minute ago, but it's done nothing to quell the lust in his gaze as he watches me undress. With far more control than I would have believed possible, he opens my nightstand drawer, perusing his options. It's a little awkward with me standing naked by the bed, so when his eyes flick to mine, I instinctively suck in my stomach, bringing my hands to cover the fleshiest, softest part of my belly. His gaze softens.

"No, baby, don't do that. Let me see all of you, exactly the way you are." Slowly, against my instincts, I let my stomach relax and my hands fall to my sides. More to himself than me, Asher mumbles, "Perfect."

He steps toward me, cupping my face and placing a sweet kiss against my mouth, which slowly deepens. I shift, becoming increasingly aroused, until Asher pulls away with a soft chuckle.

"Needy today, huh, baby?" I don't even bother to refute it. A mischievous glint shines in his eyes as he pulls not one, but two toys from the bedside drawer. The light catches on the stainless-steel plug. I bought it online as my freebie item when I spent a certain amount at my favorite sex shop, but I've never used it. The fact that Asher selected it makes me shift on my feet, a little nervous and absolutely very turned on.

"I've never actually..." I trail off, unsure why I feel the need to explain myself. Asher tips his head back and closes his eyes, as if praying for patience. When he opens them again, the golden hazel hue I love so much is almost completely swallowed by black.

"Are you telling me I get another one of your firsts, Junie?" I nod. He palms his rapidly growing erection, easily visible in his athletic shorts. Holy refractory period, Batman. He swipes a finger through my folds, groaning at the wetness he finds. His fingers are soon replaced by the plug, its coldness somewhat jarring. Still, the plug is short and stout and not nearly enough for where he's currently got it. My hips buck, seeking more. He watches the plug slide in and out of me, mesmerized. Just when my impatience crests, Asher pulls away. Grasping my shoulders, he turns me to the bed and gently bends me over.

"Still with me, baby?"

"Yes." My reply is breathy but audible. If I weren't so turned on, I might feel self-conscious, especially when he brings the plug between my cheeks, teasing my back entrance before slowly, slowly, pressing it inside. It's tight and full and somewhat uncomfortable, but not painful. After the initial intrusion, I'm able to relax and adjust to the feeling. When Asher pulls me to stand, his erection pressing against my ass and jostling the plug, I whimper. My back to his chest, he reaches down to circle my clit. I don't know if it's the drawn-out foreplay or the plug in my ass, but every sensation is heightened. I'm guessing it won't take long for me to come tonight, but instead of throwing me back on the bed and going to town on me as promised, Asher continues his reverent stroking up and down my arms, my chest, my ribcage. When he finally reaches my pussy again, I'm ready to start begging him to fuck me. I'm completely at his mercy, willing to do anything he commands.

"Asher." My plea is whiny, needy. I don't even care; Asher deserves to know how he affects me.

"You should see how beautiful you look with that cute little gemstone in your ass." I whimper again. "How do you feel?"

"Please, Asher. I need to come." He spins me around.

"I know you do, baby. You did such a good job sucking my cock earlier, I'm not going to stop until you come on my face and then my cock. Do you understand me?" I nod, unable to form words.

In a flash, Asher is on his knees, worshipfully dragging his tongue across my entrance. I grasp his head with both hands when my knees buckle.

"Fuck yes. Take what you need, Junie. I love it." My hips rock against his face as my fingers tangle in his hair. Asher hoists one of my legs over his shoulder and I lean my opposite hip on the bed, hoping I can somehow maintain my balance through my rapidly forming orgasm. When I'm turned on enough, I can come pretty quickly, but I've never come as quickly–ever–as I have with him. I swallow down the thought that the reason why might be because I've always felt safe with Asher Incaudo.

Asher flattens his tongue against my clit at the same time he curls the two fingers inside me, and I explode. The breath is knocked so swiftly from my lungs I'm afraid I'll never fill them again. My mouth opens on a silent scream as I pulse around him. My knees buckle, but his strong hand against my elevated hip prevents me from falling. He allows me to ride out wave after wave of orgasm, until the pleasure finally subsides and I'm able to suck in enough air to replenish my depleted lungs. Withdrawing his fingers and standing in front of me, he gently guides me to fall forward onto the bed.

"Still with me, Junie?"

"Yeah," I murmur into the mattress, not even caring that my ass, plug and all, is fully on display.

"Remember what I told you about how I respect you?" I hear the crinkle of the foil condom wrapper. I nod. "I'm gonna need you to remember that right about now, 'kay?" He gives me a few moments to catch my breath as he coats his sheathed cock in my arousal. He taps the head of his cock against my clit when I don't respond. My resulting moan must be a good enough response for him, because a second later, he thrusts into me in one go. I'm relaxed enough where it doesn't hurt, but the fullness is enough to steal the breath from my lungs yet again.

"Oh, fuck," I say on an exhale.

"Oh, fuck," Asher says simultaneously. "Junie, you're so tight. I can feel the plug. Oh, fuck. I'm not gonna last." As if to prove himself wrong, Asher pulls back and slams into me again. And again. And again. Each thrust shoots me forward on the bed, only for his strong hands to grip my hips and pull me back to where we started. His thrusts are rough, hard, and deep. The plug intensifies everything in a way I've never experienced before. I feel dizzy and lightheaded, yet so, so good. Spurred on by his grunts behind me, I tilt my hips, dragging my clit deliciously against the bedspread.

Sensing my movements, he snakes his hand around, his fingers strumming my clit as he continues his relentless assault from behind. It's intense and incredible. I'm a mess, drooling and babbling into the sheets when Asher replaces his fingers with the second toy he pulled out earlier. The soft vibrations of my pink wand press against my clit. I feel so close to coming, yet the release is still too far, shimmering on the horizon, teasing me.

Asher does something to adjust his posture, changing the angle in which he hits me, and it makes all the difference in the world. The head of his cock hits a new, deeper part of me, nudging me quickly toward the finish line.

"Asher, Asher, Asher," I chant nonsensically. He pulls back further and slams in harder. My vision clouds at the edges. "Again!" I instruct wildly, uncaring how demanding and frantic I sound. He must not care either, because he does exactly as I say, pounding into me. Each thrust has my clit pressing harder against the wand. A particularly hard thrust has me moaning around him, my voice and mouth making sounds I've never made before. A splash hits the ground at our feet, but I can't make sense of it; Asher is wearing a condom, isn't he?

"Fuck yes, baby. Fuck yes. Squirt all over my cock."

Oh. My. God.

The euphoria I feel is a different kind of orgasm. It's heady and happy. My orgasm hits and I dissolve into a billion pieces, disintegrating before my own eyes. My atoms float around the room, weightless and airy, before sinking back down to the bed and reassembling into me, mostly the same me, but somehow, slightly different.

Asher follows immediately after, his final grunts and groans filling the air before he collapses next to me.

Chapter Thirty-Two
Asher

"Don't move," I instruct, but I'm not entirely sure my instructions are necessary. June has melted into the mattress, her legs still dangling off the side. I burn the image into my brain, fully understanding the sentiment "fucked senseless."

June was a champ. I wasn't exactly gentle either time my dick was inside her perfect body, but she met me stroke for stroke. I've never viewed her as a fragile little bird, but I've also never wanted to hurt her. I got caught up in the moment today and am a little worried I was rougher than she could handle. I'd like to think she'd tell me if that were the case, but I'm getting in my head about this already, and my cock isn't even fully soft.

It takes longer than I'd like for the water to warm up enough to fill my oversized tub, and I probably squirted in too much of the green apple bubble bath I bought on a whim in Dallas, but the smell is comforting and intoxicating all at once. While the tub is filling, I place two glasses of ice water on the ledge before returning to June. She curled her legs up onto the bed by now, but she still seems to be in a bit of a floaty headspace.

I bend, cleaning up the fluids off the floor from the hottest moment of my life.

"Mmm, I'm sorry," June mumbles, dragging her hand down her face. I step toward her, still bent over, so I can remain at eye level with her.

"What are you sorry for?"

"It's so embarrassing. I didn't know I was going to do…" She waves her hand toward the floor. "…That."

My eyes crinkle at the corners. "Junie, that was the sexiest thing I've ever experienced. Please don't feel embarrassed. It was the highest form of flattery you could have given me. I loved every second of it." I punctuate my statement with a kiss on her nose before gently removing the plug. June emits a content little sigh when I lift her in my arms and carry her to the tub, settling in behind her.

I wince as I slide into the too-hot water, but June happily hums as if there is no better temperature in the world. My skin will be red by the time this bath is over, but at least June will be happy. I kiss her temple and trickle bubbly water across her chest. The bubbles cover the freckles there that I love so much, and she settles further into me, enjoying the warmth and sensations.

She allows me to gently wash her and I revel in the ability to touch her freely. The bath is mostly quiet. It was only after we had settled in that I realized I should have turned on some music, but if

I had, I wouldn't have been able to hear June's satisfied little noises. They might be my favorite sounds in the world.

I love the way she gets after a few orgasms. Sleepy, pliant, and so content. She deserves to feel that way all the time. There are givers and there are takers in this world, and June is a giver. I'm just glad she's allowing me to take care of her, if only for tonight.

Chapter Thirty-Three
June

"June, I need another raspberry seltzer." When I don't respond, she shakes her empty can at me, as if I'm an idiot who doesn't know what a raspberry seltzer is. My stunned silence is because I'm momentarily dumbfounded by the audacity of her request—no, her *demand*—rather than an inability to understand the words coming out of her punchable mouth.

Kill me.

Kill me right now.

Because if I don't die immediately, I might kill one of the WAGs. Talk about career suicide. Before I can formulate a politically correct, career-salvaging response, Delaney Kristoff-Benjamin opens her beautiful mouth and rescues me.

"Are you fucking kidding me, Melody? Walk your ass to concessions and get it yourself. June is not your servant." I shoot Delaney a grateful smile; I'm drawn to Delaney more than any other WAG.

"John is pitching, so I can't," she says with a shrug, as if that explains anything. My eyes widen further. If this were anything other than a work situation for me, I'd have no problem telling Melody Malone exactly what she can do with her empty seltzer can. But because this is my job–one that I like and that I'm good at, thank you very much–I'm unsure how to proceed. Melody widens her eyes at me, as if to say, *Well, what are you waiting for?*

It's humiliating. I would have thought we left the mean-girl days far behind in high school, but Melody didn't seem to get the message. She continues to stare at me, waiting for me to serve her, completely contradicting her reasoning for not getting her drink herself. She's not even watching her husband completely blow the game on the mound.

"Don't you dare," Delaney says to me out of the corner of her mouth when she sees me lean forward, preparing to stand and, I guess, go to concessions? This wasn't exactly in my job description, but Deb didn't prepare me for this situation to arise either, so I'm not sure what the right play is.

Amy, sitting in the row in front of me, turns to glare at Melody. After staring her down for several seconds, she turns around to face me, placing a gentle hand on my knee. "June, you are great at your job. You've done an incredible job taking care of us this season. But I'm fairly certain waiting on us hand and foot is not part of your job description. Please don't set that precedent for yourself."

I'm glad Deb isn't here right now. I'm not sure how she'd feel about the clear division amongst the wives when it comes to Melody. Delaney places a protective hand on her growing belly.

"I may be pregnant, but I'm not afraid to cut a bitch," she says softly, so only Amy and I can hear. I'm not entirely sure she's joking, but we laugh anyway. Sensing defeat, Melody huffs and returns her focus to the game, just in time to see Benny, the manager, jog to the mound to retrieve her husband and send him back to the dugout.

Melody stands, presumably leaving the game. Beside her, Alicia James, Hailey McClintock, and Jenny Andrews make no move to stand to allow her to get by. It's rude and petty, but not undeserved, and I can't help but feel a little warmth in my heart for the women who treat me like a human being. What a fucking low bar, but given my last work experience, at least the bar isn't in hell this time.

"I'm telling Benny," Delaney declares once Melody has exited from the other side of the row. If she were a cartoon, I'm sure little smoke lines would be coming out of her ears, the way she's fuming on my behalf. "This is fucking outrageous."

"Please don't," I beg her. I'm not sure what sort of pull the manager has, or what Benny could even realistically do in this situation, but he certainly has the power to bench Melody's husband, which not only would likely make my life uncomfortable, but could potentially impact Asher's relationship with his teammate. I don't know if Melody's husband sucks the way she does, but if he's a normal person, I'd hate to see him punished for his poor taste in women.

Amy, still turned around in her seat, squeezes my knee. "Eh, from what Jackson says, John kinda sucks, too. Maybe he'll get traded before the season is up."

"You okay?" Alicia leans over, concern etched on her face.

"Yeah. Trust me, this is not the worst thing to happen to me at work." I attempt to infuse some humor in my statement, but given the looks I get in return, it falls flat. "Not here," I rush to reassure them. "In a different job. I love this one."

"Hopefully that's the worst you have to deal with in this job," Jenny remarks.

"Trust me, it is," I assure them. "Maybe I'll get myself a raspberry seltzer to decompress, once I'm off the clock." I wink.

"Hell yes," Hailey applauds. "June, if you ever want to go out with us when the boys are out of town, you let us know. We'd be happy to have you."

"Oh, thank you," I say, genuinely touched they'd want me to join them. "I'm not sure if I'm allowed to."

"Why not?" Amy looks confused and concerned.

"I have a nonfraternization clause in my contract. I guess it really says it applies to the players, but I'm not sure about the optics of only hanging out with some of you."

"Psh, that's bullshit." As usual, Delaney doesn't mince words. "We can keep it a secret if you want. But if you're really not comfortable, we won't force you."

"No, I'm interested…just, let me think about it. I'd love to make more friends. But I also really need this job."

Alicia nods sagely. "No pressure. But you have our contact information if and when you change your mind. The offer has no expiration date."

I nod, unable to stop the smile spreading across my face. The Foxes may have lost today's game, but I can't help but feel happy and fulfilled.

Ash

Please can I eat your pussy tonight?

Jesus. I need to invest in one of those privacy screens for my phone if Asher is going to be sending me texts like this. I immediately lock the screen and put my phone down, guiltily looking around as if someone might catch me on the receiving end of a dirty text from the exact type of person I'm not supposed to fraternize with. The game hasn't been over for more than ten minutes, and I barely made it back upstairs to the offices before he started texting me.

Please?

Priya peeks over at my phone, my lock screen still lit up with Asher's one-word text. I can't exactly snatch the phone away without looking incredibly rude or like a total nutcase, so I internally cross my fingers and toes he won't send anything else incriminating.

"Ash! My childhood best friend is named Ashley, too!" I don't correct Priya. While he might be a friend from my younger days, Ash most definitely is not short for Ashley. I don't feel great about lying to Priya–yet again–but if it allows me to keep my job while Asher and I play the dangerous games we're playing, so be it.

"Let's catch happy hour," Liam suggests, sauntering over to his desk and packing up his messenger bag. I'm stunned. I've hung out with Liam approximately twice; his busy law school schedule barely allows for any social time.

"Ooh, yes! Sip is a few blocks away and has a great margarita special if we can make it in the next–" Faye checks her watch, "hour and fifteen minutes."

"Alright, I'm in." It doesn't take me long to decide, and while Asher's offer is really enticing, I also know it will take him at least an hour to get out of the ballpark. He pitches tomorrow afternoon, so he's got a workout scheduled. I rapidly send him a text, making sure I'm alone in my office before pulling up his less-than-professional text thread.

Me:

> Well, since you asked so nicely, yes.

> But I might not be home till a little later. I got invited to happy hour. I'm finally getting close to my work friends!

It takes another minute, but Asher's enthusiastic response settles me.

> So happy for you, Junie. Take your time. Let me know if you need a ride.

When we make it to Sip, we snag the last of the outdoor tables. The inside is just as busy, which isn't surprising, as the bar's location is perfectly situated to catch a lot of the post-game foot traffic. Even without its perfect location, the mango margaritas are enough to maintain a steady influx of thirsty patrons.

It's not long before our foursome switches from idle work-related chatter to gossip and more interesting conversational topics. Priya shares about her relationship with Henry. She seems happy with the way things are going, so even though things didn't work out between his roommate and me, I'm glad for her sake.

"What about you, June? Are you seeing anyone?" I don't know if it's the margarita that's loosened my tongue, or the isolation I've been feeling, harboring my own secret, or the sense of camaraderie I finally feel at work, but I find myself wanting to share what Asher and I are doing–even if I can't tell them all the details.

"I've kind of sworn off dating for now," I tell them honestly. "It's exhausting, and kind of always a letdown, you know?" Faye nods. Liam shoots me a sympathetic look. "I have been hooking up with my roommate a little bit, though," I add, before taking another gulp of my fruity drink.

"*What?*" Priya exclaims loudly, drawing attention to our table. I flap my hands and attempt to shush her.

"It's not a big deal," I tell her in hushed tones. "It's just sex, but it scratches that itch, ya know?" Even as I say the words, they burn my throat. I hate reducing whatever it is between Asher and me to such crude terms. Liam and Faye nod enthusiastically. A little too enthusiastically.

"What is this?" Priya points back and forth between the two of them accusingly.

"Well, if you must know," Faye says with a shrug. "We're fucking." Liam laughs at Faye's bluntness but makes no move to correct her. "So, June, I say go for it. Explore what's going on with your roommate."

"Whoa, let's just talk about the bombshell you just dropped in the middle of the table." Priya settles her face on her steepled fingers, glaring at our coworkers for keeping secrets from her. I'm happy to have the attention off me and my own secrets.

"Not much to tell." Liam's blue eyes twinkle. "Neither of us is interested in dating, and between our course load, work, and studying, we really don't have time for that sort of bullshit anyway." Faye nods along.

"Kill two birds with one stone. Release some stress, get your rocks off, that sort of thing," Faye finishes for him. Honestly, I'm impressed with both of their nonchalant attitudes toward the entire situation. I'm not sure Asher and I are quite so flippant about what we're doing, but our situation isn't really all that different from Faye and Liam's, right?

"It just seems so...transactional," Priya says, almost sadly. "Yep. It is." Faye is unashamed as she sips her mule. "That's what we both wanted. That's why this–" she moves her hand between herself and Liam, "works. The second he starts wanting more, I'm out."

"And if she wants what I can't give her, I'm out, too. It's honestly the most mutually beneficial arrangement I can think of. No one gets hurt."

I mull it over. I'm not entirely confident I can say the same about Asher's and my arrangement. It's hard to foresee us extricating ourselves from our situation without someone getting hurt, even though I want to convince myself otherwise. Would I really be okay with Asher suddenly wanting to date others? Is he already dating others? I realize I never asked, never considered the possibility. We got into this as a teachable situation. I didn't even really teach him all that much; it was more of me allowing him the space to find his own confidence. Sure, when you break it down to its basest level, our situation isn't that different from Faye and Liam's. We're both getting our physical needs met.

But what happens when one of us wants more? Or something different? Or, god forbid, someone finds out?

Chapter Thirty-Four
Asher

"Great game tonight, son," a balding man in a blue sport coat says to me as he shakes my hand.

"Thank you; I appreciate that," I tell him. He's the fourth man in five minutes to tell me essentially the same thing. I don't mind. It's nice to be praised, and if rich people feel like they have easy access to the players, it makes that much more money for the charity.

The Foxes have their own charity foundation, but tonight's event is for JJ's charity, Game of Hope. The Foxes encourage their players to get involved in charitable giving, even if they don't set up their own foundations. I like the idea of having my own charity, but I'm early into my career and recognize I'm not a big enough name yet to draw enough funding. Now Devin could draw some good money, if he ever wanted to start his own charity. I laugh internally, thinking of June's reaction to the idea of Devin hosting a charitable foundation. She'd probably make some joke about the money going toward testing young, naive women for venereal diseases.

JJ's charity is legit. It links local organizations with funding to do incredible work preventing child abuse and neglect. Before I came to Chicago, I guess shit really hit the fan with JJ's mom, and a whole bunch of information came out about his less-than-ideal childhood. You'd never know it from talking to the guy, but I guess that's what years of therapy do for you. I couldn't be prouder of my teammate for turning a fucked-up situation into a good thing for others. It makes it easier to put on a suit and mingle with strangers after a start, when all I really want to do is go home and rest.

It also is easier knowing June is here tonight. Of course, she insisted we arrive separately, which worked out okay, considering my treatment from today's game went long and I had to leave straight from the field. I haven't seen her yet tonight, but you can bet my head is on a swivel for her.

Crawford saunters up to me as soon as the balding man leaves. This isn't JJ's biggest event, and tonight is a more relaxed affair than his annual winter gala. Still, the place is crawling with fans, players, and staff members. The attire is slightly more relaxed, too, which I appreciate. My mother is a saint, but there's no denying I was raised on a shoestring budget, so there's something inherently uncomfortable about a suit and tie for me. Luckily, I'm not the only one forgoing a tie tonight, as I glance at Crawford's unbuttoned collar. He clinks his beer bottle against mine, leaning against the bar table and scanning the crowd. It's not lost on me that we're both searching for women right now; I just happen to be looking for one in particular.

"So many women, so little time," he muses, adjusting his collar. I just shake my head. I wonder if he'll ever get tired of bedding a new woman every night; the idea alone sounds exhausting to me. A flash of sky blue catches my attention. Crawford isn't wrong; the room is packed with beautiful women in cocktail dresses, but somehow, like a magnet, my eyes are drawn to one.

June's head is tipped back in a laugh, her blue cocktail dress showing off her round ass. She's wearing sky-high, strappy silver heels which make said ass look incredible. I wish she would turn so I could see the rest of her. Her brown hair is pulled up into a sleek ponytail, making her look classy and sexy while somehow remaining entirely professional as she speaks with Deb, who I recognize as the head of the Foxes Family Program and June's boss.

Crawford catches me staring. I quickly avert my gaze. I'm not ashamed of wanting June, but I know if she is caught with me, her job is on the line, and I don't want anyone getting a whiff of impropriety between us (despite my tongue doing all sorts of improper shit to her this morning).

He tilts his beer bottle toward June. "You know her?"

I'm a deer caught in the headlights. Do I lie and say I don't know her? Say yes, I know her, but there's nothing going on between us? Crawford is no snitch but seeing as June and I haven't really discussed a cover story, my brain is in full-on panic mode.

"Relax, man. I'm not gonna tell her you want to fuck her or something," he says, incorrectly interpreting my panicked silence. "I am an excellent wingman, though. In fact, watch a master at work."

He takes a step in June's direction before I snatch his wrist in my hand. He blinks down at where I'm holding him.

"Sorry." I release his hand slowly and sigh. "She's my roommate." I decide on a half-truth to prevent Crawford from making an awkward situation worse. "She works for the Foxes Family Program, too. She's got some bullshit clause in her contract that says she can't fraternize with players, so as far as you or anyone else knows, we don't even know each other."

I watch June's graceful neck as she swallows a sip of her gin and tonic. She chatters away happily, shaking hands and schmoozing with the people near her. I love seeing her in her element like this. She thrives off meeting new people and sharing her energy. She turns and immediately catches my eye, offering me a quick smile before turning back to Deb. My breath momentarily stills in my lungs. She looks stunning tonight. Her cocktail dress is one-sleeved, a ruffly material crossing over her chest and one shoulder. Her arms are adorned in blue and silver bangles, and her ears hold spirally blue and green glass earrings. Her whole outfit is fun and different and entirely June.

I turn back to Crawford to find him watching me carefully. "Does your roommate know you want to fuck her?"

My beer bottle is halfway to my lips; if I had drunk any, I'm sure I'd be choking on it right now. I sputter an excuse halfway between "that's preposterous" and "I don't know what you're talking about." Obviously, Crawford doesn't buy it.

"So, what I'm hearing is that she doesn't know," he says, tipping his own bottle back and drinking leisurely. He must read the panic on my face. "Relax, Incaudo. I'm not gonna tell her." My eyes drift back to June, where she's talking and laughing with a sandy-haired man about our age. His blue eyes twinkle in amusement, laughing at some shared joke between the two of them. I watch June's eyes crinkle in the corners, a sure sign that her laughter is genuine. I wonder how many times I've made her genuinely laugh since she moved back to Chicago, and if it's more or less than the man standing across from her.

"You wanna ease up on the grip there, buddy? If you white-knuckle that bottle any more, you'll shatter it, and I'm not looking to get accidentally shanked here." Crawford, for all the shit we give him about only being interested in women and his next pitch, is really fucking observant. More observant than I'd like him to be. In the interest of his safety and those around me, I set my bottle down. I no longer feel like drinking anymore anyway.

"Wait, this is the roommate who's been helping you with...the books and stuff?" Crawford's eyes widen in realization. "Holy shit! The dirty talk!"

I whip my head around, aggressively shushing my teammate and mentor. If he doesn't keep his voice down, he might have to worry about an intentional shanking this time. He adjusts his volume and hisses, "*The dirty talk!*"

There's no point in denying it further, but I refuse to admit to anything without getting the go-ahead from June first. I'm sure my silence speaks volumes anyway, given the way Crawford's eyes continuously bounce between June and me.

"Can you not?" I sigh defeatedly, running a hand through my hair. This night is quickly turning into a disaster. All I want to do is go home, eat the new brownies June made me (peanut butter cup), and maybe eat out my roommate, too. Instead, I'm stuck shaking hands with strangers while I try to keep the shit-eating grin off my teammate's face.

The next set of fans walks away, after shaking our hands and telling us how excited they are for us to make it to another World Series, despite us not even being halfway through the season. Crawford seems ready to burst, as if holding in the knowledge of what he discovered tonight just might kill him. In fact, it might work out favorably for me if it does cause his demise.

"So, you are fucking her, right?" I half-expect him to start clapping his hands and bouncing on the balls of his feet like an excited teenager. I drag my hand down my face, trying to gain some semblance of control over the runaway train that is this conversation.

Another group of fans approaches us, and we smile for pictures. As soon as they leave, Crawford starts in again.

"I'm not answering that," I tell him, which is pretty much an answer itself. I glance at my phone. Only one more hour of this before I can go home.

Chapter Thirty-Five

June

I'm not sure how I made it home from JJ's event later than Asher, but by the time the rideshare pulls up outside our apartment, I can see the glow of the lights through the window. Asher caught my eye as the night was winding down. He nodded toward the exit but was promptly ambushed by another group of fans wanting photos and autographs before the night ended. He must have been able to slip away from them easier than I realized while I was waiting for the car. I climb the stairs to the third floor. I'm not sure if I'm more excited to get out of my shoes or my shapewear, but I'm ready to relax.

Asher is standing in the kitchen when I walk in the door, his sport coat discarded and shirt untucked. It feels oddly domestic, like he is home from working a normal, corporate job instead of being a bigshot major league pitcher. After seeing him interact with fans all night, I absentmindedly wonder how many of those female fans are unknowingly jealous of me for getting this view of Asher, relaxed and genuine.

I hold onto the counter with one hand while I attempt to unbuckle my heel while standing. I'm wobbly and uncoordinated, which has nothing to do with the single gin and tonic I drank tonight. Asher rushes over, lifting me easily onto the counter so he can gently remove my shoes himself.

"Easy there, Grace," he teases. I shove him playfully.

"I could have done that, you know. I almost had it."

"Yeah, but I'd rather you not break your neck in my apartment. The landlord would probably raise the rent, and the paperwork I'd have to fill out? Forget it." He winks, the action incinerating my panties.

He presses a soft kiss to my lips. "Tell me I'm allowed to eat the brownies you made."

"Go ahead," I wave toward the pan and make to slide off the counter. "I'm ready to get out of this dress." He stops me, helping me gently to stand and tugging at my zipper himself.

"I can help you with that." His eyes are hooded. When the zipper reaches the bottom of the track, he slides the fabric off my shoulder. The dress pools at my bare feet, revealing my black shapewear underneath. Asher stares at it for a moment, probably trying to figure out the world's least sexy lingerie.

"It's shapewear," I explain. "It holds everything in, smoothes it all out so it's more flattering when I wear tighter dresses."

"Is this for you? Or are you wearing it for me?" he asks.

"Easy there, Ego. Not everything is about you," I tell him, eyebrows raised.

"I meant, are you wearing it because you want to, because you like it? Or are you wearing it to appease someone else?" When I don't say anything, it gives him the answer he needs. "Take it off," he growls.

Happily, I think. I'm ready to breathe a little easier outside of this contraption, but pulling off shapewear qualifies as the world's most ungraceful task. When I hesitate, he grows impatient.

"You're either taking that off in the next ten seconds, or I'm ripping it off you–literally, ripping it."

I stare at him, but the hard glare he gives me in response lets me know he's serious. Hooking my thumbs near the top, I shimmy it down my torso, stretching and pulling and huffing and tugging before finally letting it drop to pool at my feet next to my dress.

"There she is. My beautiful girl." Asher's voice is soft, almost reverent. I briefly wonder how much he's had to drink if he's saying things like this.

Later, when we're sitting on the couch in comfortable clothing, brownie plates containing nothing but crumbs, Asher revisits the topic.

"I don't like you hiding yourself or changing yourself because you feel like you have to do so to fit in." I roll my eyes and give him a flippant remark about him not being the boss of me, but inside, a small flame flickers.

With his words, his genuine demeanor, and his constant, affirming presence, Asher is slowly healing the insecure little girl inside me.

"I'm mostly confident in my body. I'm not the same awkward, self-conscious teenager you once knew," I tease, but Asher's face is serious.

"Yeah," he agrees, tucking a strand of hair behind my ear. "OG June was great, but June 2.0? Unstoppable."

It's an odd compliment to make me blush, but it does. I spent years wondering what it would be like to be on the receiving end of Asher's attention, his compliments, but nothing could have prepared me for the full body glow it elicits.

CHAPTER THIRTY-SIX
Asher

June's face shuttered a bit when I told her I didn't like her wearing that deathtrap that was almost certainly squeezing the air out of her lungs. Sure, she looked fantastic tonight in her pretty blue dress, but she looked just as fantastic standing naked in my kitchen.

I'm not an idiot. I know June was uncomfortable with her body in high school, but weren't we all? I've always been on the lankier side, and it took me years to grow into my limbs, resulting in an awkward, gangly look for much of my high school tenure. Being raised by a single mother, though, I'm somewhat more aware of the societal pressures on women, because my mother made a point to inform me of them. I wasn't lying when I said I didn't like June wearing it just to conform to what society thinks her body should look like; if she wanted to wear it because she liked it, great. But her lack of response told me she wasn't doing it for herself. Still, she's apparently not done arguing about it.

"But you can't tell me that the dress looks better without shapewear. I know we're not dating or anything, but your type can't be lumpy and bumpy compared to smooth, even if there is a bit of softness."

"Type? I don't have a type," I tell her truthfully.

She gives me a deadpan look. "Everyone has a type."

How do I explain to this woman that my type is just her? It's not her perfect face, her sexy curves, her dangerous freckles…those features could show up on any woman, and they wouldn't do it for me. I don't have a type; I just have *her*.

All-encompassing her. All the particles, the tiny atoms that somehow collide and form the perfection that is June Demoranville. There's no replicating the perfection. There's June, and then there's every other woman. How could I possibly have a type, knowing June exists and every other woman is not her?

I don't know how to say any of that, though. At least, not without totally freaking her out and sending her running for the hills. So instead, I just silently shake my head, unwilling to push the argument further.

She's quiet, poking at the crumbs on her plate, nudging them around instead of looking at me when she speaks next. Her words are quiet, almost as if she's talking to herself, and maybe she is.

"It's just hard sometimes for the bigger girls to get the win."

I want to pull her into my lap and hold her, remind her of how perfect she is, tell her that I find her absolutely sexy, but I don't know if it's my place to do any of those things. Let's face it, the lines are so blurred between us these days that I hardly know the right thing to say or not. I kiss June freely in the privacy of our apartment, but that's typically because it leads to sex. Do I have any right to hold her in an attempt to comfort her? I wouldn't have done it before we started hooking up; what makes me think I have the right to do so now?

What I do know is a safe topic, though, is sex. This is hardly the time to bring up sex, but maybe that's what June needs to hear to convince her that her body is as sexy as I find it.

"Junie, do you remember the first night of our agreement? When you showed me...how you liked it?" In the bedroom nowadays, I can dirty talk with the best of them, but out here? In normal conversation? I'm still awkward.

"Yeah..." June's tone is suspicious.

"You were so sexy. Your body is so incredible. And I'm so sorry I ran out on you right away after you finished." She huffs a laugh. "I don't know if you know this, but the reason I ran out is because right when you finished...I did, too."

She side-eyes me, but I can see the exact moment my words sink in.

"Wait. Did you..." She looks pointedly at my lap, as if there would still be evidence, all these weeks later.

"Come in my pants like an overexcited teenage boy? Yes, June. I did. Because of you and your banging body." I run a hand down her arm because that seems like the safest place to touch her without making myself look like a total pervert.

Her smile is soft and small, but I have the pleasure of watching in real time as it slowly takes over her face until she bursts into giggles. I take her brownie plate away as she bends forward, doubled over in laughter.

"Laugh it up, June," I tell her, but there's no bite behind my words. I'll take this girl laughing at my expense any day if it gets her to forget about her misplaced self-consciousness. I poke her in the ribs and she squeals, trying to get away from me. She attempts to tickle me back, but she's forgotten I have the reflexes of a professional athlete, and in no time, I have her pinned beneath me on the couch, begging for mercy as my fingers dig into her soft, perfect sides. When I finally relent, we're both winded and panting. I gently brush the loose strands of her hair out of her eyes.

I can't help but stare into the pools of deep blue. I don't get intimate moments like this all the time with June, and I want to soak it up as much as I can. Yes, we've been having a lot of sex, but these small, intimate moments are more important to me. It's when I feel the most connected to her, and I don't even care that the thought makes me sound like a complete sap. I've been a complete sap for June since I was seventeen; I'm used to it now. So, I allow myself to look, to get lost in her eyes, to count the freckles across the bridge of her nose. She traps her bottom lip between her teeth and I'm hit with a sudden, intense wave of nostalgia.

Gently, I use my thumb to tug her lip free, and just as she did so many years and again a few weeks ago, June inhales a sharp breath.

"You probably don't remember–" she starts, her voice barely a whisper. "You did that right before you kissed me for the first time."

I make sure I'm looking June directly in the eyes as I tell her one of my deepest truths.

"I remember everything."

Chapter Thirty-Seven
Asher

Over the last few weeks, since the night of JJ's event, I've slowly been letting a bit of my guard down when it comes to June and my feelings toward her. It's freeing and terrifying all at the same time. A part of me wants to lay it all out there for her, to tell her I've been in love with her since I was seventeen, and another, equally intense part of me wants to lock that information away forever, certain she would never reciprocate the feelings.

I can't stop thinking about her though. Little things remind me of her when I'm on the road. When I was in Kansas City and the team toured a distillery on our off day, I couldn't resist buying her a dark green shirt with juniper leaves and berries on it. I left it for her on her bed the week before her birthday, immediately before we left on another road trip. I played it off like it was a birthday gift and not something I bought her because I couldn't stand the thought of not doing something for her while I was gone. I made my note as nonchalant and unattached as possible. *A few of us visited a local distillery in Kansas City. I saw this and thought of you. Happy birthday.* She was grateful and seemed surprised that

I'd remember her favorite cocktail was a gin and tonic. As if I could forget a single detail about her.

I can't hide what I'm sure is the longing on my face when it comes to June. If Crawford was able to pick up on it before ever having met her, I'm sure I'm doing a shit job of hiding it when I'm alone with her. She hasn't said anything directly to make me think she knows the depth or longevity of my feelings, but little comments here and there make me think she might be trying to let me down easy.

Like when I told her I wasn't interested in dating random women and she told me that I'm probably just loyal to her because I lost my virginity to her. That maybe sleeping with her for the first time made me confused. She said it in a casual, flippant way, but it pissed me off nonetheless. I'm not confused about June. I'm anything *but* confused about how I feel about her. But telling her that would require me to tell her exactly what my feelings toward her *are*, and I'm still too scared to do that.

It's not only because it would likely cause June to move out and spill the beans about everything to Devin (and even if she didn't tell him, I have a sneaking suspicion he'd find out anyway, eventually, if things go south between June and me). June is finally in a stable, happy place with a job she likes and, from what I hear from my teammates with partners, a job she's incredibly good at. It would be selfish of me to rock that boat.

I don't know much about June's previous job. I know it was her first out of college and it was in Tampa. I know that she was there for about a year and a half before it somehow ended in a "disaster." Or at least that's how Devin described it.

So when June came home from work tonight gushing about her idea for WAGs yoga in the park and how much she loves this job compared to her previous one, I finally had a way to ask her about it without hopefully coming off like a total jerk.

"June, whatever happened with your last job? All Dev told me was that it ended badly."

"Ugh, that place was a hellhole." When I don't let her off the hook with that explanation, she takes a fortifying breath, coming to sit next to me on the couch. She tucks her legs underneath her and pulls her hair over her shoulder, fiddling with the ends of her braid. I wait patiently for her to find her words.

"Honestly, it was my dream job for most of the time I worked there. It was this psychology clinic that did evaluations for kids with disabilities, and I was the care coordinator. That meant that I got to do a lot of the fun, relationship-building things after the children received their diagnoses. I helped to connect them with community resources and local therapists. We planned a lot of social events, too, as a way for families to connect with one another and find support in the community. I organized a lot of charity events, too. It was good work that I really believed in."

I smile; it sounds exactly like the kind of dream job she would seek.

"It was good. I even started dating Trevor, one of the office admin assistants. We had been flirting for a long time, and when he finally asked me on a date, I was ecstatic. I never thought I'd be interested in dating a coworker, but I'm telling you, this job was just so great, and Trevor was fun, so I didn't really see a downside. The pay was incredible, too. I was able to afford my own apartment without needing a roommate. I should have known everything was too good to be true."

I watch as her face darkens, hating whatever is about to come next.

"I stayed late one night, which wasn't that uncommon for me. I didn't mind putting in longer hours because I believed in the work, you know? So, if a family couldn't make it in to meet with me until after hours or on the weekend, it never bothered me to stay late or come in on a day off, if that's what they needed." She takes a deep breath. Her words take on a rapid quality, as if she's trying to rip the bandage off and say the next part as quickly as possible.

"Anyway, I was there late, and the clinic owner was there, talking to the CFO and Trevor in the front office. They were saying a lot of things that I didn't understand about billing codes, but I never worked on the insurance end of things, so it didn't raise any red flags at first. But then the owner's voice kept getting shriller, more panicked, so it was kind of hard not to listen. And she, Trevor, and the CFO were basically talking about how to commit massive insurance fraud, billing for services they never provided, like counseling. The people that worked in the office were psychologists, but they just did evaluations, not therapy. The owner was talking about billing people for sometimes two or three more evaluation sessions than what they attended, billing for testing that was never conducted, and all sorts of fraudulent charges that would allow them to bring in a lot more money to the clinic.

"For a long time, I stood there frozen, unsure what I was really hearing. My job was amazing. My coworkers were amazing. *Trevor* was amazing, and he was a part of this? I didn't trust what I was hearing. I figured there had to be something I was missing, or something I just didn't understand, because I'm not a psychologist and I've never worked with insurance before. So, for a couple weeks, I did nothing. I pretended I hadn't heard anything, that I wasn't even there that night. The guilt and anxiety ate me alive, until I finally broke down one night and asked Trevor about it.

"He was so angry when I asked about it. He made me feel so stupid, asking the questions that I did. He told me I had no business asking about things I didn't understand."

I ball my fists, wishing Trevor were here so I could show him what I think of him.

"Looking back, I realize he was only angry because he was scared he got caught, because there was something certainly unethical, probably illegal, going on in the office. But it called into question everything I thought I knew. I thought I had the perfect job, that I was helping to make a difference for so many families." At the look on my face, she adds, "I know, I'm sure I was making a difference. But that's not everything." She sighs deeply.

"I couldn't just sit with that knowledge. I met with one family that told me they ended up paying for their evaluation out-of-pocket because their deductible was so high, and even paying the thousands of dollars in cash for the evaluation was preferable to increased insurance premiums. And all I could think was, did they charge this family double or triple as well? It broke my heart. I couldn't keep coming into work, complicit in the knowledge that what they were doing was so *wrong*.

"I placed an anonymous call to the state licensing board, which determined an investigation was warranted. I basically became a whistleblower against my own clinic." I want to pull June into my lap and tell her how proud of her I am. What she did took so much courage, so much mental fortitude, and it was unquestionably the right thing to do. Before I can do any of that, she continues.

"The clinic got shut down while the investigation was ongoing, because they immediately found cases of fraud or wrongdoing, or something bad enough to warrant shutting it down at least temporarily. So many people I considered my friends lost their jobs. Because of me. Not to mention the countless families in the community who could no longer get the evaluations and diagnoses they needed to get their children necessary services."

I watch as a slow tear trickles down her cheek. Her fidgeting with her braid is becoming frantic. She's looking at her fingers, but I'm not sure she's really seeing them. Gently, I pull her hands into mine.

"It's not your fault, you know." She startles, as if that's the first time anyone has told her this.

"But I benefited from their fraudulent practices. I had a great salary because they stole from the insurance companies and families with disabled children. They took advantage of vulnerable populations, and I helped them."

"Stop. You did not." I'm not willing to hear her self-blame because even I, so far removed from the situation, can so obviously tell that it is misplaced. "The clinic owners made their choices. It's *those* choices that lost people their jobs, that didn't help families in the community, not yours. You stopped families from being taken advantage of."

The tears are rolling down June's cheeks now and I couldn't stop them if I tried. It's odd, seeing her like this. I've never seen her as anything other than confident, so fully herself. The contradiction here, as she sits quietly crying on my couch, is jarring.

I already hated where the story was going before she said a word, because I hated what it was doing to her body language. Her shoulders slump and curve forward, almost like she's folding in on herself. No longer content to fidget with her braid, her fingers toy with the hem of her tee.

I link my fingers with hers, anchoring myself to her. If she's going to fold in on herself, she's going to have to take me with her.

It takes a long time for June to settle after she divulges her work history to me. She cries for a little bit, but for a long time, she sits silently on the couch, lost in her own thoughts. When the sun sinks below the horizon, she doesn't stop me from scooping her up and taking her to my bedroom. She doesn't fight me when I undress her and pull her body into mine underneath the covers. And she doesn't leave my bed when we don't have sex, curling into me and staying the whole night.

CHAPTER THIRTY-EIGHT
Asher

June
> Hey, I'm running out to book club. If you get home in the next little bit, be careful. I just mopped the floors, so they might be wet.

Me
> Why are you mopping the floors?

> It rained this morning and I tracked a bit of mud in. Don't slip and crack your head open.

> I'd have to fill out so much paperwork for the landlord. And then I'd have to re-mop.

> Cute.

> Have fun at book club. Can't wait to see my face in the reflection of our shiny floors.

> So shiny you could eat off them.

I made it home about an hour after June texted me, our flight having been slightly delayed due to the earlier rain. I took my shoes off outside our apartment so as not to ruin her cleaning. I'm glad she was able to make it to book club; with our nontraditional work schedules, she doesn't make it every week, but when she goes, she comes back in a good mood. I'm happy for her, and not just because she usually comes home from book club horny as fuck; she loves meeting new people and is starting to make friends. She's always been outgoing and good at making friends, but after what she told me the other week about her old job and losing the friends she made at the clinic, her friendships here have taken on a new level of importance for me.

I'm sitting on the couch, reading the mafia romance she finished last week and lent to me when I hear her unlock the front door. She's started tabbing the book for the scenes she is interested in "practicing." At this point, neither of us needs any help in the bedroom, but the practice has been fun nonetheless. Whenever she recommends a new book to me, I flip to the tabbed scenes first before opening to chapter one.

She's a little flustered, the wind having picked up in the last few minutes. I'm sure we're in for more rain later tonight. She shuts and locks the door behind her, toeing off her adorable galoshes adorned with yellow ducks. June flashes me her bright smile, her eyes turning hooded when she sees me sitting on the couch without a shirt on. This girl is the biggest ego boost.

"Hey, how was book club?" I ask innocently, as if I don't know the kind of thoughts running through her mind right now. She starts to walk toward me, but I hold my hand up to stop her. She pauses, a little confused, but answers anyway.

"It was good. We're going to be discussing that book in two weeks." She points to the book in my hand, where I've conveniently left it open to one of her tabbed pages.

"Mm," I acknowledge. "Maybe I should refresh your memory on the chapter I was just reading." June's face morphs from confused to flirtatious, but she doesn't move from her position at the door.

"You probably should."

"I just finished reading a good one. It's the part where Amelia is caught leaving Dante's house, not knowing just how much she needs his protection. He rescues her and brings her back to his study." June's chest rapidly rises and falls, telling me she needs no refresher on the content of this particular chapter. "Do you remember what happens next?"

June pulls in a shallow breath, but her answering response is clear, confident. "Dante makes her crawl naked to him." A slight flush graces June's chest and cheeks, a beautiful, rosy shade. I nod, closing the book.

"It's interesting, June. You've left that page marked for me on the same day you make a point to tell me you've mopped the floors." I raise my eyebrows at her, but she gives away nothing. It could very well be a coincidence; the weather really is terrible. But it also could have been an intentional choice on her part, and if it was, who am I to stop her little fantasies?

"What a strange coincidence." This time June's voice comes out breathy.

I recline further in my seat, setting the book aside. I discreetly try to wipe my sweaty palms on my shorts; I'd be lying if I said reading the scene myself didn't work me up a bit as well.

"Junie," I croak. "Take off your clothes and crawl to me." It's a risk, asking her to do something like this. We've played around with rough sex and slow sex. We've hooked up more times than I can count, but this seems to have an intensity to it that our other sessions lacked. I don't know if it's my dominance, or her immediate submission, or something entirely different that I haven't even considered.

I'm in awe as she slowly pulls her tee, emblazoned with something quirky that I don't even register, over her head. She drops it unceremoniously at her feet while shaking out her hair. I barely remember to breathe as she shimmies her pink shorts down her legs, followed by her black thong. Reaching behind her, she slowly unclasps her bra, her breasts spilling out as I grow impossibly harder in my shorts.

Without a word, she sinks to her knees. Her heavy breasts hang low as she starts to move toward me, hips swaying with each movement. I lick my lips and June catches the action, mirroring the movement of my tongue with her own. I sprawl on the couch like a king, but if she takes a second to consider things, she'd realize that I'm the one worshiping her.

At times, I catch myself, amazed that I'm so comfortable with June. We weren't living together long before we started hooking up, and we weren't hooking up long before we moved to sex. I wouldn't change any of it for the world, but as someone who has dragged their feet about jumping into bed with a woman, it is a little surprising. But to me, it makes perfect sense.

I avoided dating women in college and after because I didn't want to constantly second-guess their intentions. Don't get me wrong–I've wanted to date. I felt heaven when I kissed June in her parents' kitchen when I was eighteen years old and I've been chasing that high ever since. It's my lack of trusting others that's always gotten in my way. But June isn't interested in me for my connections, my fame, or my money. She could technically get all of that from her brother.

But there's a lot she can get from me that her brother can't give her.

As shaky as my confidence with women generally is, I *know* there's no one who will treat June better than I can. Because she might be crawling to me, but that's only because *she* allows it, because she wants this the same way I want it. And if she asked me to, I'd crawl over broken glass to the ends of the earth for her.

June slinks over to me, coming to kneel between my sprawled legs. She runs her hands over my tensed quads. My muscles are coiled and taut, as if I'm holding myself together with muscle tension alone, waiting for her to make her move. She licks her lips and I release a groan.

"You look so fucking beautiful, Junie. I don't know what I'm going to do with you," I praise.

"You should probably figure it out," she taunts. I reach forward, lightly grasping her throat. Her eyes darken immediately in response.

"Get up here." I tug upwards once on her neck, and she follows my command. "Sit on my face so I can appreciate you properly." She hesitates as I slide myself to a lying position. "June Demoranville, get over her and sit. I want to taste you. I need your cum on my tongue."

"Are you sure?" Her voice is a tentative squeak.

"I've never been so sure of anything in my life." I'm fully reclined, but my knees are bent. It's the only way I fit on this couch lying down, but as long as I'm enjoying June, I don't care about my own comfort.

She swings a leg up and over my shoulder, propping herself up by the foot still on the floor. I reach my arm around her thigh and scoop her fully onto the couch. She hovers above me, a few inches away from where I need her. I sigh.

"June, sit." She hesitates again. I'd feel more impatient if I didn't know this goes back to her self-consciousness about her perfect body. My tone softens. "Please sit down, baby."

"I don't want to suffocate you." I want to laugh, but June is too vulnerable to risk her misinterpreting my amusement.

"First of all, what a fucking way to go out. I'd happily suffocate between these thighs," I say, jiggling the backs of her legs. "But you're not going to suffocate me, I promise." I tug her closer. She lowers herself an inch, but it's still too far away from me. I lift my head and drag my tongue through her center, relishing the noises she makes. She pitches slightly forward and catches herself with an arm on the back of the couch. Her hips, however, stay locked in place.

It doesn't bother me. I know June is fighting years of conditioning that has told her her body is somehow–ridiculously–inadequate when in reality, it couldn't be sexier. Now is not the time to try to change her mind. I'm not naive enough to think that just because I tell her once to sit on my face, years of self-consciousness will disappear. But I'm not a man easily deterred and if June isn't convinced of how much I love her body just yet, that's okay. I'm willing to spend the rest of my life convincing her just how much I treasure all parts of her.

I reach my arm behind me and grab a throw pillow. Wedging it under my neck, it brings my head up a few more inches. June can hold herself up all she wants, but in this position, her pussy is pressed against my mouth, and I finally have her where I need her. I take another long lick before sealing my mouth against her, swirling my tongue through her folds. She's so wet and tastes so sweet, I really wouldn't mind suffocating like this. Or drowning.

June moans above me as my tongue flicks against her clit. From underneath her, my fingers slide into her entrance. I curl them, tapping against her front wall in time with my tongue.

"Asher!" June's cry is sharp as she clenches around my fingers. I groan at the sensation as my dick hardens and my hips buck against nothing. I love her sounds. We've already established I can come without her touching me, just from watching her come undone, but I stave off my release for now. I pull her swollen clit between my lips, rolling and nibbling at it as she pants above me. My fingers continue tapping out a rhythm against her G-spot.

"Ash, please!"

I fucking *love* when June begs. I love all her sounds, but when she gets to the point of nonsensical begging, it's my own personal version of heaven. I double down on my efforts as she chants my name above me. I'll never get tired of hearing the myriad ways she says my name, but the repetitive, frantic chanting of it as I bring her to the brink is my favorite. The pillow is supporting my head and neck, but I lift my head a centimeter further, burying my face in her cunt as I hum, knowing the vibrations will push her over the edge.

"Ash!" June's scream is loud, her hips bucking against my face and her fingers tugging my hair painfully, but I fucking love it.

Gone is all her self-consciousness as she rides out her pleasure and soaks my face.

"Fuck yes, Junie. Take it. Drench me," I urge. She falls forward in pleasure, supporting herself on the arm of the couch behind my head, breathless and sated. I slow my swirling tongue as I gently pull my fingers from her. She does a slow roll off me and onto her knees on the rug before the couch. She buries her face in the couch cushions as she slowly comes back to earth. I sit up, pulling my fingers from my mouth where I've sucked off her release. I can't get enough of this girl; I'll take every drop she gives me. I scoop her up and place her on the couch, where she curls into me, almost automatically. I shouldn't read too much into this post-orgasm snuggle, but I can't help it. There's something so comforting, emotionally and physically, in the way June lets me hold her like this. I feel both strong and gentle, with both arms wrapped around her.

Later, after another round of mind-blowing sex, followed by leftover brownies (coconut caramel), June surprises me by bringing up my whispered *Juniper* the first time we had sex. I freeze, unsure how to respond. I don't exactly want to lie and tell her I didn't say it, because I did. But I'm also not ready to explain myself.

"You caught that, huh?" I decide for lighthearted, playful.

"Yes. You know my name isn't short for Juniper, right?" The confusion and consternation on her face have me feeling guilty. I hate that she thinks I don't know her name. Or worse, that I do, but I called someone else's name in the throes of passion.

"I know it's not, Junie. I promise, it's not because I don't know your name, or because I was thinking of someone else. That's all I can tell you right now, though. Please don't ask me why. I'm not ready to explain."

June looks at me for a long time, expression inscrutable. There's no judgment or malice, not even confusion. It's almost as if she's considering how serious I am. I guess it could be because I've never not given her everything she's asked for, whether it's been an answer to a question or a place to live. A part of me feels terrible for not giving her a response, but another, larger, louder part of me recognizes my own need for self-preservation. After a few moments, she nods her head once, indicating the subject is closed, and I breathe out a sigh of relief.

CHAPTER THIRTY-NINE

June

Asher wanted boundaries between us when we started this whole thing. He made me promise that I wouldn't look at him differently when this was all over. Unfortunately, that's a promise I'm afraid I've already broken. While I don't judge him or look down on him after all I've learned about him, I view him differently than when we started. Or maybe I view him the same as I always have, but haven't allowed myself to acknowledge it.

The fact that he's not willing to share every bit of himself is a completely appropriate response; we moved into this thing with no expectation of deepening our emotional attachment to each other. But my reaction to his boundary is what scares me. I feel sad, disappointed even, that he didn't explain the Juniper thing. I can also recognize that that is a wholly disproportionate reaction on my end. I've always been okay with boundaries, so why am I suddenly sad that he's erected one between us?

Oh.

That's right.

It's because as much as I try to hide the effect he has on me–the effect Asher has *always* had on me–it's an impossible task. The number of times in high school that I convinced myself that I no longer had feelings for him is too high to count. Because every time I talked myself out of my feelings, Asher had to go and do something stupid, like pitch a great game, or strum some chords on a guitar, or *smile* at me, and I'd be right back at square one.

I'm not sure what I was thinking, agreeing to this hookup situation with my brother's best friend. At this point, Asher is obviously my friend, too, and honestly, he was my friend in high school, too. But creating an awkward situation by introducing sex to a friendship is one thing; blurring the lines when multiple relationships are involved? I'm not sure what sort of hubris I was experiencing to think I could handle this.

My feelings for Asher hit me this past week while he was on his road trip, but if I'm really being honest with myself, they've been growing since I moved in with him, I've just been experiencing a clinical case of denial. All this past week, I found myself wondering what he was doing when he wasn't at the ballpark. If he was thinking of me when he wasn't texting me (which, admittedly, was a decent amount). If he was reading my tabbed chapters of the romance novel I lent him. If he was eating the brownies I know are available in just about every clubhouse and wondering if they're as good as the ones I make him. I realized I really was in trouble, though, when I found myself wanting to sleep in his bed, just to smell him while he was gone.

I didn't.

Obviously.

Because that would be literally insane. But the thought, the desire, was still there. And those are not the thoughts that a roommate or even a friend with benefits should be having.

I tried to talk to Faye about it, thinking that if I slipped up, and she discovered my roommate was a Foxes player, that I could invoke some sort of attorney-client privilege to save my own skin. I didn't slip up, but Faye's advice to me was the same as it was a few weeks ago at the bar: live it up, fuck your roommate, and take no prisoners. YOLO, essentially.

It wasn't exactly helpful, but it was the straw that broke the camel's back that made me realize my feelings for Asher have spun out of control. It made me realize that sex with Asher was beginning to feel less like fucking, less like scratching an itch, and more like making love. And despite how we started, I now view him through the undeniable lens of love.

That's not what he signed up for. It's not what *I* signed up for, either, but here we are. Perhaps it was naive of me to think my old feelings wouldn't resurface. If I am really being honest with myself, I considered it a possibility when the opportunity first arose, but my reckless heart jumped in with both feet, because it's *Asher*. I've had a weak spot for him for almost half of my life.

Now, instead of taking everything at face value, I'm reading into everything he says and does. He cooked dinner tonight? What does his selection of chicken parmigiana *mean*? He told me he didn't feel like going out after the game with Crawford, despite the invitation. Does that mean he'd rather spend time hanging out with me instead?

I'm annoyed by myself.

Which is a sign that I'm in too deep, and it's not fair to either of us. It's not fair to Devin either, and he doesn't even know he's *in* a situation with us. I can no longer ignore Asher's effect on me. A quick brush of his body against mine as he squeezes behind me to get to the fridge causes goosebumps to rise on my skin. A welcoming smile as he walks through the front door has butterflies erupting in my belly. Asher telling me he's not traveling for the midseason break, and instead spending his time here in Chicago, golfing with a few teammates and hanging out, causes me to think maybe it's because what he really, secretly, means is that he wants to be with me instead of literally anywhere else.

I'm in trouble.

Asher is on a road trip now, his last one before the midseason break. For me, the schedule works out great, because it means more days off. The extra days give me time to think, but what I need isn't time; it's a new heart. Possibly a new brain that doesn't offer devastatingly handsome pitchers opportunities to learn to get better at sex.

I check my bank balance for the third time this week, hoping somehow I've become independently wealthy overnight. I'm in a better financial position than I was when I first moved to Chicago (hello, free rent), but from my online sleuthing, I can tell the limited financial wiggle room I've gained isn't going to be enough to afford me a decent place to live.

As much as I want to move out and pretend all of this never happened, I know that's not realistic. I love my job. I love living with Asher. The only thing I don't love is the ache in my chest when I crawl out of Asher's bed each night he's home, wishing he would stop me, beg me to stay, say or do anything other than let me creep back into my own room once the fun is over.

I know the only logical conclusion is the one we agreed upon from the start. The only real rule we put in place was communication. At the beginning, we agreed that if one of us no longer wanted to do this anymore, for any reason, we would stop. As much as it's going to break my heart, I need to ask Asher for an out from our current situation.

It might break my heart to ask for it, but it will hurt even more if I don't.

Chapter Forty
June

Today is the day. Asher came home around eight o'clock last night, which was plenty early for me to have the conversation with him, but instead, I chickened out and hid in my room, pretending to have fallen asleep early.

I can't remember the last time I fell asleep at eight o'clock, but Asher didn't question me. He didn't knock on my door to tell me he was home, although I swore I felt his presence on the opposite side of my bedroom door. Even I know that's wishful thinking, though. My cowardice, Asher's lack of interaction with me last night, and my desire for him to behave otherwise all confirm what I already know. It's time to put on my big girl panties and tell Asher I can't do this anymore.

When I step outside of my bedroom, my favorite mug is filled with fresh coffee, steaming and sitting on the kitchen counter. My favorite person leans against the kitchen counter as well. My first thought is that I can't tell which is hotter: my roommate or my coffee. Shaking my head to remind myself those are not the kinds of thoughts I need running through my head right now, I step into the kitchen. Asher greets me with a sweet smile, and I catalogue the tilt of his lips, knowing all the while it shows his blissful ignorance of my true feelings.

"Morning," he greets. It's a totally normal, non-romantic greeting, but still, the butterflies take flight.

Enough.

I clear my throat. "Morning. How was St. Louis?"

"Hotter than Satan's asshole, but that's St. Louis in July for you. How was your weekend?"

"Good." I give him a half-truth, because I can't tell him I got a lot of work done, read an amazing book, finished my lopsided cactus project, and spent the rest of the time missing him.

"Hey, I was thinking, since I've got some time this week, maybe you'd want to check out the beach or something? Crawford and I are golfing on Wednesday, but I don't really have any other plans for the break. I mean, if you're not busy or anything."

I swallow. My heart wants nothing more than to go to the beach with Asher and pretend to have a good time. My head knows that's not a good idea. Extra time with him, when my heart is so tender and fragile, is only going to hurt more when I am inevitably reminded, once again, that while Asher and I are sleeping together, I'm not really his, and he's not really mine.

It's time to rip the bandage off.

"Hey Ash?" He sets his coffee down, sensing my serious tone. I clear my suddenly dry throat. I take a deep breath. "Remember when we started all this?" I wave my hand back and forth between the two of us, as if that could fully encompass all that we've been doing the last few months. "We said we could stop anytime. That either of us could just say the word, and we would stop."

Asher's face softens immediately. Oh god, he's going to be nice about this. If he were annoyed, or outwardly disappointed, I could handle it better. What I can't handle is Asher being sweet.

"Yeah, June. I remember." His words are soft, but the smile he gives me is genuine. "You don't have to say anything more. It's done. No hard feelings."

Just like that, it's done.

I wish it were that simple, but I'll take the out he offers me. Because of course he's being sweet about the whole thing when I need him to be a dick. It'd make it easier for me somehow.

"We could have always stopped, whenever you wanted. I'd never force you to do anything you didn't totally feel comfortable with. But can I ask one thing?" His voice is pleading, so I nod, hoping he's not going to ask me why. "Did I do something wrong?"

Oh.

My eyes fill with tears. Of course he's being so considerate of me right now. It's Asher. He's never not looked out for me. He must see the emotions swimming in my eyes.

"Hey," he coos. "It's okay. I'm so sorry for whatever I did."

He stands in front of me, rubbing my arms in a comforting gesture that makes me fall even more. This is why you don't get involved with a man like Asher. You'll never get out alive.

"Tell me," he insists.

"It's nothing," I lie. "I just think it would be for the best. I promise you did nothing wrong." At least the last part is truthful.

"Your face tells a different story, Junebug."

Maybe it's the way he uses my dad's childhood nickname for me, or it's the sincerity in his eyes, the way he's looking at me so earnestly, that I want to tell him the truth.

I take a deep breath, knowing that as soon as I tell him my truth, I'll need to start looking for a new place to live. Maybe even a new job.

"Ash." My voice breaks. He pulls me to his chest. I take in a shaky breath, trying to pull in air without breathing in the comforting scent of him.

"I'm sorry, baby. Whatever I did, please tell me so I can fix it." He presses a kiss to the crown of my head, and I know now I have no choice but to spill my guts. I can't have him feeling guilty, like this was somehow his fault.

"You didn't do anything, Ash. I just…can't help my feelings. I'm so sorry. This was just supposed to be an arrangement and my feelings got tangled up and it's not fair to either of us."

Asher's chest expands on a rapid inhale. "What are you saying, June?"

I shake my head against his chest, savoring this moment, knowing it will be the last time he holds me like this. The last time I get the privilege of holding him in return.

"Junie. Please. Tell me–*exactly*–what you're saying." It's his turn for his voice to crack. I know it's because he's worried what Dev will say if he finds out I'm moving. I press my face further into his warm body, unwilling to look him in the eyes as my heart breaks.

"I'm sorry, Ash. I ruined things. I can't keep doing this because…I have feelings for you."

The breath wooshes audibly out of him like a balloon.

"Juniper," he whispers, clutching me tightly. "Junie. My Juniper." He holds me tightly for a moment before pulling back. Confusion swirls around me. When he ducks his head to look into my eyes, mine aren't the only ones blanketed in emotion. I look away, sure he's about to break my heart.

"Look at me." I drag my eyes back to his. "I need you to look at me when I tell you that I have loved you since I was seventeen years old. I have been *in love* with you since then."

My brain grinds to a halt.

"What?"

"It's killed me to watch you date others, post your happy little pictures on social media, knowing I couldn't have you. And now you're telling me you finally feel the same way?"

A tear slips down his cheek. I catch it with my thumb before nodding, causing my own tears to spill over the lashes. He starts to laugh, a deep rumble forming in his chest, one that I feel in my own, pressed against him.

He picks me up, my legs automatically wrapping around his waist, as he walks with me to the couch, depositing both of us together on top of the soft cushions. I'm straddling his lap, but this moment is more intimate than sexual. I'm crying, but I know I haven't fully processed his words. He seems to sense this, because he starts explaining, his words punctuated by disbelieving sighs.

"I fell for you my senior year. I don't know how I didn't really notice you as more than a friend before then, because you were always there. This happy, glowing beacon, but I suddenly couldn't look away. There were these small moments when I'd look at you, and I'd swear you felt it too, but you were always so kind, so friendly, that I knew it was just that."

He shakes his head at himself, but I bring my hands to cup his cheeks, shaking my own head at him. Maybe at myself, too, for so much wasted time. He keeps talking.

"And then we had that kiss, in your kitchen, right after graduation. That was when I really thought you felt it too, but after that kiss, I hardly saw you. We never talked about it."

"You avoided me," I tell him quietly. "I would have talked about it if you bothered to bring it up, to come talk to me." Asher's head hits the back of the couch, his gaze on the ceiling.

"June, I wanted to so badly. But I was leaving for school, and Devin had always said that you deserved better than what anyone on the team could give you, and it was hard to argue with that. I felt so guilty for kissing you that I was convinced Devin almost catching us was a sign that what we did was wrong. I don't know how to explain it." I sit further back on his lap, taking him in. Emotions flicker across his face, one after another, as both of us replay our own memories, seeing them in a new light.

"Asher. I've had a crush on you since I was fifteen. Nine years ago, I would have done anything to hear you tell me you liked me, but you never did. So, I convinced myself to move on. It was so hard finding anyone who compared to you. When you kissed me for the first time, I thought I'd finally have what I always wanted. Until you pretty much stopped acknowledging me until I moved in here." I throw my hand out, displaying the room.

"I'm so sorry, June. I was a confused kid. I didn't know that I could ask for what I wanted when your brother was so adamant about us staying away from you. Plus, I was leaving! By the time I did something about my feelings, I was only sticking around for, like, six more weeks. You deserved better than that."

I glare at him, still holding his face between my palms. "I deserved to know how you really felt and to make my own decisions."

"You're right." Asher pauses, reminiscing. "But can you blame me? You were the most beautiful girl I'd ever seen, and I'd been told for years that you were off-limits. I didn't want to risk my friendship with Devin, and I know that's a shitty thing to say."

I want to be mad at him for choosing Dev over me, but I can't really blame him. One of the stipulations for our hooking up was that Devin could never find out—because I knew as well as

Asher that Devin wouldn't take the news of us having any sort of interaction beyond friendship well.

Devin's overprotectiveness has been little more than an annoyance in my life over the years, probably because I never liked anyone enough to have his overbearing nature really take hold. I've had boyfriends, dated frequently, even fallen in love a time or two. But Devin's grumbles about my love life never bothered me because I knew they were mostly empty threats. Even now, though, I'm not so sure.

"So, what now?" I ask, almost afraid of the answer. I was soaring so high, learning Asher finally reciprocates my feelings, but now that we've brought up my brother, I'm not sure my excitement is warranted.

"Kiss me, June. Kiss me because you want to, not because of some bullshit arrangement or because you think–"

The words aren't fully out of his mouth before my lips are on his. I woke up this morning thinking I'd never feel his comforting touch again, and now he's asking me to kiss him, to touch him, and to do it without the guise of our previous agreement. I'm tired of hesitating around Asher Incaudo. The man has occupied my thoughts for years; I'm no longer allowing either one of us to second-guess ourselves.

He kisses me back with equal enthusiasm, but that is nothing new for us. We've been passionate together and we've been sweet together. We convinced ourselves we moved in sync in the bedroom because of our hormones and not our emotions, when the reality is, we never could have taken our feelings out of the equation if we tried.

When we finally break away from each other, our foreheads touching and our lungs desperately sucking in oxygen, I can't help my giggle.

"We're so stupid. This whole time, our one rule was to communicate with each other, and if we'd done that? We would have saved so much time."

"Yeah, but this way is okay, too," Asher admits. "Baby, you've been living in my brain, my heart, rent-free for eight years. You were gonna be in there till long after you moved out of this apartment. Which," he adds, squeezing my sides and pulling me closer, "is never going to happen without me now."

"What are you saying though? Are we doing this? Dating?" I didn't allow myself to consider this possibility. I didn't account for this in my rehearsed speech or my weekend preparations. Asher has been unattainable for so long, I never truly considered he could be mine.

"There's got to be a better word than dating for what you are to me, Junie. But if there's only dating, then that's what we're doing."

"Oh, is it now? When did you get so bossy?" I tease. His eyes grow hooded.

"I seem to recall you like it when I'm a little bossy," he snarks back. A moment's hesitation, then his smile falters a bit. "Is this what you want?"

My sweet Asher.

"It is." I could have used hyperbolic language or even sarcasm in response to his question, but his vulnerability kills me. I don't know if it was years of hearing Devin's overprotective bullshit or his recently publicized dating reviews, but something has my normally confident roommate faltering, and I need him to know clearly, plainly, simply, that there is nothing more I could want than him. I kiss him softly, attempting to saturate my emotions, the years of longing for him, into it.

"And Devin?" He looks so goddamn hopeful as he asks the question, but I give him a deadpan stare.

"Are you really bringing up my brother while I'm on your lap, after you declared your love for me, and after I admitted I'm in love with you, too?"

Asher's eyes widen before they soften, a huge grin overtaking his face. "You love me, too?"

"Yeah, I kind of thought that was obvious." He stares at me, as if to say there was nothing less obvious in the world. I laugh. "I'm sorry. It's just so obvious to me that I assumed everyone knew." I grow serious. "Ash, I'm in love with you, and I have been since I was fifteen. I convinced myself I wasn't, but you have this way of wiggling back into my heart, even when I'm trying not to love you."

He laughs. "You're my Wendy Peffercorn. It's always been you," he admits, referring to our favorite childhood baseball movie.

Now it's my turn to laugh. "But I'm not older than you," I point out.

"Yeah, but you are off-limits. Or were off-limits. Unattainable. Till now."

I sigh. "We'll tell Devin. I can call him right now if you want, but I kind of would rather spend the night doing other things..." I give him a mischievous grin. "With my *boyfriend*."

"Hell yeah," he whispers against my lips.

Chapter Forty-One
Asher

I can't fully describe what it feels like to be loved by June. It's like waking up to bright, warm, automatic sunshine after months and months of cold darkness. Apparently, I've been loved by June for years, unbeknownst to me, but knowing about it? It's incredible. It's like the best drug, and one that I could get addicted to very, very quickly.

The only problem is her nonfraternization clause. I'm fairly fucking certain what we were doing before our love declarations would be frowned upon by the Foxes, but now that there's emotions attached, there's no question that what we're doing crosses that line. I want to say fuck it, the Foxes can deal with it, but I know it doesn't work like that. If the Foxes find out, June is getting fired, and after the way her last job ended, there's no way I'm entertaining that idea, despite my commitment to financially supporting her…well, forever. Because June *is* my forever. She may not realize just yet that's how deep my feelings go, but she'll understand eventually.

Still, June is amazing at her job and it gives her a sense of fulfillment that few people experience in their careers. I'm not going to be that asshole that rips it away just because I can't keep my mouth shut about how much I love her.

We agree to keep the relationship out of the public eye, for now. I'm following her lead on this one, because I recognize the status that comes with my position as a player with the Foxes. While I'm sure other Foxes employees can date each other relatively easily, as long as they notify human resources, I know they put those clauses in all contracts because they don't want the players to be harassed. Which is normally great, but June can harass me all day long. I love it when June harasses me.

We also agreed we'd tell Devin about our relationship first, but that we'd do it in person. The Mustangs are in town at the end of next month anyway. I would have offered for him to stay in our apartment instead of the team hotel, but there isn't really a way of communicating why we suddenly have a spare bedroom in the apartment without spilling the beans about June's nightly presence in my bed.

Yesterday, after consummating our admissions, we attempted to talk about things before getting sidetracked, now that we can kiss freely. Let's be honest, we were playing pretty fucking fast and loose with the rules beforehand, but now that I can kiss and touch June anytime I want, without needing a reason or some sort of excuse, we tend to fall into bed even more than we did before.

It's been incredible. And now that June is mine, all I want to do is show her off. But I'm a patient man. I've waited eight years for her to love me back; I can wait a few months to figure out what we're going to do about disclosing our relationship. Last year, I was close to being traded to the Mustangs right before the trade deadline. It would have been fun throwing to Devin as my catcher again, but I doubt I would have ended up with his sister in the same way if I had been. All that to say that I could get traded again this year, and maybe the clause would be a moot point, since I'd no longer be a Foxes player. Or maybe after a year, June would be okay leaving her job on her own terms or moving into a different role. Or any of a million other things could happen that we don't exactly have to worry about right now. Because right now, I've finally got the girl, and that's all I care about.

"Morning, sleepyhead," I greet as June walks out of my bedroom. Her hair is adorably sleep-mussed, and she has pillow lines on her cheek and chest. She's never looked more beautiful, more mine, than when she steps up to me and places a soft kiss against my lips. She goes to step away, but I pull her close, attempting to deepen the kiss. She pulls away, turning her head and covering her mouth when she speaks.

"Asher! I haven't brushed my teeth yet. I've got morning breath." She squirms with embarrassment.

"I don't care. I finally can kiss you whenever I want. Give me your morning breath, baby."

"Gross," she laughs, pushing off my chest, but when I cup the back of her head and pull her toward me once again, she doesn't fight it. My tongue plunges into her mouth, stroking hers as our hands roam each other's bodies once more. We spent most of last night doing just this, but I still can't get enough. June is pressed close enough to me that there's no doubt she feels my growing erection. Her hands glide down my torso and hook into my waistband. I gently stop their journey, grasping her wrists.

"Baby, ignore him," I say as my dick gives a defiant twitch. "I just want to enjoy this moment with you."

She hums happily into my mouth. I tangle my fingers further into her hair, savoring every second of the way her mouth feels on mine.

"Let me make you breakfast," I demand. She nods against me, pulling back to let me gather the ingredients. "And go brush your teeth, you have morning breath," I tell her playfully, swatting her ass as she laughs at me once more.

Spending the day with June as my girlfriend is somehow different from spending it together when we were hooking up as roommates, even if our activities are similar. After brunch, we hung out on the patio, soaking up the sunshine. She started a new knitting project, swearing she was going to get a jump on more winter gear by starting in July. I tinkered around with a few new songs on my acoustic guitar. We came inside to watch a movie when the sun became too much, but both of us ended up napping on the couch, June with her feet tucked into my lap.

"What do you want to do for dinner? I can order delivery, or I can make us something?" I offer. "What about carbonara?"

"Meh, there's something about eggs that makes me feel queasy today. Normally, I'm all in on that, but I'm not feeling it today."

We settle on burger delivery from a greasy spoon diner down the street. It's early in the evening, but an early dinner gives us plenty of time to relax before bed, and given how late we were up last night, an early night sounds okay to me.

"I don't know if we should be celebrating our new relationship with sex tonight," June says abruptly, shoving a fry into her mouth. She looks at my face, which must showcase the surprise I'm feeling, because she laughs. "My boobs have been so sore this past week. I'm pretty sure I'm starting my period.

"I don't mind a little extra lubrication," I tease with a wink. She puts her palm on my shoulder, giving me a gentle shove.

"Gross. I never should have agreed to have sex with you. I've created a monster." She rolls her eyes. I've enjoyed flirting with June this year, but there's something about the relaxed teasing we've been doing since disclosing our feelings that feels even more comfortable. "I should probably hit the grocery store tomorrow since I have the day off. I need to buy more tampons. I should see how many I have left."

As if she's afraid to forget to make a mental list, June pops another fry in her mouth and stands to go to the bathroom, presumably to check her supply.

The gooey cheese, paired with the not-so-secret burger sauce and a particularly soft slice of tomato, makes for a slippery mess of my dinner. I try to hold my burger together with both hands while attempting to discretely wipe my mouth against my fist. June only just agreed to date me; I don't need her regretting her decision not even twenty-four hours in because I eat like a mongrel. Giving up, I place the remnants of the sandwich on my plate, standing to get a fork and knife, when I see June frozen, halfway to the bathroom and a look of pure panic on her face.

Chapter Forty-Two
June

Oh no.

There's a reason why I don't remember the last time I bought tampons. Because I haven't in a really, really long time.

Oh no. Oh no. Oh no!

"What's wrong?" Asher freezes, halfway to lowering himself back onto the couch where we're eating, knife and fork in hand.

Breathe, June.

You're totally overreacting. You've been stressed about the new job.

Oh god, please don't do this to me right now. Not today.

I snatch my keys from the counter and shove my feet into my flip flops before sprinting from the apartment.

"June!" Asher yells before the door slams shut.

I take the stairs as quickly as I can, sliding a little bit on the second landing and forcing myself to slow down. No need to add an injury to the situation.

Above me, I can hear Asher curse as he fumbles to lock the door. My mad dash out of the building isn't really that fast. Asher's long strides eat up the distance between us in no time. I'm only two buildings down from ours when he catches up, spinning me around and crushing me to his chest.

"No, June. Whatever just made you panic, I want to know about it. I need to know. We do this together, you and me."

My eyes rapidly fill with tears and I clutch at him tightly, knowing he's going to regret that statement as soon as I tell him what I think is going on. He pulls back just enough to see the panic on my face. He cups my cheeks so tenderly. It breaks my heart a little bit.

"Juniper. Talk to me."

It's the use of that pet name, the one I still don't fully understand, that breaks me. I can't stop the tears from rolling down my cheeks.

"I haven't gotten my period in a really long time, Asher." I close my eyes, afraid to watch reality crash over his face. He nudges my cheek.

"Hey. Look at me." I open my eyes. "What do you mean, in a long time?"

He's going to make me say it. He's going to make me break his heart.

"How long, Junie?" He jostles me gently when I don't respond. "Say it," he whispers.

"I think I might be…pregnant."

CHAPTER FORTY-THREE
Asher

I watch the tears spill over June's lashes. They course down her cheeks and into my palms and at this moment, I know. I know I want to be the one to catch her tears for the rest of our lives. A part of me has always suspected that June was the one for me. That's why I stayed away for so long. Because she deserves someone perfect. And my best friend deserves someone who doesn't prey upon his sister.

For years, my biggest fear around sex has been getting a woman pregnant. It's why I avoided it for so long. The irony isn't lost on me that the first person I have sex with in my entire life now might be pregnant. The universe has a twisted sense of humor.

But instead of the rising panic I thought I would feel blooming in my chest when I envisioned this exact scenario, a wave of calm washes over me. It's June. And I know, as much as I am sure that I love her, that I will do whatever she wants to do in this situation. I'll support my girl.

And right now, my girl is scared. I crush her to my chest.

"It's okay, baby. We'll figure it out." I hold her like this, in the middle of the sidewalk, for a long time. Her tears soak my shirt as she clings to me while I stroke her hair and whisper reminders that I'm here, that I'll take care of her, that I've got her. After a few minutes, she straightens, wiping away her tears.

"Come here, beautiful girl." I kiss her tenderly, hoping to infuse my love and trust into every molecule behind the kiss.

"I need to know, Asher."

"Okay, then let's go find out."

We walk, hand in hand, to the pharmacy two blocks away. June is skittish and nervous in the family planning aisle, and I squeeze her hand in reassurance. There are several types of pregnancy tests, and I don't really know which one is best, so I throw a few different brands into the basket I grabbed when we walked in.

"Come on baby. Let's get you some ice cream." Tugging her to the frozen section, I watch as she makes her selection. Regardless of the outcome of the tests, we're going to need some sugary dessert to take the edge off.

"Do you want me to do the checkout without you?" June's voice is barely a whisper. I give her a quizzical look. "In case you get recognized."

"Nah, baby. I'm with you. In all senses of the word." I press a kiss to her temple. I take the route to the cashier through the snack aisle, tossing a few of June's favorites in the basket as I go. Cheeto Puffs, DOTS candy, sour gummies. I briefly debate a chocolate bar, then second-guess whether June should be having caffeine or not.

Fuck it. I'll eat it if she can't have it. I toss it in the basket and make my way to the cashier.

I don't know if the cashier takes pity on us, sensing June's obvious discomfort, but she bags up our groceries without any comment and hands them to us with a soft smile. I thank her before taking June's hand once again and walking her home.

Chapter Forty-Four
June

Never before has three minutes been so long. Asher created a little assembly line for us in the bathroom, lining up and unwrapping the seven (seven!) different pregnancy tests. I was skeptical about being able to pee long enough to use all seven, but I'm a nervous pee-er, which came in handy for once in my life. If the situation weren't so dire, I'd laugh at Asher's efficiency. As soon as I finished peeing on one stick, I'd hand it to him, and he'd swap it out for another. He'd cap it and set it on its box before prepping the next stick. Years of Kegel exercises also paid off, allowing me to stop mid-stream. I should probably be self-conscious, having Asher in the room while I pee on various sticks, but at this point, I want to throw up. I'm petrified, so having him around is helping me maintain the tiniest bit of sanity.

I can't wait in the bathroom, though. I want to take the tests and shake them like a Polaroid, hoping it will speed up the results. I doubt they work that way, but given the excess nervous energy zipping around my body, I'm tempted to try it anyway.

It's not just the fact that I could be pregnant that makes me want to throw up. Asher has been so vocal that his biggest fear around sex is that the woman gets pregnant, using him or getting stuck with him forever. And then I go and seduce him, the first woman he's ever slept with, and possibly get pregnant, confirming his worst fear.

I don't even want to think about what I'll do if I'm pregnant. The Foxes provide decent benefits, but I've never looked into their healthcare coverage for pregnancy. I don't know what their maternity leave looks like. I've never had to consider these things!

I pace the living room, waiting for the timer on Asher's phone to go off. He stands in the doorway of the bathroom, watching me. He's oddly calm, but they say there's a calm before the biggest storms, and I'm bracing myself for its impact.

I know it takes two people to get pregnant. I understand how sex and biology work, but somehow, I can't help but feel like this is more my fault than Asher's. Realistically, biologically, I know that's not true, but I can't help but feel like he should blame me. Like I tricked him into sex, allowing his worst fears to come to fruition.

The tinkling sound of his alarm pulls me from my thoughts. I know panic is written all over my face as the moment of truth is upon us.

"I can't look. I'm gonna be sick." In two strides, Asher is behind me, his strong arms wrapping around me and holding up my buckling knees.

"Breathe, Junie," he instructs gently. When I don't say anything, he gives me a soft squeeze. "Do you want to look together?"

"Can you just do it?" I whisper. I don't know if I can handle it.

"Yeah, baby. Of course I can."

I hate that I'm asking him to do it, for him to be the first one to find out. But I really, truly, can't get my feet to move.

He steps into the bathroom. I can hear the click of the plastic sticks against each other as he gathers them and turns, facing me from the threshold of the doorway.

Chapter Forty-Five
Asher

I'm not a gambler, but on the mound, I can access a hyperfocused place in my mind in order to convey a great poker face. I've watched enough game tape of myself to know that when I'm in that headspace, I look intense, but relatively emotionless. Once I get back to the dugout, I show more emotion, whether it's yelling and fist pumping in celebration, or gritting my teeth and seething in anger. It's that place of hyperfocus that I need to access right now.

I school my face into neutrality.

There's no world in which I let June see my true feelings about these test results. She's scared, that much is clear.

When I return to the living room, she is standing there, eyes squeezed shut. She peeks one open to peer at me but clearly can't read my expression. I usher her to the couch and sit her next to me.

"Just tell me." Her voice is hollow, devoid of emotion, bracing for the worst. I take in a deep breath.

"We're pregnant."

Chapter Forty-Six
Asher

The first night, June cried in my arms for hours. I'm fairly certain the initial tears were from fear and the overwhelming emotionality of our situation. Then her tears morphed into a different kind of fear. The kind that didn't just break my heart, but absolutely destroyed it.

I held her in my arms, rubbing her back when she inhaled sharply with realization. She looked up at me with watery, red-rimmed, wide-as-fuck eyes and begged me to believe her, that she didn't do it on purpose. Her voice was high-pitched and her words were panicked as she pleaded with me to believe her that she would never do this intentionally.

It wrecked me.

It took several minutes of me begging her in return to believe *me*, that *I* knew she didn't do this on purpose. Reminding her that she didn't do this alone either didn't seem to help. Honestly, nothing seemed to help, and that's what destroyed me more than anything else. I understand how June could think my reaction would be one of fear or anger, especially after all I've told her about my sexual history (or lack thereof), but I'm still gutted to think she would believe I would put this all on her.

The second day, she seemed to be in a fog. She walked around the apartment in a daze. She didn't eat or sleep. She cocooned herself in a blanket on the couch, practically catatonic. I canceled my golf outing with Crawford. I laid with June on the couch, coaxing her to at least drink some water every few hours. We watched movies, although I'm not sure how much she absorbed while I held her.

On the third day–today–June turns into an information-seeking machine. She becomes a master Googler, researching all her options and constantly asking me what I think we should do.

I don't allow myself to answer honestly. Because in the grand scheme of things, my opinion doesn't matter all that much. I don't say that to be a martyr, or to be dramatic, but the reality is, June will be the one dealing with all the major consequences of this pregnancy and whatever we decide to do about it. June's body is the one that is going through this. June will be the one needing to take time off work if we go through with everything. June is the one who society expects to give up her career if we have the baby. And if we don't, June is the one suffering the judgment from those who say they would not have made the same choice in a nearly impossible situation. So yeah, I might have played a part in getting us in this situation, but I don't have the same consequences as June.

I don't allow myself to feel anything about our situation either. No excitement, no fear, no happiness, no anger. Because regardless of what I feel, she needs to make the best decision for herself. There's no question in my mind that I will support her one hundred percent with whatever we decide to do, but I refuse to let my own emotions color the biggest decision she will likely ever have to make.

On the fourth day since finding out we are pregnant, we both are going stir-crazy.

"We need to get out of the house. Let's go for a drive. Go grab lunch. We can take a day trip to one of the suburbs and do some shopping. What sounds good to you, Junie?"

She lets out a sigh of relief. "Anything sounds good. I need to get out of these four walls and out of my head."

We spend the day shopping at an enormous mall in one of the suburbs. When I'm not wearing a baseball hat, I'm less recognizable, and I haven't been playing for Chicago long enough to be recognized in the suburbs the way I get recognized in the few blocks in the immediate vicinity of Foxes Field. I don't really care if I get recognized normally, but I want to spend the day with my girl with as few interruptions as possible. In the suburbs, we have a reduced chance of running into any of June's coworkers, which is the only real threat to our relationship right now, as far as I'm concerned.

We get dinner together at a nearby restaurant and spend the rest of the day not talking about babies or pregnancies or changing bodies. It feels normal and nice. But when we get home, we can't seem to avoid the inevitable.

"What do you want to do, Asher?" June's eyes are pleading, begging me to give her some sense of how I feel.

"June, I can't tell you what to do about this. I'll never be in your shoes, and I can't make the decision for you. What I can tell you is that I love you, and I will absolutely support your choice, one hundred percent."

She nods, her eyes watery. "You can't tell me which way you're leaning?"

"I won't, June. I can't influence you to make a choice you don't want to make. But let's talk out the options. I don't know if it helps you to hear me say this, but I need to say this. If you want to keep the baby, I am going to be there. Every single day. My mom was a single mom, and I had a great life. I'd kill for my mom; you know that. She did everything for me, but she also had a lot of help from her parents, because she *needed* a lot of help from her parents. But I will never, ever put you in the situation that my dad left her in. So, if we're doing this, you can expect me to do it right and to be by your side, supporting you, hand in hand, for the rest of our child's life. But Junie, if that's not what you want, then I will sit with you in every medical appointment to get you the outcome you do want. I will hold your hand and love you through it all and

I will never, ever judge you because whatever choice you make will be the right choice."

She's silent for a long time after that. I don't know if my words helped, or if she's sitting there hating me for refusing to give my opinion. The truth is, I'd love a family with June. I've fantasized about building a life, a family, with her. But in my fantasies, children typically came after a few years of being married and traveling the world first. I don't have the right answer here, but I'll accept and be happy with whatever we end up doing, and that's the most honest truth I have.

After several minutes, she climbs onto my lap. She straddles me and kisses me deeply. It's not what I am expecting for us tonight, but it feels good. It feels like a little bit of normalcy after feeling like our lives were upended the last few days.

"Make love to me, Asher," June whispers, rocking her hips against me. I'm instantly hard because it's June.

"I'd love to. Let me just go grab a cond–" I stop myself. She raises an eyebrow and giggles, and after the heaviness of the last four days, the sound is so, so beautiful.

"I guess I can't get re-pregnant right now, huh?"

"Fuck. You're going to let me take you bare?"

"Doesn't really seem like a reason not to, right?" She shrugs and her nonchalance is refreshing, too.

Sex with June is amazing. Sex without a condom with June is otherworldly. It took everything in me not to come immediately as soon as I got inside her. Now, after two rounds, our heartbeats have slowed back to a normal pace, and our breathing has adjusted. I turn toward June, nestled adorably in my comforter, head resting on my pillow. I sling my leg across hers, pulling her even closer. We're a breath away from each other and it's still too far for me.

"Asher?" Her voice is strained, hopeful.

"Yeah, baby?"

"Would you hate me if I said I wanted to keep it?" My heart cracks at the vulnerability in her tone.

"No, Junie." My voice comes out in a soft, honest whisper. "I could never hate you, but especially not for that." I wrap my arm around her shoulder and pull her chest flush with mine. "Are you sure? I'm asking not because I don't believe you or because I want you to change your mind. I just want to know if you're certain."

She tucks a strand of hair behind her ears. "I don't want you to feel stuck with me." She doesn't look at me when she says it, as if she's embarrassed to voice this particular thought.

There's no "getting stuck" with June. There's only getting blessed with the privilege of her presence–something I'd happily work toward every day of my life.

"Juniper. First of all, I want you around, so *you're* kind of stuck with *me* no matter what you decide, okay?" I wait for her to nod before I continue. "Second of all, I've said this before, but it bears repeating. This is not on you. This is what happens when people have sex. Granted, we took precautions, but I guess we're just part of the lucky few that serve as the reminder that no birth control is one hundred percent effective." I kiss her swollen lips. "So let me ask you again, are you certain?" She nods against me. "Baby, I need to hear you say it."

"I want to do this with you, Asher. I want to have your baby."

The words are barely out of her mouth before they're replaced with a squeal of laughter as I pounce on her, covering her with kisses. Her laughter fills the room immediately before mine joins it.

"We're having a baby!" My smile is triumphant as I feel it take over my face. I fist pump the air, bouncing on the bed while June giggles alongside me. My emotions are genuine, but I wasn't lying earlier when I said I would support and be happy with whatever she chose. But I'm ecstatic now. Sure, it's not exactly in the order I would have planned things myself, but it's with her, and that's all that matters to me.

"We still need to get it confirmed by a doctor," she reminds me. I level her with a deadpan stare.

"Seven, June. Seven pregnancy tests all said I knocked you up. I'm pretty sure it's official." She tips her head back and lets her laughter ring out once again.

It takes several minutes for me to get my euphoria under control again. Once I do, I turn my body toward her again, pulling her close and tracing small designs on her back, the way I've learned she loves. She presses her lips to my chest as I speak into her hair.

"I thought I reached peak happiness a few days ago when you told me you loved me, June. But I'm having a *baby* with you, and I couldn't be happier. Because it's with you."

Chapter Forty-Seven
June

Being pregnant is weird. At my first appointment, the doctor confirmed I was eight weeks along, so I was barely pregnant, but it now seems to have taken over my brain. Not in a forgetful, pregnancy-brain type of way either. It's like my brain constantly wants to remind myself that I'm pregnant. Sometimes, I feel like I forget, like when I ordered a gin and tonic at happy hour with Priya last week, and I had to chase down the waiter while I pretended to go to the bathroom and ask that he secretly switch it to just tonic water. Other times, I'm consumed with wonder over what my body is building inside me.

My doctor gave me so many pamphlets to read through. She didn't need to though, because Asher has been obsessive about purchasing every pregnancy and baby book he comes across. It's a little excessive, but it's also adorable and comforting. He's traded in his romance reading for devouring baby preparation books in secret, and while I was initially disappointed to discover the switch, it's done nothing to dampen his libido. I'm not sure if it's the fact that we can have all the bare sex we want without consequence (because, hello, the consequence has already happened) or if my boyfriend has a little bit of a breeding kink, but the sex is off the charts. Asher's favorite threat these days is that he's going to put another baby in me. I can't say that I mind.

Ash no longer lets me lick the spoon or the bowl after making brownie batter because it has raw eggs in it. He's modified our grocery delivery order to include vegetarian meats so I can still enjoy lunchmeat; it's not a great substitute, but he insists it gives him more peace of mind than if I just microwaved real lunchmeat. He's taken to researching and purchasing the best decaffeinated coffee beans, so I always have options in the morning. He's so sweet and protective that it's hard to be annoyed.

I can't hide my enthusiasm for my boyfriend. While some people have noticed a general uplift in my mood, Devin has pestered me about it to no end. We talk regularly and it took him nearly no time at all to notice my giddiness. I wasn't about to tell him it's because I'm secretly dating his best friend. That news needs to be delivered gently, in person. But because I couldn't not give him an explanation when he pressed for it, I told him I had a new boyfriend but didn't want to share too much, not wanting to jinx things. He seemed genuinely happy for me, which caused a flash of guilt to run through me before I remembered that he and Christine slept together without telling me. While Dev peppered me with questions, I gave him a little bit of information, all of it true. I refused to tell him my new boyfriend's name, obviously, so Devin started referring to him as "Mystery Guy."

"I'm happy he makes you happy," he tells me one night after his game. I had just finished sharing that Asher–ahem, *Mystery Guy*–just had a huge bouquet of peonies delivered to the apartment, and that Mystery Guy wanted to bring me dinner tonight. Devin's positive reaction to my secret boyfriend gives me hope that maybe Asher and I have nothing to worry about when we eventually do tell him the full story.

He comes to town next month. While we initially decided we would tell him about our relationship first, before disclosing it to our parents or friends, being pregnant changes things a little bit. Now, we have to not only drop the bomb that we're dating, but that we're starting a family. I haven't decided if Devin will take the news better or worse when he realizes there's a baby involved. It might soften the blow, but it also just might push him over the edge. In a way, I don't care what his reaction is, because I'm happy. Fear of Devin's reaction was a huge contributor to what prevented Asher from ever disclosing his feelings toward me in the first place; I'm tired of Devin's influence on my life in that regard. On the other hand, he's still my brother and one of my biggest supporters. I'm not thrilled about keeping two secrets from him for so long.

It's weird that Asher and I are having a baby when we can't publicly date each other. I don't know what I'm going to do at work when I start to show, but I'm hoping it will already be the offseason at that point. I wonder how long I can hide a bump under baggy clothes? Hopefully by the time I start to show, we will have come up with some sort of plan. I hate lying to my coworkers, but I really don't want to lose this job either.

I'm in this sort of limbo state, where I want to share my excitement about the two biggest pieces of news in my life with the people I care about most, but I can't tell people about my relationship with Asher, and I shouldn't tell people about the pregnancy because it's still early days. Still, I feel like I'm going to burst out of my skin if I don't tell someone soon, which is why I scheduled a joint Zoom call with Whitney and Christine this afternoon. Asher is in Atlanta, but when he comes home later tonight, we'll be video calling both of our parents, because I can't hold it in any longer.

I could have predicted Whitney's and Christine's individual responses and, as I knew they would, they reacted with shock, excitement, and lots of screaming.

"Girl, can you *imagine* how fifteen-year-old June would have reacted to hear that twenty-four-year-old June is pregnant with *Asher Incaudo's* baby?" Christine is practically shouting. She can't seem to channel her excited energy because she keeps shifting around in her chair before standing up, sitting down, and repeating the whole process all over again.

"She'd for sure shit a brick," Whit adds inelegantly. "Wait!" she shrieks. "You have to let us throw you a shower. Oh please?"

I laugh. "I'm only ten weeks along, I technically shouldn't even be telling anyone yet. It's so soon. But I feel good about things. Not that I'd really know how I'd feel if things aren't going according to plan..." I trail off, getting lost in my head.

"I'm sure you'd know," Whitney reassures me. Her eyes take on an overbright sheen. Christine's brown eyes are soft and comforting.

"Your secret is safe with us. You deserve to celebrate this. Two big wins rolled into one week. Guess you weren't really expecting a surprise baby when Asher told you he loved you, huh?"

"Not at all," I laugh. It's the truth, but I'm glad it happened the way it did. I'm confident Asher is with me because he wants to be, because apparently, he's wanted to be for the last eight years, not just because I'm having his child. "He definitely wasn't expecting it either. But here we are," I add with a shrug.

"Here you are," Christine agrees.

CHAPTER FORTY-EIGHT
Asher

I've wanted to get home right away after games all season, to get to spend more time with June. But now that she's carrying my baby, I can't leave work fast enough. Still, the police escort bringing us from O'Hare to Foxes Field is not moving us fast enough because we're still somehow not moving at the speed of light, which, as far as I'm concerned, is the only acceptable speed at which to travel when I'm trying to get home to my girl.

Tonight, we have video calls scheduled with each of our parents. We agreed that even though it's somewhat early in June's pregnancy, our parents probably need a lot of time to adjust to us not only being together, but to them being grandparents.

When I finally make it home to June, she's already started the call with her parents. I watch in real time as her smile morphs from one of happy amusement in chatting with her parents to joy upon seeing me walk through the door. Loving June is good for my ego.

"Asher just walked in," she informs her parents, and they each call out their hellos to me. Tossing my backpack aside, I sit beside her on the couch. Her parents' faces appear on the screen, and June angles her laptop toward me so I can see them. I gently angle it back to its original position on her knees and settle in closer to her. I catch a flash of something in Mrs. Demoranville's eyes, but it's gone as soon as it appears.

"Nice game, son," Mr. Demoranville says. "Ten strikeouts! Is that a career high for you?"

I nod. For much of high school and college, the Demoranvilles have served as second parents for me. They came to all our games in high school, and while I know they were there to support Devin, they always made sure to cheer especially loud for me when my mom couldn't make my starts. I feel a twinge of guilt for what I'm about to tell them and hope they don't think too poorly of me for impregnating their only daughter.

"Junebug was just telling us how much she loves her new job," he continues. "We're so glad she has someone in the city with her."

"We tend to worry less, but not because we don't think you can't handle yourself," her mother adds quickly. "But it's nice to know if something does happen, you aren't alone."

"Yeah, about that," June starts. Her parents share an anxious look. "Asher and I have started seeing each other."

I'm not sure what her parents were expecting her to say, but the relief when she tells them we're dating is palpable.

"Junie, that's wonderful! I thought you were going to tell us something awful!" Mrs. Demoranville's eyes sparkle. "It's about time," she teases. "June had the biggest crush on you throughout high school."

In the small window reflecting our own faces, June's cheeks blush and she groans in embarrassment. I put my arm around her shoulder and tug her closer to me.

"So I'm hearing! It's okay, Junie. June is also discovering that those feelings weren't exactly one-sided at the time either." Her mother laughs, but her father's smile is knowing.

"I had a feeling," he murmurs.

Honestly, this reaction is so much warmer than I was expecting. The Demoranvilles have always been good people. They've always made me feel like a part of their family. His mom even sent me a card when I finally got the call up to the show last year. In my head, though, I anticipated them reacting poorly to the news that I had taken advantage of their baby girl and them telling me they hated me. It's a relief to know I'm wrong, but we aren't done dropping bombs on them yet.

June turns to look at me, silently confirming if I'm ready for the next piece of news. I give her an encouraging smile and nod. This needs to come from her; the Demoranvilles are her parents, after all.

"We haven't told Dev yet. We were going to wait until he's in town later this month to tell him in person." I don't miss Mr. Demoranville's soft whistle under his breath, as if to say *good luck with that.* June's mother rolls her eyes and softly shakes her head; they both know what Devin is like about June. June has never given him a reason to doubt her. She's perfectly capable of picking a suitable man to date, and I felt that way long before she ever chose me. "So, I would ask that the next thing we tell you also remains just between us. For now."

A pall of seriousness falls over the conversation, her parents' faces matching the change in tone. June begins fidgeting with the hem of her shorts, and I cover her fingers gently with my own. I smile softly at her through the computer screen.

"We're pregnant."

A moment of silence falls before us, stretching long enough that for a second, I am tempted to check if we lost the connection on the call. June's parents' faces are frozen, immovable, before her mother's suddenly cracks and she shrieks.

"Ah! Junie! My baby!" Her mother bursts into tears. Mr. Demoranville immediately moves to comfort his wife, and I'm struck with the terrifying realization that I don't know if he's comforting her due to her distress or excitement.

"Congratulations, honey," Mr. Demoranville says with a smile that is soft but genuine. Mrs. Demoranville sniffs, shaking out her hands. Their stunned expressions slowly transform into excitement. June and I both release the breath I wasn't aware we were holding. June lets out a watery laugh before dissolving into her own tears, and I find myself mimicking Mr. Demoranville as I pull June to my chest to comfort her.

It takes a long time for the four of us to get a handle on our emotions. Her parents have lots of questions, only some of which we know the answers to. We haven't decided if we want to know the sex of the baby, or what names we're starting to consider. June hasn't been feeling too tired and hasn't experienced any morning sickness so far. In fact, if we weren't constantly and excitedly talking about the fact that she is pregnant, we wouldn't be able to tell in any real, discernable way.

Never once in our conversation did her parents express disappointment that I ruined her future by knocking her up. They never brought up concerns about her career, her raising a child, or the massive life changes ahead for each of us. That doesn't mean they don't think or feel those things, but for both our sakes, I'm thrilled that their reaction is one of joy.

My mother's reaction is no different. Her tears came a little faster and a lot harder than Mrs. Demoranville's, but pride and excitement fill every word she speaks. She insists on speaking to June alone near the end of the call, and when I tell you I could handle the anxiety spike in telling the Demoranvilles we were pregnant, but not the terror of whatever unknowns my mother is going to discuss with June, I'm being one hundred percent truthful. My mother is my favorite person in the world, aside from June, but still, I have no idea what she could possibly want to say to June alone.

After she hangs up and emerges from the privacy of her room, June's eyes are puffy and her nose is pink. It takes everything in me to pull her into a hug instead of immediately calling my mother and demanding an explanation. I've never been a hot-headed guy, but I am ready to yell at my own mother–something I've never done in my life–for making the mother of my child cry.

"No, I'm good, I promise. Just emotional," June insists. I narrow my eyes at her as she burrows further into my arms. I don't believe her. "I promise, Ash. She was nothing but supportive."

Chapter Forty-Nine

June
Age 16

"Hey, aren't you supposed to be on the field already?" It's twenty minutes until Asher and Devin's game starts, and I'm running late, having lost track of time while I attempted to complete all my homework in the library before gametime. Apparently, I'm not running nearly as late as Asher.

"I can't find my...I have a bit of a good luck charm," he finishes quietly. Devin is the definition of superstitious, and he always plays while wearing the same pair of socks each season. Once, he had back-to-back games last season and forgot to do laundry between them. I watched him, holding back my own vomit, as he stuffed his feet into crunchy, day-old, sweat-dried socks, lest he tempt fate by playing in a pair of fresh, clean socks.

Automatically, I glance toward Asher's feet, clad in high socks and red cleats. He smiles as he catches me, knowing what I'm thinking.

"Lucky for both of us, my good luck charm is a little cleaner than Devin's. But I always have it with me on my starts and I'm going out of my mind not having it now."

"What is it?" I know some people are cautious about who they divulge their superstitions to, so I won't be offended if he tells me to mind my own business. "I can try to look around for it?" I offer.

"Nah, that's okay. If it's not in the locker room, it probably fell out of my bag at home." He rolls his neck as he walks toward the door, his cleats clacking against the floor of the school's front hallway. "I'm just going to have to suck it up."

The distress on his face is so evident, and I feel helpless to make it better. I may be actively trying to distance myself from Asher and this ridiculously unrequited crush I have, but I still feel for the guy.

"You sure?" When he nods and readjusts the cap on his head, I continue my lame attempt at cheering him up. "I'm sure you'll do great. Dobbins Valley has nothing on you!"

"Thanks, June," he says softly, but I can tell his mind is back on his missing charm. "It's a note from my mom," he blurts suddenly. At my look of confusion, he clarifies. "My superstition. She writes me a note at the beginning of every season. She always signs it the same way. She's done it ever since I started little league, so each year, I rip out the signature and put it in the inside brim of my hat." He sighs deeply. "After my last start, I thought I'd mix it up and tuck it into my shoe instead. Which is apparently the worst idea I've ever had, because now I can't find it."

Oh.

My heart clearly didn't get the memo about dislodging this crush, because that's the sweetest thing I've ever heard. Asher is one of the most popular guys in school, universally loved by everyone, and all he wants is his note from his mom. My heart squeezes in my chest.

"I'm sorry, Asher." I don't know what else to say.

"It's okay. Not your fault. My mom is working at the diner tonight, though. It would have been nice to have a piece of her here, you know?"

I nod, because I do know. Asher is a boy who loves his mom, but Ms. Incaudo is an easy woman to love. I've never heard him talk about his father, so I'm not sure when he left, or if he was ever in the picture to begin with. His grandparents are really involved in his life, but they're even busier than his mom, trying to run the diner as well. I'll tell Devin to help Asher look for the note later and redouble my efforts to get rid of this crush, all the while knowing that the more I learn about Asher, the harder it will be.

CHAPTER FIFTY

June

PRESENT DAY

"I want pink slime! With glitter!" Scarlett Benjamin is back in town and making her presence in the Foxes family room known. Her stepmom dropped her off an hour ago, and my favorite six-year-old has been flitting from activity to activity ever since. I've taken to spending the first hour or two of each home game helping in the family room before making my way to the family section at the field, where the WAGs and other family members sit for the games.

Today's activity is on the messier side, so I'm hoping none of the parents will be disappointed if their children come home a little more...colorful...than when they arrived. Most of the parents are great. In fact, the only parent who ever gives me a hard time is Melody, and according to the whispered gossip Delaney delivered as she dropped off Scarlett, she may not be sticking around for long.

The trade deadline is looming, and the Foxes, much like every other team in the league, are hard at work finalizing their roster for their postseason push. There's still a lot of baseball left in the season, but it looks like the Foxes are solidly on track to repeat last season's October performance. By the time Devin comes to town next week, the trade deadline will have passed, which means both Dev and Ash should be solidly confirmed with their teams.

Not that there's a chance either of them will be traded. Both are playing well. Devin leads the Mustangs in batting average, and barring injury, that trend will likely continue for the rest of the year. Asher has been solid on the mound for the Foxes, too, which is no surprise. Ever since I've known him, Asher has been rock solid in everything he does. Now that I see a different, more private, side of him, I can confirm that's him in every sense.

Deb reminded me of the trade deadline this morning, as if I needed reminding. While she's not privy to the ins and outs of negotiations and deals, we both hear the same rumors about trades because we live in Chicago. John Malone is a name that's been tossed around as a trade possibility quite a bit in the last few days. I almost feel bad for being excited about the possibility, but the potential for Melody being in the family section seats each time I head there makes my stomach ball up with anxiety. It's hard to remain professional when she's just so horrible!

I may not be able to fraternize with the players, but there's nothing in my contract forbidding me from fraternizing with their wives. While I haven't hung out with any of them outside of Foxes Family Program sanctioned events, the core group consisting of

Delaney, Jenny, Amy, Alicia, and Hailey always includes me in their conversations. It strikes me suddenly that even though no one knows it, I am one of them. Normally, I'd be tasked with ensuring Asher's girlfriend feels welcomed to the team and to the city. Seeing as she is me, and no one affiliated with the Foxes is allowed to know, I justify my taking of a second cookie from the tray in the family room kitchen.

Heading back downstairs to help Scarlett and the other children mix their individual cups of slime, I hear her adorable voice projected loudly over the hum of the other children pouring, stirring, and chatting.

"Delaney is having a baby boy. I wanted a girl, but Daddy said that there's already two girls in the family, and now Kai won't have to be the only boy." Tracey, one of the family room babysitters, smiles and nods as she assists the curly-haired boy next to Scarlett pour more glue into his cup.

"Scar, what do you think Delaney and Daddy should name the baby?" I ask, coming up behind her and gently taking the bottle of glitter from her hands. She's poured about half of it into her cup already.

"Pegasus!" she proudly announces.

"Pegasus?" She nods enthusiastically.

"Isn't that the most beautiful name you have ever heard?" She looks at me with wide eyes, completely serious.

"Absolutely. I think Pegasus Benjamin would be lucky to get that name." I stifle my grin when Tracey catches my eye, her loud cough covering her own laugh. "I think you should tell Delaney that's your vote when she picks you up."

As I help Scarlett stir, adding more ingredients gently to her cup so glitter doesn't fly everywhere, my mind drifts to Asher's mom's words from yesterday. Asher started to panic when I emerged from my room, clearly having cried when talking to his mom, but what he didn't understand was that my tears were mostly happy ones.

Lorelai Incaudo has a heart of gold, but I have to admit, I was nervous speaking to her alone. It's not the first time I've talked to her alone, but seeing her at Asher's games and at the local diner growing up, our conversations consisted of social niceties, not serious conversations about her grandchild. I needn't have worried.

She spent several minutes thanking me for making her son happy. She told me she started to sense a shift in him a few months ago, noting that he's seemed lighter, happier this season. I'm not sure I can take credit for that, and when I said as much, she promptly shushed me and told me I was wrong. She then explained how Asher's father was never involved, leaving as soon as she told him she was pregnant. She acknowledged how raising Asher mostly solo was difficult, but something she wouldn't trade for the world.

She saw the panic on my face when she started talking about the challenges, but she immediately alleviated it by telling me how she knows Asher is different. She volunteered that he has loved me since he was a teenager, and if Ash hadn't already disclosed that, the earnest way in which Lorelai looked at me as she said it would have convinced me it was the truth. She knows her son, which is also why she asked for a moment of privacy with me. Because she spent the next few minutes telling me that she would have respected the hell out of me for whatever choice I would have made in the face of this unexpected pregnancy, but that she was so proud of the path I chose.

"You've made me a grandmother," she told me with tears in her eyes. "I don't know what your plans are, or if you've even thought that far ahead, but if you decide to spend the offseason in Philly, I'd like to be as involved as you'll let me. My own parents were so helpful with Asher, but I also want to respect your journey and don't want to overstep. I'm just so proud of you both."

I blink back my own tears at the memory. During that conversation I really, truly, realized the impact of what Asher and I are doing. We're not just changing our own lives and the life of this baby, but we're changing our families' lives, too. It may not have happened exactly the way we would have planned, but the love and support we've received from the few people we've told has been inspiring.

An idea sparks. I want to make sure that Asher feels that love in the same way. I know he does, but especially with Devin and my job being a bit of a wild card, I feel like I need to ensure he really feels it when he's the most stressed. I shoot a quick text to the Foxes equipment manager, who confirms my plan and agrees to keep it a secret. As Foxes Family Program assistant, he didn't balk at my plan or why I'd want to do this for Asher. I just hope it can get done before Asher's start next week.

The rest of the game, I find myself lost in thought. My brain has had to process so much new information in the last few weeks, and I haven't had a lot of people around that I can share it with. Aside from Whit and Christine, none of my friends know I'm pregnant. And aside from them, none of my friends know I'm hopelessly in love with Asher.

I never stood a chance against Asher Incaudo. I've loved him since I was fifteen, and as much as I tried to replace him with countless other men, Asher was and still is incomparable. I never had a choice in the matter; Asher and I are inevitable.

CHAPTER FIFTY-ONE
Asher

I flip the glove in my hand, twisting my wrist once, twice. I tap the toe of my right cleat against the rubber and breathe out deeply. It's part of my windup, so ingrained in me now that I'm not sure I could throw a pitch off the mound in fifty years without going through the same motions. Tonight, though, it feels different.

At the beginning of each season, I get a few new gloves. I play with only one all season, but there are a couple backups ready for use in the off chance something happens to my everyday glove. Nothing has so far, but I make a point to pull out my backups regularly to work with them so they're broken in by the time I'll need to use them in a game.

My glove tonight is the trusty, well-worn one I've used all season, with one tiny addition. Embroidered along the outside pinky in cobalt thread, the words "I love you always" sit in the loopy script of my mother's handwriting. When I found my glove, with the new addition, sitting in my locker this morning, there was no note attached to it explaining why I couldn't find my glove to practice with yesterday. But I know who's behind this gift.

June is the only person who knows the details of my mother's note. Devin knows I tuck a piece of paper under my cap before each start. I'm sure my teammates have noticed me rubbing the soft paper between my fingers before each game. But no one else knows the contents of the note, and June's thoughtfulness is just one more reason that girl can bring me to my knees. If June ever wakes up and decides she no longer wants me, I'm in trouble. Because my heart belongs to her forever.

Tonight, when I get home after securing the win, June greets me in the kitchen with more than just the caramel popcorn topped brownies she made me. She hands me an envelope with a somewhat sheepish expression.

"What's this?" I ask, my thumb already lifting the flap to peer at the greeting card inside.

"I thought it might be hard on you, not being able to tell a lot of people about us, about the family we're creating. I thought maybe you'd want something to remind you of what you're coming home to when you're on the road."

I run my fingers over the cover of the card. In metallic script, words proclaim that she's excited for what's to come for us. The card is commercially produced and purchased, but it feels like it was written especially for us. I open it and a glossy photograph slips out. I catch it before it falls.

"June." My gaze is heated as I take in the photograph. It's June, but from behind and at a slight angle, cradling her not-yet-existent baby bump, wearing my jersey, with forty-five–my number–but Incaudo is not the name emblazoned across her shoulders. Instead, the word DADDY is stamped across her shoulder blades. The picture is somewhat innocent; although June isn't wearing pants, the jersey is long enough to cover everything but her dimpled thighs. She wears a mischievous smirk as she looks over her shoulder, the definition of *up to no good*. I'm instantly hard.

June ducks her head, as if she's embarrassed, but her eyes mirror the lust I know is shown in my own.

"Holy shit, June." Awe-struck is the only appropriate word to describe what I'm feeling. My eyes bounce from the June in the photo to the June in real life, both equally sexy. I trail my eyes up the real June, slowly cataloging the expanse of skin on display in her sleep shorts and *Rosebud Motel* tee. Her nipples harden under my gaze. Snapping my eyes back to the photo one last time, I stalk to the fridge and pin it, front and center, to the freezer door with a magnet.

"I'm getting this blown up to hang above my bed."

She laughs. "Shut up," she says, pushing my chest as I stalk toward her.

"Never. Now get over here so I can put another baby in you." I pull her gently toward me by the shoulders. We haven't decreased the intensity of our bedroom activities since we discovered June's pregnancy, but I have been more careful in my movements around her outside of it.

I tilt her chin toward me before pressing my lips to hers. She whimpers when I deepen it, wrapping my hands loosely around her throat. It will be at least six more months before I choke her the way she wants me to, but I know that simply laying my hand across her throat gets her halfway there.

"Thank you," I whisper, pressing my hips against her, letting her feel what she does to me.

"You're welcome," she whispers back, hands roaming across my shoulders.

"Not just for the photo, even though that's the hottest fucking thing I've ever seen. For my glove, too." Her eyes crinkle at the corners. She's so fucking adorable I want to spend the night kissing each of her freckles. After I fuck her into the mattress.

"I hope I didn't overstep on that. I remember how you lost your mom's note once when we were in high school, and I wanted to ensure you always had a piece of her before stepping on the mound."

I close my eyes. The thoughtfulness of this woman knows no bounds. I have no words to adequately convey just how grateful I am for her, but I hope my body can show her. Because tonight, she needs to know just how much she has altered the course of my life for the better. Not just with the baby she's growing for me, but for the ways in which she makes me better all around.

I dot kisses across her jaw and pause to gently nip at the soft skin below her ear. It's her most sensitive spot and I know it drives her wild. My stomach growls, rudely interrupting us.

"Did you eat after the game?" she asks, breaking away from me and stepping toward the fridge, as if to make me something.

I did eat after the game, but the amount of calories I expend on the mound keeps me hungry for hours after the adrenaline wears off.

"What are you hungry for?" she asks, opening the refrigerator and peering at the ingredients. I press my hand on the door, closing it and stepping in front of her. I let her see the lust in my gaze as I peer down at her, crowding her space.

"You know what I'm hungry for."

"Asher," she whines. "You need to eat." She's suddenly sounding like my mother, which is *not* the kind of thought I want to be having before I devour the mother of my unborn child. I step further into her space, pressing her back against the counter. She doesn't push me about food anymore, correctly reading the look in my eyes. Later, I'll go out and grab us some ice cream, but right now, there's a different hunger I need to sate.

In one quick movement, I have June's shorts on the floor and her ass on the counter. Standing in front of her, I grasp her ankles and place them on the edge of the counter in front of her. She's forced to lean back on her elbows, which puts her fantastic tits on display for me. She's still wearing her shirt, but I don't care; I pull her nipple into my mouth through the fabric. It elicits a deep moan from her, so I repeat the action on her other breast, my fingers finding their way to her slick center.

Slowly, torturously slowly, I circle the pad of my thumb over her clit while my mouth toys with her nipples. June is gasping and writhing beneath me and I know my gentle ministrations on her clit aren't nearly enough.

Too bad.

Tonight, we're not shooting for quick. June deserves to feel worshipped for all she's done for me. I'll get her off–multiple times–but I plan on drawing her pleasure out for at least an hour before we leave the bed. Or, in this case, the kitchen. What can I say? There's something about this girl in a kitchen.

I lock eyes with her as I slowly kneel in front of her. She adjusts herself, pressing up slightly higher as my little voyeur watches as I press my mouth to her glorious pussy. I groan at her taste. I eat June's delicious pussy just about every day, yet each time, I forget just how good it is.

I suckle. I nip. I kiss. I trace every inch of her with my tongue. I was made to eat this pussy. I flatten my tongue and slide it over her clit. I pull the whole thing into my mouth, gently sucking before tapping my pointed tongue over it repeatedly. Her breaths stutter and I know she's close. I release her clit and slightly angle my body so I'm now eating her sideways. The new angle puts my mouth completely parallel to the shape of her cunt. She practically shoots off the counter in response. I chuckle to myself. I love that I can try new things with her but love even more when she responds so enthusiastically. I feel like a god, the way she is so responsive to me.

"Just like that," she moans breathily, as if I don't already know what she needs. I point my tongue and thrust it inside her, nibbling her clit with my lips. Her hips rock against my face, reaching a frantic pace as her hands tangle in my hair, pushing my face deeper into her soaked cunt. I feel her spasm against me as her first orgasm takes over her. I enjoy every second of lapping up her arousal; I wasn't kidding when I said June is delicious.

When her tremors subside and she collapses flat against the counter, I gently untuck her legs and wrap them around my waist. I pull her to my chest and carry her to our bed—because it's not just my bed anymore. As far as I'm concerned, June will never go back into her bedroom for anything other than a change of clothes. As it is, she might as well move her closet in with mine.

June clings to me as I walk. My cock is pressed against her sopping entrance, and the knowledge that she'll leave a wet spot on the crotch of my pants makes me impossibly harder. There's nothing this woman can do that I won't absolutely love. She could spit in my face and tell me to get fucked and I'd thank her and ask her when she can do the honors.

"Baby, you're so beautiful. I love making you come." She sighs deeply, the content sound worming its way into my bloodstream and heating me from within. "What else can I do?"

She murmurs, something between nonsensical words and a hum. My chest expands in pride, knowing I've rendered her speechless.

"I can do that," I promise her, having no idea what I'm committing to but knowing no matter what she asks for, I'll deliver. I set her gently on the bed and hover over her. My right arm shakes, its muscles having more than reached their limit tonight. I shift to hold my weight up with my left arm as June runs her fingertips softly up and down my biceps. If this was all she wants to do the rest of the night, I'll be happy, too. Any way she touches me feels amazing. Her eyes take on a sleepy, satisfied look.

"You tired, baby?" I ask. "I'm gonna need you awake if you're going to take my cock tonight," I tease. She widens her eyes instantly, as if to prove she's not tired in the least. I can't help but laugh.

"I need you," she says, rocking her hips against my fully clothed lower half. As if those were the magic words I needed to hear, I undress in record speed. She follows suit, discarding her top. Her breasts are more sensitive with the pregnancy which, on the one hand, means I need to be gentler with them. On the other hand, she gets off so much quicker on the smallest amount of nipple play. It makes me want to suck on them to see if that alone can make her come.

I come to rest between her thighs, my favorite place to be. Keeping most of my weight on my left arm, I coat myself in her arousal as she groans in approval. I tap the head of my cock against her clit a few times, her moans becoming more desperate, before I notch myself at her entrance.

June is more than warmed up for me, but I still take it slow. Tonight, though, it's apparently too slow, because she wiggles underneath me, urging me to move.

"How do you want it tonight, baby? Hard and fast or soft and slow?"

She gives me a devilish smirk. "Both."

God, I love this woman.

I give her what she asks for, thrusting hard into her. I press her knee toward her chest, careful to maneuver her breast out of the way. Anchoring my hand against her knee, I thrust deeply, bringing my own knee to the side to give me even more leverage. June's hands are tangled in my hair once more, tugging at the strands. She's not gentle and neither am I. We share a hard, passionate kiss, all tongue and teeth. Her nails claw at my back. I'm sure I'll have marks tomorrow and I'll wear them like a fucking badge of honor. Simultaneously, without a word being spoken, our movements slow. As if we've gotten our fill for now of hard and fast and now it's time to move to soft and sweet.

Pressing a hand against her abdomen, I apply a gentle, steady pressure. It's incredible. It heightens every sensation for me, making her feel tighter, but it also allows me to feel my cock move inside her with my hand. It's an incredible sensation that spurs me to fuck into her harder, faster, deeper.

"Oh fuck, Asher. Fuck, fuck, fuck!" *My thoughts exactly.* I love when she gets like this, when she's so wrapped up in her pleasure that she just chants one word, usually *fuck* or my name, over and over. When I look back on my first full season in the MLB, June's throaty moans, whispered repetitively, will be the soundtrack to my memories.

A rush of additional wetness gushes around my cock and spills out onto the sheets below us as she squirts.

"Fuck yes, baby. Fuck yes," I praise.

"Ohhhhhhhh." June's resorted to sounds instead of actual words, and I've never felt prouder. Her pussy ripples around me and I wonder vaguely how much sensation my cock can take. As it is, I feel my balls drawing closer to my body, ready to explode. I wanted to hold off until June came at least three times, but I'll have to eat her pussy again later because there's no way I can hold out even a little bit longer.

"Juniper," I groan as I spill into her. A mixture of our releases squeezes out of her, and I watch it drip onto the bed. We're going to have a huge wet spot on the bed tonight, but I can't bring myself to care. Thank god for in-unit laundry. When I pull out, I watch in awe as our cum mingles together at the apex of her thighs. I gather it on my thumb and push it back inside her. June told me about breeding kinks the other day. I'm not sure if that's exactly what this is or not, but the sight of my cum inside her is simply stunning.

June herself looks incredible. Her sleepy, sated look from earlier is back. Her hair is a mess, just the way I prefer it. Her tits heave as she catches her breath and smiles dreamily at me. The love in her eyes floors me and I know the way I look at her isn't dissimilar. I have no idea how we're going to hide our feelings from Devin when he's here in a few days. We'll only have to keep it from him for a little bit, until we spill the beans, but he deserves to hear it from us instead of guessing it just from looking at us.

"Come here, beautiful." I pull her to sit after I clean her up. "Let's get some ice cream."

CHAPTER FIFTY-TWO
Asher

"Give me one more, baby. Soak my hand." I'm well on my way to coaxing a second orgasm out of my girlfriend when the front door to the apartment opens. I spring from the bed so quickly you'd think I sleep on a trampoline.

"Ash? You home?" My best friend's voice carries through my small apartment.

Fuck.

The door to my bedroom is half open, so I slide out of it, pulling it closed behind me and adjusting my cock in my shorts. When I talked to Devin after today's game, I told him to come over whenever. I also gave him my address and the front door code to the building. I didn't expect him to be here so soon.

"Hey man," Devin begins, just as the door fully shuts. It clicks satisfyingly behind me, giving me the reassurance I need to know it won't be popping back open to reveal his naked sister sprawled across my bed. Devin's eyes widen. "Oh shit, do you have someone in there?"

I palm the back of my neck before realizing my hand is still covered in June's arousal. I surreptitiously wipe it on the back of my shorts, praying for a miracle.

"Uh, yeah. Shit, I'm sorry. I didn't realize what time it is." I catch the time on the oven's digital clock. Devin isn't early. He's exactly on time from when he said he'd be here, but June's magical pussy must make me lose all sense of the passage of time. It's never been an issue before.

"Is June home?" Dev cranes his neck to look past me into the rest of the apartment. I don't say anything. I don't want to lie to him, but I can't exactly say *yeah, she is. I was actually two knuckles deep in her pussy just now; wanna come back in five after I make her come again?*

"Uh..." I respond stupidly. Devin laughs.

"I guess you wouldn't know if you've been busy yourself." He walks into the living room before tapping on the doorframe outside of June's old bedroom. "Junie, you in here?" When she obviously doesn't respond, he peeks his head around the corner, finding the room empty. "Does she normally work this late?"

I still don't answer, fumbling over my thoughts. I'm so close to blurting out the truth. The only thing stopping me is imagining the look of disappointment on June's face at the way her brother finds out.

"Fuck, sorry. I'm standing here cockblocking you. I'll just text her. Want to meet up in, like, an hour for dinner?" I cringe internally as Devin pulls out his phone and begins tapping out a text to his sister. I can only hope June can hear this conversation through the door and has already put her phone on silent. The only thing worse than me blurting out that I'm sleeping with his sister is him finding out for himself when he hears her phone go off from inside my room.

I clear my throat, hoping it might mask any sounds from her phone. "Uh, yeah. That'd be great. Thanks."

Devin waves me off, typing away. "I'll let you get back to your girl. I can see myself out."

With his face buried in his phone, I hurry back into our bedroom, squeezing through the barely-opened door, closing and locking it behind us. June's panicked face reveals she heard everything. I press my finger to my lips in a totally unnecessary gesture. She stares at me, wide-eyed and now fully clothed, as we both wait with bated breath for her brother to leave. My heart thumps against my chest, and I swear it's loud enough for Dev to hear it through the door. I'm still standing with my back against the door, as if that somehow could afford us more protection against him finding us out.

It's that exact position I'm in that allows me to hear his whispered, "What the fuck?" followed by footsteps. I don't know what he's still doing here, but knowing him, he's still engrossed in his phone. A few minutes later, we hear the door slam, followed by the pounding of feet in the stairwell. Just to be safe, I give it a few minutes before I stride across our bedroom and peek out the window to see Devin walking quickly down the block.

I breathe out a sigh of relief. June's shoulders slowly drop from her ears as she falls backward against the pillows. I open the bedroom door to lock the apartment door, just in case Devin gets any ideas about coming back. I flip the deadbolt and walk two steps back to the bedroom when something on the kitchen counter catches my eye.

Sitting in the center of the counter is my favorite photo of June, mostly naked and wearing my jersey, DADDY emblazoned above my number on her back.

Fuck.

Chapter Fifty-Three
June

Devin hasn't answered my calls or my texts. He won't pick up for Asher either. There's no way we can hope he didn't see the picture; it's been hanging on the fridge since Asher put it there the night I gave it to him. It didn't magically jump onto the counter of its own accord on the exact night Devin happened to be in our apartment.

My brother and I have always been close. We've never really been in a fight. Sure, we've argued before, but I can confidently say this is the first time Devin has ever truly been mad at me. I don't know what to do with myself. My (unanswered) texts and voicemails to him have all been vague, asking him to call me. I know he already knows, but he deserves to hear it directly from me, so I refuse to admit to anything in a voicemail or a text. I don't know if that makes him angrier or if he's even listened to my messages. After a few hours of alternating attempts to reach him last night, both Asher's and my calls started going straight to voicemail, so Devin either blocked us both or turned off his phone. Today hasn't been any different.

Asher and I hardly slept last night. I felt him tossing and turning long after we turned out the lights. He's starting today and I'm not sure he got any sleep. I woke to him already gone, his bowl of mostly uneaten Frosted Flakes sitting in the sink. My body can't decide if it wants to cry or throw up. I couldn't eat anything last night, so even if I tried to throw up now, I'm not sure it'd be of any use.

I pour myself a sad little cup of decaf coffee. My favorite mug feels silly and stupid. The knit cactus I displayed on the kitchen windowsill looks juvenile. *I* feel silly and stupid. Not because of our relationship, but because I was naive enough to believe things would be okay as long as Devin heard the information from me first. Now that that didn't happen, I don't know how it's going to affect my relationship with my brother. Even worse, I don't know how it will affect Asher's relationship with my brother. Eventually, I might be able to convince Devin to forgive me, but I'm not sure he'll be so willing to forgive Ash, which is ridiculous, because we're both equally culpable here. But I know my brother, and I'm fairly certain his knee-jerk reaction will be to cut Asher out following this betrayal.

The bright sunshine seems to mock me on my walk to work. I briefly debate calling my mother to see if she's heard from Devin before immediately quashing that idea. There's not a way I can talk to her about this without making it seem like I'm tattling on my brother for not taking my calls, and as much as I don't regret my relationship with Asher, there's no doubt that the way Devin found out about us was just plain wrong.

My jeans feel sweaty and tight as I sit in the stands, watching my boyfriend and my brother warm up on opposite sides of the field. Asher looks as handsome as ever, but even from my seat two sections back from the field, I can see the worry lines etched into his beautiful face. Devin practices further down the right field line so I can't read his face, but his body looks stiff and tight. I tell myself I'm just reading into things, but I have my doubts.

"Ready to watch big brother again?" Jenny asks, taking a seat next to me. Yesterday, a few of the WAGs found out that Devin is my brother. Deb said I could take the series off, knowing he was in town, but I declined. I'm going to be at the ballpark anyway, so I might as well get paid for it. The only difference is that for this series, my ass is firmly planted in the seats for all nine innings. I haven't visited the family room, which Deb insists is fine. If Asher wasn't pitching today, I might be spending the whole day in the family room just to distract myself from the gnawing pit in my stomach.

It's guilt. I know it is. I fucked up, and until I can talk to Devin, I can't make it right.

By the end of the third inning, I want to crawl out of my skin. As a pitcher, Asher doesn't make any plate appearances, so he and Devin stay at least sixty-six and two-thirds feet away from each other at all times. Asher has already pitched to him once, and he's about to do it again.

In the bottom of the fourth, Devin glares at Asher as he steps up to the plate. I can't possibly be the only one picking up on the tension on the field, right? Edwards tosses the ball back to Ash as Devin steps in the box.

The pitch he delivers is high and inside. From this angle, I can't tell if it was accidentally thrown that close to Devin's chin or if it was one of those "accidentally on purpose" things. Devin doesn't seem to have trouble deciding which it is as he drops his bat and charges the mound.

The crowd is instantly on their feet. I want to scream but all I can do is hold my breath, knowing Devin has at least fifty pounds of muscle on Asher, even if Asher has more height. Tyler Edwards attempts to get between Devin and his pitcher, but I swear, Devin doesn't even see him as he pushes Edwards to the ground to get to the mound.

It's pandemonium. As soon as Edwards leaves his feet, both benches clear. The game has devolved into an all-out brawl. I can see Devin's mouth moving immediately before his fist connects with Asher's jaw.

Chapter Fifty-Four
Asher

"You fucked my sister!" Devin roars. In my periphery, I see Caleb Andrews stiffen where he's shoving a New York player. "Friendship over," Devin declares as he punches me in the jaw.

I knew it would come to this.

Okay, I didn't anticipate the benches-clearing brawl. And maybe throwing a little chin music at Dev wasn't the most mature way to handle things, but the guy is pissing me off. He can be mad at me all he wants, but he needs to talk to June. He doesn't get to treat her like this. He puts her on this pedestal, makes her infallible and untouchable. I get it. June deserves to be on a pedestal. But when she makes her own choices about who she wants to touch, she shouldn't be met with the silent treatment from her brother. Yes, we should have told him. *Yes,* the way he found out was fucked up. I'll own that. But the way he's been glaring at me all game, muttering god knows what under his breath, has been pissing me off for the last hour.

His words don't surprise me. The punch to my jaw doesn't really surprise me either. Devin's stockier, with his classic catcher's build, and he knows how to throw a punch. As soon as he charged the mound, I was ready for it, but all I could really do was plant my feet in preparation. I'm not going to hit him back, but I'm also not going to let him get more than one shot in.

I rock back on my heels with the force of the blow but somehow manage to stay upright. I stumble into the bodies behind me, everyone jawing and shoving. As soon as the hit lands, though, the atmosphere changes. Electricity crackles in the air as my teammates rally around me, closing ranks. In all of the shoving, I get turned sideways, and I see the bullpen emptying out onto the field, Crawford leading the charge. Foxes and Mustangs players pull Devin back, and I seize the opportunity to leap forward toward him, but Benny throws an arm around my chest and hauls me away before I can do anything stupid.

It takes a few minutes, but eventually, everything settles down. Devin and I are both thrown out of the game. I'm sure we'll both be fined, but I don't give a fuck. Both teams are issued warnings, and play resumes, but I have to watch it from the clubhouse, my presence expressly forbidden in the dugout.

The television replays taunt me, repeatedly replaying the "fight." It's not much of a fight. Devin got the jump on me from the get-go. But it's the announcer's comments that make watching the replays so difficult.

"It makes you wonder, Bruce, what's going on here. Devin Demoranville and Asher Incaudo are—or *were*—famously close friends. They went to high school together and played on the same baseball team growing up. I can't imagine the falling out that led to this."

I can.

All it takes is for one best friend to act on the longstanding feelings he's had for the other best friend's sister.

As much as I want to get in the car and leave the game, it would make me a pretty shitty teammate. I have to stay until the end of the game; I owe it to my teammates and coaches. Besides, if I left, I'd be going home to an empty apartment. June's still here at work and I have no doubt she'll be trying to get ahold of Devin after the game. I'm not technically allowed to be on it, but I sneak my phone into the bathroom stall. When I power on the screen, it's filled with texts and missed calls. Most of the missed calls are from my mother, and each seems to have its own voicemail attached. I thumb past the notifications and open my texts.

Juniper

> Oh my god. Are you okay?

> I know you can't respond right away, but holy shit. This is such a mess.

My heart aches, knowing what I'm putting her through.

> I don't know if you can text while the game is still going on, but please tell me someone is putting ice on your face. You're too pretty to be disfigured.

I smile, wincing at the pain it elicits in my jaw. She always seems to know what to say. I appreciate that she's not mad at me about the fight; technically, my pitch started it, even if Devin threw the first (and only) punch.

> **Me**
> I promise I'll ice it, but I'll heal faster if you kiss it better.

> Ash! Oh my god! How are you feeling?

> **Me**
> I'll be fine. Are you okay?

> My phone is blowing up. My parents have called twice. I can't talk to them until I talk to Dev.

> Would you hate me if I went to his hotel after the game today?

I smile again, this time my mouth decidedly more lopsided, shaking my head. I knew she'd want to do this, and she needs to repair her relationship with her brother. He can hate me for the rest of our natural lives, but I'll never forgive him if he doesn't talk to June.

Sliding my phone in my pocket, I return to my locker and get ready to shower. There's not much I can do at this point but wait. Wait for my teammates to finish the game without me. Wait for Devin to agree to talk to June. Wait for the love of my life to feel okay with being with me when I just caused a massive rift between her and her brother.

Chapter Fifty-Five
June

"What are you doing here, June?" Devin's voice is heavy with disappointment and exhaustion. He looks like he slept about as much as Asher and I did last night. Dark half-moons shadow the skin beneath his eyes.

I cock my hip. "What do you think I'm doing here, Dev? Let me in." I don't wait for him to open his hotel room door further; I push my way in. He doesn't stop me. When I walk in, he moves to stand in front of the windows, taking in the view of the city skyline as the sun begins to set. It's a magnificent sight. Beneath us, the Chicago River flows steadily outward. Tourists fill an architectural tour boat below. I wanted to arrange that tour for the WAGs at some point this season. Now, with everything going on, I'm not sure if I can keep this pregnancy and my relationship with Asher a secret. Who knows if I'll even have a job next week.

"What the fuck, June?" Devin says softly as I come to stand next to him. I squint out at the sunset, careful not to look at him.

"I'm so sorry you had to find out that way." He releases a heavy sigh. "I never meant for you to discover our relationship that way.

You deserved to hear it from us, from me. That was awful, the way you found out." He nods curtly beside me.

"Your relationship? Is that what that is?" He barely hides the derision in his voice. His anger about how he found out about the relationship is more than justified, but he does not get to judge the existence of said relationship. Anger sparks in my chest.

"Yes, of *course*." I take a deep breath and will my fingers to stop fidgeting with the hem of my Foxes work polo. "This isn't just us messing around, Dev. I'm in love with him–and before you say anything," I add, correctly interpreting his open mouth. "He's in love with me, too. Did you know he's been in love with me since your guys' senior year of high school? And that I've been in love with him since my freshman year?"

Devin finally turns to look at me, disbelief written all over his face. I swear I see a flash of something else, guilt maybe, before his expression hardens once more. It's that look that has me fighting to bite back my temper.

"I know this is a lot to process right now, but you better get used to it, Devin. Because like it or not, Asher and I are stuck together for at least the next eighteen years, in love or not."

Realization dawns on his face as I cradle my barely-there bump.

"Junebug," he croaks. "You're having a baby?"

I decide not to give him a hard time about what he thought the DADDY on the back of my jersey meant.

"Yes."

"And Incaudo is the father?" I glare at him. If he wasn't my brother, I'd be tempted to hit him for the sheer audacity. "Shit, I didn't mean it like that. It's just...wow. Fuck." I move to put my hand on his arm, but he steps away from me, apparently not ready to be friends again yet.

"Devin," I sigh, finally giving into the exhaustion that's been pulling at me all day. "Make it right or don't. It's your call. But you're going to have to live with the consequences of your choices."

I'm out the door before he has a chance to process my words or lecture me for what he clearly views as reckless behavior, because I'm done.

It's late at night, the sun set hours ago, and I'm still curled against Asher's chest. We're still seated on the couch, where I collapsed into him as soon as I got home. I'm exhausted but too emotional to sleep. Every few minutes, another tear escapes my eyes just as I think I'm finally calming down.

I don't know how to exist with my brother mad at me. I don't know how to deal with my boyfriend losing his best friend overnight. The guilt for the latter is eating me alive. Asher was adamant this is not my fault, but it's hard not to feel that way. I still don't regret our relationship, but I feel responsible for the dissolution of his and Devin's friendship, at least to some degree. Devin's hardheadedness is a major factor, too.

"Let's go to bed, Junie. I can hold you better in there," he suggests after I stifle another yawn. A knock on the door echoes through the apartment. "Stay here," he instructs, as if I have the energy to do anything but remain right where he tells me. He looks through the peephole before sighing deeply and with a resigned shake of his head, opens the door.

Devin stands at the threshold, laden with white plastic bags. Asher leaves the front door open and rejoins me at the couch, as if he needs to touch me, hold me again, in the face of my brother's return. Devin's face is tortured as he watches Asher cross the room and position himself next to me, swiping the last of my tears off my cheek. Asher tilts my chin slightly, establishing eye contact and nonverbally checking that I'm okay.

I'm not, but I'm okay with the idea of Devin being here.

"I'm sorry, Junie. You're right. I overreacted. I'm so sorry." Devin steps inside, placing the bags on the side of the couch furthest from me, as if he's afraid to come much closer. Diapers and onesies and bottles spill out of the bags. "I didn't know what stuff you guys needed." He gestures toward the bags of baby items.

"I can provide for my own child, dickwad," Asher says with a glare. Devin grips the back of his neck and visibly cringes.

"I know you can. I just...I've spent my whole life looking out for June. I can't just turn it off."

"It's my turn now," Asher says, his hand closing over mine in a manner far gentler than his tone suggests. "I've been doing it all season."

"Fuck, I know. You're Mystery Guy. And I liked you before I knew it was you. I liked how she told me you treated her. And she deserves someone like you...and so does her baby."

"Our baby." Asher's growl is lethal.

"Your baby," Devin hastily corrects. "Can I please just sit down? I didn't know it was love. I didn't know there was a baby."

"Baby or not, I'd walk through fire for June. I've loved her for so long, Dev. I'm finally, *finally* getting my June. And we are making a family. And if I have my way, we're going to have so many more babies."

I blush furiously as Devin groans. I know Asher threw in that last little bit to twist the knife the tiniest bit, but when he looks at me after he says it, I know it's the truth. Devin's eyes are pleading as he looks at me.

"June, can we please talk about this?" I nod, wanting to put us both out of our misery, and Asher takes it as his cue to give us some privacy. Before he leaves, he gently grips my face and presses a tender kiss to my lips. My eyes close softly and I feel the sting of tears once more. When he pulls away, he stands, glaring at my brother, silently daring him to see what happens if he makes me cry again.

"Sorry about your jaw," Devin mutters, looking sheepish.

"It'll take a lot more than a weenie little hit from you to ruin this beautiful face." Devin rolls his eyes, but I can't help feeling a little relieved that they're joking again. Asher grabs his keys from the counter and gives me one last long, lingering look, before shutting and locking the door behind him.

Devin sits heavily on the couch next to me. Needing to do something with my hands, I begin picking through the bags. My head has been consumed with thoughts of this pregnancy, and we've done a lot of planning, but until I pull the onesies out of the bags, it doesn't totally feel real. I'm growing a human inside of me. Asher's and my human. A wave of emotion rolls through me. Luckily, I'm distracted by the contents of the bag before I can start crying again.

"Baby Jordans?" I say skeptically, pulling them out of the bag. They're tiny and adorable, but entirely impractical for an infant. Devin shrugs.

"I wanted to buy him or her their first pair of Js, so sue me."

"You do realize infants don't wear shoes? This is a complete waste of money." I roll my eyes but don't let go of the tiny black-and-red high tops. The sides are flimsy and flexible, and I can't get over how cute they are.

"I've got enough money. One pair of baby Jordans isn't going to break the bank." My smile slowly fades as the heaviness of today bleeds back in.

"Dev, what happened to us? We used to be thick as thieves, and now you don't even trust me to know what I want in a relationship?"

"Thick as thieves? Is that what you call it when you hide that you've been in love with my best friend since you were fifteen?"

"Oh, get over yourself, Devin! I wasn't hiding shit. The whole world knew I was in love with Asher." He has the courtesy to look abashed. "Did you know he was my first kiss? My first kiss after *two years* of pining after him. And when he finally, *finally* started noticing me, his fear of your reaction held him back from doing anything until just recently!"

Devin raises his eyebrows and rears back as if I've slapped him.

"Don't even try to pretend you wouldn't have gone all overprotective big brother on him. Your actions right now prove you would have! You can be mad all you want that I didn't tell you about us, or about the baby, but you don't get to be mad about us falling in love. And while you're sitting there, stewing in your anger, don't forget that I'm mad as hell at you, too."

For a long time, Devin doesn't say anything. He sits there, staring at the floor. My chest rises and falls as I start to calm down. I didn't realize how much anger I'd been holding toward him. Finally, when he starts to speak, his voice is quiet, thoughtful.

"You're right. You're right. I'm sorry. There's only so many times or ways that I can say it. I've just always wanted what's best for you, and I'm sorry that it came across as me not trusting you to know what was best for yourself. I do trust you, I promise. It's also hard for me to see you hurt. After that bullshit with your last job, and your last boyfriend, Tommy—"

"Trevor," I correct.

"Whatever, that guy sucked." I don't argue with him because he's not wrong. "I just want you to be happy." I open my mouth, but he holds up a hand to stop me. "I know. You are happy. It just took me a sec to see past my own bullshit to realize it."

I nod, unsure that there's anything left for me to say right now.

"I love you, Junie." I swallow back more tears. "It's going to take me some time to get used to seeing you guys together, but I won't stop you." I hold myself back from audibly scoffing; as if Devin could stop us from being together. I swallow my retort, choosing to take the high road. Devin is still adjusting, and as much as I want to call him out on his dickishness or hypocrisy, I know it won't help in the long run.

"I love you too, Dev." He pulls me into a tight hug I didn't realize I needed from him.

"I'm going to head back to my hotel."

I walk him to the door with promises to call him tomorrow before he leaves. The Mustangs will head to the airport right after tomorrow's game, so I will only get to see him briefly at work. Right before he heads down the stairs, he leans back.

"Be careful with him, Junebug. He's one of the good ones."

I nod, because I know.

Chapter Fifty-Six
Asher

"Can I get you another round?" The bartender at Sip asks, eyeing us suspiciously. She looks vaguely familiar, but I can't place her. I'm two double whiskeys deep after not having drank for the last several weeks in solidarity with June; admittedly my problem-solving skills are a little lagging tonight. I'm physically and emotionally exhausted, and as much as I would never admit it to Devin, my jaw hurts like a bitch.

"No thank you, D," Crawford says. I wonder if he flirted with her to get her name. If he's giving her a nickname already, he must feel like he's got this locked in. Interesting, seeing as she's fairly pregnant. She's pretty, but she's nothing compared to my June. Her tight tank top rides up on her stomach a bit and it reminds me how much I can't wait for June's belly to swell.

Tonight, I'm drinking my emotions. Because even though things between June and me are good, and things between Devin and me are possibly getting on the right track, I didn't miss the way my teammates looked at me after filing into the clubhouse today. They heard what Devin said before he socked me in the face, and some of them didn't bother to pretend they weren't judging me.

"So, are we going to talk about it or are we just drinking tonight?" Crawford eyes me warily over the top of his whiskey glass. I'd already finished two drinks before he met me, and the rest of this one is going down quickly too. I kind of wish he hadn't told the bartender no on the additional round.

"What's there to say?" I ask evasively.

"Hmm, I don't know, Incaudo. Maybe you could have told me that the roommate you were fucking is Devin Demoranville's sister!" His words are a quiet hiss, only for me to hear, but I still whip my head toward him as if he shouted.

"Watch it. I'm not *fucking* her. I'm in love with her. I'm having a baby with her. Which, I guess does mean I'm fucking her, but it's not like that."

Crawford pauses, his drink halfway to his mouth. He stares at me in stunned silence, as if he's trying to figure out if I'm messing with him or not.

"No shit? You're having a baby?" I can't help my grin, not even caring that it causes my jaw to throb angrily.

"Yeah. June is due in February." I swipe through my phone, pulling up a picture of the sonogram. At this point, it doesn't look like much, but to me, it's the most beautiful thing I've ever seen. Crawford nods and acts impressed, which is nice of him, seeing as the photo looks kind of blobby and only vaguely human if you have someone point out the body parts to you.

"So...does Demoranville know? About the baby, I mean?"

"Yeah," I sigh, running a hand through my hair. "He didn't exactly find out the way we wanted him to. We wanted to tell him, give ourselves a chance to explain that we've been in love with each other, unbeknownst to each other, since high school. It didn't exactly go according to plan."

Out of the corner of my eye, the bartender is wiping the counter exceedingly slowly with a rag. She seems to be lingering closely, but at this point, I don't even care. The cat's out of the bag and unless this bartender also works for the Chicago Foxes, I don't care that she enjoys listening to our salacious gossip.

"No shit?" I nod. Crawford is thoughtful, pensive before he says more. "I just thought you were hooking up with your roommate so you both could get off, then you went and fell in love with her. I didn't realize you've been in love with her since you were a kid."

I grin. Nostalgia is a powerful emotion, and one of my favorites. Teenage June was beautiful, but so is twenty-four-year-old June. She's so sure of herself, so kind and generous, that even if I didn't already love her from a young age, falling in love with her now would have been the easiest thing I've ever done.

"Yeah. She's it for me, man. I can't believe I get to have her. She's finally mine. And we made a baby together. A *baby*." I keep repeating the word in a tone that demonstrates just how awe-inspiring the concept is.

The whiskey is fully hitting me now. I've never been a big drinker, but after abstaining for a while, these heavy pours are getting to me. Suddenly, another reality comes slamming into me, one not quite as pleasant as making a baby with the woman of my dreams.

"Do you think the whole team hates me? I crossed a line. My best friend's sister and all..." I trail off.

"Nah," Crawford says, waving the air in front of him to dispel any notions of hard feelings. "You should probably tell them that you love her and there's a baby on the way, though. That'll probably help convince anyone who's still on the fence."

Another round and twenty minutes or so later, or maybe longer, because I'm officially drunk now, Crawford heads out. He says something to the bartender, who smiles and shakes her head. I guess for once, he couldn't close the deal with a woman.

I sit at the bar for a while longer, until the lights in the place start to turn on. June texted me an hour ago, letting me know she was heading to bed. In that time, I've been trying to sober up, but I'm fairly certain I'll be taking a rideshare home and leaving my car in the bar parking lot.

"Finally." The bartender looks over my shoulder at whoever walked through the door. "Come get your boy. He's a bit of a mess tonight."

Suddenly, Samuel Benjamin's face is swimming in my vision. "C'mon, Ash. You've had quite the day." Coming to stand beside him, the pregnant bartender stands on her tiptoes to greet my manager with a kiss. I blink, looking back and forth between them.

"Ohhhhhhh," I say, suddenly aware of how loud my voice is in the empty bar. "That's where I know you from. You're Benny's wife! You ran after him last year! I saw you!" I watched from the back of the team bus as the black-haired beauty ran after a heartbroken Benny last season. The next day, he was late to our road game in Milwaukee, but he appeared in much higher spirits.

"See what I mean?" she says to Benny, before saying, "*Messy*" in an exaggerated whisper. Turning to me, she holds her hand out. "Give me your keys, Rocky. I'll follow behind in your car while this one takes you in his. Don't puke in my husband's car, please."

"Okay, but I need an apple first."

CHAPTER FIFTY-SEVEN
June

"Please. Don't move." Asher is starfished face-down on the bed, an arm and a leg casually slung over me. His voice is muffled by my hair as he speaks into the crook of my neck. He groans as I wiggle my body out from underneath him. Normally, I love being as close as possible to him, but right now, my bladder is not a fan.

"Junie. If I don't move, my hangover can't find me." I giggle, Asher's dead weight pressing me further into the mattress. My laughter is not helping the overfilled bladder situation; I freeze, hoping the lack of movement will allow me to regain more muscle control so I don't pee the bed. Pressing my legs together, I heave him off me and waddle to the bathroom.

When I return, he is still face-down, but he lifts an arm when he hears me enter the room. I slide underneath it and settle in just as my phone vibrates with an incoming text.

"Noooooo," Asher moans when I jostle him, stretching to reach my phone. I run my fingers through his hair. He came home late and very drunk in the early hours of the morning. I couldn't make out who helped him through the front door, but a large man, probably one of his teammates, got him into bed and took off his shoes. Asher had been trying to take his pants off over his shoes and was generally being a menace before whoever it was just shoved him into bed and finished the job for him.

"Look at my Junie," Asher had whined to his friend as I sat up, attempting to help him under the covers. "Isn't she so beautiful?" I don't want to know what I looked like; I was dead asleep until he crashed into bed. "She's the most perfect woman in the world. Hey, Skipper, did you know I've loved this girl since I was seventeen?"

The man at the foot of our bed chuckled softly. "So I've heard," he replied agreeably.

"Skip, I'm gonna marry her one day. She's forever for me, man." I started shushing Asher before he embarrassed himself even further. He reeked of whiskey and wasn't thinking straight. We haven't talked about marriage; we've barely talked through the logistics of raising a baby together. We're still in that excitement and wonder phase. While I assume he and I will live together in the offseason, we haven't exactly talked about it. After the fiasco of Devin finding everything out, I'm not sure I'll have a job to worry about anyway.

"I'll flip the lock on my way out," the man had told both of us. I murmured my thanks and focused my energy on placating an increasingly sappy Asher.

"Junie, do you want to be my forever?" In the dark, I could make out his hopeful eyes. "Be my forever, Junie."

"Let's talk about this in the morning, baby." I doubted he would remember, and I knew he was blitzed out of his mind, but my heart couldn't help but hope that the old saying of a drunk mind speaks a sober heart rang true here. I would consider myself lucky to be able to spend the rest of my days with Asher.

My phone buzzes with another text as my fingers grapple with it. I'm dreading the cold reality hit I'm about to get. I still haven't talked to my parents after the chaos of yesterday. I can only hope the texts aren't work-related. There's not enough coffee in the world to prepare me for that disaster, especially now that I'm drinking decaf.

Delaney Kristoff-Benjamin

> So…Asher Incaudo, huh?

> In the spirit of full disclosure, I may or may not know about the pregnancy, too.

My stomach bottoms out. I thought the last few days of walking around, ready to puke, were mostly over, but apparently not. It's one thing for me to have to reckon with Deb for dating a player. There was a small part of me that hoped no one would connect the dots between the fight yesterday on the field and me, but when Whitney sent me a fan analysis video lipreading his words prior to Devin's punch, that part of me crumbled to nothingness. The video, in which the fan correctly reads Devin saying "You fucked my sister! Friendship over," has close to two million views already. The comments section was so out of control, I stopped reading after the first page. I know it's futile, hoping somehow the video doesn't make it across the desk of any of the Foxes office personnel.

I don't know what to say to Delaney. She's always been my favorite of the wives. I can't lie to her, but I also have no idea how she knows everything. Should I play dumb and hope she forgets what she knows?

> Me
> Um, what?

It's the best I could come up with, and even I know it's a lame attempt at deflection. Asher's phone begins to ring, vibrating incessantly on his nightstand. He silences it, only for it to begin vibrating again a few seconds later. He groans, oblivious to my inner panic about how to respond to my boyfriend's boss's wife.

> Don't worry. Your secret is safe with me, but if the internet today is any indication, it's not me you have to worry about.

> Want to grab a coffee? Now that you're pregnant too, we can suffer through decaf together!

The texts keep rolling in. I barely have a chance to process them, let alone read them, before another comes in.

> I'm outside your apartment, by the way. Come on down. I'm sure Asher needs to put out fires or sleep off his hangover (or both).

I groan but decide I better face this head-on, barely registering that Delaney somehow knows where I live. I roll out of bed again, brush my teeth and hair quickly, and throw on a pair of leggings and my favorite green shirt. It has a cartoon avocado running away crying on it, while a second avocado runs after him, saying "I said you were the *good* kind of fat!" I need a little levity in my morning, but I have a feeling this shirt is as much as I'm going to get.

I smile at the apple on the counter; Asher has brought me home a single piece of produce each week to coincide with the size of our baby. Week fifteen, they must be the size of an apple. I set the newest fruit next to last week's lemon. Asher already ate the plum from week thirteen. I think it's weird to eat the fruit, knowing it represents our child, but he doesn't have an issue with it. I'll save the apple for him, too.

Armor on, I descend the stairs to determine just how bad my fate might be. Hopefully better than Asher's, who, by the look on his face as he listens to whoever is on the phone, either might vomit or pass out. He shoos me away with what I'm sure he thinks is a reassuring smile, but it does little to relax me.

Delaney's smile is warm when she sees me. I'm hit by an instant wave of relief. I'm not sure what I expected, but the fact that she isn't yelling at me or telling me that I let everyone down in this job, too, is a small comfort. She links her arm through mine and steers me to a coffee shop a few blocks away. I'm relatively silent on the walk, grateful that she chooses to fill the void with conversation that doesn't require me to respond with anything more than "mmhmm." She tells me about how she helps her friends and former employers by moonlighting at their bar every once in a while during the season. She talks about her latest Ob-gyn appointment and how excited Benny is to have another baby. She rambles on about how she's going to make different custom liqueur-filled chocolates for the holiday season once she can start drinking again. She informs me of her latest pregnancy craving, which would sound incredible if I weren't so nauseous thinking about losing my job. She chatters brightly about how if you mix the pizza rolls with the Caesar salad *after* you put the dressing on, they stay crispier, serving as delightful little exploding croutons.

I'm barely listening by the time we receive our order. Delaney requested the barista add a cranberry muffin to my order before paying for the whole thing herself. I'm not sure if I'm permitted to allow her to pay for me, given that it might blur some professional boundaries, but I'm tired of constantly questioning what I can and cannot do in my personal life because of a job I may no longer even have.

We settle into a booth in the back corner of the coffee shop. It's a Sunday morning and the place is noisy and bustling, but I suppose that bodes well for me, because there's less of a chance our conversation will be overheard.

"Remember how I told you I moonlight tending bar for my friends?" I nod. "I was the one serving Asher last night." She holds up a hand, as if to stop me from speaking, but I'm still a little numb from the past thirty-six hours or so, so I wasn't going to try to formulate words. "Before you say anything, I'm not sorry he got so drunk on my watch. After everything he's dealing with, the man deserved to get good and drunk. Although he might hate me for the hangover I'm sure he's feeling today."

I'm hit with a pang of guilt. I've been so focused on how everything has been impacting me that I didn't stop to think about how stressful this must be for him. Sure, I knew his relationship with Devin is on shaky ground, but they seemed to have reached something of an understanding last night. I didn't think about how the fight and getting tossed from the game was going to impact Asher's career. I instantly feel sicker than I did when we walked in here.

"Okay, let's start over," Delaney says, sympathy etched in her features. "Asher will be okay. I promise. The next few days are probably going to be a headache for him, according to everything Benny told me last night, but he'll be fine. These things happen." She shrugs, as if a benches-clearing brawl, contract violations, betrayals of friendships, and secret babies are everyday occurrences.

I nod and swallow, pulling in deep inhales while trying to will the nausea away.

"Let's go through everything, one by one. You can tell me as little or as much as you want, and I'll tell you everything I know, which isn't a lot, but it all comes from my husband, who, by the way, is kind of a big deal around here." When I don't say anything, she pops off a corner of my muffin and tosses it in her mouth before taking a sip of her coffee and diving in. "Okay. Last night, Asher said that he's been in love with you since you were in high school?"

I can't help but smile. It might have sucked at the time, thinking my feelings for him were unreturned, but now it's my favorite part of our story. Somehow, it makes the path we took to find each other again worthwhile.

"Yeah. We grew up together. Ash is two years older than me and the same age as my brother. As I'm sure you know now, Devin and Asher are best friends. Or were best friends." My smile fades. Delaney waves her hand in front of her face.

"They're men. They'll fight and get over it. And they've already gotten through the fighting part, so they're probably already back to being friends." I'm not sure if that's true, but for everyone's sake, I hope she's right. "So, when did you really get together?"

I tell Delaney the highlights about finding a job with the Foxes, moving in with Asher, and falling back in love with him. I skip over the parts about our friends with benefits situation, but given the way her eyes sparkle, I'm sure she can connect some of those dots when I tell her we discovered I was pregnant the day after we confessed our true feelings for each other.

"It's been a bit of a rollercoaster," I admit.

"Yeah, but there's a reason why everyone loves rollercoasters. They're fun as fuck." I'm startled by the laugh that bursts out of me. It feels good to laugh–really laugh– after the heaviness of the last few days.

"So why all the cloak and dagger? I get why you didn't want your brother to find out until you knew if it was serious, but you didn't tell us." She tries to hide the hurt on her face. Over the last few weeks, especially since Delaney and the other girls stood up for me against Melody Malone, I felt like we were becoming closer. I understand why she might feel a little betrayed, especially seeing as she's the only other pregnant one in the family section. It would have been nice to be able to share my pregnancy journey with her. I remind her about the nonfraternization clause in my contract.

"What the fuck." Her eyes bug out when I inform her of the details. "What a fucking antiquated rule. I get that you don't want people, like, sexually harassing the players but a clause like that makes it seem like you're automatically unprofessional. Like you only signed up for the job to be a cleat chaser."

I never thought about the message that sends, only thinking about how the players must be relieved to not have to worry about getting hit on at work or being used for their status...but if any of that happened in a regular workplace, HR would get involved right away anyway, because it's not appropriate or professional, regardless of a clause. In a workplace full of consenting adults, they should be able to make their own decisions about who they hang out (or do more) with. The Foxes could still protect their company's assets by having their employees inform HR if things moved beyond friendship, the same as any other business does.

For the first time, I'm finally allowing myself to feel angry about my situation. Asher certainly doesn't have a nonfraternization clause in his contract; he can hang out with anyone he wants. It's only me who will suffer any consequences.

"Isn't that always the way?" Delaney voices my thoughts. "You can't hang out with Asher or any other player, but there's nothing that's stopping players from sleeping with each other—which, by the way, would be far more impactful on clubhouse interactions, I would imagine." She winks.

"It's already a power differential," I realize aloud. "All of that to say, of course, that it's probably too little, too late for me. I went into my relationship with Asher knowing I was breaking my contract. It's hard to argue it's not fair at this point."

"Maybe. But don't you think it's still worth fighting?" I shrug. After Tampa, I'm confident I don't want to stick around a job where I'm not wanted or appreciated. It probably doesn't matter that I got this job on my own merits, prior to reuniting with Asher: all anyone will see is that I'm with him now. I don't know if that's better or worse than people thinking I took this job to gain access to athletes, in search of a potential baby daddy. I sigh.

"There's no winning here," I tell Delaney honestly.

"Maybe not at work, but it sounds like you got a pretty good prize in Asher in your personal life." I smile.

"Yeah, that is true. When I think of it that way, I almost don't care about my job. I mean, other than the paycheck. And benefits. And the sense of personal fulfillment it gives me." Delaney laughs.

"I guess we can't always have it all." She thinks for a moment, then adds, "But maybe if you get fired, you can just sit in the stands with us all game anyway. You're a WAG now, you know."

My grin widens. "Yeah. I guess I am."

By the time I make it home, I'm feeling much lighter. A large part of me really will be disappointed if I get fired, but an even bigger part of me doesn't care as long as it means Asher and I are okay.

My lightness shatters when I walk through the front door. The stress is apparent on Asher's face as he paces the apartment, still on the phone. When he finally hangs up, he heaves out a sigh before greeting me with a soft kiss. I push his hair back from his forehead.

"How are you feeling?"

"Nothing scares away a hangover like a PR specialist." His lips quirk into a small smile, but his words fall flat. Asher and Devin have the same sports agent, and I'm pretty sure they share the same PR person, too. Asher's such a golden boy; I'm not sure he's had to use her too much beyond standard media training.

"Mariah is pissed at me and Dev. She's working overtime to spin the story, but there are lipreading videos all over the internet that are working against us." I cringe, having watched said videos a few times myself. "And I'll probably get my sentence today. My agent, Sean, thinks I'm looking at at least a five-game suspension, so that I miss a start."

Yep, all that earlier lightness is gone. My heart breaks for Asher and the consequences he's incurring for being with me. I'm not enough of a martyr to suggest we break it off, but I can't help but think I'm supposed to be making his life easier, not more difficult. As if he can read my thoughts, he pulls me into his chest.

"Listen to me. This is not your fault. I threw at your brother; that's on me. He punched me; that's on him. None of this is on you. Do you understand me?" He tilts my chin, forcing eye contact as I swallow, lost in the intensity in his hazel eyes. "We're going to figure this out. We'll weather the storm for a few days, and after that, we'll be good. And when all this is over, I am going to take my girlfriend on a very public date. I'm going to feed her the best Italian steakhouse meal before I come home and put a few more babies inside her."

I choke out a laugh. "You can't put another baby inside me. I'm already growing you one. I'm not a damn kangaroo." Any further arguments I have are cut off by Asher's gentle kiss.

CHAPTER FIFTY-EIGHT
Asher

"Incaudo, my office when you're done running. And you better not puke on my field!" Benny's words would be a lot more intimidating if he said them with any sort of bite, but the man is mostly a teddy bear.

The day after a start is filled with light jogging and lots of treatment, but seeing as I didn't even go three and a third innings yesterday, my strength and conditioning coach works me a little harder than normal. And seeing as I'm still working on my hangover recovery, practice today seems to be punishment enough. That and the slight bruising of the left side of my jaw.

Benny offers me a seat when I enter his office. I choose the chair closest to his desk instead of the lumpy couch that dwarfs the rest of the furniture in the room. The shelf behind his desk is littered with photographs of his family. A large photo featuring him kissing his wife in front of a river sits in the center in an ornate silver frame. Delaney is wearing a white sundress and purple Converse; it must be their wedding photo. Their foreheads are pressed toward each other, but their happiness radiates around them.

My eyes flick back to Benny, whose face is uncharacteristically solemn. He is usually serious during the games, but rarely solemn.

"I just heard from MLB. You're being fined two thousand dollars and suspended for five games. You'll miss your next start. You can try to appeal and you might get your fine reduced, but I'm guessing they won't reduce the suspension."

I nod. "I understand. For what it's worth, I'm sorry. I didn't mean to let you guys down or make this harder on you."

"Thanks for saying that. I appreciate it. We'll have to shuffle things around to cover your start, but it won't be too bad. From what I understand, Demoranville is suspended for six games and fined five thousand. He'll likely appeal, but at least MLB is viewing him as the aggressor, rather than you. Even though you threw at his head." I smirk.

"I wasn't going to hit him with my pitch. I knew what I was doing."

Benny snorts. "Spoken like a true pitcher." He stands. "The suspension will be officially delivered to you at four o'clock, which means you will not be allowed in the dugout, bullpen, or clubhouse. You can still work out, but once game time starts, you have to be out of here." I nod, knowing the rules all too well.

When I exit his office, Stephen, one of our clubhouse attendants, finds me. "Hey, Incaudo. There's someone here to see you." My heart lifts, thinking June has finally made her way down to the clubhouse. I haven't had my phone with me, but I grab it from my locker and stuff it into my athletic shorts as I follow Stephen down the hallway and to the clubhouse entrance. Devin leans against the wall, waiting. Any other week, I'd be thrilled to see him. Today, though, I can't help but feel disappointed.

"Wow, don't look so excited to see me," he deadpans.

"I was hoping for a different Demoranville," I tell him honestly.

"Jesus Christ." He shakes his head. "You make one baby with my sister and suddenly I'm no longer your favorite Demoranville."

I laugh. I appreciate that he's here, that he's trying. "Let's be honest, Dev. June has always been my favorite Demoranville." He rolls his eyes.

"I'm learning that." I walk with him to the end of the hallway. "Can we talk somewhere private?"

"Yeah. I'll find us a conference room." I hit the elevator button. It opens immediately and we stride in. We're both in our practice gear, decked out with our respective teams' logos, both of us a little sweaty from our conditioning work.

"Suspension hits soon, so I'll try to make this quick," he says, following me off the elevator and down the hall. There's no shortage of empty conference rooms; with game start only two hours away, meetings have already wrapped up for the day. I've never been allowed to visit June at work before; I'm not sure if her office is even on this floor, but I already feel closer to her. Neither of us knew what to expect for her today. I pull out my phone and confirm I don't have any messages from her yet. That either means she's hard at work or she's been fired and is so distraught she doesn't want to talk to me about it. My stomach turns to lead thinking about the latter.

When the door to the conference room closes quietly behind us, Devin stands in front of the floor-to-ceiling windows, looking out onto the foot traffic below. If any of the fans below us looked straight up, they'd see both of us. I imagine the social media frenzy that would make, given that just over twenty-four hours ago, the two of us caused a benches-clearing brawl and now here we are, standing together. Not quite friends, but not not-friends, either.

"You would have been the exception, you know." My head flies up, but Devin won't make eye contact with me. He stares out the window, as if he's still not sure he wants to look at me.

"What?"

"I wouldn't have minded if you dated her in high school." Devin's words are quiet yet firm.

"Bullshit." I refuse to let my mind wander, to visit all the what-could-have-beens. It would be too painful.

"Well, I might have minded. But it would have been better being you than fucking Greg." I can't help but smirk at that. Devin runs his hands through his hair, exhaling deeply. "I didn't know. How could I not know?"

I don't know if he is referring to my feelings for his sister starting when we were kids, or if he's talking about more recent events.

"I didn't want you to know. Fuck, I didn't even want *her* to know, because I knew, even then, that I wasn't good enough. It's why I forced myself to lose touch with her in college and why I wasn't outwardly thrilled about her moving in. I felt like such a fucking masochist, agreeing to her moving in, knowing it would only end up breaking my heart." My eyes burn as I stare hard at the design in the carpet, refusing to blink.

"I didn't know." Devin's words are soft, barely audible. He sits heavily in a roller chair, rubbing his knuckles. "If I had known, I wouldn't have pushed this on you..." He lets his words hang in the air.

"I'm glad you did." A small smile creeps onto my mouth. "Dev. I know this is a lot for you to process, but this is everything I've ever wanted. I have the girl I've loved since I was seventeen. We're having a *baby*." The tears building in my eyes finally spill over, but I don't wipe them away. For once, I don't hide my feelings from my best friend. He deserves to see my joy.

"Fuck yeah, you are," he tells me, not bothering to hide the pride in his voice. My laugh is watery but genuine.

"Fuck yeah, I am."

Devin and I stay there for a while, him seated, me standing, staring out the window. We seem to have reached an understanding. It might take a bit to get us back to normal, but I think we'll get there eventually.

"I'm glad it's you, you know. If it had to be anyone, I'm glad it's you."

I bark a quick laugh. "How much did that burn to say?"

Devin offers me his own small smile. "Not at all. It's the truth."

The only place Devin and I are technically allowed to go on MLB property, now that our suspensions are in effect, is the stands of the game, and neither of us are stupid enough to attempt that. I wasn't sure how he was going to respond to my invitation to come back to my apartment to watch the game together from there. I half-expected him to tell me to fuck off, that I was pushing the friendship thing too fast after the events of the last few days. To my surprise, he readily agreed and hopped in my car to go home with me. I still haven't heard from June, so having Devin with me helps to assuage some of my anxiety, even if I know it's just a distraction.

Last night, not wanting to abandon our tradition, June made me brownies after Devin left and while I was at Sip. She covered them in aluminum foil and I forgot about them until now. I pull the pan toward me, preparing to cut slices for Devin and me as he makes himself at home on my couch. When I peel back the covering, I'm met with a tiny flag in the middle of the pan, constructed from a sticky note and a toothpick. I tip my head back and laugh loudly, thoroughly absorbing June's presence.

"What's so funny?" Devin asks. When I don't immediately respond, he launches himself over the back of my couch and approaches the brownie pan. His eyes widen when he sees the peanut butter pretzel topped pan, with a tiny pink flag sticking out the top, proudly pronouncing "The Knockout Brownie." There's a tiny stick figure punching another, taller, stick figure.

Once again, I'm reminded that if I hadn't already put a baby in June, her sense of humor would cause me to want to do it all over again.

I frown when I hear June's key in the lock. It's the fourth inning of tonight's game, which I know, because Devin and I are watching it live in my living room. June typically makes it home from work earlier than me, but I've never known her to leave work prior to the end of a game. Which means things probably did not go well for her at work today. I'm standing and striding to the door before she even crosses the threshold. I catch her in my arms as she drops her purse onto the counter. She doesn't even fight me, allowing me to pick her up and carry her to the couch. Devin is standing too, alarm on his face.

I sit with her straddling my lap, not caring that Devin might be uncomfortable seeing this. It's not sexual anyway; if there was a way I could sit where I am more wrapped around June, I'd be doing it, because right now, everything about her body language is screaming that she needs protection. She's not crying, which is almost more alarming. She's shed so many tears the last few days that I wonder if she's all cried out. I sit, stroking her back. Devin puts the television on mute. We both just wait.

Finally, she releases a shuddering sigh. She's no doubt exhausted. In all the baby books I've read, there's a clear theme of the exhaustion that comes with creating another human, but I also know she hasn't been sleeping well. Our lives have been completely upended the last few days; it's a wonder she's even standing half the time.

"My employment with the Foxes is 'under review,'" she tells us, using air quotes. "Deb asked me to work the day as usual, but to meet with her and HR once the game started. They asked for the truth, and I just couldn't lie anymore, Asher. I didn't want to hide this part of our lives. I'm tired of it." I can't help my smile; I'm not happy about the situation, but I've been hiding my love for June for years. I've been ready to shout it from the rooftops for a long time now. Still, loving me is not a reason for June to lose her job.

"What does that mean, under review?" Devin, per usual, plows past the fact that this is a somewhat emotional topic and gets straight to business. June sighs, turning her face toward him.

"I'm basically suspended, pending a review of whether my conduct violates my contract enough to warrant termination."

I hate the cold, professional language she uses, clearly parroting what was said to her. I've always liked Deb, from my limited interactions with her. I have a feeling this is coming more from HR than anywhere else. June's eyes widen, as if she's finally taking us in and the fact that we're at home in the middle of a game.

"What are you both doing here?" She covers her mouth, imagining the worst. Devin and I wear matching smirks.

"Looks like you're not the only one suspended, baby girl." Before she can panic, I pull her close again. "It's nothing to worry about. Just a few games and two thousand bucks."

"You got fined two thousand dollars? What the fuck? I was fined five thousand!" My smile is triumphant.

"I've been on the phone with Sean all morning, who obviously relayed the circumstances to the MLB suspension committee. They clearly believe I'm an upstanding guy who fell in love, and you're the unhinged brother who can't let it go and likes to crowd the batter's box." Devin glares at me.

"Lucky for you, I already told the commissioner's office I'd pay your fine for you," he grumbles. At my look of surprise, he simply says, "Save your money for the baby."

Later, after the Foxes pull off a resounding win and Devin leaves, grumbling about having to carry the team with his batting average, June sinks into bed with me. Devin and I spent a few innings convincing her that everything would be okay as far as work is concerned. She mentioned that Delaney had Benny go to bat for her, so to speak. There's a reason why Samuel Benjamin is a beloved manager across baseball.

I know June isn't okay with things the way they are at work, and I'm going to do whatever I can within my power to make HR see that this isn't June's fault (because it's not anyone's fault) and that losing her would be a huge detriment to not only the Foxes Family Program, but, as a result, to the morale of the team. I fired off a few texts as soon as the game ended, saying as much, but I haven't heard back yet.

"Hey baby?" June's back is pressed to my chest. My favorite time of day is when I hold her in bed each night. It makes for lonely road trips, but the times we are physically together are that much better.

"Hmm?" She responds sleepily.

"I'm sorry." June startles, shifting to face me. "I'm sorry that I let my fear of losing your brother's friendship prevent me from seeking you out sooner. I'm sorry that we're finally getting together now, instead of eight years ago."

She presses a soft kiss against my lips.

"I'm not. Maybe we would have gotten together then and grown together, but being apart also allowed us to grow into the people we are now. Maybe it wouldn't have worked back then." She grins. "But it's working now."

I press myself onto my elbow to hover over her. I run my nose along the length of her jaw, her nose.

"Yeah," I agree. "I want it to work forever."

"Forever?" Her words are breathy, but I hate the tiny sliver of doubt I hear in them.

"Yeah, baby. Forever. Someday soon, if you let me, I'll show you how serious I am. And instead of being stuck with me for eighteen years, you'll be stuck with me forever."

June's voice is sleepy, content when she answers me. "Forever sounds good to me."

Chapter Fifty-Nine
June

Now that the two most important men in my life are both suspended from work, and I am too, it's been a relaxing yet confusing couple of days. Since Devin isn't allowed in the clubhouse during games, he was given permission to stay in Chicago for a couple days, working out here while he serves his suspension. It's weird and nice to have him here in the middle of the season. It's also weird having some free time at the same time as Dev and Ash. We went to the beach and checked out a few new restaurants. We even took an architecture cruise along the Chicago River, and I can confirm that it would be a great thing to plan for the WAGs if I ever get my job back.

A few of the WAGs have reached out to me, offering their support. I'm not sure there's anything they can do, but it's nice to hear their words of encouragement. Delaney has been texting me every morning reminding me that she's always available to grab lunch or a prenatal yoga class. She always follows this text with a reminder that she doesn't really want to do yoga, but feels like it's something she should offer anyway.

Today, Asher is taking me to lunch with him and Devin. I finally feel a little more pregnant, now that cravings have started to hit me. Luckily for Asher, I tend to crave Italian food the most, and he's been thrilled with the turn this has taken. He supports me in ordering every variation of garlic bread at each restaurant we go to. Devin's appetite is as big as Asher's, so I haven't heard him complain either. It's nice, being able to hang out with my brother and Asher, just like old times. Only unlike old times, Asher holds my hand or squeezes my ass on the regular. Devin tries to pointedly ignore the latter.

"Why are you wearing a blueberry bush on your shirt?" Devin asks me around a mouthful of garlic knot.

"It's not a blueberry bush, you uncultured heathen. It's a juniper bush. Asher got it for me." He glares at me.

"How the fuck am I supposed to know what a juniper bush looks like? I'm not a botanist." I shrug. After a beat, Devin's eyes widen, as if finally connecting the dots to a long unsolved mystery. "Juniper..." he murmurs. "Fucking hell, Incaudo. *She's* Juniper?"

Asher's eyes dance with mirth, while mine reflect confusion.

"What does that mean?" I ask both of them. "He got me this shirt in Kansas City, at a distillery. It's because I like gin and tonics!"

"No, that's not what it fucking means, and he knows it." Devin points across the table at Asher, who doesn't deny it. I turn to my boyfriend who is grinning like the cat that got the canary.

"Explain."

CHAPTER SIXTY
Asher
Age 18

I can't ignore her. I've tried. I feel like a terrible friend. I *know* I'm a terrible friend. Trust me, if there was a way I could rid myself of my ridiculous crush on my best friend's sister, I would. I constantly feel guilty.

June's been around forever. Of course, June was always around, but I never viewed her as anything other than my best friend's sister. The shift from friend to fantasy happened so slowly that I didn't realize it was happening until it was too late. Until now, when I can't look at my own best friend without thinking about his sister, wondering if she is going to be hanging out with us, or watching our games, or just breathing the same air as me.

There is no way I can explain that to Devin. I'd caught his raised eyebrows when I asked one too many times about what June's plans were and whether she'd be joining us. Since then, I've kept my previously passing interest in June's social life to myself. Now that we've kissed, though–that one, slow, stupidly good kiss–it's becoming harder and harder to keep her name off my lips.

I slip up once, and only once.

I create the Juniper nickname on the fly, out of necessity—an act of survival, really.

Devin asks why I'm not interested in Sierra Ridgway, who practically threw herself at me after a summer bonfire last night.

"Because she's not June...iper."

It's the lamest, most feeble recovery in the world, but somehow, Devin doesn't catch it. Chalk it up to being distracted or divine intervention, but somehow, Devin never puts two and two together, and for the rest of the summer, he believes I am talking to some girl online named Juniper.

I obviously never correct him.

Chapter Sixty-One
June

Asher's eyes narrow as he stares down the batter. Okay, I can't see his eyes narrowing from my seat in the stands, but I *imagine* his eyes narrow, homing in with laser-like focus on his target. It's sexy as hell.

I watch his glove twist and his toe tap before he goes into his windup, swinging his leg high and delivering a ninety-eight mile per hour fastball.

Ugh, the crowd collectively sighs with disappointment. It was a great pitch, landing solidly in Tyler Edwards's glove with a smack I can hear from here. For the last two innings, Asher has been throwing gold, and his fastballs are hovering just under one hundred miles per hour. The sweat glistens on his forearms. When the jumbotron in center field displays a close-up of his face, I involuntarily lick my lips. He's hot in all senses of the word, sweat trickling down his temple.

"Do you need a fan?" Delaney asks, using her napkin to waft the humid air toward my face.

"I wouldn't say no," I admit. And not just because I'm a pregnant woman sitting in ninety-degree weather. Asher initially didn't want me to come to the game due to the weather forecast, but after I promised to hydrate well, he relented. I think it helped that Alicia James promised to keep me supplied with a steady stream of waters and Gatorades.

I'm still technically on leave from work. If I don't think about it too much, I can almost convince myself I'm on sabbatical, earning myself a nice little vacation thanks to all my hard work during the first half of the season. Denial is not just a river in Egypt, my friends.

Between the core group of wives, Amy, Jenny, Alicia, Delaney, and Hailey have kept me busy enough during Asher's road games that I don't dwell on my employment status too much. I've joined their book club, even though I still belong to the one held at the indie bookstore in Roscoe Village. These days, I seem to have an abundance of time on my hands, so reading for a second book club is hardly taxing.

The umpire punches out another batter. Let's face it, when you throw nearly a hundred miles an hour with even the smallest bit of accuracy, you're going to get out of the inning. It's hard to get a fast enough bat speed to match what Asher is hurling from the mound, which is why this game is moving at a faster clip. We're in the seventh inning, and while Asher hasn't thrown a ton of pitches, he's been throwing with such force that I'm not sure how much longer Benny is going to keep him in the game. His pitches look good, though.

Devin left to go back to New York the other day. This is technically Asher's first start since his suspension, and the extra time off seems to have done him good. I watch as he shakes off Edwards's initial pitch suggestion, then nods at Edwards's second attempt. He moves into his windup and releases the ball. Almost immediately, I hear the smack of leather against leather as the ball lands in the catcher's mitt. My eyes, along with every other set of eyes in the stadium, swing toward the radar display.

102.

I leap out of my seat, my cheers drowned out by the roar of the crowd. Asher looks around, surprised, as if he wasn't even aware of the crowd hanging on his every pitch. I can't help my grin; there's that famous Incaudo laser focus.

His next pitch results in a popup back to the mound. He takes it himself easily before tossing it to JJ when he jogs past him to go to the dugout. Before Asher turns to follow his shortstop, he pauses on the mound, flips his glove open, and lightly kisses it.

Right where the new stitching rests.

While Asher was gone, I asked the equipment manager for one more favor. This time, when he said yes, he added a winky face emoji to his text, letting me know he knew I was asking as Asher's girlfriend, not as a Foxes Family Program employee. Nevertheless, he delivered.

Because now, in addition to his mother's words stitched on his glove, Asher's leather is sporting a new word, right over the heel of his palm.

Forever.

CHAPTER SIXTY-TWO
Asher

I feel bad, keeping June waiting after my game. It was a media frenzy in the clubhouse after we won. I pitched my first complete game, which is celebration enough, but today, my pitch speed topped triple digits, so every reporter in the locker room wanted to talk to me. That is, of course, after I completed the official press conference afterward. By the time I was done with media and treatment, the postgame activities lasted almost as long as the game itself.

I can't complain. I was nervous to start today, wondering how the crowd would receive me after my suspension. My teammates, once they found out that June and I were in love and I wasn't just an asshole taking advantage of a situation, all made sure to let me know there were no hard feelings either. Crawford, however, still takes it upon himself to frequently remind me that I'm never allowed around his sister.

He doesn't even have a sister.

I finally check my phone for the first time since I texted June, informing her of all the press attention I needed to field.

Juniper

> Don't worry about it. Take your time. You deserve the attention.

> Proud of you.

By the time I make it up to the lobby, June is the only WAG left waiting. She's sitting on a bench, chatting with someone who looks like another employee, if her Foxes polo is any indication.

"Ash, this is Faye. She's one of the Foxes' legal interns. I worked with her upstairs," June says when I get close to them. I don't miss the way she uses the past tense to talk about work. We're still waiting to hear back from them and it's hard not to feel angry at my employer for dragging their feet on this. It's not about the money, or the benefits. I'll marry June in the next five minutes, and not just to get her on my benefits. I hate what this is doing to her spirit.

I shake Faye's hand before she excuses herself. June watches her go with an almost sadness in her eyes. When she turns her gaze back to me, she hides it well, covering it with excitement for my game today.

"That was quite the performance, Mr. Incaudo!" she gushes, and I know her reaction is genuine, even if she's sad for herself. I pull her into my arms.

"Thank you, Junie. What do you say we get you home? I bet you're ready to get off your feet and into the shower." Her eyes heat. "Because you've been in the sun all day, you nympho." When she turns, I make a point of grabbing her ass. There's no one else in this room anyway. I lean into her space as I murmur, "But you better believe I'm going to devour that pussy while the water runs down your body."

Any time June is lying in my arms is a good moment, but when she's lying here, hair a mess with a sleepy, satisfied grin on her face after her third orgasm of the night? That might actually be my favorite.

"I meant to tell you," she says around a yawn. "Faye told me she thinks Deb is going to call me tomorrow. She gave me a head's-up when I saw her after the game tonight." I brace myself. June had to do a lot of relationship repair with her coworkers, especially Priya, who understandably felt a little betrayed for not having known about our relationship. I hope Faye didn't hold it over her head.

"Did she tell you anything else?" I ask, trying to come off as unworried and nonchalant. I'm not sure what I'll do if the Foxes fire her. I love my job, and the Foxes have been good to me, but now that June is an extension of me and part of my family, if she's not treated well, I've already talked to Sean, my agent, about the possibility of requesting a trade. It won't happen this season because the trade deadline has already passed, but there's a good chance, especially after my performance tonight, that more teams will be interested in me during the offseason. I haven't brought any of this up to June yet, though. I don't want to worry her unnecessarily.

"Not really anything concrete. She just kind of talked about the directions things could go in. She said the nonfraternization clause is pretty airtight, though." June sighs deeply against my chest. "There's not really any way around that, even though I knew you before I signed my contract. Even though they knew I was Devin's sister when they hired me, too. It's kind of hard to argue that I didn't fraternize with you when I'm living with you and having your baby." She makes a good point. Honestly, any point she makes that includes her having my baby is a good one.

"That's still bullshit." I don't care what her contract says, I'll defend this woman until my dying breath.

"Yeah. Basically, the only thing we can hope for at this point, if I want to keep my job, is that the Foxes agree it's not a fireable offense." I nod. I personally feel that what June does in her free time should never warrant her losing her job, but she and I have nontraditional jobs, with very nontraditional hours and responsibilities. I truly don't know which way this is going to go, and while I know, ultimately, we'll be okay no matter what the outcome, it doesn't make the situation any less stressful.

Just as Faye predicted, Deb calls June the next morning and asks her to come in for a meeting later that morning. I'm annoyed instantly. It's an off-day for the team, and I can't help but feel they purposely asked June to come in on a day where a lot of people wouldn't be around. Before she confirms the meeting with Deb, I answer as well. June has had me on speakerphone. We talked about the possibility of me joining her whenever a meeting was scheduled, so I know she doesn't mind me butting in.

"Hi Deb. It's Asher. I'd also like to join your ten o'clock meeting. I'm sure you don't mind." Deb sounds flustered, like she might not mind, but isn't sure how the others in the meeting might feel about my presence. Deb, however, is the head of the Foxes Family Program and she acts like it, ensuring that my presence in the meeting would be a welcome delight.

I stroll into the building, June's hand clasped in mine, at nine-fifty. We're brought immediately into a conference room. I'm not sure if it's because I'm with her, but we are both offered drinks and snacks while we wait, which we both decline. June's fingers twitch, like she's itching to play with the hem of her pretty little sundress. I give her hand a gentle squeeze.

Finally, Deb files in with a blonde guy and a balding man I've never seen before. I recognize the blonde guy from JJ's event. He's the one that made June laugh.

What? I might be a little obsessed with her.

He catches June's eye and gives her a friendly wink, eliciting a small smile from my girl. It has the effect of immediately setting her at ease, and I decide to forgive whoever this guy is for making her laugh without me so many months ago. He introduces himself as Liam, another legal intern. The bald guy is Joseph, head of human resources. We all shake hands, exchanging pleasantries, before we sit again.

Joseph takes a deep breath and begins.

"June, you've been waiting long enough, so I'm going to cut right to the chase." Finally. At least this Joseph guy seems to know what he's doing. "Unfortunately, there's no way around the violation in your nonfraternization clause."

I hate Joseph.

June's face falls. I start to scoot my chair back, ready to leave. There's little they can say here to fix things now. My fingers are practically dialing Sean's number.

Liam holds out a hand across the table.

"Hang on a sec, Asher. Mr. Incaudo." I shake my head. Liam smiles. "Fine, Asher. From a legal perspective, June violated her original contract." Even through the haze of my anger, I don't miss his use of the word original. He continues. "Again, speaking from a legal perspective, the nonfraternization clause is clear. That being said, we know there's a lot more to a person's employment than the legal impact of a contract."

From across the table, Deb smiles at June and opens a manila file folder. She pushes it toward June. June adjusts the folder so it's sitting between us. The file contains pages and pages of what look like printouts of emails. The first one is from Samuel Benjamin. The second is from JJ Jeffers, followed by Amy Jeffers, Caleb and Jenny Andrews, Tyler Edwards, Delaney Kristoff-Benjamin, Hailey and Elijah McClintock, Crawford, the Warners, Kaito Soji and his wife, and a few others. It takes us several minutes to scan the pages, but they all basically say the same thing. They sing June's praises for her work. They commend her on her professionalism, her communication, her ability to sense what the families need and provide it without being asked. Samuel Benjamin's email includes a photo attachment, which is printed and stapled to Benny's email; it's a drawing and letter from Benny's youngest daughter, Scarlett.

There's even emails from Priya, Faye, and Liam, all detailing what a wonderful coworker June is. Priya's email even notes that June never once disclosed her relationship with me, never using it to her advantage despite numerous opportunities to do so.

I'm as speechless as June right now. A drop of saltwater hits the email we're reading from Priya together. I let June have her moment. Because even if she does get fired, at least she'll know she's good at her job and she is so, so loved.

Joseph clears his throat again. "At the risk of sounding like the bad cop, I'm going to say what I need to say first very quickly, and I would ask that you allow me a moment after I say it in order to hear everything. June, given your violation of your original contract, we would like to give you the opportunity to resign from your position–"

"I beg your finest fucking pardon?" I interrupt, but Joseph, that ballsy motherfucker, simply holds up his hand and continues.

"A resignation would allow you to quietly distance yourself from breaking your contract. You would not be required to disclose it as a termination, should any future employer request such information." I can feel my blood boiling. My normally even-keeled temperament is nowhere to be found. June is squeezing the life out of my fingers, trying to maintain a facade of calm, but I know she's moments from breaking down. Still, Joseph continues.

"With your resignation of your original contract, we would then be able to move forward in offering you a new position."

Silence blankets the conference room.

Wait, what?

Deb smiles again, this time directing her words toward the beautiful woman to my left.

"June, you've done a fantastic job this year. These emails prove as much. Given that you clearly never set out to use your position with the Foxes to take advantage of a relationship in your personal life, I've been working with HR and legal to find a way to keep you on, while also not setting any precedents for future employees that we may end up regretting." June's swallow is audible. "If you'd like to hear it, I'd be happy to tell you about the new position?"

"Please," June squeaks out. I encouragingly rub the back of her palm with my thumb.

"Much like your previous position, should you choose to resign and accept your new role, you'd still work in the Family Program. This time, I'd like your role to address the new status and situation you find yourself in." Deb gestures to our clasped hands. "The hours are a little more flexible, should you find yourself needing...different...hours, if your life changes require it." Deb glances at June's stomach but otherwise makes no indication that she's aware of the pregnancy. To her, at this point, everything is just rumors. "You would be a consultant, rather than a direct service provider. We'd like you to use your unique position as both an athlete's partner and a Family Program employee to develop unique opportunities, not just socially for our families, but for things that would ease a family's transition to a new city and a new team. Perhaps revamping the Family Program website with our tech team, recruiting concierge medicine providers, curating a list of hospitality providers in the city that can work with our families on a semi-permanent basis. Of course, we'd like you to work closely with the other partners and family members to develop the most robust Family Program possible, but we would not require you to come into the office every day, or work in the family room."

June nods along, her eyes sparkling not from tears, but this time excitement. To be honest, the new role sounds a lot like her old role, just with more flexibility, but if June's happy, then I'm happy.

"Given your rave reviews," Deb continues, gesturing to the stack of emails, "I'd like to review the benefits and compensation plan available to you. The benefits obviously would remain the same, as those are standard across all full-time employees. While you would not be expected to work a full-time schedule in a consultant role, we anticipate the hours and needs of the role to fluctuate, necessitating the provision of benefits." I know this is Deb throwing June a bone, but I don't question her on it. If she wants to give away benefits to June, be my guest. It's only a matter of time before she's on mine anyway. "I'd like to propose you shift to an hourly consulting fee, rather than a salary, to reflect your new workload."

Liam opens the folder in front of him. He slides a stapled stack of papers toward June.

"You are not obligated to make any decisions anytime soon, but here is what we're offering. If you are in agreement, you can sign whenever you're ready, but take it home and mull it over for a few days. You also are not expected to make a resignation decision today, either. Take your time, Junie."

My eyes flash to his at the use of her nickname, but June looks back at him with nothing but platonic love. And with that, everyone rises and leaves the room, Liam shutting it behind him as he goes.

I sit back down, pulling her chair toward me so she comes to a stop between my spread knees. I cup her face gently, peering into her eyes.

"You good?"

"So good," she nods against me. I kiss her fiercely, letting her feel my relief. There are many ways this meeting could have gone, but if we're being honest here, this was not even close to what I was expecting.

"I can have my lawyer look over the contract and negotiate on your behalf, if that's what you want?"

"I don't know what I want. I just want to breathe, knowing that I'm not fired. And maybe get some garlic bread," she says as her stomach growls. A laugh tumbles out of me as we stand. I press a kiss to the crown of her head.

"Let's get you some fucking garlic bread, then."

We walk out of the room together, hand in hand, and I know no matter what happens moving forward, it will be good, because we're doing it together.

Chapter Sixty-Three
Epilogue: June

NINE MONTHS LATER

There are many, many things in my life that have not gone as planned. My ignorance of Asher's feelings toward me for several years, for one. Having a surprise baby, for another. While I'm not one of those people who believes everything happens for a reason, it's hard not to feel some sort of universal or karmic intervention has allowed some of the most unexpected twists of my life to be the best things that have ever happened to me.

Daniela Lorelai Incaudo was born a couple weeks early, in late January, and much like the discovery of her growing in my belly, her timing could not have been more perfect. A late January birth meant that Asher's Spring Training schedule was minimally impacted, and it allowed for Daniela, my parents, our new pitbull puppy, and me to travel to Arizona with him after a couple of weeks.

A week after my job was solidified with the Foxes, Asher came home with another surprise for me. Another pregnant mama dog was rescued from the street by the animal organization Caleb and

Jenny work with, and when she had the puppies, Asher practically tripped over himself to put his name on the list. Once he reached twelve weeks old, we officially adopted him and named him Champ. Ash even bought me an adorable "Show Me Your Pitties" pitbull window sticker for my car; when Champ rides in the backseat, he perfectly mimics the dog outline on the sticker. He's thrilled with the laughs and smiles it elicits when people notice him. And Champ couldn't be more in love with Daniela. Seeing my boys interact with our girl warms my heart in a way I didn't realize was possible.

Asher sings Daniela to sleep every night, which isn't all that different from the way he sang and played guitar for her while she was developing in my womb. Still, every time I see him do it, I fall in love with him a little more.

Significantly less exciting than the birth of our child, but still important, was the call we received from Asher's agent this offseason. The Foxes offered him an enormous contract extension, complete with a hefty raise, ensuring our stay in Chicago would be a semi-permanent one. It wasn't a surprise; Asher finished last season with the Rookie of the Year award. I guess that's what happens when you pitch a complete game, top triple digits in pitch speed, and establish yourself as a consistent force to be reckoned with all in your first complete season.

We still plan to spend our offseasons in Philly, where Daniela will have plenty of access to her very devoted grandparents. Lorelai, while still working as a dental hygienist, doesn't seem to know what to do with herself now that her parents' diner has sold. She's found plenty of shopping and cooking to fill her free time, judging by Daniela's closet and our freezer. It's impossible not to feel the love surrounding us.

Once Asher told me, I've never doubted his love for me, but I've got some fierce competition in our daughter. She's only nine weeks old and she's already got him wrapped around her tiny finger, but I couldn't ask for anything more. My pregnancy with her was relatively easy, all things considered. She made up for it in spades, though, fighting the delivery every step of the way. Asher jokes that she wanted to come early to surprise us, then decided I'd created such a nice home for her in my belly that she changed her mind on coming out. Twenty-two hours of delivery had me inclined to agree, but now that she's finally here, we couldn't be more in love.

So far, she's got my dark hair and Asher's height (clocking in at the ninetieth percentile in length!); I can't wait to see whose eyes she will favor. For as much difficulty as she gave me during the delivery, she's been a fairly easy baby, but I couldn't have done it without our parents' support. The season is barely underway, and I'm already dreading Asher's first road trip. Christine and Whitney have already booked their flights to stay with Daniela and me for that week.

"How's she doing, Junebug?" My dad plops a soft kiss on my daughter's beanie-clad head. She's dressed in an oversized onesie with baseball stitching on the side and little Foxes socks, both gifts from Deb when she was born. I brought the smallest pair of infant headphones with us in the stroller, but I doubt she'll need them in the skybox we're in. Asher packed her diaper bag last night, right before he packed his own backpack for the first game of the season. He happily hummed along, Daniela strapped to his naked chest as he did so, and I've never seen a more apt description of domestic bliss.

Asher has settled into fatherhood like a champ. Not that I'm surprised; he has always taken such good care of me that adding another person to the mix was an adjustment he happily made. When he's at practice, I get a text almost once an hour asking for an update on our little princess. There's only so many different ways I can tell him that she pooped, or that she's still napping, or that she still is a bit of a fussy eater. I can't even complain about his doting: every move Daniela makes is a miracle. Asher and I together created the most beautiful baby the world has ever seen. Even I can't believe it sometimes.

"She was a little fussy this morning while you and mom were at breakfast, but I think she just missed her daddy." Smart girl; that makes two of us.

"Good thing she's about to see plenty of him," my mother remarks, nodding toward the television in the corner of the room. Highlights of Asher's season last year spin past on the screen in preparation for Opening Day.

In addition to securing a new contract and an increased salary, Asher earned the Opening Day nod. His laser-like focus and the calm he settled into during the second half of last season served him well, and it wasn't a surprise to anyone that he came out of Spring Training with the honor of starting the home opener.

I've never been prouder of anyone in my life (except for maybe when Daniela holds her head up during tummy time). Somehow, Asher has struck the perfect balance of devoted family man and dedicated athlete, and the dividends it pays are seemingly endless.

It's not all sunshine and roses, but even late nights and Daniela's latching challenges are easier to handle with Asher's gentle presence at my side. Christine was right. If my younger self could see me now, she wouldn't believe it. I couldn't have fantasized about a more perfect twist of fate.

My mother pries my daughter from my arms so I can sit outside to watch Asher warm up. The chill in the early April air in Chicago isn't something I'm thrilled about exposing my newborn to, and I'm grateful that the Foxes provided the box for the WAGs and that my parents joined us. I love my parents, but they could have also done their own thing today, given how much the other WAGs are cooing over our baby girl. Sure, most of them have met Daniela before during Spring Training, but there's something about seeing a new baby, decked out in baseball gear, for her daddy's Opening Day that makes a lot of the women in this room go a little bit crazy with baby fever. Even Delaney, whose own baby is only a few months older than Daniela, gets sucked in.

"She's just got the most gorgeous cheeks!" she gushes about my child as Hailey holds hers. Roman (not Pegasus) Benjamin was born mid-September, the same day the Foxes secured their playoff berth.

This time, unfortunately, the playoff run didn't end with another World Series win for the Foxes, but they made it to the League Championship round before losing to Phoenix in five games. Devin's playoff run fizzled out too, but he and Asher have already placed an informal "bet" on whose team will make it further this year. While betting on your own sport is strictly prohibited, the boys have agreed whoever's season ends sooner will have to fund Daniela's first year of T-ball, including sponsoring uniforms, snacks, and coaching staff for the league, once she is finally old enough to swing a bat. Nevermind the fact that she is half genetically mine and therefore, she runs the risk of inheriting my coordination and balance–or that she may not even be interested in baseball. When I pointed out her potential lack of interest in the sport to Asher and Dev this spring, Devin covered Daniela's ears and looked as if I had just spewed the most foul, vile curses at my daughter. Asher looked at me, open-mouthed, as if he couldn't believe he could procreate with such an uncultured heathen, so I guess our daughter will be playing baseball or softball until the day she dies.

I flick my gaze to the mound, where Asher tosses his last warm up pitch. He looks good, and I'm not just saying that as the mother of his child. He entered Spring Training, and now this season, with an air of relaxed confidence. Asher has always been poised and certain in his athletic skills, but there's something a bit more *settled* about him now.

I want him to do well today, but only because I want good things for my boyfriend. For so long, he was suspicious of others' motives for getting close to him, out of fear that they didn't want him, but just wanted a piece of him. If baseball didn't run through Asher's veins and soul, I wouldn't care if he never pitched another game in his life. To me, Asher is not Asher Incaudo, baseball pitcher extraordinaire, whose fastball now regularly reaches triple digits. No, my boyfriend is just Asher, the lanky, sweet, loveable boy I fell in love with before I could legally drive. He's just Asher, the same rock-solid man I've loved since I met him so long ago.

The breeze floats through the ends of Asher's hair as he taps his right toes and begins his windup. He started the season with a new glove, but he made me promise to get him the same embroidery on this one as his old one. I did, of course, but added "Daddy" in small script across the top of the webbing. He sees it, along with our *Forever* promise, every time he adjusts the ball in his grip, and it makes both of us smile. Soon, though, he won't need the stitching on his glove to remind him that we belong to each other.

It's always been Asher for me. I may have gotten sidetracked by detours and other relationships along the way, and his route to me was equally tortuous. For me, it was like hiking through a particularly humid jungle. You can't really make out your surroundings; it's just shadows up ahead. You still walk, following blindly, mostly through faith alone, hoping that you'll still end up at your intended destination. As you take more and more steps closer to the end goal, your surroundings really don't get clearer. There's just another layer of mist. So, you keep your fingers crossed and you keep going. And when you get to the end of the trail, and it ends up opening to paradise, you don't know whether to laugh or cry with relief that you did finally make it. That you did get to the right place, even though it felt scary and nerve-racking at times. Loving Asher is like that. Asher is my paradise.

Much like the main characters in Asher's and my favorite romance novels, we found our way back to each other. Tonight, after the game, we have an appointment to make it a bit more official.

I've never needed a marriage proposal to know Asher is mine. Maybe we'll get married one day, but I don't need that to know that what he and I have is forever. And yeah, the matching tattoos we're about to get aren't strictly necessary either, but there's something about the cursive font spelling out *forever* stretching across my ribcage and down Asher's forearm that is both romantic and exceedingly hot. Asher initially proposed the idea on a night in which I was feeling particularly guilty about my inability to breastfeed my daughter.

"Just because you can't feed her the exact way you want doesn't mean you're not feeding our daughter. She's healthy and happy, and that's what matters most." I had given him a weak, watery smile that convinced no one. He tucked my head under his chin and held me for a long time before saying, "Think about it this way. Now you can drink and get as many tattoos as you want, whenever you want!"

Thus began the planning for tonight. After the game, Asher is taking me out on our first night away from Daniela. I'm petrified to be away from her while also looking forward to spending some time alone with my man. After tattoos and dinner, he's taking me home and making love to me for the first time since Daniela was born, and if his dirty talk and the texts he's been sending me all morning are any indication, my body is not ready for what he's got planned for me.

I can't wait.

THE END.

Want More?

C an't get enough of June, Asher, and the Chicago Foxes?

Sign up for Meghan French's author newsletter to get access to an exclusive bonus chapter! Scan the code below:

Acknowledgements

I talk a lot. I write a lot. But I'm going to keep these acknowledgements short.

As always, thank you to my readers for taking a chance on an indie sports romance author. It means so much to me that you would choose to spend your time with my books. If you enjoyed it, I'd love if you would review it—reviews and ratings are so critical to authors!

Thank you to my alpha readers, Aleshia, Jill, Alexa, and Jimmy. Between your suggestions and unwavering support, you make book writing fun!

To Neil, for once again seeing my vision on the cover when I give you so very little to go off of! And Katie at Inked and Bound in Phoenix, who designed the most adorable scene breaks ever (I've never had so much cuteness aggression in my life!). You sure know how to make a girl feel special!

To David (and your lovely wife, Cathy). I know you'll probably never read this, since my book isn't about math or physics or history, but you still provided me unending support with all things Meghan French, The Brand, and I'm so grateful for you.

As always, all my love and thanks goes to Mr. French, for keeping me sane, loved, and accounted for when I'm drowning in chapters and self-imposed deadlines. You're a good one and I'm lucky to have you.

About the author

Meghan French loves writing authentic romances about strong female characters and the swoonworthy, dirty-talking men who love them. Her stories typically feature accurate mental health rep, heat, and heart. A self-professed foodie and dog lover, she lives in Arizona with her husband. When she's not in a writing cave, she spends her time as a school psychologist, practicing yoga, and reading all the romance novels she can get her hands on.

Join Meghan's Facebook group, Meghan's Francophiles, for updates on all things Meghan French.

You can also stay up-to-date by following her on Instagram, Threads, and Facebook under @MeghanFrenchAuthor.

Also by Meghan French

Casual Now
Book 1 of the Chicago Foxes Series

I'll Look After You
Book 2 of the Chicago Foxes Series

The Way You Say Good Morning
Book 3 of the Chicago Foxes Series

MEGHAN FRENCH

Reckless Behavior

Book 4 of the Chicago Foxes Series

Billionaires' Row Series

(Coming Soon!)

Mafia Series

(Coming Soon!)

www.ingramcontent.com/pod-product-compliance
Lightning Source LLC
LaVergne TN
LVHW010306070526
838199LV00065B/5454